THE
SHATTERED
WORLD

OTHER BOOKS BY MICHAEL REAVES

Darkworld Detective
I Alien

WITH BYRON PREISS
Dragonworld

WITH STEVE PERRY
Samurai

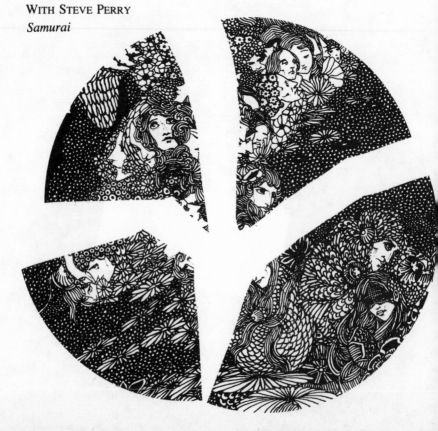

THE SHATTERED WORLD

by MICHAEL REAVES

TIMESCAPE BOOKS
Distributed by Simon and Schuster
New York

Simon & Schuster Building
Rockefeller Center
1230 Avenue of the Americas
New York, New York 10020

Use of the TIMESCAPE trademark is by exclusive license from Gregory Benford, the
trademark owner
SIMON AND SCHUSTER is a trademark of Simon & Schuster, Inc.
Designed by Christopher Simon
Manufactured in the United States of America

10 9 8 7 6 5 4 3 2 1
10 9 8 7 6 5 4 3 2 1 Pbk.

LIBRARY OF CONGRESS CATALOGING IN PUBLICATION DATA

Reaves, Michael.
    The shattered world.

    "Timescape book."
    I. Title
PS3568.E269S5   1984   813'.54   83-23085
(Library of Congress numbers)
ISBN 0-671-49942-4
0-671-49943-2 Pbk.

For Brynne
who got the "J" —
and the rest of me.

At each moment of our becoming (becoming older, wiser, other than what we were in the previous moment) we are being acted upon alternately by a pulse of autochthonous existence and a pulse of consciously perceived and intellectually evaluated existence; each alternating pulse modifying the next, so that, as with the sound of a flute, we are conscious, finally, only of the continuum, the thin, beautiful, and resonant sound of the self—the self, alive.

—John N. Bleibtreu,
The Parable of the Beast

BOOK I

Darkhaven

Insubstantial, the bear appeared—monstrous, shadowy in the smoky, foggy gloom, like some djinn emergent from the fire and brooding darkly above it...

> —Richard Adams,
> *Shardik*

Chapter 1

The Thief

He was running, had always been running. Though he crouched, still as a stone gargoyle, in the shadows atop the wall, listening to the night sounds and the slow beat of his heart, yet he was in flight. So it had been for years—he could never outrun that which pursued him. "Why are you so damned cool about all this?" Suchana had asked him once, when they were hiding in a dank cistern and guards were searching the streets and a fat merchant was screaming offers of rewards and there seemed no possible escape for them. "If they catch us," she had said, "it's torture and death." And he had laughed and said (just before he had figured out a way to save them both— as well as the loot): "This is nothing. Nothing. Wait till you've been chased by a bear."

She had not known, at the time, what he meant. She learned all too soon.

The thief balanced delicately between rows of serrated spikes. Below, in the dim twilight that was Oljaer's short night, lay the grounds of the baronial mansion. In the daytime the grounds were beautiful, filled with patterned gardens and walks, streams that shimmered with fish, trees that rang with birdsongs. At night they were deadly. At night the manticore prowled.

The thief waited, his loose, dark clothing the perfect shade for blending with the dim light, the hood concealing all but his eyes. His breathing was shallow and noiseless. What breeze there was carried his scent away from the grounds. He waited patiently, though he knew it would not be long before the castle Darkhaven would rise and make the night brighter still. He thought of the legends he had heard of the time when there had been real night for thieves to work in—real night, and stars sparkling like sunlight on the sea. He shrugged mentally. The world was no longer whole; he sometimes wondered if it had ever been so. It did not matter. The lack of darkness made the game more interesting.

He heard the approach of the manticore when it was still some distance away. Soon he glimpsed it, its loose-limbed body padding through the shrubbery. The thief held an egg in his left hand. He waited until he could see clearly the grotesque scowling man-face, the scorpionlike tail held ready to strike anything that moved. He felt a momentary sense of kinship with the manticore. You wear the face of a man, he thought; and I, on occasion, the body of a beast.

When it was below and slightly to the right of him he tossed the egg. It broke upon a walkway and the thief held his breath. The shell, emptied of its original contents, had been filled with sleep-spice. His eyes watered momentarily as the breeze was laced with the dusky powder. He heard a choking growl and saw the manticore collapse. The feline limbs twitched and the poisoned tail spasmed against the ground. Then it was still, the only sound a slow, heavy breathing. The thief waited another moment, then climbed easily down the wall and into the garden.

He knew only one manticore patrolled the grounds; the beast had been brought at great expense all the way from the fragment of Calamchor. He moved past it, making his way silently through the maze of hedges and topiaries toward the mansion. The gardens were open to the public during the day, and he had come several times in various disguises to wander through them and enjoy their beauty while memorizing their paths. It had been easy. There had been times in his training when he had been led once through a labyrinth of Bagerah's narrow, twisting alleys and then been expected to retrace his steps. As he grew proficient a blindfold was added. If he failed, old Maenen would snake the iron hook he wore on his left wrist about the young thief's neck and wonder aloud if perhaps he were not better suited for beggar's work—appropriately maimed, of course. It had been an effective learning aid. The memory of those hot, dusty streets came to him now in vivid contrast to his present cool, fragrant surroundings. Only once, in those days, had he dared to rob such a mansion as this. He put that memory aside quickly.

The thief came to the south wing of the mansion and found a small barred cellar window. Around one of the bars he wrapped a thin strip of basilisk hide and began to saw. It made very little noise and it cut through the iron bars as though they were wood.

He had to remove four of the five bars before he could lower himself into the darkness, and at that it was a tight fit; he was a large man—when he was a man. From the heavy scents of syrups and preserves he knew he was in a stillroom, the one the maid had told him about. He took a tiny cruet of oil from one of his pockets and oiled the hinges and the massive spring lock of the door before trying his ring of skeleton keys. None worked, but a prybar against the bolt did. The door opened quietly.

He climbed wooden steps, stepping to each side and pressing his hands against the stone walls to lighten his weight. He felt fairly sure no one would hear the creak of old wood down here, or, if they did, not bother to investigate. But his precautions, ingrained over the years, had become more instinct than reason.

He was in unfamiliar territory now, relying on the information he had charmed from a maid of the house a few days previously. He wondered if she was waiting for him again in the Golden Gryphon Tavern, and grinned slightly at the thought. She would wait a long time this night.

He passed the kitchen and the larder and crossed the dining room, entering the huge main hall, and there he stopped. The chandelier was unlit, but hooded wall sconces of starcrystal gave more than enough light for his sharp vision. He looked at the tapestried couches and the tile-inlaid tables, the staircase of marble and onyx; he smelled the polish on stone and wood. He listened to the silence that only houses built of quarried stone and long years can contain. I have been here before, he thought. Of course, he knew it was not so. He had never been to the fragment of Oljaer before. But he had been in the house of Rorus Hanach in Bagerah, in an attempt to plunder it. He had been there with Suchana.

The house of the Baron Torkalis of Oljaer reminded him far too vividly of that other mansion.

He moved quickly down vaulted corridors, passed through dimly lit chambers and rooms, every sense alert. His soft boots made no sound on carpet, wood, tile, or marble. He had perfected stealth by walking on brittle paper until he could do so in silence. The leather of his garb was well oiled and supple; it did not creak. He took care never to let his shadow cross a doorway before he did. Suchana had taught him all this, and much more—she and the others of Thieves' Island. She would be proud, he knew, to see him now.

He would have given all he had ever stolen to make that possible.

The thief knew his way now. Two days before, his skin darkened with berry juice and his eyes slanted by tiny bone pins pinching the skin over his temples, he had been given a tour of the mansion. He had posed as a wealthy merchant and art fancier from Shigha. Baron Torkalis himself, mustache quivering with pride, had shown him the works of art he had collected over the years. The thief had expressed his amazement and envy over such things as a painting of the Shattering by the great Dalriana, or a panoply of demonskin armor, reputedly from Xoth itself—and, at last, the greatest treasure of them all: the Crystal Crescent. It was kept with the baron's favorite possessions, not in a strongroom or treasury, but in the master bedchamber.

During his tour the thief had memorized the floor plan of the mansion. Four guards patrolled the four floors; he had tried to keep track of their comings and goings during the tour, and had also spent several nights spying on the mansion's windows and timing the guards' appearances. But he could not know their routes exactly, as he now realized. As he slipped across the length of a spacious drawing room he suddenly heard footsteps approaching a doorway.

He looked about. The furniture offered no concealment. Tapestries hung flat against the wall. The door opened outward, so he could not hide behind it. And he could not reach the other exit in time.

The door opened. The guard entered and stood for a moment, surveying the room. He bent and tugged at his greaves; then, tapping a finger against his scabbard in some simple tune, he moved slowly across the floor, boots scuffing loudly, and passed through the curtains at the far end.

The thief waited a moment, then dropped to the floor from his hiding place. He had swung up to and balanced on the door's lintel. He breathed deeply several times to calm himself. He was not fearful—what he felt was exhilaration. In situations like this he felt totally alive; the danger and the challenge charged his blood. There was another way in which that feeling came to him, but he did not like to think about that. It was when he was not a thief—when he was not a man.

He continued his surreptitious way, hiding, waiting, moving like a ghost. At last he stood before the master bedchamber. The open door was at the far end of a hall ten strides long. There was no apparent danger, but the thief did not take the first step. From his tour he knew that the wooden floor of the hall had been laid so that it would shriek like a riven vampire beneath the slightest weight.

He carried a rope, woven of unicorn hair and equipped with a grapnel made of a gryphon's claw, but there was no beam or chandelier on which to swing across. There was another way, however. The walls were of dark wood carved with frescoes of hunting scenes that stretched the hall's length. Though there was little light, the thief could make them out: one forested scene showed the slaying of a catoblepas, a fierce beast that seemed born of boar and buffalo; another scene set a group of hunters against a bear. The thief looked at that one with a rueful shake of his head. Then he stepped to the wall, found and seized suitable holds with strong fingers and toes, and began to work his way down the hall.

It was hard work. For all his nimbleness and strength the thief was a heavy man, and the woodworker had been a delicate artist. There were few holds deeper than a finger's width, and the wood was oiled. But though his progress was slow, not once did he stop until he had stepped into the safety of the bedchamber.

There he realized something was wrong.

There was light where he had expected darkness. A flickering pearly radiance came from the étagère against the far wall by the chamber couch. The light illuminated the chamber fitfully; the thief could see the sleeping forms within the canopied bed, the sheets of vellum that lay upon the small writing desk, and his own reflection in the mirror on the near wall.

The shelves of the cabinet were filled with artworks: dragonsteeth scrimshaw, a casting sphere with fragments of gold, silver, platinum, and the like. But the glow surrounded a silk cushion on the center shelf, and on the cushion rested what the thief had come for: the Crystal Crescent. It was an artifact that had survived the Shattering: a meld of sapphire, tourmaline, lysophaum, chrysoprase, and other rare gems, somehow blended yet retaining their individual beauty, formed into a delicate faceted shard by a magic no longer known. And protected, now, by that shifting sphere of light.

Magic, thought the thief in disgust.

The light had not been there when he had been shown the Crescent by Torkalis. It was obviously a final defense against a resourceful thief. He had no idea how he was going to deal with it, but there was one other matter to take care of first.

He stepped to the huge bed. Through the gossamer curtains he could see the Baron Torkalis and next to him his wife. He knew by the rhythm of their breathing that they slept deeply. In a moment they would sleep more deeply still.

From a hidden pocket he took a small, bulbous object: the rubbery pod of the sirlyet plant. He held it over their faces and squeezed, then drew the bed curtains to keep the sleepspice from reaching him. They would feel no ill effects in the morning other than a headache, but for now the dead would not sleep more soundly.

Now he could devote his attention to the Crescent.

He held his hand close to the shimmering light. He felt nothing, but that did not reassure him. He had a healthy respect for magic. In Balisandra he had studied briefly in the Taggyn Saer system,

almost attaining the second rank of warlock before he was forced
to abandon it in a hasty departure from that city. He had not kept
up the practice, and so had forgotten most of the simple passes and
cantrips. But he had learned nothing to help him against a spell like
this.

He took from his sleeve a delicate ivory-handled hook and carefully probed the light. In theory anything could happen; in practicality
he did not seriously expect the release of a roaring cacodemon or
the devastation of a thunderbolt. Torkalis would not be likely to
keep such power in his bedchamber. What did happen was impressive enough, however; with a hiss the hook glowed and disappeared.
The thief smelled the sharp tang of vaporized metal.

He tried several other tools, from string to leather to bone—all
incandesced and became ash. Time was growing short; he still had
to make his escape before the morning bells sounded.

There was a way, there had to be a way. He had not come this
far to be stopped with the Crescent almost in his hands. There had
to be *something* not affected by the spell. The Crescent was not, of
course...

And neither was the silk cushion it rested upon.

That was the answer. His shirt, beneath his robes, was also silk.
He tore a strip from one of the several pockets in which he carried
some of his tools and tied a noose in one end of it. He lowered the
strip of silk into the light and quietly exhaled in satisfaction as it
descended unscathed. He tugged the loop tight about the faceted
surface of the Crescent and lifted it toward him.

Another moment and he held it in his hands.

But there was another problem. He had brought an imitation
crescent to leave in its place, a forgery for which he had paid dearly.
It would not fool the baron for long, of course, but it would not
have to; by morning of the following day the thief would be on a
dragonship in the Abyss, on his way to a man in Salakh who was
willing to pay handsomely for this prize.

But would the bogus crescent be consumed by the magic? Even
as he wondered this, the thief saw the light suddenly flicker, fade,
and die. With the Crescent no longer there to protect, the spell had

vanished. The thief, acting on a hunch, quickly brought forth the forgery and placed it on the cushion. A moment of darkness, then the glow reappeared, cradling the imitation crescent as defensively as it had the real one.

The thief grinned. He had heard that the baron was a miserly man, and here was a proof of it: he had been unwilling to pay for a more discriminating spell. As was so often the case, the thief's job had been made easier by his victim's penurious foolishness.

He left the chamber and the hallway as he had come, clinging like a great dark spider to the wall, and retraced his route through the house. The most difficult part was over, but he did not relax. He could still be seen by a guard, and if that happened, he was as good as caught even if he escaped the mansion. Oljaer was small, with few places for a stranger to hide. He had to be on a dragonship before the theft was discovered.

He heard the rattle of pans and the voices of the cooks before he entered the dining room. The maid had told him no one stirred until after dawn. She had lied or been mistaken, but that did not matter now. The door to the kitchen began to open; in the reflection of a candlestick holder he saw a serving girl coming through with a platter of covered dishes. He faded back into the hall and started up the staircase. He had to find another way out.

Halfway up he heard footsteps descending beyond the curve of the staircase, matching those of the ascending serving girl. He was trapped.

The rope and grapnel went quickly about one of the balusters, and in an instant he hung in the shadows of the hall below the staircase, above a potted goldenleaf tree. The servants passed each other above him, and he heard their day-greetings. Then the one descending crossed the hall, removing the shades from the starcrystal sconces as he passed. Light filled the hall. The thief hung upside down, curled into a ball that blended with the few shadows left. He felt his tools shift within his pockets, but they made no noise.

When the servants were both gone he pulled himself up, retrieved his rope and quickly reached the top of the stairs. The house would be stirring first on the lower levels, he knew. The only way out would be through an upper window.

Just as it had happened before...

The thief shook his head in an animal gesture and continued his flight. He came to the fourth floor without further incident. And there, in a room full of furniture covered with dusty muslin, he found what he had hoped and dreaded would be there: a single oculus window set high in the wall.

He looked at it and shivered. Such a similarity to what had happened before was eerie. Memories came back to him, cold as the tide: Suchana and he, discovered in the midst of their burglary of the house of Rorus Hanach; the flight through chambers and corridors, up stairs and into a room so like this one, with a single window...

He had locked the door with one of his keys, holding the guards off for a few precious moments. Then he had climbed to the window and shattered it. He did not have to break this one. He unlatched and opened it, clinging one-handed to the sill, and looked out. A tree rose halfway between the house and the wall. The last time it had been a cornice on a facing wing of the building.

The opening was too small for his shoulders to pass through. Without hesitation and with very little pain the thief dislocated the right one. It was a trick Suchana had taught him, and it had come to him easily; his joints and ligaments were quite used to stretching in most unusual ways.

He wriggled out and onto a small ledge just below the roof. He could see dawn beginning to lighten the close horizon. In a moment morning bells would sound. There was no more time.

And yet he stood, immobilized for a moment by memory of what had happened ten years before. It had not been his fault, he told himself. He could not be blamed for keeping the secret from her. He had kept it for three years, giving way to the bear only when he had to, no more than once a Bageran month. He had wanted to tell her, but the thought of her fearing him, leaving him—he could not face that. She had been the first woman, the only woman, he had ever dared to love.

Perhaps she had believed that, but it had not stopped her from being jealous. She had demanded to know where he took himself every so often for a day or more, and when his excuses and inventions had run thin she had watched him, followed him. She was good at it; she was a thief. He could never be sure if she was spying on him.

And so he had held prisoner too long that which had to be free.

It was the only time since the beginning that it had happened without his willing it. He had broken the window and hurled the grapnel about the cornice. The guards were about to break down the door; he could see the wood splintering beneath the blows of their pikes and axes. He had crouched down and reached for Suchana's hand . . . and she had screamed at the sight of it.

He had known what she saw; he could feel it beginning within him. His vision had begun to blur, but not before he saw the door give way before the guards' assault. He had shouted to her, his voice already rough and growling, telling her to grab his hand. Her choice had been simple: the guards or him. She had chosen the guards.

She had fled from him into the arms of her captors. When they looked up and saw him at the window, their cries of triumph changed to fear and disbelief. An arrow hit the wall next to his head. He could not have attacked them; they would have killed him before the metamorphosis was complete. And so he had done the only thing he could do. He had turned, seized the rope, and leaped.

Halfway through the arc he had to take the rope in his powerful jaws to hold it, as he could no longer grip it. He had cleared the wall and landed in the shrubbery beyond, and had fled through crowds of screaming people. The house of Rorus Hanach had been near the river, and into it he had plunged, seeking and finding one of the many underwater entrances to the city's sewers. His memory was not too clear after that. But by the time the bear had left him, he had left Bagerah, never to return.

The thief started as the first peal of the morning bells sounded from the palace. The sun was rising from the Abyss. He slapped one hand against his chest to make sure that the Crystal Crescent was still secure in its harness, and hurled the grapnel toward the tree. The curved claws bit into a large branch.

The thief shook his head savagely until he felt the blood pounding. It does not matter, he told himself. All that matters is not getting

caught. He had not been caught. He had run.
He had always been running.
The thief took a deep breath that sounded very much like a sob, and leaped.

Chapter 2

The Enchantress

The city of Oljaer had been built on one edge of the fragment of Oljaer. It had been raised on half of the ruins of a nameless older city which had been torn asunder by the Necromancer's final spell. None of the ancient buildings had been left standing, but enough stone and metal had been recovered and reworked to make Oljaer a place of considerable majesty for that small land.

The city overlooked the Abyss, a promontory supporting it like a gigantic corbel. A wall surrounded it on the sides that faced the fields and pasture, not out of fear of the farmers and herders of Oljaer, who would never challenge the role of Troas, but out of respect for the fierce catoblepas. The beasts' bellows and squeals could often be heard in the small wood of poplar and aspen that covered the far half of the fragment.

From the forest's depths a rain-fed stream wandered through the tableland and divided the city before falling in mist and rainbow into the Abyss. Perched on the land's edge, the buildings crowded each other as if for a glimpse into the depths. The inhabitants enjoyed a temperate climate, and days and nights of comforting regularity. The sun crossed the middle of the sky, and few other fragments blocked its rays.

The city was not large. From the palace, with its columns carved of dragon ivory, seven avenues radiated. They were lined with the manors of the nobility and merchants, each with their mullioned windows and porticoed entrances. Beyond that were the streets of the guilds and crafts, and the marketplace, with its flyridden open stalls and sweet smells and clamor. The buildings after that, for the most part family dwellings, became quickly more ramshackle. Flagstone streets gave way to cobblestone, tile vanished and shingles began, and finally adobe and thatch were the rule on those patchwork structures crowded against the wall.

Though not large, Oljaer was nonetheless varied; there was an opera house and a theatre, and several temples consecrated to several gods. There were also alehouses and inns, for the land was large enough so that to journey from forest to city required a night away from the hearth. It was also close enough to the rest of the world that dragonships docked regularly, and people of other fragments were commonplace. They wandered Oljaer's streets, or hunted the catoblepas, or sat in the patio of the Land's Edge Tavern, sipping wine and perhaps staring moodily into the cloudy blue depths of the Abyss.

Which is what Beorn was doing.

When memories of a tragedy long past sour one's pride in a job well done; when one has just braved considerable danger and shown much ability and ingenuity and cannot find pleasure even in reminiscing about it; then there is little left to do but go someplace and drink. At least, this was Beorn's view of things as he lifted his fifth glass of cloudberry wine to his lips. It had taken that many glasses to put even the slightest blunting on his melancholy. It would be his last glass; he dared not let himself drink too much. The bear would not allow him that.

Beorn tossed down the last of the clear blue liquid, smacking his lips and holding the goblet aloft to coax down a final reluctant drop. The cloudberry wine of Oljaer was excellent, even better than berries fresh from the vine. He lowered the glass and looked glumly about the small patio, finding no pleasure in the beautiful gnarled wood tables or the starflowered tolsis plants set about. He was, he reminded himself, lucky to be free to see these things; the episode at the house of Baron Torkalis had brought him as close to capture as he had come in some time. And he had the Crescent safe within his jerkin, next to his chest. Money for it awaited him in Salakh, enough for a lifetime of indolence. In Tamboriyon, perhaps, he thought wryly, sadly. Yes, there would be money enough for the dream he had once shared with Suchana.

Perhaps even money enough to free him from his curse.

With a petulant flick of his large hand Beorn tossed the goblet over the low stone railing. He watched it drift away, his hair fanned by the constant breeze that spilled up from the Abyss. The goblet sparkled in the sunlight, and he was able to keep it in sight until it disappeared into a cloud.

Eventually, he told himself, amused by the pettiness of the thought, it may dash someone, somewhere, on the head. Good.

"Now then," a woman's voice said beside him, "I'm afraid that goblet'll cost you a piece of the palace."

Beorn looked around and saw the serving girl, her dark hair threaded behind her through two carved alays pods and her bodice stitched with a scene of geese in flight. She looked at him sternly.

"You can't tell me," he said, spreading his hands, "that no one's ever thrown a goblet into the Abyss before."

"Of course they have; so many that the owner's hard put to stay in business replacing them. Nay, and that's not all they throw. Likewise goes food that doesn't meet their liking, or coins for wishing, and often the bill."

Beorn turned his gaze back into the Abyss. Far below something black flickered for a moment between clouds; a bird, or possibly a vampire.

"And sometimes they toss each other, I'm sure," he said.

"It's happened." The serving girl looked behind her. The sun was still low and there were few other customers. Impulsively she set a new goblet down before him from the tray held at her hip. "I'll let on I didn't see it. After all, you're a guest in Oljaer."

Beorn grinned up at her. When he grinned as he did then it seldom failed to draw a like response, nor did it now. She smiled back and stepped closer.

"Join me," he said, indicating the seat opposite him. Her companionship would be better than his own dark thoughts.

"Nay, it might be my job." But she made no move to leave, and from the way she was looking at him he knew that she wanted to sit. "What land be you from?" she asked him.

"None in particular. I was born in Aēslovèclan, but I left there at an early age. I take my living where I find it."

"Ah, I'd noticed the foreign way you had with Talic. Osloviken, then? That's many a fragment from here." She looked at him with an interest heightened by his remote origins. "And what work has you ranging so far?"

"I'm adaptable. Any form of labor suits me, so long as fighting isn't a part of it."

"I'd have thought you a soldier," she said. "If you don't mind my saying so, you've a build—"

Like a bear, he thought.

"Like a bear," she finished.

Beorn grinned again. He felt himself cheering up somewhat; the conversation and her smile was what he needed. He had not let memories of Suchana depress him so thoroughly for several years; had thought, in fact, that he had finally almost come to a time when he could think of her and smile.

He noticed the serving girl looking at him curiously. "Sorry," he said. "Drifting like a cloud in the Abyss." He lifted another goblet from her tray and held it up to her. "Are you sure you won't join me?"

She glanced swiftly over her shoulder, the motion lashing a braid gently against one breast. "Well, 'tisn't the time for many customers, and my feet will like me the better." So saying, she slipped into the seat. Beorn poured her some wine. "A sip only," she cautioned, "or my breath will betray me." He glimpsed himself in the curving pewter as he poured. The distorted reflection made him appear even more squat and broad than he was. He was built like the trunk of an oak, with huge shoulders and a barrel chest, and arms that filled the large sleeves of his shirt. Women evidently found his face attractive, though at times he was hard put to understand why; it was solid and craggy, with a broad nose and a wide, expressive mouth. His hair was cinnamon and curly, as were his thick brows and beard. Beorn poured the wine slowly, aware that she was watching him, feeling her gaze warm his chest where the shirtneck opened to reveal more hair.

He handed her the drink and lifted his own. "What shall we toast?"

She shrugged. "Your pleasant stay in Oljaer."

"Alas, I'll be leaving on the morrow for Salakh."

She smiled slightly. "In that case, let's drink to a most pleasant night."

He decided he was willing to drink to that.

A shadow crossed the table and the patio. Beorn looked up and saw a small fragment which, appearing from beyond the jerkin-head roof of the tavern, had eclipsed the sun momentarily. It had a strange shape to it; he saw it distinctly with the sun's rays behind it. The bottom of it was rough and irregular, but the top was a sawtooth silhouette of architecture. His companion saw the shadow also, and without looking up made a gesture to ward off evil.

"Why do you do that?" he asked.

She looked at him in slight surprise. "You've not heard, then, of the castle Darkhaven and who dwells there?"

"I know only the castle's name; nothing about its inhabitants."

"Only one of them causes our woe; the sorcerer Pandrogas. A diabolical man, responsible for most of the ills of Oljaer. Just last week a man I know was gored in the leg by a catoblepas outside the gate, right at the time that Darkhaven crossed the sun! And two months ago a rock the size of a hogshead was hurled from those battlements; it near destroyed a farmer's house..."

Beorn watched as the floating castle passed by. Distances were deceiving in the Abyss, but he had the impression that the structure was huge. He did not know if its inhabitants were in fact responsible for the woes the girl was recounting or not, but he tended to doubt it. The impression he had gotten of sorcerers during the short time he had studied magic was that those devoted enough to reach an advanced rank were seldom prone to toying with others for spurious reasons. In any event, it was not his concern.

He had begun his practice of magic because there were certain aspects of it that could help him in his thievery. Many items of value were protected by spells, as the Crescent had been, and he could not always count on his wits to bypass them. The casting of spells also required concentration and some knowledge of misdirection and manipulation, all of which were important to a thief as well. But there had been another reason behind his investigation of the art: a dark and shambling shape that padded always a step behind him . . .

". . . there are even those who say Pandrogas is responsible for sending Ardatha Demonhand to seduce and befuddle the Lord King."

Beorn realized he had not been paying attention to her words. A part of his mind remembered them, as he had trained himself to do, and he smiled pleasantly while he quickly reviewed her last sentences. She had merely been recounting legends of the sorcerer of Darkhaven. But her last statement interested him. He raised a bushy eyebrow to invite more on the subject, but she had already clapped a hand over her mouth in mock horror. "That wine's loosened my tongue, and saying such things might lose it for me completely!"

"I take it Ardatha frowns on such talk."

She shuddered. "That woman will be whole in hell, and no mistake." But another swallow of wine made her chuckle. "They say she's a shapeshifter, you know, as well as an enchantress."

"Really?" He asked it a trifle too sharply, but the wine made her miss it.

"Even so, and that she becomes all manner of beasties for their mutual amusement. Myself, I've never cared for that sort of sport." A patterned fingernail toyed with the fine hair on his knuckles. "Though I must admit I'm growing fonder of bears by the moment."

That brought an instant of coldness to Beorn's chest before he realized she was only referring to his appearance. But that knowledge brought a new kind of apprehension. He knew that she was his for the asking this night, and a familiar uneasiness came with the thought. It was a fear he had lived with for over ten years, and it stirred whenever a woman cast an admiring gaze his way.

Nothing would happen, he told himself. Why, after all, should this night, this woman, be different? And if anything were to happen—well, who was she, after all? No one; a serving wench. He did not need her; he only desired her.

He grinned back at her then, and captured her small hand in his large one. "Speaking of beasties then," he said, "there's a particularly fabulous one I've always been fond of."

"Might it be the one with two backs?"

"You take my meaning," Beorn said. He was about to ask her when her work was done, when suddenly there was a shout from the arched entrance to the tavern.

"Yonder he is! Take him!"

Beorn whirled about and saw five men wearing hauberks with the catoblepas, Oljaer's symbol, emblazoned on them. They moved quickly toward him at the direction of the sergeant who had first shouted. He heard the cold hiss of steel leaving scabbards. He wore no weapon but a poniard; to draw it would be almost an insult. He felt panic welling inside him, the familiar unreasoning fear of a cornered beast. As he had done many times before, he clamped down on it. He could not lose control now, or ever. Somehow he would find a way out of this.

He reviewed his possibilities quickly. He could leap into the Abyss; a rash move. Even if he were not feathered with arrows he would likely float helplessly until he starved. He could seize the serving girl and use her for a hostage. That course seemed calculated to gain him no more than a few moments of freedom. Where could he run to on this small fragment? There was only one port for the dragonships and it was well guarded.

The thought occurred to him that perhaps they had mistaken him for another criminal, but he discounted that immediately. He stayed alive by always assuming the worst.

The soldiers approached him warily. Beorn stood up, a look of annoyance on his face. His clothing was not that of nobility, but he could pass for a wealthy man. He still carried with him the forged letters of passage naming him a merchant of Shigha, though he no longer wore the makeup. It was worth a try. The sergeant stepped up to him and Beorn said haughtily, "What is the meaning of this? My name is—"

"Your name doesn't matter," the sergeant interrupted him. "You're a thief." He seized Beorn's shirt and jerkin at the collar and ripped downward, tearing the shirt and popping the coral buttons of the jerkin. The Crystal Crescent, held to his wide chest by a leather harness, sparkled in the sunlight as the sergeant pulled it loose.

A fence of swords was raised about him. There was nothing he could do—to call upon the bear would take too much time. He could not count upon the sight to cause enough fear and panic to stop them from attacking. He was almost glad; in a very real way he feared the bear more than the soldiers.

Beorn raised his arms. At a gesture from the sergeant a man attempted to fit a pair of manacles about his wrists. The clamps would not close. "His wrists are too big, sir."

"Use rope, then," the sergeant directed. "Mind you," he added, looking at Beorn, "bind him securely." The soldiers obeyed, wrapping Beorn's arms in layers of hemp, much more than necessary. It would hold the bear, he thought. Then a hand against the middle of his back pushed him forward roughly and he stumbled up the broad, flat steps and into the tavern's coolness. As his boots crunched across the sawdust floor he turned and caught a last glimpse of the serving girl, still staring in disbelief after him. He had never learned her name.

Beorn was marched from the Land's Edge Tavern to a gaolwagon waiting in the street. The soldiers, for the most part young men trying to look grim and official, stared at him with ill-disguised curiosity. Beorn wondered if thievery was that rare in Oljaer.

He took deep, slow breaths, trying to calm the pounding of his heart. He had been captured before, he reminded himself, and he had escaped. There was no reason he could not do the same this time. No reason, save that he was trapped on a small fragment with no friends to turn to.

He wondered if he should have taken his chances in the Abyss.

The sergeant was watching him. He was a thin man, whose ropy muscles twitched slightly like a horse shaking off flies. He stepped toward Beorn, holding the bars as the wagon moved swiftly past the colonnaded buildings and splashing fountains of Oljaer's wealthier section. Beorn looked at him and wondered about bribery. He abandoned the thought; the man had the look of a fanatic, and besides, his men would have to be included. Beorn had little left of the ivory currency the people of Oljaer referred to as "pieces of the palace."

"Animal," the sergeant said.

Beorn noticed the peculiar emphasis given to the epithet, and apprehension turned him suddenly cold. He said nothing, but the sergeant nodded as if his suspicions were now confirmed.

"Didn't think we knew you was a shapechanger, did you? Why'd we bind you so tight, then, eh? Take my word on it, beast—you're being brought before Ardatha Demonhand, and she knows how to deal with demifolk. When she's finished with you, you'll wish you were in Xoth, make no mistake!"

There was no time to wonder how they had learned his secret. He had heard tales of the enchantress and her talent for torture. Their superstitious fear of shapechanging would bind him to a slow, excruciating death. The only chance now was the bear. If he could take them by surprise, hold them off until the metamorphosis was complete, break his bonds and the bars and somehow reach the city's edge . . .

He would sooner be drained by vampires in the Abyss than be tortured as Suchana had been. He began to feel the tingling, the dizziness, the pains deep within his bones. The sergeant's face rippled as though seen through flowing water, and the sneer on the thin lips changed to shock. Beorn spun about, snarling, watching the others shrink back in terror. Then something damp and soft was clamped over his face, and an overwhelming smell whirled him into darkness.

A time of floating, surrounded by clouds, caressed by sunlight, gifted with the ease of complete thoughtlessness and relaxation, was Beorn's. He knew that he was adrift in the Abyss, floating through the gulf between the world's fragments, but he was not afraid. It was as if he had left all his cares behind him. He wanted simply to float forever.

That, however, was not to be; beneath him, out of the clouds, he saw the greens, browns, and blues of some pastoral land swim into view. He felt it tug at him, at first leisurely, then insistently. He began to fall. Clouds tore at him with ghostly fingers. He clutched at the air in futile terror. The light surrounding him, instead of the comforting blue of the sky, was now actinic, harsh, blinding. Beorn wanted to scream, wanted desperately to scream at least once before he hit . . .

"He awakes."

The light became the golden glare of the afternoon sun; the horrible sensation of falling transformed into the cold of the marble floor on which he lay, breathing raggedly. Beorn opened his eyes and stared up at a coffered ceiling rich with designs and tinted skylights.

"Don't gasp so," a languid male voice said. Beorn realized that a woman had spoken before. The male voice continued. "You sound more like a beached whale than a bear. Put your legs beneath you and face us."

He stood carefully; the room he was in had an unsettling tendency to suddenly dip and spin. It was obviously a minor throne room, not small but not large, with walls of crystal panes and polished rosewood, the latter carved with battle scenes. High on one of them a panoply of armor hung; he could see dust dulling the gleam of the mail and weapons. Before him was a dais of onyx which supported two wooden thrones, and on one of them sat Troas, Lord King of Oljaer. Beside him stood Ardatha.

Beorn stared at Ardatha. From the amused twitch of her lips he knew she was quite used to such staring, but he could not help it. Her hair was white as the beard of a patriarch, though she was surely no more than thirty. She wore a gown of dark green, on which filigreed dragon's talons rose from a belt of gold and cupped her breasts. Demonshead earrings leered. She stood in a strangely demure pose, hands clasped behind her back.

Troas cleared his throat impatiently and Beorn looked at him. On his robe was a stylized design of a catoblepas, stitched in silver thread in a *rampant* pose. Beorn thought it looked faintly ridiculous. A thin cloth-of-gold circlet confined the Lord King's black hair. His ringed fingers tapped the throne arm, where a small scroll lay.

"Proceed, my dear," he said to Ardatha.

Ardatha's right hand came into view; her left remained behind her back. She opened a small potion pouch that hung from her waist and took from it a handful of white powder. This she blew at Beorn. The powder surrounded him in an acrid mist; he sneezed violently twice. Troas looked away in distaste, touching a scented foulard to his nose. I'm not making a proper first impression, Beorn thought ironically.

When his vision cleared he looked again at Ardatha. She smiled at him, cocking her head slightly to one side; the white hair, which reached to her waist like a winter's frozen waterfall, fascinated him. The demonshead earrings peered out from it as if through fog; they seemed to be laughing. He did not like the way their jeweled eyes sparkled.

"Be at rest, changeling," Ardatha said. Her voice had all the qualities of a cat's purr except its warmth. Her large, green eyes held his gaze easily. She was a woman who had polished and perfected her power as a swordsmith crafts a blade, layer by loving layer of tempered metal.

"Be at rest," she said again. "If you have any thoughts of calling upon your powerful alter ego, dismiss them; the dust coating you is the ash of a bear's bones, admixed with other ingredients. If you attempt to change before bathing thoroughly, you will fail—most painfully." She paused, then continued briskly, "Now, on to matters of justice."

Beorn tried to control his breathing. He was sure his heart was pounding hard enough to make a visible pulse beneath his hairy chest. Part of that was the drug the soldiers had given him, of course, but most of it was fear. He did not want to die, and most particularly not in any of the ways he was sure that Ardatha could devise.

Troas reached for the scroll. "Your sorcery has covered the tiles with dust," he murmured to Ardatha in a petulant tone, and Beorn very nearly began to laugh.

"Far better than to have them covered with blood," she replied pleasantly. Troas flashed a suspicious and slightly frightened look at Beorn, who thought, If there was any mercy in his mind, it's gone now.

The Lord King glanced perfunctorily at the scroll. He was a powerfully built man, handsome except for his face, which had too much nose, not enough chin, and eyes that would not stay still. It was as if someone else's head had been set upon those shoulders by mistake. "You are a shapeshifter," he said to Beorn. "To be precise, a demibear. You are also a thief, and you have stolen the Crystal Crescent from the house of Torkalis, Baron of Oljaer. There is no use in denying this."

Beorn said nothing. He simply waited. As long as he was alive, he told himself, there was still a chance.

"I see no reason to waste more time on this," Troas said. "I leave his fate to you, my dear." He tapped a ringed finger against a small bronze gong that stood beside the throne. The tones shivered through the air; from a curtained entrance behind Beorn came four burly guards to surround him. As they laid hands on him he looked again at Ardatha, receiving again her smile.

"It will not be brief, changeling," she said. "But it will be most interesting." And, for the first time since he had seen her, she brought her left hand from behind her back to lightly stroke her cheek. Her left hand was not made of white skin, delicate veins and manicured nails, as was her right hand. At her wrist human flesh melded into a thing of scales and ridged cartilage, of six lean fingers tipped with curved talons. It shimmered, blue-black, in the sunlight. On the ring finger he saw the silver ring that named her enchantress. All this, in a single, shocking glimpse—and then he was hustled from the chamber.

The curtains settled after the guards took Beorn away. Ardatha turned to the Lord King, the meditative smile still on her lips.

Troas did not look nearly so content. "I fail to see why you take such an interest in designing the punishment of a lowly thief." His tone was snappish, but also diffident; his infatuation with Ardatha was tempered with a healthy dose of fear, which only large amounts of wine could occasionally overcome. The enchantress had worked hard to cultivate that fear.

"But my lord," she said in mock surprise. "He has robbed a noble of the realm."

Troas named a portion of a goat's anatomy which, in his opinion, contained more nobility by far than the Baron Torkalis.

"You know I frown on other practitioners of magic in Oljaer," she murmured. She lightly stroked the reptilian skin of her clawlike left hand with the nails of her right, knowing that the sight and sound of it made Troas shudder. It made her shudder as well, but she confined that sensation to deep within her, letting no tremor show on the surface.

"Magic? He wears no ring of rank! He is merely one of the werefolk. What threat is he to you, Ardatha?"

"None at all, I'm sure; still, one does not have to cast the sphere to know that it is always best to keep one's powers honed, and to keep the public awed."

"Well, no matter. All that's important is that the affairs of court are done for this day. There are needs of a more personal nature to attend to now, wouldn't you say?"

"Of course, my lord," Ardatha murmured. She had won the argument, as usual. She began to stroke Troas's hair, using the hard bony palm of her claw.

"*Ardatha!*"

"My apologies, my lord." She switched to her right hand, smiling slightly. Her eyes were fixed on the spot where Beorn had last stood.

Beorn was led down a wide corridor beneath spandrelled arches lit by chandeliers of starcrystal. They turned down another, smaller corridor, and then through a series of passageways that wound and snaked about until even his acute sense of direction was confounded. A stairwell of cold iron lit by torches guttering in a constant breeze came next. The air, though laden with incense, nevertheless had an underscent of moist decay.

They marched him along a narrow tunnel floored with wet stone, passing the wide columns that supported the palace. Doors banded with iron were set periodically in the walls; behind some of them Beorn could hear coughs and curses, the rattling of chains, and once shrill laughter. He walked with a straight back, every muscle tense, breathing through clenched teeth. Added to his natural human distaste for the dungeons was a measure of the bear's unreasoning fear and rage. It was this that he was hardest put to control.

A large key creaked in a rusty lock; hinges shrieked, and Beorn was pushed into a darkness that was like madness. The door was shut, the guards' hasty footsteps echoed to silence, and Beorn was alone.

He stood immobile for some time, making an effort to relax. He tested his bonds; they had not been made so tight or so many this time. He set to working them over his hands, patiently stretching them and twisting them, developing a sheen of perspiration that aided in their eventual passage over his knuckles. He was almost sorry when they fell away from him—in his concentration he had been able momentarily to forget his surroundings. Now, however, there was nothing to do but feel the panic and the terror and attempt to deal with them the best he could.

He felt his way along the damp wall until he had paced off his confines—the cell seemed little larger than a crypt. The walls were of large stone blocks, roughly hewn. He pressed at the door. It moved ever so slightly against the jamb, but its weight told him that not even the bear could knock it down. There were no hinges on his side of it. He checked his clothing, confirming that he had been thoroughly searched while unconscious. All of his weapons were gone, including the knife in its bootsheath and the garrote in his sleeve hem. They had taken his money also, so there was no chance of bribing the turnkey.

The cell was empty save for a small mattress made of stitched hides; it felt as if it were stuffed with seashells. Beorn sat gingerly on it.

How had they known? He had left no traces, no clues; his performance had been that of the complete professional. And yet they had known not only that he was a thief, but that he was a shape-changer. Magic was the only way they could have known, and that meant Ardatha. He saw her enigmatic face again clearly against the cell's darkness, and shuddered.

He stood and explored his confines again. He suddenly realized he was very tired and very hungry; he had eaten only a light breakfast, and nothing at all the previous day. He ran his fingers over the rough surface of the wall. The mortar between the stones was old, but he had nothing with which to dig it out, and very likely no time in which to do it. He thought of pitting the bear's strength against the walls or the door—what did he stand to lose?—but then he remembered the powder Ardatha had coated him with.

He thought about the bear.

The creature had ruled his life since it had first come upon him, when he was thirteen. The memory of a young girl's terrified face, framed by woods and an iron-gray sky, made him shake his head until he saw red spots in the darkness. He felt suddenly dizzy and weak, and half sat, half fell onto the mattress. It occurred to him that perhaps he had not entirely recovered from the soporific the soldiers had used on him. But he could not allow himself to sleep now; there was too little time...

He was dreaming of flames roaring through a farmhouse, threatening the nearby pines, leaping toward dark clouds, when a sound awoke him—a key rasping in a lock. Beorn was on his feet before he was fully awake. He stared blindly at the door, heart thumping, waiting. He was sure he had slept through what little time he had had, and that now she had come for him.

There was a creak, and cold silver light bracketed the opening door. Beorn realized that he was right. He inhaled thinly, suddenly overcome with terror, feeling on the verge of soiling himself.

Ardatha stood in the doorway, the claw that was her left hand glowing like the fabled moon. She looked quickly over her shoulder, then beckoned impatiently to him.

Beorn realized he could not move. He backed up against the damp wall. A whimper escaped him.

Ardatha looked at him, and he was sure that he was misreading her expression—there seemed to be pity in her face. "Bear-brained fool," she murmured. "Come in thrall, then," and she added a phrase and a gesture with the glowing claw. Beorn suddenly felt his legs moving, despite all he could do to stop them. She led him down the corridor and into another cell. There she pressed a stone in the back wall, and a concealed door swung open with the grate of stone against stone. Behind it was a narrow, steep staircase.

Beorn followed her up it. He seemed supernally aware of everything: the drip of moisture from the low, rounded ceiling; the scuttlings of spiders in their gray webs as the light passed them; the scent of the air, at first stale, now growing fresher, with a hint of strange, exotic scents (chemicals for torture? he wondered); the beating of his heart. He tried to perform the relaxing exercises, the rituals of thought that the thieves had taught him. Perhaps there would at least, somehow, be a chance for a quick death.

At the top of a climb all too short was a landing, and a partially open door. Ardatha swung it wide and Beorn stepped through it into luxury.

He realized that he must be in Ardatha's chambers. He glanced about; even in such a situation he could not help taking in with an appraising eye the rich wall hangings and the sumptuous furniture. On a table of gemwood in the center of the room a feast had been spread. The enchantress said, "It is set for you."

At her words the spell she had laid on him vanished. "A strange way to begin my torture," he replied, making no move toward the bounty, not yet daring to hope...

Her next words almost buckled his knees. "There will be no torture—at least, not if you cooperate with me. I regret the necessity for deception, but I have a role to play. Now eat, but sparingly. You have some work before you; the type of work you do best. Do not bring a heavy stomach to it. After you have eaten, bathe; cleanse yourself of the werebane. Hurry! We have little time."

She turned and was gone through a curtained archway.

Beorn tried to eat. The food was excellent; a variety of meats and breadstuffs, cheese soup and wine and a frumenty. But as hungry as he was, he did not enjoy it. He tried to adopt a fatalistic attitude; after all, did he not appear to be in much better circumstances now than an hour before? But he could not stop speculating about what

Ardatha wanted. He had heard tales of her ever since arriving in Oljaer: how she was the real power behind the throne, how she had contrived to eliminate all other schools of magic from the city, and, of course, of her imaginative cruelty to those she disfavored. The serving girl had said she was a shapechanger. Beorn doubted that; he had found, over the years, that he could recognize other demifolk, be they werewolves, catfolk, serpent people, or bear kind. How he knew he could not have told, but he was sure that Ardatha was not one. Any shape she took would only be illusion. Her claw, however, was no illusion; he did not know how she had come by it, and hoped he would not learn.

But what made him more uneasy than the claw was her assured manner. He was used to being in control of a situation. She had manipulated him quite handily, and he did not like that. Not at all.

He bathed in a sunken tub of marble and gold leaf, in scented water. As he dried himself the door opened and Ardatha entered, carrying garments. "Pardon the intrusion; it will save time."

Beorn hesitated, then continued toweling; if she was not bothered by the circumstances, neither would he be. Ardatha looked at him, green eyes faintly amused. Beorn felt uncomfortable, and the fact made him angry. He showed no sign of it. Though it galled him to admit it, she still had the upper hand—or claw, in this case.

"How very bearish you are, even in your human shape," she commented. "The muscles are hard, but limber," she added as Beorn bent over to dry his feet. She handed him the garments. "These should fit you. Your weapons have been sewn into them."

He dressed in dark tunic, leggings, and boots, with light mail. Then Ardatha led him from the bath chamber into what was obviously her laboratory. He snorted as he entered and smelled the heavy scents rising from alembics, censers, and tripods. A circle of golden tiles stood out from the dark green floor. An ivory bookcase was filled with scrolls, tomes, and codices. In one corner stood an altar of starstone with dark stains upon it. Candles set in ebony holders lit the chamber.

Ardatha said, "I have a job for you." She sat cross-legged near a bronze mirror in which played shifting hues. Beorn noticed that

she sat on air as if on a cushion, hovering above the tiles. He said
nothing, determined to be unimpressed.

"A job," she continued, "for which you are most admirably suited."
She pointed above him, and Beorn looked up and out of a skylight.
In the night sky, its turrets glowing like pearl in the last rays of the
sun, the castle Darkhaven floated.

"I must have a certain talisman from that castle. You may have
heard that Darkhaven is the sanctuary of a sorcerer. It will take a
thief to penetrate it, and it may take a bear to win a way back out.
It is a difficult job—but it can be done, and you are the one to do
it."

Beorn felt a wave of dizziness not due entirely to the fumes of
alum and assafoetida. It was also relief that made his head spin
momentarily. She needed him. He wanted to throw back his head
and laugh, but he did nothing. She needed him!

She continued: "You have little alternative, you know. Your
profession and your nature have condemned you to torture in Oljaer.
It required considerable work on my part to have your disposal
assigned to me. Accomplish this task; return with what I desire, and
you will be rewarded. I know your deepest desire, bearling. I learned
it from your drugged dreams. I know that you fear the beast within
you, that you would like nothing better than to gain total control
over it. The talisman I want can give you that, with my help. You
need no longer fear the bear, Beorn. What do you say to that?"

"I have been told by mages before that such a cure is an impos-
sibility," he replied. "If you can do it, it would be worth any risk.
But how do I know that you speak the truth?"

"You do not," Ardatha said, unruffled. "You must take my word.
It is that, or a lingering death. I could make this a geas, but such
might impair your abilities. So you must decide—obey me and win
freedom and your heart's desire, or refuse and die. Will you attempt
it?"

"Of course," he said. He knew she would not put him under a
geas. He knew he had her where he wanted her now. She needed
something that only he could provide, and that meant he controlled
the situation, though she did not yet realize it.

It meant he could begin plotting his revenge.

Ardatha stood and turned to a table. From the neatly arranged paraphernalia she took a necklace and a ring. The ring was a drop of hardened resin, and imbedded in it was a thin sliver of black stone. "This is a fragment of the talisman which you must steal," she said. "How I gained even this much of it would make a long tale. It is not enough to spell with, but like draws like, and it will serve as a siderite to lead you. Watch the resin; the brighter it glows, the closer you are to the stone."

Beorn put it on his finger. Ardatha hung the amulet about his neck; he tried not to shudder as the claw brushed his hair. The amulet was of copper and zinc, inscribed with cabalisms. "This should afford you some concealment from the spells of security which Pandrogas has doubtless placed over his domain. But it will not protect you from danger. No spell can do that in Darkhaven." She pushed him toward a curtain of beads. "Now you must go."

"Wait!" Beorn protested. "Thievery is not a matter of impulse! I must have time to prepare, to learn more—"

"There is no time! This must be accomplished tonight. I cannot risk Troas's discovering your absence."

"Tell me one thing, then," he said, stopping and facing her. "How did you know it was I who robbed the baron?"

She looked at him in exasperation. "Does it really matter?"

"It does," he said, not moving. She looked at his face for a moment. "Yes," she said, finally. "I can see how it would."

From a cabinet full of thaumaturgic equipment she picked up a small burglar's tool—a drill made from the polished thorn of a spiralspike plant. "This was found on the leaf of a potted tree in the baron's main hall," she said. "From it, by use of Senarum's Incantation of Association, I deduced your identity."

He looked at it and nodded. He recalled hanging upside down to avoid the servants, recalled feeling his tools shifting within his pockets, including the pocket he had torn to lift the Crystal Crescent. "Thank you," he said. "Now I know the mistake I made."

"Come then; and do not be alarmed by what you see and hear."

They went through the beads and into the cool night air. They were on a small balcony high on the palace wall. Below, he saw the lights of Oljaer spread out; above, the lights of the heavens— the diffused sunlight and distant glowing fragments. Darkhaven was by far the largest of the fragments; it rode aloof and majestic through the air, seemingly close enough to touch. Its rippled reflection crossed the river that bisected the city.

Ardatha lit two candles on the balcony ledge. Beorn stood back as she began to move in a form of adjuration. He watched fascinated by the serpentine twists and writhings of the dance, and, somewhat to his surprise, felt a sudden intense desire for her come over him. His breeches were abruptly tight and uncomfortable. Despite his hatred of Ardatha, he wanted at that moment, more than anything, to seize her, to take her on one of those pelt-covered divans inside. He felt slightly stunned by the intensity of the feeling. It was probably a reaction to the summoning spell she was performing, he told himself. It was meant to call things inhuman, and perhaps this was some form of side effect.

He did not want to admit that there might be another reason.

The coruscant glow of her claw was bright enough to hurt his eyes. She began to chant in a belling voice, "Balandrus, you are summoned by the power of my left hand, under the name of Sestihaculas the Demogorgon, he who rules the Chthons; come with dispatch and perform the service to which I set you..."

There was a sound of winds and a muffled shriek, and the flames of the candles suddenly burned blue in the stench of sulfur that surrounded them. Beorn involuntarily closed his eyes; when he opened them, a vast and shadowy shape crouched on the crystal ledge.

He swallowed, but he was determined not to show or feel fear again. He had encountered manifestations of magic before in his career, but he had never faced a cacodemon, had never before known of any mage with the power to control one. Its massive body blended with the darkness, save for two glowing eyes. The burning gaze shifted from him to Ardatha, and a voice like a dying dog's howl said, "Three journeys are yours. What would you have of me?"

"Ferry this one to yon castle," Ardatha replied. "Take no sport with him, nor betray him in any way. Deposit him securely at the

Spire of Owls and wait for his return. Bring him then back to me under the same conditions."

"That is the first journey," Balandrus said. It extended an arm toward Beorn; talons the size of a young dragon's encircled the thief's waist, almost hot enough to burn. He was lifted, not gently. He reminded himself once again that she needed him; and also that he would, somehow, have his revenge. Then he looked at her and thought he saw, suddenly, the same look of concern he had seen on her face in the cell. For an instant she seemed no longer aloof and cruel, but instead a human being, concerned for the welfare of another.

Then, with a quickness that drained the blood from his head, the balcony fell away and the night wind screamed in his ears.

The candles burned normally again. Ardatha stood by the ledge, looking up at Darkhaven. Now there was nothing to do but wait. The light breeze brought a faint scent of rain to her. Beyond Oljaer the sun shone, illuminating a black line of clouds. She hoped the storm would not strike before the mission was done.

She realized her concern was not entirely for the mission. That was not as it should be. The bear man was not important; only the stealing of the Runestone was important. She repeated that to herself, over and over, but still she felt sorry that Beorn had to die.

Her sadness made her angry. Why should this death upset her after all the others she had caused? She had not felt grief over them. So she told herself, ignoring the fact that there had been few nights over the past year in which she had not awakened from dreams of accusing voices and pain-filled eyes.

The enchantress traced in the air before her a circle, the sign of the One God, with her claw, and turned away from the sight of Darkhaven. It was necessary to do this. It had all been necessary. It was for the greater good. He would not be the first, nor the last, to die before the world was redeemed.

She hoped she could trust the thief. She thought she had given him sufficient incentive, and there was no way of escape from Darkhaven save in the cacodemon's grasp. But he was a cunning man, this demibear, and a proud one. She knew he hated her because she had used him, and because she had seen him filled with fear.

Still, she had divined his motivations well. He would return with the Runestone because he wanted more than anything else to be cured of the werespell that haunted him. And she had promised him that.

And instead she would give him death, because she could not take the chance of Pandrogas's finding him and learning who had stolen the Runestone. The master of the Circle, the man she knew only as Stonebrow, had so ordered it, and Ardatha knew that he was right.

It was for the greater good. Everything had been for the greater good . . .

Chapter 3

The Castle

Though night never cloaked the castle Darkhaven, it was seldom day within it. The huge structure was a potpourri of architectural styles and excesses, its wings and towers having grown slowly and haphazardly over the centuries before the Shattering. It had only one constant: the darkness within it. Candles, starcrystal, and torches did what they could to lessen it, and windows and skylights admitted some sunlight that seemed always reluctant to touch the ancient stone. Those who lived in Darkhaven lived in shadow.

Not many lived there, and not all who did were human.

The ancient cycle of day and night was preserved by the massive bells in the Boriun Tower. They tolled every hour. The time they spoke of now was an hour past midnight, and their peals tumbled and reverberated throughout the vast structure, reaching to the tops of the towers and, more felt than heard, the depths of the caverns within the castle's rocky foundation. Most of those in Darkhaven, habituated by many similar nights, slept through them, but one heard: a lone figure, hurrying down a hall of grim splendor.

It was a woman; she carried a thin rod of starcrystal to light her way. The soft blue light made her pale skin even more pallid, and made cold the warm dark gold of her hair. She hugged a robe about her to protect her from the castle's chill air, for she was dressed in nightclothes. The route she took was a maze of intersecting passages and chambers, but she did not hesitate at the many crossroads. She knew the way well.

Her way led over floors of polished onyx, jade, and petrified wood; past murals by artists long dust, and panels carved into scenes of battle and conquest; past treasures to make or break a kingdom, which were not one ten thousandth of all the treasures of Darkhaven. She knew these few well by now, and did not look at them as she passed. She did not look back either, though she was alone and the moody halls seemed designed to play on nightfears. But familiarity had made her somewhat used to Darkhaven; she knew she would never feel entirely at ease in its depths. There were too many alcoves and unlit ways and rooms, too many unexplained sounds, and, she knew, too many real dangers that lurked in the miles of caverns and corridors beyond the tiny inhabited area used by Pandrogas and his servants.

There, for example—that noise as she passed the vaulted opening to a dark passageway. A strange sound of movement, now scrabbling, now slithering. She paused, peering into the passage's depths. The starcrystal did nothing to illuminate them. The sound came again; she could not tell if its origins were close or far away. She continued quickly on her way.

He would let no harm come to me, she told herself. But she knew that not even his sorcery could encompass and control all of Darkhaven. She was only relatively safe. And she also knew that she preferred it that way, that whatever peril there was in walking Darkhaven alone added to the excitement, the pleasure that awaited.

She descended a short flight of stairs, staring at the entablature over it as she did so. It was marble, decorated with a brilliantly worked frieze of an orgy. The participants were cacodemons, werefolk, and hideously malformed humans. She always looked at it as she passed beneath it, and always wondered if she deserved a place among its characters.

She always wondered, as well, how she could love a man who could live in such a place, a world such as Darkhaven.

Another flight of steps, these ascending, and she stopped at the corridor's end. A huge door stood partially open beneath an arch on which could be seen the remnants of a defaced emblem. As always, she wondered what it had been. In the starcrystal's light she could barely make out the form of an equilateral triangle, but whatever had been carved within it had been effaced.

She looked at the door. It was open, as usual. As always, she thought, I could still go back.

Her name was Amber Jaodana Chuntai Lhil, and she had been a marquise. And, in a room almost a mile away, a man who had been a marquis slept.

She put her hand against the door and pushed, always surprised at the ease and silence with which it swung open. It was dark within; thick hangings covered one of the castle's few chamber windows. The small rod of starcrystal showed her the outlines of the massive furniture and bed.

A shadow crouched on the bed. It rose, seeming to grow as she saw it, and a voice like distant thunder spoke: *"Limnus diam!"*

At the words four candles set in sconces on the walls flared with intolerable brightness, illuminating the room in stark black and white. Amber gasped, covering her eyes with the brocaded sleeve of her robe. Then the light was gone as quickly as it came; only the soft radiance of her starcrystal remained, and the smell of melted wax. And Amber laughed.

She stood in the middle of the room and let her laughter fill it for a moment. Then she crossed the carpet to the bed. The starcrystal turned the shadow into a man seated cross-legged on the silken sheets. He looked somewhat embarrassed, but as Amber continued to chuckle amusement pulled at his lips as well.

Amber put the starcrystal in an empty candlestand on the bureau. "You know that spell never works," she said to him. Then she let her robe fall away from her and met his embrace.

The passage from Ardatha's balcony to Darkhaven was over in a moment. Even so, it was one of the most uncomfortable journeys of Beorn's life, as bad as the time he had escaped the Duchy of

Darqnehs by hiding in a corpse cart after robbing the duke.

For an instant that seemed like forever his lungs had been filled with the stench of sulphur, his eyes tortured by the wind, his midriff almost crushed in the cacodemon's grasp. But then it had been over, and the thief was released. He fell half his height to strike a rough stone surface. Winded, he crouched there for a moment, fighting nausea, before attempting to stand.

He got halfway to his feet before he froze, realizing that he was poised on a rim of stone scarcely wider than he was. One sloping side dropped at least five stories to a dimly glimpsed rooftop; the other disappeared into the blackness of the interior. The Spire of Owls was octagonal in shape, and the top of it had crumbled long ago, leaving some of the walls higher than others. Stone steps lined the inner walls, fading into the darkness below. The interior and the rim on which he stood was mottled with bird droppings, which seemed appropriate to the spire's name.

Beorn made sure he was standing on a fairly secure part of the rim before turning to look out over the castle. He had no fear of heights and could easily keep his balance now that he had recovered from the flight. The spire was one of the higher points of Darkhaven, and he could see the stone world spreading out before him for what seemed like forever. Though it had been night on Oljaer, here the sun's rays lay obliquely across the fragment. At the moment the light was obscured by a cloud, but he could still see well enough to make out the rise and fall of countless towers, parapets, bartizans, domes . . . it was an ocean of masonry, gray and crumbling. At another time, in another situation, he might have stood for some time contemplating the majestic panorama. But as he turned slowly, taking it all in, he saw again he whom the spectacle of Darkhaven had caused him to forget for a moment—Balandrus the cacodemon.

It crouched on the stone lip in the shade of the wall, talons gripping it like a falcon holding to a perch, hiding from the sunlight that was deadly to its kind. Lambent eyes watched him. Beorn could make out its form somewhat better than in the night of Oljaer. He wished he could not. The cacodemon was scaled and muscled like a rude clay sculpture. As the thief watched it, trying again to control his fear, the sun shone through the clouds and turned the gray light ruddy. The cacodemon scowled, revealing a flash of yellow fangs, and shrank deeper into the shade. "Make haste!" it growled at him.

Beorn turned away quickly and began to descend the stairs. They seemed sturdy enough for the most part, though the excrement coating them made footing perilous. Beorn stayed close to the wall, testing each step before putting his weight on it. As he entered the spire he felt the amulet about his neck grow momentarily warm. This, he knew, was a result of its absorbing the warning spell that no doubt guarded the castle's many entrances. He looked at the ring on his hand; it glowed with the faintest hint of crimson.

He had not gone far before he heard a strange sound below him: a rushing, flapping sound, like the beating of hundreds of rugs or the skirling of leaves in a gale; he had an instant to prepare, to huddle against the cold stone, protecting his head with his hands, before the air about him was suddenly alive with feathers, beaks, and claws. A hollow shrieking, endlessly multiplied, filled his ears. Then the moment was past. Beorn glanced up, dazed, to see the last of them catch the sunlight on their feathers as they disappeared into the cloudy sky.

He shook his head to clear it. The Spire of Owls indeed, he thought. If this was the entrance Ardatha had chosen as a safe one, he wondered what lurked in other parts of the castle. Things, perhaps, that not even the bear could deal with.

He had no further encounters during the long descent. When he finally reached a narrow corridor at the spire's base he saw that the glow of his ring had become slightly stronger. He stopped in the shadows before venturing further and composed himself. Nothing could be on his mind now but his task, his entire being had to be geared to it only. He breathed deeply, filling his lungs with musty air and letting the tension in his mind and body flow away from him as he exhaled. It was a technique he had perfected with years of practice, a way of emptying his mind and turning his attention entirely outward, ready to evaluate every sound, every movement, every scent, every change in temperature. Thus prepared, he continued on his way. He had no idea what this talisman he was to steal might be, but whatever it was, he did not doubt his ability to steal it.

He found himself in a confusion of intersecting halls and corridors, marked everywhere by the ravages of age and neglect. Rotting tapestries and pennants hung from walls and ceilings; furniture crumbled, forgotten, in shadows; curtains and hangings were patched with cobwebs. Light from an occasional dormer or lancet window in the high ceilings, or from a rare ever-glowing starcrystal, showed him his dim way. Beorn followed the route dictated by the waxing and waning of the ring's glow. He saw no one, and heard only the scurrying of rats and the distant drip of water.

The ring's glow led him through a long-forgotten arsenal for one wing of the castle, and he paused to admire the weapons that filled the room. Though rust-pitted and dulled, they still showed the care and workmanship of their ancient makers. The walls were shingled with blades of every type, with shields of dragon leather and arrows tipped with hydra's teeth. Pikes and halberds stood in corners, and casques, breastplates, and chain mail were arranged on racks. Beorn was tempted to take one of the small daggers, but decided not to; his own weapons, concealed among his clothes, were in much better condition. Besides, if he started lifting things in Darkhaven he would soon be too heavy to move; even in this uninhabited part of it, full of mold and decay, were treasures to match any he had ever stolen.

The vivid memory of the enchantress writhing in her summoning dance kept rising before him; he could almost see her spinning on the dusty floor. He hated her and yet he desired her. He had not wanted any woman so badly for a long time—and, as always, the desire frightened him.

He had not wanted any woman as badly since Suchana.

Suchana, he thought, how I wish you were here with me now. He alternated that wish with one putting him anywhere else, even back in decadent, temple-ridden Bagerah. He had come to the desert metropolis as a lad, his few belongings in a sheepskin pack that had promptly been stolen. He would have starved had not Suchana, in the act of lifting his moneypouch, taken pity on him and offered him dinner. She was four years older than him and a century wiser.

He had shared her knowledge, her quarters on Thieves' Island, and—reluctantly but finally—her bed.

She had been a good thief, Beorn thought, though she had at times been plagued with a conscience, something that had never troubled him. Lying on stolen silk, her hands tangled in the hair of his chest, she had spoken sometimes of her fears of despoiling moneylenders and merchants—not fears of being caught so much as fears for her soul. She had been a sometimes adherent to the teachings of Hothoth, who held that individuals were but shattered pieces of a single oversoul, and that harm done to any kept all from joining in spiritual harmony and peace. She had longed for that peace. He hoped she had finally attained it.

As for himself, he had troubles with his soul only when it wrapped itself in fur and threatened a berserker's rage. He had no qualms about being a thief; indeed, he considered it a more honest way of life than that of many of those from whom he stole.

A sudden flash of warmth from the amulet on his chest stopped him. He looked about in surprise and dismay, realizing that he had no idea how he had come to the dark and moldering bedchamber in which he stood. By the Necromancer, he had been wandering blindly, his mind full of thoughts of past and self-pity! It had been purest luck that he had not stumbled straight into a brace of guards, or Pandrogas himself.

He looked about him. The vast chamber had obviously once been the sleeping quarters of someone important. A huge bed, canopied now with webs, set on a raised dais before him. Carved on the wall above it was a strange emblem; within an equilateral triangle was a likeness of a head with two profiles, one that of an aristocratic, bearded man, and the other a grinning death's-head. Cabinets and bureaus now made nesting places for rats. On either side of the bed stood two statues, one a warrior in archaic battle dress, the other a woman in a long, flowing gown. They stared at each other across the bed, their marble expressions full of ineffable longing.

Beorn felt suddenly nervous. There was nothing alive in the chamber, and yet he had the distinct sense of movement, of life. He fought rising panic, the panic of the bear, as he squinted through the dim light at the statues.

Then he realized where the movement was coming from: the shadows of the statues, cast by a small starcrystal sconce almost obscured by webs, were lengthening. And not only that—they seemed to be thickening, solidifying somehow, as they crept slowly across the rotting bedsheets. Beorn stared, hypnotized at the creeping darkness.

The shadows touched. Something began to move beneath the sheets.

A rat, the thief thought, still unable to move. It had to be a rat. But it was too large for a rat, and it did not move like a rat. Instead, he could see in languorous motion beneath the sheets the outline of two people locked in love. And he could hear, faintly, as though muffled by many walls or years, the cries of passion, rising in time with their movements. The bodies arced, froze for a moment—

He heard a scream that echoed and re-echoed through the chamber and through his head. From beneath the sheets another, darker shadow pooled and moved. It reached the edge of the mattress, and blood fell in slow, loud drops upon the tiles.

Beorn turned and ran from the bedchamber down the long hallway. He seized a column, stopping his panicked flight, and held on to it, gasping, like a lashed prisoner grips the whipping post. For a long moment he leaned against it, oblivious to his surroundings. Then, with a start, he looked about him for enemies both natural and supernatural. He stood in a vestibule at the intersection of two hallways. All was silent; he was alone.

Beorn straightened his shoulders, shaking his head as would his angry alter ego. What was wrong with him? Ardatha had intimated that there were strange occurrences in Darkhaven. And he had seen things as inexplicable and as terrifying during past escapades. Alone he had entered the Cists of Aum and stolen the ruby-eyed skull of Tallan-zun; the sights in those subterranean vaults would have driven many mad. He had kept his wits then; he had remained professional.

He had been asked to rob for adepts before, though never under such bizarre circumstances. And he had stolen from adepts, though never from a sorcerer of Pandrogas's standing, and certainly never without any preparation for the theft. But that was no excuse for letting memories and thoughts pollute the clear stillness of his concentration. He had lost control. No, it was worse than that. He had not been in control from the start. It was Ardatha who controlled him, as surely as though he labored under her geas. She had manipulated him, had toyed with him most cruelly, and yet he could not stop thinking of her or letting her lead his thoughts away from his work. She was making a fool of him, and he would not have that. He would almost rather remain on his present terms with the bear and deny her the talisman she wanted so badly. But perhaps there might be a way to gain both his reward and his revenge.

He would find this talisman, whatever it was, and then he would plan further. He would think of a way to turn the tables on the enchantress. He could do no less. It was a matter of honor.

With all the noise of a shadow, the thief continued his search.

In another part of Darkhaven, the man who had been a marquis was not asleep. Instead, he, too, walked the corridors, coming at last to stand before two ironbound doors. He paused before them for a moment, then stepped forward and put his hand on the latch. Mounted above the doors was a brazen head which stared at the far wall. The face was handsome but empty, lacking expression. The man who had been a marquis felt his stomach tighten as the eyes of the sculpture suddenly blinked and looked down at him. The head spoke in a metallic voice.

"Who enters my master's laboratory?"

As he answered, he was proud that his voice did not tremble. "Your master's guest, on your master's business."

The answer was evidently satisfactory, for the metal face became immobile again. He sighed, opened the doors and entered.

The huge chamber was still quite dark, even after he had uncovered the starcrystals. He did not feel all that eager to see some of the things in the room, but he preferred the light to the dark.

That was his problem, he thought bitterly; he had always preferred the light to the dark.

He sat in a comfortable highbacked chair near one wall and looked at the room. Despite his feelings about the one who owned it, he had to admit it was impressive, if somewhat lacking in order. Cab-

inets and shelves lined the walls, stuffed with a variety of books,
scrolls, enchiridions and the like, as well as carved bowls and boxes,
vials filled with liquids and powders, and many devices for which
he had no name. The long table in the room's center was likewise
strewn with appurtenances and instruments. Various robes and vest-
ments hung on the backs of chairs or from standing candelabra.
Golden censers hung by chains, faintly scenting the air with cinnamon, galingale, and black mint.

He stood and wandered nervously about the room. He looked at
a complicated set of orreries and armillary spheres designed to represent the myriad orbits of the fragments through the sky. The seven
major fragments—Toul, Rhynne, Salakh, Calamchor, Twilan, Kulareem, and Pandor—were highlighted in gold. Elsewhere were
globes upon pedestals, basins and mortars stained with various chemicals, alembics and chests, a great charcoal-blackened athanor in
one corner of the room...exhausted, his head swimming, he sat
down on a workbench. What am I doing here? he wondered in
despair. Where should I begin?

He shivered and pulled his feathered cloak tighter about his shoulders, though the temperature was comfortable. I am cold because I
have no blood in my veins, he thought. That was obvious; had he
blood, he would not be there. He would be at the sorcerer's bedchamber, pounding on the door, challenging the sorcerer to a duel
for the satisfaction of honor.

But the sorcerer had saved his life.

His name was Tahrynyar Zokhan Chuntai Girihan. A year before
he had lost a marquisate. And now he had lost his wife.

His life had not prepared Tahrynyar for any of this. He had been
the Marquis of Chuntai, an estate in the Empire of Turrith on Toul.
He had had lands, title, and fortune; until little over a commonyear
ago he had been used to ease and order, with nothing more dangerous
than a fencing lesson or more strenuous than an afternoon's ride
through an espaliered wood. He had been dressed in velvet and sable
by servants, had dined on roast swan and wines of remarkable vin-
tage, had slept on cloudlike goosedown.

And he had made enemies.

He had paid too little attention to the various intrigues that were a part of all governments. He had made no special attempt to use the power and influence he had for good or ill; he had assumed that by maintaining *status quo* he was maintaining good will. He had not realized that having can be its own reason for losing.

And now here I am, he thought, with nothing more to lose.

The sorcerer's laboratory wavered as tears of frustration came to his eyes. He looked at an ambry nearby, saw in it a statue of a woman carved from gemwood. He stared at it, seeing instead of its delicate features the face of Amber, his Amber. She had been his wife for five years—even now he could recall some grim echo of the happiness he had felt when she had agreed to marry him. That she had been of lesser nobility than he had not mattered to him; even the fact that she had bore him no children he had accepted with equanimity. Tahrynyar had always considered himself a plain and uninteresting man, and blessed by all the gods there were to have a wife of such talent, wit, and beauty. He remembered the countless times he had listened to her play a flute crafted from a unicorn's horn, the awe and ecstasy it had never failed to give him. No sorcerer ever made greater magic. And she had loved him; that had been the greatest magic of all.

He stood abruptly, resolutely, and crossed to the table. Several dozen huge volumes of lore, obviously centuries old, lay upon the wood. He saw the scattered fragments of a casting sphere as well, and was tempted to gather them and toss them. But he had never been good at reading the fallen pieces. He draped his cloak over the back of a chair and turned to the books.

The covers were embossed with such titles as *The Book of Stones* and *The Red Grimoire*. He hoped that the latter was a codex of spells and formulae which comprised the Lorian System, the school of magic in which Pandrogas had attained the rank of Sorcerer of the Tenth Ring. Tahrynyar had never studied magic, had always been suspicious and afraid of it. But he had been told once by an old conjurer that the potential for it lived within everyone to greater or lesser degree.

Perhaps now was the time to test the old man's words.

He opened *The Red Grimoire*.

He had no idea what he was doing, no plan, no intention. He was a hurt and angry man, and he merely wanted to strike out somehow, using the weapons and knowledge of the man who was his enemy and his friend. With no more than that in mind, Tahrynyar began to read the book.

What surprised him at first was that he *could* read it; he had been sure that the ancient tome would be in a language unknown to him. But the characters, set down in precise, small lines on the curling pages, the margins referenced and annotated by numerous hands, were in Rannish, like the titles; it was a dead language, and the spelling and diction were archaic, but he had learned a great many things in his childhood he had never thought would be of use to him, and reading ancient tongues was one of them. He was surprised and slightly disconcerted; in the back of his mind he had seen himself giving up when faced by a foreign text. Now, however, he had no choice but to read on.

He flipped over several pages. They seemed to settle almost without his help, and he found himself looking at a picture. It was finely drawn, quite faded but still easily made out. It was the face of a Chthon.

Horns rose from the temples, and small, snakelike tendrils extended from the jawline. Though the inks used on the page had faded with the book's age, he could still sense the glossy coloration of the scales. The lidless gaze held his. It was an effort to look away, to turn to the next page. And that was his mistake.

The first line of the spell seized him. "This is the means of summoning Sestihaculas," he read. "The Demogorgon, Lord of Snakes, he whose blood melts iron, whose breath is a pestilence upon the land..."

He did not want to continue reading, but he could not stop. He heard the words; they seemed to be shouted in a cold voice from far away, growing louder and louder. He could hear a soundless pounding—his heart, or some infernal drum?—that increased in tempo, drowning out the sound of the summoning as he spoke the final words. And then the starcrystal light vanished.

At last he could scream; but it was too late.

At first there was nothing but darkness and waiting. Then he became aware of a faint, cold light, a phosphorescence like that found on rotting wood. He could see the stone floor beneath his feet, but nothing beyond it. He heard a distant wind beginning, felt a breeze tug at his blouse. Dimly glimpsed clouds seemed to be swirling about him, faster and faster. The wind was like the screaming of children now.

And then, quite suddenly, there was no longer a floor beneath his boots, and he was falling into a funnel of whirling clouds.

Tahrynyar screamed, and could not hear his screams. He fell, and the wind tore at him and spun him, and the smell was of ancient earth, rich with decay and putrescence, overpowering. The sound of the wind now seemed more like dry, whispery laughter, or like the rustling of scales and the hissing of snakes.

Over it, he thought he heard from far away a voice shouting words too distant to understand. From the corner of his eye he saw a warm golden light, unlike the foxfire of the clouds. Tahrynyar could make out the form of a man outlined in fire, glimpsed momentarily through the clouds. At the same time he felt the floor for an instant beneath his doeskin boots, like a man dragged by an undertow will occasionally feel the sand. He seemed no longer to be falling, but rather floating. And all the while the voice grew louder, strong and comforting, speaking words he could not understand, but which overpowered the hissing and wailing.

He felt a moment of relief, but only a moment, for tendrils of smoke began to creep up toward him from the clouds. They wrapped about him, pulling him down. He shouted for help, and the cry was cut off as one of the wraithlike ropes tightened about his neck.

Then a hand reached to him through the clouds—a pale hand in a sleeve of pale gold that did not flap or tear in the winds. On the fifth finger of the left hand was a crystal band. Tahrynyar seized the hand with both of his and hung for a moment, still pulled downward. Then, reluctantly, the tendrils' hold on him slackened, and they faded away.

He still hung from the hand as though over a vortex. He looked down into the cloudy depths. And from the depths a voice spoke. Its tone was rich and courtly, full of civility, and yet somehow it suggested to Tahrynyar the hissing of snakes.

"I am not summoned lightly," the voice said, "nor will I leave without something for my trouble. Dare you offend me, recluse?"

And the voice which had saved Tahrynyar, the voice which he now recognized, asked, "Dare you battle me in Darkhaven, Serpent Lord?"

"I can still take this one," the Demogorgon replied. "He has summoned me without protecting himself. I shall not meet you on your home ground. But I exact this pledge: that you give me leave to come to you in a place of equal power, for there are matters unsettled between us. And I see Darkhaven giving you up at long last."

The sorcerer replied slowly, "I do so pledge, Sestihaculas."

"We will meet again," the Demogorgon said, and on those words the winds rose to a final shriek. Tahrynyar closed his eyes and cried out, and suddenly felt his knees strike the stone painfully. He opened his eyes.

He knelt before the man who had now saved his life twice. He still held his hand.

The laboratory was as it was before, illuminated by Pandrogas's other hand, which burned with golden fire. Tahrynyar rose to his feet with difficulty.

"What happened?" he gasped.

"You summoned the Demogorgon," Pandrogas said. He stepped up to one of the starcrystals and stroked it with his fiery hand, causing it to glow again, then extinguished the hand by shaking it as though it were a brand. He closed the book on the table; the sound was like a door slamming. Then he looked at Tahrynyar and said, "Why?"

Tahrynyar tried to meet the sorcerer's eyes and could not. Then there was a footstep from behind them, and both turned.

Amber stood in the doorway, her robe clutched about her, her hair disheveled. She said nothing, nor did they, for a long moment. Then Tahrynyar left the room, brushing past her roughly. Amber raised a hand as though to stay him, then let it fall to her side. She crossed to Pandrogas and put her head on his chest as Tahrynyar's bootfalls faded into echoes. The two stood there, saying nothing, for long after the silence was complete.

Chapter 4

The Casting of the Sphere

The sorcerer was afraid.

He stood with Amber before the crenelated walls of a battlement, looking over the castle. The always evening sky of Darkhaven looked ominous; a storm was approaching. Dark clouds covered part of Oljaer, dimming the many colored lights of the city. From the point of view of the two on the battlement the fragment seemed to float at right angles to Darkhaven. More clouds obscured the sun beyond it. The storm was moving toward Darkhaven.

The sorcerer watched the clouds billowing like smoke, chaotically, with no possibility of prediction or control. Were the fragments of the world to career like that, unordered and unrestrained, life would soon cease to exist. It was a fearful concept, to be sure. But it was not what he feared most.

I should be better able to take the long view, Pandrogas thought cynically. After all, I am a sorcerer. But he was also human, and it seemed that as he grew older he grew more human—and more afraid. And so the message he had received earlier that day from

56

Thasos of the Cabal did not frighten him as much as the threat of Sestihaculas, illogical though he knew that to be. For his old friend and mentor on the Cabal had spoken of a danger too vast and impersonal to really feel, despite its onrushing inevitability—while Sestihaculas was a danger he knew.

He also knew that, in a way, he had brought the impending confrontation with the Demogorgon upon himself.

He almost wished he had let Sestihaculas take Tahrynyar. Immediately he felt ashamed of the thought. One of the many things that made it all so difficult was that he liked the former marquis, though the man was somewhat a weakling in several ways. (But am I not also? he thought.) The knowledge that he was in part responsible for the hurt and the anger that had almost sent Tahrynyar to Xoth was not an easy load to carry. For all his abilities and powers, for all his insight into mysteries beyond the comprehension of most people, he felt as foolish and bumbling as the newest apprentice in this matter. And he could not help feeling resentful of the situation at times, if only because there were so many other urgent matters that required time and energy.

Sometimes he found himself impatient with his humanity; sometimes he let himself become angry because he, a Sorcerer of the Tenth Ring, had become involved in such petty matters as love, and guilt, and grief. But, no matter the pain or the price it cost, he thanked the many gods of this fragmented world that he was lucky enough to love Amber.

Pandrogas was very aware of her standing beside him, not touching, but close enough that he could feel her body heat in contrast to the cool, rain-scented air. They had said little since what had happened in the laboratory. She had questioned him about what had taken place, but he had told her nothing outside of reassuring her that there was no longer any danger. She had sensed that he was not ready to talk about it yet; she was always so very receptive to his moods. That was a part of the talent she had, the talent she was learning to develop, under his guidance. It promised to be a most formidable talent. He thought of the two of them as they had been so short a time before, lying together on damp silk, he in his robe and she still naked. She had been playing her flute, that beautiful instrument carved from an alicorn, and he had been listening . . . no, Pandrogas corrected himself; there had to be a better word for it than that, a word that gave a hint of the willing utter abandonment with which he gave himself to her music. And "music": that, also, was altogether too pallid and insipid a word; what Amber created with thin, delicate fingers and carefully measured breath on the spiraled ivory instrument could never be subsumed under such a paltry heading as "music." But, for lack of better terms with which to describe it, she had made what must be called music, a simple, pure melody that was perfect for the calmness and the afterglow that they both felt, and he had listened. Until she had stopped jarringly, in mid-refrain, looking confused. He had asked her what was wrong and she had said, "I felt a sudden chill, as if a door had opened." And then he had felt it, known it for what it was, and dashed from the bedchamber toward the laboratory. But even in the shock and surprise of the realization that his sanctum had been breached by Sestihaculas, he had been aware that she had felt it before he had.

He had studied for many years, under many tutors, to develop slowly and painfully what she possessed innately. Of all the students he had taught over the years, she had by far the most potential. At times he felt almost frightened for Amber, for the power he knew she possessed. And at other times—too many other times—he felt jealous.

After Tahrynyar had left the laboratory, the two of them had come to stand upon the battlement. He assumed she felt, as he did, the need to stand in the wind, and perhaps the rain as well. He wondered what she thought as she looked out over Darkhaven. She had come here by accident, while he had come for a specific purpose over five years ago (and the message from Thasos had reminded him most pointedly of the urgency of that purpose). He knew that the castle frightened and repelled her; what she did not know was that it still had the same effect on him at times, even after five commonyears. But he was sure Darkhaven still held the answer to his quest: a way to save what was left of the world without recourse to Necromancy.

But was there any time left?

* * *

Amber stood next to him, looking out over Darkhaven. A canvas
of chimneys, gables, fenestrated walls, colonnades, and an infinity
of other structures, the roofscape appeared even grimmer than usual
against the coming storm. Already the far boundaries of it were
obscured in the clouds. Gusts of wind tugged at the acres of ivy and
moss that covered some shaded walls, and tore leaves from the
orchard and garden Pandrogas's servants had cultivated on the top
of a nearby building. As Amber looked toward the Spire of Owls,
she thought she saw movement in its broken turret. A moment later
the birds, made mothlike by the distance, appeared in a cloud that
dispersed into the storm. She had lived within Darkhaven for over
four commonmonths, and so still found much about the view that
was new to her. The castle's longer axis measured more than two
leagues, and its widest part almost half that. Its highest tower was
over three hundred feet. What amazed her the most about these
dimensions was that the castle had once been larger still; Pandrogas
had taken her once to the Boriun Tower and from its belfry shown
her the broken walls and timbers lining Darkhaven's circumference.
No one knew how big it had been before the Spell of Shattering had
torn this part free of the disintegrating world. How many centuries
had it taken to build it? she wondered, as she had so often before;
how many quarries had it exhausted, how many generations of laborers had it consumed? There was no way of knowing. Perhaps
somewhere within its many libraries and record chambers, brittle
pages recorded the statistics of its growth, revealed the mysteries of
its origin, the name of whoever had ruled over this domain of cold
stone and darkness. But a thousand scholars might search away their
lifetimes and not find those pages.

She feared Darkhaven, it was true; feared it and yet was fascinated
by it. She could not conceive of living here for the rest of her life,
or any appreciable part of it, and yet she did not want to leave
Pandrogas. He was here for some specific reason, but refused to
speak of it save as "research." For five years he had pursued this
research. He had come here the year she was married, she realized.
He had told her of his explorations within the gray vastness, had

spoken of its myriad styles of design and decor; how some areas
were nothing but miles of unadorned stone corridors with monasterial
cells opening off of them, while in others the very walls were gold-
gilded, the door latches platinum and diamond, the floors carpeted
with cashmere. There were rooms within larger rooms; houses, complete with grounds, covered by welkinlike roofs; secret ways and
corridors in bewildering complexity; so much so that several different
communities could—and apparently in times past did—live inter-
mingled and yet unknowing of each other.

He had told her also of other, more sinister aspects of Darkhaven:
of the many apparitions that haunted its unused areas, and of the
more material but still blasphemous creatures that rose occasionally
from the pits and caverns in the fragment of Darkhaven's foundation.
Within the castle proper there were areas where even he, Sorcerer
of the Tenth Ring in the Lorian System, as well as sorcerer and
enchanter of lesser rank in other styles of magic, found it prudent
not to go. Darkhaven had held many secrets over the ages.

These thoughts brought her mind to one of the latest of those
secrets, one which had until recently, she thought, been successfully
kept. But Tahrynyar had obviously been motivated to whatever fool-
hardiness he had committed by suspicion, anger, and pain. Amber
blinked, sudden tears blurring her vision of Darkhaven like the rain
now sweeping toward them. She had only been deceiving herself
these past few months in believing that he had been fooled; Tahrynyar
might be a coward, but he was not a stupid man. Even within a
castle the size of a city it was impossible to conceal such an affair
when the population was no more than the three of them and ten
servants.

So he knew, and now she knew that he knew. And what was to
be done about it?

It was not a question that she wanted to face. She had succeeded
fairly well in the past few months in not facing it. But now the
choice was no longer hers.

She was not sure when she had stopped loving Tahrynyar, and
there was some doubt in her mind if she had ever really loved him.
Certainly she had never felt about him the way she felt about Pan-

drogas, had never reached the giddy heights of emotion that characterized her time spent with the sorcerer. And she was not merely thinking of their lovemaking, but of their long conversations, their explorations of the small bit of Darkhaven that was his, the teaching in the basics of magic, a hundred other things . . . she was endlessly fascinated with him. But this was not infatuation, for she did not find him perfect. At times he was moody and remote, seeming almost to use prestige and power as a cloak behind which to hide. At first she had been reluctant (Be honest, she admonished herself; not reluctant, afraid) to accuse him of that. But not long after their first clandestine bedding she had done so, and to her surprise and relief he had admitted it, and apologized. And he thereafter had made an effort to be more accessible to her. If he had not succeeded all of the time, well, that was to be expected, considering the anchoritic life he led. He was not a man one grew to know easily; but she thought he was all the more worth knowing for that.

She looked at Pandrogas; he was watching the storm. His profile against the clouds seemed a part of the castle's skyline: craggy and grim, full of secrets. It was weathered as well, as though in the past he had spent much time outdoors; she had been faintly shocked to realize how much of a recluse he was. He did not particularly like the outdoors, she knew; for him to stand thus was unusual.

His hair was a black mane laced with stone-colored streaks; it fell almost to his shoulders. His loose robe did no justice to the body beneath it, the body she knew quite well. It was still lean and supple, though he was approaching his fifth commonyear decade. He put himself through a rigorous program every other day that combined exercise with spell-casting and meditation. Sorcery, he had told her, like any other discipline, must be constantly practiced.

He lifted a hand to brush back his wind-stirred hair. She noticed the crystal ring on the last finger of his left hand—the tenth finger, counting from his right hand. He was one of the foremost living adepts. And he loved her.

As did Tahrynyar.

A faint spatter of rain stung her cheeks. This storm looked to be a bad one, like the storm that had brought Tahrynyar and her to Darkhaven. That one had hurled their dragonship against the stone walls and buildings and broken it like a kite in a gale. She had a dim memory of staggering and sliding over the rain-slick shingles and slate tiles, until at last she had fallen. Numbed by the rain, confused and disoriented by the storm-tossed flight and shipwreck, she had taken out her flute and, hardly knowing what she was doing, begun to play a piece she had learned as a child, called *The Light upon the Water*. That the music might attract rescue had not occurred to her until Pandrogas had appeared out of the mist and rain before her; she had done it for the strength it had given her. He had saved her and Tahrynyar. No one else had survived.

Amber put her hand over his where it rested on the merlon. He turned and looked at her, and she knew his thoughts had been somewhere far away.

"Do you fancy getting wet?" she asked him, smiling. "Myself, I fancy breakfast."

He smiled slightly also, then hesitated as though about to speak. When he said nothing she turned him toward her, putting her hands on his hips. "I did not thank you for saving him," she said.

His expression was ironic. "Neither did he," he said wryly.

"Pandrogas—"

He touched two fingers to her lips, but she pulled away from them. "No, I'll not be silent now. Nothing has changed; it is merely out in the open, as it should be. It can't be resolved by ignoring it. I love you, not Tahrynyar, and I owe him the honesty of telling him so. I have been weak these past months; I'll not be weak any longer."

Pandrogas looked at her, his gaze unreadable. No, Amber thought, Please—now is not the time to retreat. "So you will tell him," the sorcerer said. "And what will happen then?"

The question disconcerted her. She hesitated over the answer, which she knew would sound harsh and uncaring of her husband. "Why . . . then he will go his way, wherever it takes him, and I shall remain here with you." Until I can convince you to leave, she thought.

He looked out at the coming storm again. "And if I were to tell you that I might be leaving Darkhaven soon?"

Astonishment kept her silent; astonishment, but not hope. There was something in the way he spoke that did not bring joy at the prospect of leaving Darkhaven. Then he sighed and told her in detail what had happened in the laboratory, and of the pledge exacted by Sestihaculas.

She had learned something of magic from his lessons. "How could Tahrynyar have called the Demogorgon? He has no magical talent, and you say he performed none of the necessary preparations—"

"Exactly so. Sestihaculas did not have to come, but the reading of the Summoning Spell gave him license to enter Darkhaven. He did not want Tahrynyar—he wanted me."

The wind seemed much colder to her. "Why?"

"We know each other of old; the details do not matter now. This is not the first time he has used an excuse to enter Darkhaven. He wants access to the knowledge, the power, within these walls. The point is that I agreed to battle him, somewhere, somehow—I had to, to save Tahrynyar. I would rather the meeting be of my choosing than his."

"But how can you battle him?" Amber said, shivering. "The Serpent Lord is evil incarnate!"

Pandrogas shrugged. "Evil? Are snakes or spiders evil? Or any of the other creatures we consider loathsome, and which the Chthons, for reasons of their own, protect? I would not say so. Chthons, and the cacodemons which serve them, are ruthless, cunning, and vindictive, true. But think—Sestihaculas and his kind existed for ages beneath the crust of the whole world, taking no notice of humanity save when troubled by us. Then the Necromancer shattered the world and they tumbled out into the light and the void like wasps from a broken nest. They resent and torment humankind for their present state of affairs—and who is to say they do not have a right?"

"I'm in no mood for a debate," Amber told him. "You're evading my question. But it doesn't matter. If you intend to meet Sestihaculas outside of Darkhaven, I shall go with you."

Pandrogas raised one eyebrow, and Amber felt an absurd sense of triumph in having finally surprised him. "Out of the question! It is too dangerous!"

"That isn't a reason."

He stared at her for a moment; then suddenly his grave expression gave way to a smile. It made his face both older, by the wrinkles it brought to his eyes, and younger, and as always Amber could not help but smile back. "Well," he said, "if that isn't a reason, then surely no reason exists. But this is a discussion to have over breakfast, rather than in a cold rain," as another wave washed over them. They turned and re-entered the vast, still body of Darkhaven, Pandrogas holding the loose folds of his robe protectively over Amber. A moment after they had gone in the rain began in earnest, and soon the storm in its full fury was lashing the unrepentant stone.

The long table was supported by dragon's legs carved of dark wood. Pandrogas and Amber sat together at one end of it, dwarfed by its length as the table itself was dwarfed by the size of the huge refectory. Amber looked at the dull reflection of the starcrystal chandelier in the table's polish and thought about the first time Pandrogas had shown her the dining hall; she had impulsively kicked off her slippers and leaped onto the table to dance its length, playing an impish, skirling tune on her flute. Pandrogas had stared at her, first in astonishment, then in humor, and then had vaulted nimbly up to join her, his boots and clapping hands counterpointing her music. Tahrynyar had gaped in shock and then looked somewhat ill at the damage being done to the ancient wood. It had taken several of the servants over a week to restore the finish.

One of the servants entered now, carrying a trayful of covered dishes which he sat before them. "Thank you, Kabyn," Pandrogas murmured, and the man withdrew with an impassive face. Amber watched him exit noiselessly; like all of the sorcerer's servants he was dressed in somber green livery, and was tall and thin, almost gaunt. The women had hair much darker than her own honey-colored locks, and most of the men were bald. She had never been able to guess the age of any of them—they could have been from forty to sixty commonyears. As she had done before, she leaned toward Pandrogas and whispered, only half-jokingly, "I don't like any of them. You should dismiss the lot."

"They were here before me," he said as he lifted the cover from a dish of sweetbreads. "The retainers of the previous owner, and the owner before him."

He had never mentioned their origin before. "And he was?"

"Another sorcerer—does that surprise you? He offered me custody of Darkhaven when I resigned from the Cabal. He said there was much here for a man devoted to study and learning." Pandrogas poured fresh juice into a mug carved from a single giant beryl. "He was right, so much so that I nearly despaired of starting."

A container of iceberry jam was beyond his reach; he made a small gesture at it and murmured, *"Elim, toom."* The command was spoken in Payan, a language well suited for magic of no great consequence, and his gesture and expression, Amber knew, had been perfectly executed for all their casualness. But the dish of jam, instead of floating obediently to his hand, trembled and suddenly tipped over, spilling itself on the table. Amber chuckled, but when she looked at Pandrogas's face she stopped.

Later she would wonder about that look. There had been anger in it, and embarrassment, as she had seen earlier when he had tried to light the candles in his chamber in a moment of mock drama. But there had also been a great sadness, quickly masked.

Pandrogas looked at the results of the failed spell, then startled Amber by asking, "Would you like to know why I resigned from the Cabal, and why I came to Darkhaven?"

It was the question she had always asked, and which he had never answered. She nodded, suddenly unsure if she wanted to know.

"Well, then," Pandrogas said. "I won't waste time with prefaces; everybody knows what the Necromancer did, though none know why he did it. The speculation is that the mages and rulers of the time refused to acknowledge his supremacy. But the why does not matter now; he summoned a fire from beyond the sun that broke the world like a clay urn, and scattered the potsherds to the heavens, and were it not for the efforts of all the mages then alive (or most of them, anyway), that would have been the end of the world. As it was, it was the end of the moon."

"What was the moon?"

"Some other time. But due to the combined efforts of five thousand (give or take a few) sorcerers and sorceresses, enchanters and enchantresses, and so on, the world was saved in the fashion we now know it. Their spells gave power to the Runestones, setting the fragments in complicated but safe journeys about each other and the sun, ordaining that each one, no matter how small, exert an attraction as did the original sphere, and surrounding them and filling the Abyss between them with air."

"I thought," Amber teased gently, "that you were forgoing the preface."

"I thought it necessary to reinforce your learning," he replied imperturbably, then made a face at her before continuing. "The secrets of Necromancy, along with almost everything else of civilization, were lost in the apocalypse. The rest of the magicians did what they could with what they had, but they knew, as their descendants know now, that it is a losing battle."

"What do you mean? That—"

The sorcerer nodded. "That the destruction of the world was only delayed, not defeated. This morning I received a message from Thasos of Rhynne, my mentor in the Lorian System. He was the only one who had supported my decision to leave the Cabal." Pandrogas took a deep breath and said, "I left because members of the Cabal had decided to actively seek out the secrets of Necromancy and use them to maintain the fragments' precarious dance. Only a trace of the knowledge remains, widely scattered in ancient Rannish volumes such as *The Red Grimoire*. One or two had even gone so far as to resign and join the ranks of the Circle."

He was silent for a moment, brooding. Amber debated asking questions, afraid he would suddenly feel he was telling her too much. But her curiosity was too strong. "What is the Circle?" she ventured.

"The adherents to the One God, who claim that their deity has commanded them in dreams and visions to return the world to a state of grace by re-forming it once more into a sphere. They seek more than ancient volumes of Necromancy to accomplish this; they search for the Necromancer's tomb, hidden since the cataclysm, in hopes of reviving him under their control.

"All of these concepts, I felt, were much too dangerous. I thought

another alternative could be found. And so I came to Darkhaven to
search for one.

"Darkhaven, you see, was in past centuries the home of many
magicians. Hundreds of schools of sorcery and enchantment were
held within these walls, and many the man and woman who came
here an apprentice left a sorcerer or sorceress. The libraries are filled
with concordances and compendiums of different styles, different
approaches—a thousand ways to achieve the same end. Magic works
at cross-purposes today, Amber. The Shattering fragmented everything. If all the different systems could be integrated, the powers
behind them unified..." For a moment Pandrogas's face seemed to
shine. Then he sighed. "I thought—I hoped—to find a way to do
that here."

"But you haven't," Amber said.

He shook his head. "And now Thasos joins the others in pleading
with me to help them. The ectenic force behind the Runestones is
weakening. Five weeks ago, a fragment the size of a dragonship
collided with Kormalion. The impact took place in a rural area; even
so, several hundred were killed. Kormalion now pursues a new orbit,
one that brings it steadily closer to Twilan. There have been other
collisions and near-misses. Things will get worse. Thasos and the
Cabal want me to help them collect and decipher the texts of Necromancy, to use the power of the dead to save what is left of the
world."

"I have heard it said," Amber said slowly, "that the Necromancer
is whole in hell." She was referring to the religion of Jantaism,
which held that the good and evil parts of a person are separated
after death, so that only extreme saints and sinners remain whole in
the afterlife.

"If any man was evil, he was," Pandrogas agreed. "And so is his
magic. Do you see why I am against it?"

She nodded, looking down at a breakfast for which she suddenly
had no appetite. She wondered how he could sit there so calmly,
bearing this burden, and the threat of Sestihaculas, and the situation
with Tahrynyar... "What will you do?"

He sat silently for a moment, as if pondering the question. Then he stood and, crossing to a sideboard, took from it a casting sphere that sat upon a wooden stand. The sphere was also wood, the size of two fists, its fragments interlocking pieces of gemwood, walnut, mahogany, and others, all polished with loving craftsmanship. Pandrogas held it out before him in his two hands, then let it fall to the table. The sound of it striking and shattering was very loud.

Amber watched as he bent over and studied the positions of the fragments. She had never seen anyone read a spherecasting without recourse to the book that explained the images formed by the pieces. He had taught her over the past few months to use this sphere; it was not one of the cheap, simple ones used by common folk, with only twelve main pieces, and those weighted and planed so that there were only a limited amount of symbols that could be formed when the sphere was cast. This one shattered into more pieces than could easily be counted, and *The Book of Stones* was filled with studies and interpretations of the patterns discovered so far. She recalled how hopeless it had seemed to make anything out of it when she had first studied it. But, as she had looked over the pieces that first time, she had seen a subtle symmetry in their positions. There was an order, though what it meant or how it had come to be she had not known then. Still, she had felt that if she had stared at the pieces long enough, if she did not study them, but simply let them fill her mind, let them be within her, then whatever inherent meaning there was would become clear to her. And subsequent castings had made this feeling stronger.

Then she heard Pandrogas exhale sharply; she looked at his face. What she saw shocked her: he was pale.

"What is it? What do they say?"

He was silent for so long that she thought he had not heard her. Then he pointed to the arrangement of the fragments. "See here," he said in a low voice. "See how Toul, which represents change and strife, presses down on Zarheena, which stands for pride or prosperity. And here: Salakh, the symbol of stability, is in the shadow of Calamchor, the jungle fragment, the sign of bestial destruction and chaos. I could consult *The Book of Stones,* but there is no need; I know this configuration. The translation reads: 'Reason surrenders to savagery; knowledge is lost, and equanimity overturned. Houses fall.'"

Amber could hear thunder sound faintly through the many stone walls, and a part of her marveled at the intensity of the storm. She looked at the motionless wooden pieces, feeling that there had to be something that she could do or say to comfort him. But she had no idea how even to begin. "What can I do?" she asked gently.

Pandrogas sat down. "Play," he murmured after a moment. Amber nodded slowly and took the flute from its casing on her belt. She put it to her lips and began to play. She had intended the music to be light and lilting, something to bring him out of the despondency. Instead she found herself filling the air with a quiet procession of notes, a slow and measured cadence that was stately without being solemn. She watched him as she played; he sat with forehead resting against clasped hands, his eyes closed. Amber wanted very badly to take him in her arms, to hold and comfort him, to reassure him. But at this moment all she could do was play for him.

And Pandrogas, sitting at the end of a long table in a refectory larger than most people's houses, in a castle almost the size of a kingdom, found himself wishing very strongly that the vaticination of the spherecasting meant nothing, or that it meant any one of a thousand things, none of which were important. But he had never read a casting wrong since he had gotten his fifth ring. Added to the fears of the Cabal and the words of Sestihaculas, the conclusion was inevitable.

Darkhaven would fall. And with it would go the last chance to save the remnants of the world, save through Necromancy.

He could not let it happen. He had to stop it, somehow. After all, he was a sorcerer.

But he was also human, and afraid.

Chapter 5

The Runestone

Beorn crouched before the small arched outline of a door set in the dim, musty corridor. Ardatha had returned to him most of his weapons and tools, but had neglected the cruet of oil. With a mental curse at her he wet down the hinges with urine and pushed the door. He froze as he heard it grate slightly. Light spilled in.

The other side of the door was a concealed panel in the back of a walk-in fireplace. The door had grated on ashes, which meant that he had reached, at last, an inhabited area of the castle.

There was no one in the suite, but it was obviously lived in; by its size and furnishings he assumed it was a servant's quarters. He made his way cautiously through it and proceeded down a well-lit hall. Though he knew that the danger of discovery was not decreased, he felt relieved still to have left the dusty, shadowy maze of the unused portion.

He came to a crossing of two passages and chose the right-hand route. He watched the glow of the ring on his finger and he followed the twisting way. After a moment he saw the light lessening in intensity. He returned to the intersection and took the left-hand path. The glow remained steady, and after a time increased.

He had made his route in that way from the Spire of Owls, hours ago, and now felt that at last he was drawing close to his goal. Surely the ring could not glow much brighter; it dazzled his eyes now. Soon he would have the talisman in his belt pouch. Then, instead of returning to Ardatha via Balandrus's viselike grasp, he would seek another way of escape from Darkhaven. A castle this size had to have dragonships moored somewhere. He would take the safest revenge upon the enchantress; he would simply disappear, and take with him the talisman she desired so greatly. He had no guarantee, after all, that she would keep her word and cure him of the werespell—he had long ago made it a point not to trust anyone. He could bargain with another adept for a cure. Yes, that was what he would do. He would leave Darkhaven somehow, and...never see her again.

Beorn thought of her dancing; thought of her as he had first seen her in Troas's throne room, with that hideous demon's hand hidden behind her. He thought of her frostlike hair, her green eyes, beautiful even—or especially—while they taunted and mocked. He thought of the way the dragon's talons on her dress cupped her breasts, and felt his fingers curving in imitation of those talons. He shook his head and almost growled out loud in the silence of the hall. He would *not* let her make a fool of him!

And yet he knew that he would take no pleasure from this revenge.

At last he stood before two massive doors, above which was mounted a head cast from bronze. He looked up at it and thought he saw the brazen face twitch; at the same time he felt the amulet against his chest grow momentarily hot again. The bronze head made no further move. Feeling that he had somehow narrowly escaped detection, Beorn opened the doors.

He was in the sorcerer's laboratory. One starcrystal sconce dimly lit the huge room. The thief held the ring out before him as he moved about the chamber. It grew brighter, and brighter still, as he approached a table strewn with books, scrolls, tablets, and note-covered parchment. In the middle of the untidy pile—so unlike the neat orderings of Ardatha's table, a small part of him remembered—sat a small box, inlaid with marquetry and inscriptions. Beorn extended the ring toward it, and the glare was like the fire of dragon or phoenix.

He opened the heirotheca and beheld what he was to steal: the Runestone of Darkhaven.

Beorn stared at it in shocked disbelief. He had never seen a Runestone before, but he had seen pictures of them, and he recognized the small oblate spheroid, smooth and black and covered with cabalistic engravings. He had had no idea that this was the talisman for which she had sent him. Such a theft was beyond anything he had ever before attempted.

He knew what everyone knew about Runestones: they were objects of great potency and value, and wars had been fought many times over their possession. A fragment's Runestone was its source of stability and life. He knew what it would mean to Darkhaven and its inhabitants if he should take it.

He stood in the dark laboratory, thinking. He was a thief, not a killer. He was not squeamish about death and did not hold life particularly sacred; his reluctance came from a sense of aesthetics. It was an admission of incompetence to have to kill, even indirectly, in the course of a job—it was bad art. There had been occasions when he had found it necessary to incapacitate someone, with a thumb gouged into the nerve behind the jaw or pressure against the neck's artery, but he had never killed. Even as the bear, he had never killed.

He closed his eyes suddenly at that last thought, hard enough to cause him pain. Quite vividly before him he seemed to see a small farmhouse of stone and timber ablaze, the peaked roof caving in, the chimney rocks glowing with the heat. He could hear screams coming from within, and he could see the bear crouched at the edge of the forest, watching, howling his grief and frustration to the cloudy skies...

But that had not been his fault—they had driven him to it. They had been responsible for the bear in the first place!

A faraway rumble, more felt than heard, brought him back to the present. Automatically he crouched, fading into the darkest patch of shadows while he looked quickly about the chamber. He was alone. The rumble came again, and he realized it was thunder. The sky had been cloudy when he had arrived at the Spire of Owls;

evidently a storm had broken. It could hinder his chances of escape.

He reached hesitantly into the velvet-lined heirotheca and picked up the Runestone, noticing a slight tingling in his fingers as they touched it. He placed it hastily in his belt pouch, and the ring with it. With the drawstrings tight the glare of the ring was gone, and he blinked his eyes against green patterns in the darkness. Then he closed the heirotheca.

He did not know how a Runestone, a talisman designed to support and maintain a fragment, could also be used to change the werespell upon him. But he knew little of magic, after all. As long as the stone represented the slightest possibility of a way to put the bear at last under control, he could not let anything stop him from taking it. After all, was Pandrogas not a sorcerer? Should disaster strike Darkhaven, surely he would be able to protect his domain.

But still he hesitated. Then, in the wake of the thunder, he heard another sound filtering through the stone walls. At first he did not recognize it; it seemed so out of place in this grim setting.

It was music; the music of a flute.

The notes tickled the edge of his hearing, fading in and out as the music rose and fell. It was a serene piece, nothing sprightly or cheering about it, and yet it was calming. It soothed Beorn with its tranquil, introspective sound. He strained his ears to hear more of it.

Someone in this castle was an artist. Without knowing anything about the person playing, the thief felt a sudden sense of kinship. The uncertainty about stealing the Runestone, forgotten for a moment, returned. Could he be responsible for bringing some form of disaster upon someone who could play like that?

Frozen with indecision, he looked about the sorcerer's chamber. He had never been plagued by such doubts before, had always been slightly contemptuous of others, even Suchana, when they expressed them. He was a thief; it was what he did, what he was. There was no room for conscience in his work.

Beorn stood there, absently stroking the feathered cloak that hung on the back of a chair. Before him, on the table, rested the fragments of a casting sphere. He had never believed in their predictions before, but now he was suddenly tempted to let it make his decision for him. The music came to him again, stronger, and he stepped quickly to the table and scooped up the sphere's fragments. They were of crystal, he noticed abstractly, exquisitely worked; he could get a fortune for them from any fence he knew...

He fitted them together hastily. It was a complex sphere, one used by masters, but he had learned something of their assembly and usage. Suchana had been a great one for consulting the sphere. Maybe she had been right in doing so—maybe it could help him now.

He was holding it out before him at arm's length, ready to drop it, when he thought of what Suchana's reaction would be to his current idiocy. Dithering about in the heart of a sorcerer's castle, about to let a casting sphere drop and make a noise that might bring discovery! Simultaneously with that thought, he realized that the music had stopped. Beorn stood for a moment, still holding the sphere, feeling like a man who has just come out of a trance. What could he have been thinking of? He would set the sphere down quietly, break it into parts as it had been before, and make his escape before he took leave of his senses again. Once again, he thought, Suchana has saved me from an amateur's mistake.

Then the doors opened.

Tahrynyar had walked the halls of Darkhaven for hours, caught in a storm of emotions that matched the storm outside. He burned alternately with embarrassment at the foolishness of what he had done and rage at the sorcerer and Amber for having driven him to it. He had wanted revenge, and he had succeeded only in placing himself doubly in Pandrogas's debt.

If only he were not such a coward, he thought bitterly. If only he could keep his head in a confrontation and not begin sweating and stammering. It made no difference if he was in the right or not; the result was always the same. It was that trait that had lost him the marquisate, and now it had lost him Amber as well.

He had been a sickly child, intimidated by his uncle, who had raised him, and his instructors. All had agreed that he was not fit to be marquis, and he had believed them. Chuntai was in a frontier province, and had long been coveted by the governors of the surrounding areas. Though nominally under allegiance to the emperor, in reality little notice was taken of them and their boundary-shuffling and deposition of minor officials as long as a strong border was maintained. Only the close ties of his uncle with the court had kept Chuntai autonomous for as long as it had been.

When his uncle had died in a hunting accident, Tahrynyar had inherited the title and the responsibilities. Until then he had not fully appreciated how tenuous a thing the emperor's favor could be. He had never quite mastered the infinite and intricate subtleties of court etiquette, and never really comprehended until too late the fact that an inopportune word or reference, or even an ill-timed step or gesture, might be enough to bring disfavor upon one's head. A frown from the emperor could completely restructure the balance of power in the marches, not by such gross means as mangonels and battering rams, but by assassins' daggers and forged cartularies.

Tahrynyar was not even sure what he had done or said (or not done or not said, as the case might have been) that had resulted in that all-destroying frown. Perhaps the time when he had been unexpectedly asked his opinion of the Kenyari aquisition; Tahrynyar blushed to recall how he had had to admit his ignorance of that excellent *coup* on the emperor's part. Or even the *faux pas* he had committed by wearing red and white together when attending the Ball of Danatar's Release.

Most likely it had been a combination of these things and more— his ignorance had effectively greased the machinery of his downfall. It had been due solely to the loyalty and bravery of a servant who had been set as a spy by Tahrynyar's late uncle in the province governor's staff that the marquis and his wife had been able to flee. They were in a small dragonship when the assassins dispatched by Sartuland Moyil Penn Taganay, the governor, reached their bedchambers. The original intention had been to leave Turrith and seek sanctuary with a cousin of Amber's in Quy. But the storm had arisen and changed that. The storm had blown them to Darkhaven, and Amber into the arms of Pandrogas.

The one thing he had felt sure of through all the uncertainty of his life as marquis and his downfall had been Amber's love. When he had seen, almost two commonmonths ago, the intensity of conversation between her and Pandrogas, the long hours she had spent learning the basics of magic (in itself a pursuit he feared to see her undertake), and, worst of all, the slow but inexorable cooling toward him, he had refused to believe it at first. Then he had tried to ignore it, because to do otherwise meant a confrontation. And now the confrontation had come and gone, and what was the next step?

As he asked himself that hopeless question a sound reached him during a lull in the storm; a sound that, though almost too faint to hear, nevertheless struck him like an arrow between the shoulder blades. Somewhere in this cursed castle Amber was playing her flute—playing it for Pandrogas, as she had once played it for him.

Tahrynyar felt himself bending under the weight of the music. He sobbed, once, harshly. Then he forced himself to stand upright again, closing his eyes against tears.

If he could not have her, and could not fight for her, then all that was left was to go. Their dragonship had been repaired weeks before; he would take it and start a new life on a new land. Perhaps it was best, after all, he thought, to lose everything before you begin again.

This, too, was a frightening prospect, but it was at least one he could face. He shivered in the cold air and made an attempt to draw his cloak about him; only then did he remember that he had left it in the laboratory. He debated returning to his chambers without it, but could not face the sight of the empty bed; besides, he knew he would get no more sleep. Best to begin gathering his belongings and packing them.

It was still early; the seventh hour had not yet sounded. If he was to reclaim his cloak, it was best to do so before Pandrogas returned to the laboratory. Tahrynyar turned and walked down the hallway. He had a destination again, if only for a moment. For now, he could only take things one step at a time.

As he approached the doors of the sanctum he slowed, his heart beating faster at the memory of what his foolish reading of the book had caused. He had never had an experience even remotely like that.

He had summoned the leader of the Chthons, Sestihaculas the De-mogorgon. As he thought of it, he was amazed to realize that, despite the terror of the memory, the vivid re-experience of being sucked remorselessly into that maelstrom which emptied, he was sure, in the mushroom forests of Xoth, there was a tiny, ludicrous feeling of pride. Though Tahrynyar had almost lost his soul in the process, still it was the only awesome thing he could ever recall doing.

He sighed. Fool, he called himself with weary familiarity.

And yet, perhaps the old conjurer had been right. Perhaps he, too, had the potential for magic...

"Who enters my master's laboratory?"

Tahrynyar answered the bronze head as he had before, faintly surprised still to be allowed entry after what he had done. Perhaps Pandrogas had neglected to instruct the head differently as to him. This evidence of forgetfulness on the sorcerer's part cheered him. He is human, despite his knowledge, Tahrynyar told himself. Per-haps I still have a chance to somehow win her back.

He reached for the latch, then hesitated with his hand on it. Nothing would happen; he would look at no books, touch nothing except his cloak. He could at least be brave to that extent.

He opened the doors and saw a man standing at the table, holding a casting sphere at arm's length, a stocky, redbearded man in dark clothes who was not, he knew, an inhabitant of Darkhaven.

Beorn saw the pale, blond-haired man in ruffled blouse and silken surcoat staring at him in comical surprise. He dropped the casting sphere and leaped over the table toward the doors, hoping to bowl the fop over and be gone into the labyrinth of corridors before an alarm could be raised. But the fellow, though obviously shocked, was still able to move; he quickly stepped back into the corridor and slammed the doors with a cavernous sound. Beorn heard the latch fall into place on the outside just before he slammed into the doors and rebounded, cursing and rubbing his bruised shoulder. He tried the handles, but the door was barred from the outside. He heard running footsteps fade away.

He took no time to curse himself for his stupidity; he was in the cauldron now and would just have to get out as best he could. He still had the amulet to protect him somewhat from magic, and if he could just escape this chamber his sense of direction would lead him back to Balandrus at the Spire of Owls. But there appeared to be no other exit from the sorcerer's laboratory. He made a quick circuit of the room, checking the paneled walls for possible hidden doors. He found nothing.

The sorcerer would be here in short order, he knew. There was only one way out, then. He could not break those doors—but the bear could.

Beorn spent another precious moment fruitlessly casting about for an alternative. Then he unstrapped his belt pouch and hung it on its leather belt about his neck, alongside the amulet. He took another deep breath, swallowing the fear he always felt at this moment. He could feel the bear surging within him, the fierce, savage joy, as though it knew it was about to be released. It would not have all of him; it never had before, and this time would be no different. So he told himself, as he prepared for the pain of the change.

Then he closed his eyes and let it begin.

Tahrynyar hurried along the hall looking for someone, anyone, to report this to. The stranger had to be a thief; it was the wealthy man's automatic reaction to an unknown face in a familiar household. If there had been any doubt, the burly man's leap toward Tahrynyar had removed it. The former marquis congratulated himself on his quickness of mind and limb. Now, if he could only find a servant to warn Pandrogas.

At that thought he stopped suddenly, chest heaving from exertion. To warn Pandrogas? To warn the man who had taken the one most dearest to him?

Ahead, at the intersection of another corridor, he saw one of the monklike servants cross. The man glanced at him incuriously. Tahrynyar said nothing, and the servant passed from view. Tahrynyar stood there, thinking furiously.

Perhaps this was his chance for revenge; a mean and petty revenge, to be sure, but such appeared to be all of which he was capable. If he were to do nothing, to let the thief, or whatever he was, carry out whatever deviltry he was engaged in...

But he had locked the man in the laboratory.

Not sure what he was doing, or why, Tahrynyar turned and ran back down the hall.

When he was almost at the doors again, he slowed down. If I release the thief, he thought, what if I am attacked? How to convince him I mean him no harm? He approached the locked doors cautiously, making as little noise as possible. Perhaps he could lift the latch and then flee before the man came out.

But as he drew closer he heard something that quickly drove all thoughts of opening the sanctum from his mind. He listened in disbelief that grew immediately to horror as he stood before the huge, ironbound doors. What he heard sounded like nothing less than what he imagined one would hear in a torture chamber. Behind those locked doors mayhem and murder had to be taking place; Tahrynyar heard a human voice groaning and gasping, combined with horrible noises of cracking limbs and rending flesh. There were popping sounds that he somehow knew were ligaments parting and tendons snapping. He heard a heavy shuffling, as of someone or something writhing in agony on the floor. Tahrynyar backed away from the door, nauseated, unsure what to do.

"Who enters my master's laboratory?"

The brazen voice burst over the grinding and tearing of flesh and bones, and Tahrynyar very nearly screamed. "Don't you hear it?" he gasped, forgetting for a moment in his confusion and terror whom he was addressing.

"I hear nothing. Who enters my master's laboratory?"

Tahrynyar was unable to speak again; his voice, like his legs, refused to function. He stared at the doors, praying that they would remain locked, would continue to conceal whatever horror was taking place within. Perhaps it was Sestihaculas, returned somehow to reclaim him. But he did not believe that. In its own way, this seemed even more terrible. The cries and grunts of the human voice within had now been joined by another sound: the growling of some huge beast. Had the thief inadvertently summoned some voracious monster and was now serving as its meal?

Tahrynyar suddenly realized that the sounds of dismemberment had stopped; all was silent within now, save for a low, regular susurration. After a moment he recognized it: the panting of an animal.

The ceasing of the sounds of torture released him from his immobility. Whatever was happening within the sanctum seemed to be over for the moment. He would run, find Pandrogas, and tell him. Perhaps he could use this to his advantage, somehow convince Amber of the dangers of staying in a sorcerer's castle.

He took two unsteady steps away from the doors. At the far end of the curving hall he saw the servant Kabyn come into view. The bald man stopped, staring at Tahrynyar with that enigmatic look that ordinarily infuriated the former marquis. Now, however, he was glad to see it. He started toward him, and then he heard what he thought for an instant was another roll of thunder. As he turned he realized too late that it was the sound of a huge animal in full charge.

The doors exploded outward; one of them struck Tahrynyar edge-on as it whirled across the hall, catching him across both knees and crushing him, for an instant, against the wall. He felt pain shoot up his legs like fire up a flue, and he collapsed. Through gathering darkness he stared upward and saw, looking down at him, the snarling face of a bear, with tattered clothing still clinging to its cinnamon pelt. Then sight was gone, thought was gone; there was nothing left but the pain.

Pandrogas and Amber sat in the refectory before the cold dishes of an untouched breakfast. She had played her flute for quite some time, but if it had comforted the sorcerer in any way she could not see it. He still sat staring at the sphere's fragments. He had not spoken since the music stopped, not even to thank her for playing.

She stood, and he looked up. "I'm going to find Tahrynyar," she said. "I have to . . . to tell him how it is between us. He deserves at least that much respect from me."

Pandrogas merely nodded and returned his gaze to the scattered sphere. Amber felt a wave of anger, followed by sadness. You should offer to go with me, she thought. To stand by me during this. Even if you carry the fate of this broken world on your shoulders, you owe me that much. She opened her mouth to say as much to him, but at that moment the door was pushed open and Kabyn burst into the room.

Even though there was obviously an emergency, Kabyn retained a measure of phlegmatic calm. "The marquis has been attacked by an animal, sir," he said to Pandrogas, and Amber felt suddenly dizzy. She sat down as Pandrogas stood up. "An animal? One of the livestock?"

"No, sir. A bear. In your laboratory."

Pandrogas wasted no time in disbelieving questions. He followed Kabyn to the door, then turned and looked back at Amber, held out his hand to her. The look on his face was full of concern; he had finally come out of his self-absorbed trance.

She arose and went with him; the three of them hurried to the laboratory, where they found Tahrynyar still on the floor. Kabyn had summoned several more servants to attend him; he had been covered with a blanket, with another bundled under his head. One of the men said to Amber, "His legs are broken. We will do what we can." She nodded and knelt beside him, still unable to think.

He blinked and looked up at her and Pandrogas. She took his hand, and he squeezed it with surprising strength, almost hurting her. "The...the man," he whispered. "The bear...he cast the sphere," and then he was unconscious again.

Pandrogas looked up at the guardian. "What did you see?"

"I saw the doors burst; I saw the man felled," the head replied in its metallic voice.

"Nothing else? You saw no one enter, nothing leave?"

"Only he entered, earlier. I saw nothing leave."

A perplexed frown on his face, the sorcerer entered the laboratory, followed by Kabyn.

Amber heard the servant explaining to his master what he had seen as she watched the others carefully lift Tahrynyar onto one of the doors and carry him down the hall. I should go with him, she thought. But instead she turned and, stepping over the wreckage, entered the laboratory.

There was no sign that anything out of the ordinary had taken place, with the exception of several shredded pieces of clothing scattered near the entrance. Pandrogas picked up what was left of a leather boot. Amber felt ill looking at it. "Could the bear have done that?" She thought how lucky Tahrynyar was to be alive at all.

"It looks more as if it had been burst apart," Pandrogas said. He picked up what had been a shirt of dark muslin, pulled a ring of keys from a pocket. Each key had been wrapped with twine about its base to prevent it from jangling on the ring. "Burglar's tools," the sorcerer said. He looked at Kabyn. "You said the bear had strips of cloth hanging from it?" Kabyn nodded.

"We seem to be dealing with a shapechanging thief," Pandrogas said. "But how could he have gotten past the entrance spells? And what might he have taken—" Then, for the second time that day, Amber saw him go pale. He pushed Kabyn aside and leaped to the table, grabbed a small, ornate box and, hands shaking, opened it. Then he stood quite still.

"The Runestone," he said in a low voice. "He has taken Darkhaven's Runestone."

Kabyn said, "It had a pouch about its neck; I saw that clearly as it turned and rushed away down the hall."

"So soon," Pandrogas murmured. "The prophecy fulfilled so soon."

Then he took a deep breath, pushed his shoulders back and said, "Perhaps not." He crossed to a cabinet and took from it a mirror set in an ornate frame. He laid it flat on the table; the glass reflected nothing of the room or of him, but instead seemed filled with slowly shifting colors. Pandrogas leaned over it and stared into it, brow furrowed with concentration. Kabyn and Amber drew close to him, peering into the mirror. The sorcerer held out his hands and performed a series of complicated, graceful gestures, knotting his fingers together in almost hypnotic patterns. "Kaliaden," he said softly; "Entaminja kom nacon wes." The mists in the mirror cleared in a flash of gold light to be replaced with a strange scene: a blurred and moving perspective of a corridor, as though they were hurrying at considerable speed down its length. With the mirror lying flat on the table, the effect was of falling down a well. The walls and floor looked oddly gray and colorless.

"We see through his eyes," Pandrogas said. "The eyes of a bear, nearsighted and somewhat color-blind. Now to stop him." He stepped back from the mirror and extended both arms, then quickly and easily began the graceful motions of a spell. Amber listened to his voice, the sure cadence as he spoke a phrase, watched him move with the precision of a dancer and, even under the tense circumstances, felt envy of his mastery. Then the spell was cast, and they looked into the mirror again.

There was no change, save for a momentary shudder in the moving vision, as if the bear had stumbled. But he continued down the corridor. Pandrogas exhaled in exasperation. "That should have paralyzed him. Very well, then. He is protected against attack, as well as some forms of detection. We shall have to stop him by other means." He looked at Kabyn. "Gather everyone and arm them with torches and swords. He must be stopped, as bear or man, before he leaves Darkhaven."

Kabyn nodded and hurried out the doorway. Pandrogas turned to Amber. "Remain with Tahrynyar," he said gently. "You will be out of danger there. And you're right—he deserves at least that much." Then he turned and was gone before she could speak, before she knew what, if anything, she would say.

Amber looked at the broken, splintered doors. A thief, a shape-changer, invading Pandrogas's inmost sanctum. Why had the sorcerer not known? And why did she feel somehow responsible for his not knowing?

A shadow fell across the doorway; she jumped, then relaxed as she recognized Undya, another of the servants. "Come, milady," she said; "I will take you to your husband." Her expression was unreadable, but Amber felt sure there was contempt behind it.

She nodded and followed Undya down the hall, trying to convince herself that she would rather do what was right, would rather stay with Tahrynyar, than try to help Pandrogas; and trying to forget, as well, the emotion she had felt when Kabyn had first entered the dining hall with the news that Tahrynyar had been struck down. It had not been horror or concern—those had come later. What she had felt initially had been a hideous sense of relief.

Chapter 6

The Bear

This was power—to charge at a barrier of wood and iron faster than a galloping horse and shatter it like the Necromancer shattered the world. To feel muscles rippling under a thick, almost invulnerable pelt, to shamble through hallways and galleries, claws clicking on parquet and stone, fearing nothing and no one. To be the bear— why had he feared it so greatly? He was alive now in ways he could never be as a man. His vision was poorer, but his hearing and sense of smell more than made up for it. And his strength—the doors had felt like reeds before him! He was always surprised at the power of the bear; the power and the sheer, savage exultation of using it. He felt filled with life; it surged and sang in his veins. He could barely keep from venting his exuberance in loud, coughing barks, or by stopping to shatter statues or rend furniture with his heavy, taloned forepaws. To do so would bring pursuers down upon him, he knew, but he felt no fear of that; indeed, he almost welcomed it. Let come what might—he was the bear now, a juggernaut of fur and muscle, unconquerable. No longer a puny thief, a puny man...

Beorn came to a stop slowly, swinging his huge head from side to side. It had been long since he had last freed the beast within him, and now he stood trembling slightly with the effort to control it. Puny he might be as a man, compared to the bear, but the mind of that man still ruled, though he could feel the animal portion of him struggling to be ascendant. This was what he feared most about the bear: the threatened loss of control, the possibility of being submerged by the small brain within the sloping skull. It was a constant war of wills he waged with the creature, and the longer he remained in the shape of the bear, the harder it was to retain the sense of self, the knowledge of his humanity, the ability to think. This was why he feared the bear—had always feared the bear. Every other aspect of his life was subject to his will, except the bear.

He thought of the man he had left back at the laboratory, his legs twisted beneath him like a discarded marionette's. He had had no way of knowing the fool had come back and was standing before the door. Still, he regretted it. Only a bare half hour before he had been praising himself for having never killed as the bear. To cause such an accident was very unprofessional, and to leave it unresolved was even more so. He should have opened the man's throat with his claws to make sure he could not speak of what had attacked him. But he had not, and the reason he had not was because he had wanted to so very badly. In that first flush of snarling rage, his bones and muscles still aching from the traumatic metamorphosis, he had come very close to rending the weakling. And that frightened him. He *had* to keep control of the bear—he knew he would not escape Darkhaven otherwise.

He listened; he could hear the scurrying of mice in the ancient walls and the sound of wind and rain filtered through many layers of stone. He heard no sounds of pursuit yet. He scratched an ear with a rear paw, snorting as the dust he raised found its way to his muzzle. The thongs holding the amulet and pouch about his neck were tight, and his clothes were gone, of course, save for a few shreds that he now carefully combed free with his claws and hid within a floor urn so that he would leave no more trail than he could help. There was little he could do about the splayfooted prints he left in the dust, or the coarse reddish-brown hair he shed.

He continued on his way, moving at a steady trot that covered the twisting ways of Darkhaven quickly. He did not know how much time he had before a pursuit would be organized. They would find the weapons and tools left within his ripped and discarded clothing and know that a burglar had been there. He should have hidden them as well, but he had instead succumbed to the bear's animal urge to escape. Too late to worry about it now; whether the sorcerer would make the connection between the thief and the bear Beorn was not sure, but he thought it likely.

At that point he felt the amulet sear the matted hair about his throat. Simultaneously a coldness gripped his limbs for an instant, and then passed. He stumbled, regained his footing and continued. He did not doubt that the amulet had protected him once again from a spell. So—the sorcerer was moving against him already. The chase was on.

He would have to find another way into the unused portion of the castle and the route back to the Spire of Owls, as he could not squeeze the bear's body through the small panel in the fireplace. It would be some time before he could shapechange again; the bear had gone unreleased for a long time, and would not easily be caged within his human form until at least several hours had passed. Also, he needed time to recover from the changing; he still felt sharp twinges of pain in his joints as he lumbered down the hall. Beorn remembered how much easier and quicker the metamorphosis had been when he had been a youth. There had been very little pain then; now each transformation was close to agony. He wondered what he would do as he grew older and the pain increased even more.

Assuming he lived that long, he thought, as he turned a corner and found himself facing several men armed with torches and swords.

There were five of them; servants of the sorcerer, he assumed. All were thin and wiry, with either dark hair or bald heads. Beorn reared back onto his hind legs, standing upright, and snarled. They were expecting a bear, but perhaps they did not know that a human mind controlled it. A roar and a charge would be unexpected; it might break their nerve, scatter them. If not, he knew from experience how a single effortless slap could disarm a man and break his wrist into the bargain.

He snarled again, dropping to all fours—and one of the men took a ball of cloudy glass from a pocket and tossed it at him. It burst at his feet, enveloping him in a dark dust. Only long years of training as a thief taught him not to gasp reflexively and inhale a lungful of the same soporific with which he had laid low the manticore in Baron Torkalis's garden. He wheeled about and took off in a lumbering run, holding his breath until he was well away from the sleepspice. Behind him he heard the shouts and footfalls of his pursuers.

He turned down a side corridor, reviewing where he was now in relation to where he had to be to get back to the Spire of Owls. Now was not the time to seek a dragonship and so cheat Ardatha; he would have to return to her and plan from there. But first he would have to get back to the Spire alive. It was difficult to recall now the route he had memorized so effortlessly while following the ring's glowing lead; memories of his time as a man became dreamlike almost immediately; only his reality as the bear was vivid. And while the bear's vision made good use of the little light in the halls and corridors, he could focus clearly only a few feet in front of him, and he had a much narrower field of sight than a man's eyes afforded. Still, he felt fairly certain that once he crossed this empty chamber— evidently, by the disintegrating high bench and spectators' galleries, once a court of justice—and passed the arch he glimpsed dimly at the far end, he should approach a rendezvous with the way he had come . . .

He had crossed a line of stylobated columns and was about to enter the arch when he heard a sound: a growing creaking rattle from above him. Then a portcullis of iron bars hurtled down to block the archway. The bear roared in surprise and dismay. He turned, quickly for all of his weight, and saw more of the castle's inhabitants advancing toward him, some holding swords, some with bows nocked and ready. Two of them carried a weighted net between them. Beorn snarled, champing his jaws together in rage. He suppressed with difficulty a wild desire to hurl himself into the midst of them, striking and biting. Instead he looked about for another way to escape. At the edge of his blurred vision he could make out an arras hanging

before a wall; it seemed to bulge oddly in its middle. More trust-
worthy than the uncertain sight was the musty smell brought to him
on the breeze; the smell that told him an opening was hidden behind
the material. Beorn turned and charged toward it, paws thudding
against the mosaic floor. An arrow struck the faded scene on the
arras an instant before he did; then he plunged into its dusty folds
and tore through it, saw too late the sweeping stairs beyond it, and
tumbled down the wide curving descent, feeling each step in staccato
bursts of pain. He was halfway down when his massive body struck
the balustrade, broke through, and fell into the endless night of
Darkhaven's lower reaches.

Pandrogas and Kabyn, with several others, had been searching
the shadows of one of the castle's many deserted cathedrals when
they heard the shouts and roars reverberating through the corridors.
An instant later a servant appeared at the far end of the nave, sil-
houetted in dim light. "The bear is trapped within the Court of High
Sentence," he said. Then he turned and led the way as the sorcerer
and his servants followed at a run.

They are so calm, Pandrogas thought as he ran. Nothing fazes or
upsets them, these functionaries. Yaladin, the sorcerer who made
way for me, said they were here when he had come to Darkhaven.
Pandrogas had a momentary fantastic conception of Kabyn and the
others having walked the halls of Darkhaven since before it was
ripped from the stable ground. But there was no time to indulge in
such useless speculations now. They reached the Court of High
Sentence quickly and found the rest of the servants gathered at the
top of the staircase, looking down into darkness. The light of starcrystal and torch showed Pandrogas that the floor at the base of the
stairs had been broken or collapsed years before; sagging timbers
marked the circumference of the pit. It gave back no reflection; its
darkness spoke of unguessed depths.

"They heard him strike water, far below," Kabyn said. "It is
unknown whether he lived or not."

Pandrogas stared into the opening. They were on the bottom floor
of the castle, which meant that the bear had tumbled into the caverns
that riddled the fragment.

Kabyn and the others waited his word. He knew he had no choice—whether the bear was alive or dead, the Runestone had to be recovered. And that meant they had to descend into those nighted cloisters of rock and limestone, where things that were in their own way even more terrible than the many ghosts of Darkhaven prowled and fought and bred. There was only one route by which they could enter the caverns below the castle; they would have to descend the Warped Stairs at the edge of the Labyrinth.

It was the only area in the part of Darkhaven he was familiar with that he feared.

It had all happened so quickly, Pandrogas thought. No time to prepare. But then a Sorcerer of the Tenth Ring should always be prepared, should he not?

How could it have happened? How could a thief have penetrated the warning cantrips and guarding spells, gotten to the very heart of his knowledge, and nearly escaped unseen? Had it not been for a chance accident—an accident that may have made a cripple of an innocent man, and that was now his responsibility also—he would not even have known of the theft until too late. It might be too late already. The predictions of the sphere and Sestihaculas might be unavoidable, inevitable. But there was a time, had to have been a time, when this could have been turned aside. A moment, an instant, when something he did, a decision he made, determined that things would come to this. What was it? And, far away or deep within his mind, he seemed to hear the strains of Amber's flute.

He sighed and looked at Kabyn. "We will descend the Warped Stairs," he said.

Amber, Undya, and two maidservants stood beside the bed on which Tahrynyar lay. Undya's skilled hands had done what they could for his broken kneecaps, and now the former marquis slept under the influence of dream tea. Amber looked at his face, pale even against the glossy satin of the pillow. The ghost of pain still haunted that face, even in drugged sleep. She saw lines there, about the eyes, creasing the forehead, that she was not familiar with. A twitch pulled at his lips—the echo of faraway agony—and Amber winced as though she had felt the pain.

She wondered why he had gone back to the laboratory; was his motive still vague, inchoate thoughts of destruction and revenge? Or had he been investigating a sound, perhaps ineptly trying to be a hero to impress her? She bit her lip at the thought.

She had hoped he was dead.

Only for a moment, when Kabyn had brought the news to them in the refectory; a moment of hope and relief. If Tahrynyar had been killed she would have been free, and she would have been spared telling him her decision. It would have made things so very much easier. But it had not happened, and now she had to deal with the guilt of being at least partially responsible for his condition, as well as the self-hatred for wanting, however briefly, to see him dead.

She could care for him, attend him, remain with him. But, try as she might, she could not fool herself into believing that she wanted to do that instead of be with Pandrogas and share whatever danger he faced.

Then she felt Undya's gaze upon her and turned to meet the calm black eyes. "He will sleep for some time," she said, and Amber was surprised by the gentleness of her tone. She knew she was being given permission to leave. She hesitated for a moment (At least have that much grace, a small, stern part of her said), and then turned and fled from the bedchamber.

Once away from there, in the vast silent reaches of Darkhaven, she did not know where to go or what to do. She wanted to find Pandrogas, to join him, to help him. But she knew that this hunt for the thief was dangerous and that he would be angry with her if she did so.

What if the thief—the bear—was not caught? What if he escaped with the Runestone? "Houses fall," the sphere's prophecy had said. It seemed incredible that Darkhaven's endless, cyclopean mass might ever cease to be. But if it did, what would become of Pandrogas—and her?

She walked the halls until she came to the laboratory again—by accident or purpose, she was not sure. With the Runestone no longer in it, it seemed smaller somehow, drained of power. Amber noticed the fragments of the sphere on the table—they were in a position different from that in which she had seen them yesterday. She frowned.

What had Tahrynyar said? "The man...the bear...he cast the sphere." Had the thief also sought a prophecy?

Intrigued, she opened *The Book of Stones* and set about translating the position of the fragments. It took her only a few moments to find the reading: "The hand of light is raised. To escape its fire, one must bring darkness to its grasp."

The cryptic saying held no meaning for her because she had no idea what question had been in mind (if any) when the sphere had been cast. She gathered up the pieces swiftly and reassembled them, then held them out before her. She cleared her mind of all thoughts except one question: What will be the result of Pandrogas's search?

The sphere fell from her hands to the table with a crash. It seemed to drop almost of its own volition, as was proper. In a few moments she would know what the oracle had to say.

When she finished categorizing and determining the many inter-relationships of the pieces, she turned to the translation in the book. She read it once, twice, and then the pages seemed to grow dark before her; she had to grip the edge of the table to maintain her balance: "The serpent waits within the darkness. From confusion and disorientation come loss and destruction. Clouds consume all of worth."

She had never read such a bleak prophecy before. She went over the configurations again carefully; she had made no errors in trans-lation.

The reference to confusion and disorientation made her think of the Warped Stairs and the Labyrinth, of which Pandrogas had told her once. The Stairs led to the Labyrinth, a collection of twisting passages, tunnels, and dead-ends full of menacing traps. Pandrogas had attempted once to penetrate past the Labyrinth, to the catacombs of Darkhaven at the center of the fragment, but he had found the maze permeated with ancient thaumaturgy which had drained his sorcerous abilities to the point that he counted himself lucky to have escaped alive.

What if he had entered the Labyrinth again, in pursuit of the thief? Might that not be the danger that lay in wait? But the oracle specifically said "serpent"...

Sestihaculas!

She had to find him, had to warn him. But she did not know where the entrance to the Warped Stairs was. She stood alone in the laboratory, heart beating wildly, feeling helpless, on the verge of panic. What could she do?

Then she remembered what he had told her during a discussion of the preliminaries of magic. "Learn that at times you will do things, not knowing why, that will nevertheless be correct. For no one learns magic so much as they remember it; it is a part of all of us, deep down. When you learn not to be afraid of what you already know, you will have come most of the way to the crystal ring of sorcery."

Amber breathed deeply, calming herself. She thought: There is a reason that I should find him. But how shall I find him? Which way lies the first step?

She closed her eyes, and let the first step be taken, and then the next, and the next, until she was walking swiftly toward a destination that was unknown, but no less sure.

She hurried down curving corridors and stairs, through boudoirs and anterooms, until she reached the lower levels of the castle, the empty, echoing stone lanes where occasional doorways opened into storerooms and butteries, for the most part now unused. Lower still, by dark passageways with low ceilings and damp walls, until she came at last to a corridor's end, and an iron gate barely distinguishable in the light of the starcrystal rod she had taken from the wall. Amber looked through the irregular interstices of the gate. Beyond it, steps led down into blackness. There seemed to be something wrong with their construction, or perhaps it was the dim light; they were of dark, glistening stone that looked oddly insubstantial. The curve of the stone arch was off-center very slightly, and the walls beyond the gate, from what she could see of them, appeared almost to undulate, as though the stone had melted and flowed.

The Warped Stairs.

The gate shrieked as she opened it, echoes hurtling away from her. Amber stepped forward. Her foot contacted the first step with a jar; it had seemed deeper than it was. She felt a moment of terrible uncertainty and fear. But she took the next step, and then the gate swung shut behind her with the reverberating finality of a gong, and she knew she had to go on.

*   *   *

Beorn had had time to feel a distinct surprise when he did not
strike the floor he supposed lay directly beneath the staircase. Something sharp had grazed a rear leg, leaving a line of pain there, and
then he had been surrounded by darkness, feeling almost as though
he were floating instead of falling, save for the increasing rush of
wind by his ears. Then, with a numbing shock, he had plunged into
icy water.

Only the thick fur and fat of the bear saved him from succumbing
to the temperature and drowning. He fought his way back to the
surface and began paddling strongly, choosing a direction at random
because he could see nothing. After some time he felt his claws
scrape a rocky shelf, and he pulled himself out of the water into air
only slightly less cold. He coughed and spat—the water tasted foul—
and shook his fur free of most of the soaking. The amulet and pouch
were still about his neck, he noted with relief.

His leg hurt where he had grazed it against the jagged edge of
something, and he was sore on his backside; fortunately he had
struck the water in a clumsy dive, rear legs first, instead of flat.
Though he limped, he could still walk. He explored cautiously. The
walls and floor had not been constructed; he seemed to be in a natural
cavern within the underlying bedrock that supported Darkhaven. The
wall he followed soon veered away from the subterranean lake, and
he was shambling along an uneven passageway filled with rocks and
columns. He had no idea where he was going; he was moving more
to keep warm than anything else. At least I have stymied my pursuers
for a time, he thought ironically.

The passage led downward, at times steeply, at times almost
imperceptibly, but always downward. If there were branches and
forks Beorn did not know of them; he followed the lightless route,
not even thinking for long periods, merely obeying the instinctive
urge of the bear to find a place in which to lair and lick his wounds.
Many scents came to him; the faint reek of sewage, the tang of
limestone and silaceous deposits, and other smells which he could
not identify, but which raised the stiff hair along his back. Though
he had assumed he was far below the level at which the first stone
blocks and pylons had been raised, ages before the breaking of the

world, to create Darkhaven, still he found it hard to believe these caverns were the result entirely of water's slow erosion through rock, or the shifting and shaking of the crust. On occasion he would brush against huge stalagmites or columns that seemed planed in regular, albeit uneven, designs, and once he bumped into a large boulder that felt to his questing paws to be carved in a grotesque caricature of a face. The floor, also, though rock-strewn and pitted, was still too even to be the result of chance. Did he, Beorn wondered, now walk the same halls that Chthons had walked before the Shattering? The thought made him shiver. He stopped occasionally and listened, but at first he heard nothing at all, and then, after a long while, the very faint sound of thunder. The storm was still going on, and he marveled at the intensity of it, that he could hear it deep within the fragment.

He heard no sounds of pursuit, but he continued moving anyway, simply because stopping in the blackness and the silence was too horrible to contemplate. I am a long way from Tamboriyon, he thought grimly.

Suchana had often spoken of wanting to go to Tamboriyon; a fragment, by all accounts, of empyrean beauty and climate, where none went wanting and no life was hard, where a thief might flee to after amassing a fortune and spend the rest of his or her life in luxury and peace. They had spoken of it many times. It had become something of a joke between them; they would rob the king and go to Tamboriyon. At least it had been a joke to him; he had never known how serious Suchana had been. But now, not surprisingly, he found himself longing very much to be wandering Tamboriyon's sun-kissed meadows and drinking from its clear mountain streams.

Thinking of Tamboriyon, for some reason, made him think of the music he had heard just before he had been discovered. Though moody, it had been lovely; he wished now that he could hear it again. Though it had been part of the circumstances that had led him into this predicament, still he was glad he had heard it. He let what he could remember of the melody play over and over again in his head; it calmed him, even soothed the bear-fear at being lost in these nighted caverns.

He stopped once again to listen, and this time he did hear a sound—a sound that raised his hackles and pulled his black lips back from his fangs in an unseen snarl. It was the sound of something slithering and scraping over the rocks ahead of him—something quite large. The bear backed up hastily, growling. A dry, reptilian scent washed over him, and he felt, with no sense he could have named, the presence of *something* malefic in the darkness ahead. A fear so primal and so all-consuming that it was like paralysis held him for an instant. And then the reflexes of the bear took over. Beorn turned to flee the way he had come when there was an explosion of movement behind him, and a lance that felt like a white-hot iron struck his left shoulder, digging into it, bringing a roar of agony from him. Simultaneously he was slashed across the back. He stumbled, rolled, hearing a hissing that seemed multiplied endlessly. He scrambled behind the base of a large column and his unseen attacker crashed into it from the other side, shaking the massive stone. The bear felt movement in the air beside him and swung a paw toward it; he hit something, knocked it away, felt a spray of blood that was neither warm nor cold and heard a shriek like torn metal echo deafeningly about him. He backed up against the wall and felt an opening behind him; a niche just large enough for him to wedge his body into. He pushed back into it, sensing the whiplike movement in the air before him of several objects weaving back and forth, seeking an opening. He had no idea what they were; he only knew that he stood little chance of defeating them in the darkness. He could only slash blindly before him with his talons until the beaks or claws belonging to whatever had gouged him reached a vital spot. There was no escape.

With a calmness that surprised him, Beorn thought: I always knew I would end as the bear.

Then, without warning, blinding light filled his eyes.

The Warped Stairs: a slow descent into madness, Pandrogas thought. He leaned wearily against the obsidian wall, one hand holding aloft the starcrystal that did little to penetrate the heavy, breathing darkness. About him on the stairs were grouped Kabyn and five other servants. They looked as tired as he. They had been on the stairs for hours, and were quite totally lost.

To say that the Warped Stairs led to the Labyrinth, the lowest part of Darkhaven proper, or to the caverns beneath the castle, was not entirely true. They led to these places, and many others, at times. The steps, uneven and seemingly not designed for the passage of human feet, and their winding, twisting course, seemed to follow the precepts of a geometry totally alien to human minds. Merely to look at the steps made one dizzy and ill; at times the loss of perspective was so intense that it was impossible to tell if one were standing on a series of steps or hanging impossibly over a chasm. The irregular length and depth of the steps was tiring, also.

When the feelings of nausea and vertigo had first begun Pandrogas had spoken a spell of stability. It had helped little, and soon not at all. The disorientation affected him less than it affected Kabyn and the others, for he was used to glimpses into other dimensions and planes. But it was tiring, for his senses were not equipped to deal with it for a long period of time. And so he had become lost on the Stairs. It had happened to him before, when he had tried to reach the Labyrinth. Following the Warped Stairs was not merely a matter of descending steps; concentration and will were needed to keep the Stairs from leading them to a dead-end or returning them to where they had started. That had already happened once. They had rounded a corner, still descending, and found themselves back at the iron gate and the passage. When Pandrogas had turned to face the Stairs again they were as they had been originally: descending. They had started again—there was no other choice.

"I know the steps will take us to the caverns," he told Kabyn. "They deposited me there before, when I was seeking the Labyrinth and the catacombs beyond. Now that we seek the caverns, of course, the Stairs are reluctant to take us there."

Kabyn nodded, his face devoid of expression in the blue and yellow lights of starcrystal and torches. "I have heard it said," he murmured, in an almost musing tone, "that when reason fails, one's instincts are best relied upon."

Pandrogas glanced at him, but Kabyn said nothing further. He is right, of course, the sorcerer thought. How many times have I told students over the years to let go, to dismiss rationality, to use the forms and trappings of spells only as guides to the power that is already within? And that is the only way we will descend these Stairs.

But he had not felt well treated of late by his instincts. For the first time in many years he felt reluctant to trust his feelings. Still, he knew that in the current situation he had nothing else upon which to rely.

He was about to lead the others once again down the Stairs, when a cry echoed faintly about them—there was no way to tell if it came from above or below, since such terms were meaningless upon the Stairs. It came again: "Pandrogas!" Faint, fading—but he knew the voice.

He jerked away from the wall as though stabbed. "Amber!" he cried.

She was lost upon the Stairs.

He hesitated for a moment, unsure which way to go. Trust your instincts, he thought. He began to descend the Stairs, Kabyn and the others following. He heard her shout again, fainter still, and inspiration struck him: "Amber!" he shouted. "Play! I can find you if you play!"

A moment of echoing silence; then he heard the flute. She was playing the piece she had played in that other storm, months ago, when he had found her clinging to the rain-washed flèche on the roof. *The Light upon the Water*. He closed his eyes, let the music fill him, let it pull him toward her. He stumbled suddenly when the angle of the steps changed from downward to upward, but he did not open his eyes. He let her music guide him. The music grew louder—then suddenly it stopped, and his outstretched hand touched hers.

They held each other, shuddering with relief, each feeling the other to be a haven of stability upon the shifting Stairs. Then she pulled away and, before he could ask why she had come to the Stairs, she told him of the sphere's reading.

He leaned against the wall as Kabyn and the others came up

behind him. "It is a bad reading," he murmured. He suddenly felt very tired; how much worse could things get?

"I feared the serpent might be Sestihaculas," she said.

Pandrogas looked at her, beautiful even in the dim, wavering light, and thought, No matter what happens, it has been worth it because of her.

"The Demogorgon cannot enter Darkhaven without my leave. I do not fear Sestihaculas here, but there are other menaces in the Labyrinth. We must find the way to the caverns as quickly as possible."

"Maybe I can help," Amber said. "My wanderings on the Stairs have already taken me there once. But I felt, somehow, that you were still descending, and so I turned back."

"I have been to the caverns before myself," Pandrogas told her. "It makes no difference; the ways of the Stairs are ever-changing. It is a matter of will, not of route."

"I understand. But still, I feel I can find them again. We may as well try." She lifted her starcrystal high and stepped past him, ascending the Stairs. Pandrogas watched her for a moment, then shrugged and glanced back at Kabyn. He was surprised to see what looked like amusement in the bald man's eyes.

He turned and followed Amber. He would not be surprised at anything she could do, he told himself. She had found him on the Stairs as much as he had found her. Perhaps she could lead them to the caverns.

But as he followed, he felt troubled, because he recalled wondering earlier what he had done or not done to bring the situation to this pass. Why had he thought of her music? he asked himself, and had no answer.

She led them to the caverns.

It did not even seem difficult; the descent was tedious but fairly direct, ending at last in a chamber that, though huge in itself, was but the merest anteroom to what lay beyond. Amber turned back to look at the rest of them as they left the Stairs, and she grinned up at Pandrogas with such a look of triumph that the sorcerer almost laughed out loud.

His amusement, however, did not keep him from being impressed. She had done what he could not in finding a way down the Stairs; had demonstrated once again the potential that lived within her. And he, once again, felt a wave of jealousy that he was ashamed to acknowledge.

He soon forgot it, however, as they made their way into the caverns. The underground corridors were like none he had ever seen before—primarily of black, glistening limestone, with stalagtites and stalagmites that curved like fangs. There were also unwholesome hints that the formations were not entirely natural; gigantic, brooding dolmens and what they thought—but could not be sure—were rough sculptures of demonic faces and bodies. Once they passed what seemed to be the fossilized skeleton of some saurian beast, longer than a dragon. They felt the weight of more than the tons of rock and construction above them—there was also the feeling of eons pressing down. "Even the Chthons were parvenus here," Pandrogas said. "These caverns date long before the days of man or demon." They proceeded cautiously, for Pandrogas knew from his studies of Darkhaven's archives that creatures lived in this labyrinth beneath the real Labyrinth—dangerous creatures.

They marked their way carefully, for everywhere tunnels and passages branched in vermicular confusion. How, Pandrogas wondered, will we ever find the lake into which the bear plunged?

The question was soon answered when they stopped for a rest. The silence was suddenly broken by the distant sound of an animal's roar. It was followed by a hissing, wierdly magnified, like a nest of snakes disturbed. Amber seized Pandrogas's arm as he arose. "The serpent," she said.

"Possibly," he replied. "But it sounds also like the bear, and so we must investigate."

The sounds of fighting led them across a wide natural bridge that spanned a chasm and through a narrow cleft in the black wall. Pandrogas led the way; the hissing and growling were very loud as he emerged from the cleft. The starcrystals and torches illuminated the scene: across the wide tunnel the bear huddled in a natural alcove of the wall, and before him loomed a hydra.

Pandrogas had one startled moment in which to view it all—the ponderous reptilian body, torchlight iridescent on the scales; the serrated spine and barbed tail, and seven bobbing, weaving heads. One of the necks was broken; the head lolled drunkenly on the end of it, tongue protruding, and blood flew like a spray of lava from the wound in the thrashing neck. Pandrogas saw another head turn toward him, saw red eyes glittering, saw the heavy curved beak open. He flung himself to one side and the beak struck the wall, bringing sparks from it. The hissing was like the sound of storm or ocean as the sorcerer rolled over and came to his feet in another rocky recess similar to the one in which the bear stood. A moment later Amber and Kabyn joined him.

The hydra shifted its position, bracing itself on four strong legs. Three of the heads continued to harass the bear; the other three, their serpentine necks stretched to fullest length, snapped beaks or stabbed with curved horns at the cleft, keeping the rest of Pandrogas's men imprisoned within it as Amber, Pandrogas, and Kabyn were trapped in the recess.

"This is the serpent within the darkness, I take it," Kabyn said calmly.

"Can you not use sorcery?" Amber asked Pandrogas. She had to shout to be heard over the hydra's hissing.

"I must have room in which to perform a spell of any consequence," he replied. "Still, we shall see what this may do." He brought the backs of his hands together sharply, pulled them toward him and thrust them, palms out, as though casting something. At the same time he shouted five Payan words; Amber recognized one of them as meaning "sand." She felt a burst of wind tear at her clothes and saw powdered black rock that had lain for centuries suddenly spin into the air, making a cloud about the hydra's heads. Four of the heads were blinded, including the three that menaced the bear. They pulled back, shrieking, their lidless eyes filmed.

Amber saw the bear take advantage of this; the huge furry body, incredibly lithe for all its bulk, leaped over the hydra's thrashing tail and galloped down the tunnel at a speed that astonished her. The bear had escaped, but they were still trapped—and now the hydra moved toward them, its two remaining heads extended.

"What sand did not do, fire may," Kabyn said. He leaped forward, thrusting his torch into the forest of heads atop the massive shoulders. The flames singed one head, and all seven reared back long enough for Pandrogas to grab Amber and pull her around the curve of rock with him and into the main part of the tunnel. But Kabyn was not fast enough; one of the heads swooped downward, slamming into his side like the fist of a giant. He was lifted off his feet and hurled backward against the far wall, where he lay motionless.

"Somashae tanyen!" Pandrogas shouted. He spun about once, twice, thrice, and brought his arms out and up with such force that the loose folds of his robe snapped against his skin. Amber saw his fingers spread wide, the tendons on the backs of his hands raised and straining, saw, for an instant, those hands outlined in golden fire.

The hydra's seven necks snapped outward and upward, and she heard the heads shriek this time in pain instead of anger. Pandrogas grabbed Amber and pulled her to one side as the beast lurched unsteadily past them and down the tunnel. Another moment and it was gone, with only the fading sounds of its passage and cries left.

Pandrogas knelt beside Kabyn and tore open the man's blouse. A large bruise was rising, and several ribs were obviously broken. The servant's breathing was painful but regular. "We will take you back up the Stairs immediately," Pandrogas told him as the rest of the servants gathered around them.

Kabyn shook his head. "Not until you have the Runestone," he said with difficulty. He put up a hand to stop Pandrogas's reply. "Go—you know I am right."

Pandrogas nodded and turned to two of the others. "Stay here with him," he told them. Then, to Amber, "And you as well."

She was about to protest, but it was not necessary. "No," Kabyn said. "She must go with you, Pandrogas."

"You're wrong," Pandrogas said to him.

Kabyn smiled painfully. "Have I ever been wrong before?"

The sorcerer hesitated, then turned and started down the tunnel in the direction the bear had taken. Amber followed, as did the three servants he had chosen. She hurried, stretching her legs to keep up with him. "What did you do to the hydra?" she asked.

"Stung it," he replied briefly.

After a moment she asked, "What will you do to the bear?"

He did not reply to that. The grim look on his face, in the light of the starcrystal he carried, was answer enough.

When his unexpected salvation had come, Beorn had felt not a moment of guilt in taking advantage of the first opportunity to run. He had certainly not expected to be tracked down even in these trackless depths, and he realized that he had, really, no chance of escape—it was a choice of being taken by the sorcerer and his men or dying in any variety of horrible ways in the caverns. Yet still he ran, colliding with helicites and stumbling on cave coral, in what amounted to an instinctive, bestial reaction to pursuit. He would run until he could run no further, and then he would turn and fight until he could fight no more—to such an extent did the bear now rule him.

He wondered if the sorcerer had been among his posse. He had caught only the barest glimpse of anyone; his vision, none too good at best, had been dazzled by the light of the torches and starcrystals. He could only hope that the hydra would delay them long enough for him to hide. And so he ran, hearing the sounds of battle dwindle behind him until once again he was wrapped in the complete silence of the underground.

Or so he thought. When he stopped to catch his breath he could hear, over his convulsive panting, the rumble of thunder. It was much louder now. He realized also that the air was no longer dry and stagnant; he felt a slight breeze, and smelled moisture. Not yet daring to hope, his wounds aching, the bear lumbered on.

The tunnel narrowed until he could not stand upright, and the fresh, rain-sweetened air washed over him. He could see, faintly, the rocks around him, and wisps of fog. He rounded a narrow turn, barely squeezing through.

He was in a small chamber, full of damp mist and illuminated by gray light. The light became momentarily brilliant, stark; and thunder deafened him. The mist was boiling up from the center of the sloping, damp floor. Then a gust of wind parted the mists for a moment, and he saw an irregular hole in the center of the floor and through it the angry iron swirling of stormclouds.

He had descended deeper than he had thought. He was at the bottom of the fragment on which rested Darkhaven. Before him gaped the Abyss.

There was too much fog in the chamber for Beorn to see if the tunnel continued. He moved carefully along the slick rocks that rimmed the opening. When he reached the other side, he found it was as he had feared—the chamber was a *cul-de-sac*. He was trapped.

He started back toward the tunnel. Perhaps there was still time to retrace his steps, to find another escape route—

A tall man with hair of black and gray stood in the tunnel's entrance. Beside him was a woman, tall but not as tall as the man. Both held torches of starcrystal. Neither had weapons, but neither, Beorn was sure, needed them. Though he had not seen him before, he felt sure that the man was Pandrogas, the sorcerer of Darkhaven.

The same instinct told him with equal certainty that the woman was she who had played the flute while he was in the sorcerer's laboratory.

He cannot harm me, Beorn thought. Ardatha's amulet protects me. But deep within he knew that made no real difference. He was wounded, tired. The chase was over.

Three more men now entered behind them; the ones who had pursued him earlier. They held torches and swords. I could still attack, Beorn thought. The room is small, no place for them to run—but somehow it did not seem worth it. The bear had retreated from his instinct slightly; it seemed now that the best thing to do would be to surrender, explain Ardatha's hold on him and hope for the best.

The sorcerer held out a hand. "The Runestone, shapechanger." His voice was hard. Beorn looked past him, to the woman who had played the flute. The music had been beautiful—perhaps there was a chance they were not the ogres the people of Oljaer thought them to be. He squinted, looking hard through the mist and the limitations of the bear's eyes at her.

"We will not harm you, bear man," she said softly. "We only wish what is ours."

As I only wish what is mine, Beorn thought. He wished that he could speak to them, to explain what was suddenly so clear to him— that all he had ever wanted was a chance at peace, peace with the bear, peace with himself, and time to walk the sunny fields of Tamboriyon. But perhaps he would be able to explain. Perhaps they would not harm him, would let him return to his human shape, so that he could tell them how it was.

He stepped forward meekly. The woman smiled and exhaled in relief, as though she realized that a battle had been won; even Pandrogas's expression seemed to soften slightly.

And then the room suddenly filled with fire as lightning flashed in the storm outside. A cannonade of thunder struck all in the room like a physical blow, followed by a swirling updraft of rain. The bear staggered, slipped on the slick rocks at the opening's edge—

And fell into the darkness of the storm.

BOOK II

flight and Pursuit

Thy thoughts have created a creature in thee; and he whose intense thinking thus makes him a Prometheus; a vulture feeds upon that heart forever; that vulture the very creature he creates.

—Herman Melville,
Moby Dick

Chapter 7

The Healing Spell

Ardatha listened to the dripping of the clepsydra, loud in a momentary lull in the storm, and thought, There has been trouble. She had waited through Oljaer's short night and most of its day, had watched Darkhaven settle beneath the cloud-darkened horizon and rise again. She had seen the storm boil over the floating castle like surf over a rock, and had been driven indoors by the rain when it had reached Oljaer. She had waited, whiling away the terrible silent hours trying to read, or going through rituals of practice and form. But nothing could make her forget, even for a moment, the unknown drama taking place across the rain-driven gulf of air between Oljaer and Darkhaven.

Thunder exploded outside her window, rattling equipment on the table before her and making her jump. She sighed. Should someone peek into her sanctum now, she thought, they would be quite surprised at what they saw: the imperturbable, sinister enchantress of Oljaer as nervous as a witch with a new brass ring.

This is foolishness, Ardatha told herself. The bearling's lateness was no sign of capture; not even a cacodemon could safely traverse the Abyss in such a storm. They were no doubt huddled in some obscure garret or tower of Darkhaven, waiting for the storm to blow

107

over. And waiting for Pandrogas to discover the theft...

A knock on the door brought her about quickly, white hair whirling about her face. She tugged fingers through it, adjusted her sleeves, picked up a decanter and began to carefully tip salts into a mortar. "Enter," she said in an absent tone.

From the corner of her eye she saw Troas enter. She concentrated on her bit of mummery as though it were the Necromancer's last spell. She often used such charades with Troas; magic made him nervous and easier to handle. It came as quite a shock to her to suddenly feel his hand on her hip, his breath on her bare neck. She stiffened, and she knew that he felt it—the massaging hand paused for a moment before sliding up to cup one breast. His other hand mirrored the action.

"Troas, your passion makes you reckless," she said calmly. "Interrupting a spell in progress can have disastrous results."

"I would face them," he said, and the richness of his voice told her he would not easily be dissuaded this time. "I would face the Demogorgon himself for you, Ardatha. Leave these foul smells and unhealthy pursuits, and I'll show you man's magic tonight." His hands closed on her breasts, kneading the nipples roughly between thumb and forefinger. They hardened in pain, which he took for pleasure, and so began to kiss her neck.

Over the scents of herbs and philters about them Ardatha could smell the wine on his breath. She tried to twist away from him, but she was trapped between the Lord King and her worktable. "Troas!" she said sharply. "This is not the time, nor the place! I will come to your chamber at nightfall—"

"Too long," he said, his voice muffled by her hair. "Were the day only a breath in length, it would still be too long to wait. I want you *now*, Ardatha." He buried his face in the curve of her neck again.

Angered beyond consideration of consequences, she spoke under her breath a short command. Troas jerked his head back convulsively and released her, clapping one hand to his ear. He looked at the slight smear of blood on his palm, then at Ardatha, and the demonshead earrings that grinned at him from the mists of her hair.

"Take care, enchantress," he said in a low voice. "I am, after all, the king—"

"And *I* am Ardatha, Troas! I have work to do and there's more to it than—" Hearing herself, she took a deep breath and continued more calmly: "—than you may think. Rest assured, milord, that I am pursuing Oljaer's interests—"

Her words ended in an incredulous gasp as he stepped forward and seized her roughly by her right wrist. "As am I, Ardatha!" He grinned. "I am king—I *am* Oljaer—and Oljaer's sword is raised for you!" He pressed her back against the table again, and began with his other hand to clumsily unbutton his robes. She felt the bulge of his codpiece against her hip. He tried to kiss her, but she twisted her face away from him. From behind her she heard a flapping sound, and it stopped her heart for a moment. Balandrus! she thought. He is returned with Beorn—Beorn, whom Troas believes is languishing in a dungeon cell awaiting torture! She knew that Troas, ever suspicious of all about him, would immediately take her duplicity as a plot. At that moment he succeeded in kissing her, forcing his tongue into her mouth. Revulsed and panicked, she brought her free hand up between his legs, grasped the royal genitals in her six scaly fingers, and let him feel, for an instant, the power of the Chthons.

Troas screamed at the searing heat. He stumbled and fell backward, bleating in agony. Ardatha glanced toward the balcony, saw that what she had thought was the beating of the cacodemon's wings was in fact the flapping of a curtain where one of the doors had blown open. She closed it, then quickly seized from her cabinet a draught of memphitis and, kneeling down beside the Lord King, forced him to drink it. He coughed and sputtered, then ceased thrashing as it took effect. Ardatha rose and moved her demon hand quickly through the air in the enspelling form of Memoryweaving. The claw left a tracery of luminous silver in the air.

"To nearly lose all that makes you a man—a shameful fate for a king. Best to take no memory from this room," she said softly, "nor come again until I bid you." She sealed the spell with the proper Payan words, applied an aloetic to the superficial burns on his scrotum while he was still groggy from the combination of the spell and the anesthetic, and pulled him to his feet. She was certain that no one had heard him scream over the tumultuary thunder of the storm. She was not nearly so sure that the simple witchery would keep him from remembering his visit to her; such a traumatic experience was not easily forgotten. But simple spells were the best where the mind was concerned—a more complicated cantrip would have required constructing a false memory for him, and that was never attempted lightly. She could only hope that, linked to his masculine ego, the memory would be too embarrassing for him even to wonder where he had lost an hour and gained a painful burn. But she did not delude herself; at most it would buy her a day, and then he would remember.

Whether Beorn was successful or not, she would have to leave Oljaer very soon.

Ardatha helped Troas out the door. "Rest now, little king," she murmured to him. She closed the door behind him as he shuffled down the hall—those functionaries who saw him would interpret his mazed behavior and gingerly walk as the result of too much wine. She collapsed on a couch beside the bookcase, her heart pounding louder, it seemed to her, than the thunder outside. She stared at her worktable, at the complicated network of copper piping and earthenware aludels, retorts, and alcohol lamps designed for lixiviation, coagulation, decoction; at the heavy bound tomes filled with magic spells; at the impressive laboratory that was her domain. What good has it done me? she wondered. What good has it done anyone? All I have used my knowledge for is to cause pain. And now I must leave everything here—everything but this. She looked at her demon's hand with revulsion, clenched it suddenly into a fist, heard the talons scrape on the palm's carapace, and began to laugh. To use such power to tickle a petty monarch's balls, she thought— how have I come to this?

After all these years she still feared the hand. She remembered the searing pain that had accompanied its formation. A gift, she thought, bitterly. Still, it was a gift that had served her well, in magic if not in life. She had never allowed herself to feel its full power, just as she had never allowed herself to feel the fullness of love. The mockery of coupling with Troas was all she had had in a very long time that even echoed of intimacy. She tried to tell herself she did not miss it; that she was devoted to her work for the One God; but though she could lie very skillfully to others, she could not lie to herself.

She noticed suddenly that the thunder had stopped. She stepped to the balcony and peered out. The rain was slackening. She could see Darkhaven, visible in the clouds like a many-masted ship in a dense fogbank. She watched it move ponderously overhead. So hard to think of it as anything but eternal. And yet, if Beorn had done his job—it would soon fall on Troas's head.

Ardatha smiled at the thought.

A dry, rasping hiss was all Tahrynyar could manage in the way of a scream. He opened his eyes. He was alone in a large windowless bedchamber, lit by starcrystal, with a tiny flue over the headboard for ventilation. Besides his bed, another, empty one, and a shared night table, the only furniture was a chair between the beds and a brazier for hot bricks. The bricks in it gave off slight heat; the room was chill, but not cold. Tahrynyar noticed all of this abstractly; the only reality at the moment was the pain.

The door opened, and one of the sorcerer's servants—Undya, he remembered—entered. She carried several red-hot bricks on a wooden-handled tray, and used thongs to replace the cold bricks in the brazier with the hot ones. This task done, she turned toward him, saw that he was awake, and quickly poured him a cupful of fragrant tea from a kettle on the brazier.

"Drink," she said softly, lifting his head from the pillow. The marquis sipped through clenched teeth, feeling the tea scorch his mouth and throat, welcoming this new pain as a distraction from the other. The tea burned its way down, and after a moment, the relentless agony dimmed slightly—just enough for him to feel he could endure it and remain sane. He glanced up at his nurse, then took a deep breath and collected his strength; it was important that he ask his question in a steady voice. "Amber... where is she?"

Undya looked at him with a gaze the color and expression of

ebony wood. "With Pandrogas," she said, "pursuing the bear."

"Leave me," Tahrynyar said after a moment.

She nodded slightly and turned toward the door. "If the pain rises again, drink more of the dream tea," she told him. "It may help you in other ways as well." Then the door closed behind her.

Tahrynyar remembered the bear looming over him, the worst of all possible nightmares. They had not told him, but he knew what had happened; his knees had been crushed. He closed his eyes on two hot tears. He had lost his title, his holdings, his wife, and now his legs. He tried to hate both Amber and Pandrogas, swore an oath to himself that he would somehow wreak a manly revenge; but he knew, even as he muttered the words aloud, that it would never happen. Revenge was for the strong, and even at his best, he had never been that. He could not truly hate Amber even now. The realization only served to further depress him.

The door opened again, and several of the servants entered, carrying another of their number on a makeshift litter. They deposited him carefully on the bed, and Tahrynyar saw his face—it was Kabyn. Undya removed his tunic and Tahrynyar looked in dull amazement at the swollen, purple bruise that spread halfway down the bald man's side. He wanted to ask what had happened, but something about the servants' silence, and their complete absorption in this accident that had befallen one of them, made him hesitant to intrude. It was an odd feeling; he had never before been overly concerned about the feelings of servants. He watched while Undya bandaged Kabyn's ribs, unspeaking all the while. She gave him nothing that Tahrynyar could see to ease his pain. Before she left, however, she made what Tahrynyar assumed was a gesture of affection, though a strange one: she touched her index fingers and thumbs together, forming a triangle. Kabyn nodded slightly and smiled with an effort. Undya left the room with the other servants. Tahrynyar watched them go, then looked back at Kabyn. The man lay on his back, eyes closed, breathing shallowly.

"What happened?" His tongue, scorched by the dream tea's heat and numbed by its effects, made his speech an effort. But the pain had subsided considerably now, though accompanying it was a strange feeling of disassociation. He found it difficult to concentrate on Kabyn's reply.

"The thief is gone," Kabyn whispered painfully. "We pursued him into the caverns beneath Darkhaven. I was struck down by one of the beasts that prowl there, and the sorcerer and your lady confronted the bear in a pit that opened into the Abyss. He was swept away by the storm, and the Runestone went with him."

Tahrynyar knew little about magic, but he knew the purpose of a Runestone. "That means Darkhaven is doomed to fall."

"Yes."

Tahrynyar nodded. He stared thoughtfully at the starcrystal rod on the wall; it seemed to have an intensity, a scintillance that he had never noticed before in one. With difficulty he brought his mind back to Kabyn's statement. The pain of his broken legs was becoming more insistent; he took another long swallow of dream tea.

"Good," he said then. "I would gladly see Darkhaven go down; in fact, I would do everything in my power to aid its fall." It seemed to him that he could hear the words resonating in the air after he spoke them. He felt ashamed at making the statement, but it was said now, and he would not take it back.

Kabyn looked at him calmly for a moment, then said in a soft, sad voice, "Such an oath must needs be honored." He closed his eyes then, and in a moment, as far as the marquis could judge by his breathing, was asleep.

Tahrynyar stared at the ceiling, which seemed higher than it had been when he awoke. He attempted to go back to sleep, but, though he was exhausted from fighting the constant pain, sleep would not come. He looked at the lean, bald man in the bed next to his, and wondered why he had the uncomfortable feeling that he had just been cursed.

Fog and clouds fled across the roofscape of Darkhaven. Bursts of rain stung Amber's skin as she huddled within the Borium Tower and stared out into the maelstrom. The scene reminded her of the circumstances in which she and Tahrynyar had come to Darkhaven, though that storm had been nothing compared to this one. Beside her she could barely hear Pandrogas say, "Impossible to launch a ship in this storm. We will have to wait."

They had hurried back to Pandrogas's laboratory immediately after the bear had disappeared, and the sorcerer had attempted to locate their quarry once again in the mirror. He had gotten only a momentary vision of swirling gray clouds and the craggy underside of the fragment, coming closer—then nothing; the bear evidently had lost consciousness or had been hurled by the wind against the rocks. They had then come to the bell tower, near the dragonship port, only to realize that they could do nothing until the storm abated.

The tower suddenly shook, and white light seared Amber's eyes. Simultaneously she was deafened by a sound like the crack of a dragon's tail, followed by the discordant ringing of the bells in the belfry above them. Both she and Pandrogas staggered, momentarily stunned. Amber coughed on powder and smoke that filled her nostrils, and then a downpour of rain drenched her to the skin. But we were inside, she thought dazedly, as Pandrogas led her down the winding stairs and away from the storm's fury. Amber looked up and saw that a piece of the ceiling had given way across the room from where they had stood; powdered masonry and rubble covered the floor. Through the hole she could see the belfry above the room they were in; the timbers of the peaked roof had been charred by a momentary blaze that the rain had extinguished, and two of the huge, age-old bells had fallen.

"Are you all right?" Pandrogas asked her. Amber blinked and peered at him; he stood next to her in a corridor. Her first dazed thought was, You've aged! Then she realized that his hair was white from the stone ground like flour by the lightning strike. "Come on," he said to her; "you need warm clothes. That was the first lightning to hit Darkhaven in more than a commondecade. This storm is one to remember."

Back in her chamber she found dry clothing. As she changed, Amber listened to Pandrogas pacing in the outer rooms. For the first time she was seeing him truly upset—no, more than that: frightened. She remembered the moment after the bear had fallen; she had thought that he was going to hurl himself into the storm in suicidal pursuit. Only the quickness of his servants had kept him from falling. His loss of control had shocked her, though she felt it was certainly understandable. She tried not to acknowledge the tiny feeling of almost-gladness deep within her that the Runestone was gone, for if Pandrogas could not recover it, he would have no choice but to leave Darkhaven. She shook her head to rid herself of the thought— she had been having many feelings lately of which she was not proud.

As she rejoined Pandrogas, she asked, "Since we must wait for the storm's end, isn't there something more you can do for Tahrynyar?"

He seemed almost reluctant to reply. "I will do what I can," he said at last. "With the Runestone gone, my power has been lessened considerably."

Amber looked at him in surprise. "I thought thaumaturgy was independent of Runestones," she said. "You told me power was something that dwells within one, not supplied by external forces except in specific cases."

Pandrogas gazed past her and said, "True, true. But I have... invested... my powers in Darkhaven's Runestone. Now that it is gone, I am incomplete. I must conserve what I have. Regaining the Runestone is the most important thing." He looked back at her and gave her a distracted smile from which she took no comfort. "Come," he said, "let us see how he fares."

Tahrynyar came back from a something that was not quite sleep, not quite dreaming, and not quite reality, to focus on the two standing before the bed. He looked from Amber to Pandrogas. The room was very quiet, save for the gentle breathing of the sleeping Kabyn in the next bed.

"Tahrynyar," Amber said gently. She placed her fingers on his hand beneath the quilt. He saw her eyes moisten as he moved his hand from hers. Her pain was more amusing, for some reason, than satisfying to him.

"And to what do I owe the honor of this visit?" he asked lightly. Some dim part of him was aware that these two people had done to his life what the Necromancer had done to the world, but that too, at the moment, was merely amusing.

"I can lay a healing spell upon your knees, to speed your recuperation," Pandrogas said to him, "but I do not want to give you false hope. Sorcery can perform what many consider miracles, but the price exacted can be high. The body is a complex mechanism; disturb its natural functions, even to its benefit, and it will oftimes rebel in unforeseen ways—"

Tahrynyar laughed, and the surprised expression on the sorcerer's face made him laugh some more. The laughter shook him, and he felt the pain begin to push at the limits of his endurance again. He swallowed another cupful of dream tea.

"You're saying you can't help me, sorcerer? How kind of you to take time from your busy schedule to inform me of this!"

Pandrogas took a deep breath. "I didn't say that. I am saying that you must be aware of possible consequences."

The dream tea dimmed the pain again, but seemed to suddenly release a flood of anger that filled every cell of Tahrynyar's body. *Consequences,* he thought. At last he felt able to hate Amber, and it filled him with a fierce joy.

He said through clenched teeth, "I should like very much to refuse your help, Pandrogas, but I can't face being bedridden for the rest of my days. You have saved my life twice, and helped to ruin it twice. I don't know which you have come to do now. I just want you to know that no matter what either of you do, I hate you, and will always hate you." The words sounded petty and ineffectual to him. Amber turned away; Pandrogas looked uncomfortable. Tahrynyar stared at him, the observing part of his mind that had been amused now registering mild astonishment at the vehemence of his hatred. He wanted Pandrogas and Amber to know how much they had hurt him, and to what reaches he had gone—would still go— to hurt them. "I wanted the thief to rob you, Pandrogas! I summoned Sestihaculas to take you, not me! I wanted him to have you both, and I still do!" He saw Amber's shoulders jerk at those words, and reveled in the fact that it caused him no pain. "I am ruined in every way, and you...you...." To his unspeakable frustration, he began to cry. He thrashed his head against the pillows, trying to deny the tears. Say something else, he thought—anything else to hurt them. "I swear to you, sorcerer, that I will see you in Xoth!" he cried. He was trying to think of a worse curse to follow that one when he saw Pandrogas make a quick, hypnotizing gesture with his hands, heard him speak cryptic words . . .

Pandrogas saw Amber turn around at the sound of his spellcasting. She looked at Tahrynyar's white, drawn face, the eyes closed now, and then at Pandrogas. "Why did you do that?" she asked. The coldness of her tone shocked him.

"I was afraid he would hurt himself," the sorcerer said. "It was a simple sleep spell—"

"He has a right to his anger! You could respect him that much, at least!"

Pandrogas stepped back in surprise. Her anger brought the power within her very close to the surface; with an analytical part of him that he could never fully suppress, he thought of how effective it would be channeled by knowledge and craft. "The dream tea had addled him," he said quietly. "He did not know what he was saying."

"He knew very well—as did you!" She was hoping that he would fight back, do anything to show some kind of emotion. But he merely folded his hands behind him and said, "We have no time for this— even now, Darkhaven is falling. Its path through the sky began to decay the instant the Runestone left. Unless we find the stone, Darkhaven will collide with Oljaer. We have priorities—we must prepare for the search."

"How much preparation can it take?" Amber demanded. "When the storm is over, take the dragonship out and find the demibear— or his body. Are you telling me that a Sorcerer of the Tenth Ring cannot find his own Runestone, no matter where it has been blown to?"

He turned away from her, clenching his hands into fists behind his back. "You don't understand," he said in a low voice. "I'll have to go outside."

Amber looked at his back for a long, silent moment. "Yes, you will," she said finally. Then she turned and left the room.

Pandrogas looked down again at Tahrynyar. Beyond the sleeping marquis, Kabyn regarded the sorcerer with calm black gaze. Pandrogas squared his shoulders. "I will do what I can to aid him— and you, old friend," he told the servant.

"There is no need in my case," Kabyn said. "Conserve your strength, Pandrogas. The winds of the Abyss can be harsh."

Pandrogas nodded. It did not seem strange at all for the servant to be giving him counsel. He raised his hands over the sleeping marquis, then hesitated. Tahrynyar had been drinking dream tea heavily. The mild hallucinogen might affect the spell somehow; no sorcerer alive could predict all the subtle and myriad ramifications of magic dealing with the body and the mind. And, he admitted to himself, he felt uncertain about his ability to cast a spell he had learned years before and practiced at least once a commonweek since. This was foolishness, he thought. But he knew it was more than that. Over the years, in his attempts to understand Darkhaven more, to probe its secrets more deeply, he had focused his powers within the Runestone. The investment had given him more strength in subtle ways, but now he was paying for it. He remembered the sphere's reading: *Clouds consume all of worth.* The Runestone had been carried away by the storm, and so had most of his power. His confidence had been badly shaken by the threat of Sestihaculas, and the impending doom of which Thasos had spoken. Now he stood with his hands raised to heal a man who was his rightful enemy, who had already made a serious effort to send him to Xoth. He sighed. And of all these threats, he thought, the one that troubles me the most is Amber's anger.

He began the healing spell. It was hard to remember the words.

Ardatha stood on the balcony and felt the evening sun on her face. The last of the stormclouds had drifted past Oljaer; everywhere, jeweled and gilded roofs sparkled with infinite color. Darkhaven was not currently in the sky; it would rise soon after sunset. But Balandrus should have returned, she thought. She could wait no longer, so by words and gestures performed with the power of her

claw she summoned the cacodemon from the Spire of Owls. It
appeared with a thunderclap of wings that made courtiers on the
floor below think the storm had returned. Huddling within the shade
of the building, it told her, "Your thief has not returned."

"You let him enter Darkhaven, and have not seen him since?"
Ardatha asked suspiciously.

"He left me at the Spire whole and unharmed, and has not returned. This I swear by him whom I sensed within the castle."

Ardatha moved her hands quickly before her in a calming pattern
for her own benefit. Her plan had gone awry—either the thief had
been apprehended, or he had somehow outfoxed her and escaped
from Darkhaven by another route. But how? He could have launched
no dragonship in the storm, and Balandrus would have seen it leave . . .

The enchantress's eyes widened as the rest of the cacodemon's
words suddenly sank in. It would not take oath on any human, even
so strong a sorcerer as Pandrogas. Balandrus would swear only by
a Chthon. "Who of your kind did you sense within Darkhaven?"

"He who rules me—Demogorgon."

Ardatha stepped back in shock. The evening bells sounded as the
fragment showed the sun its hind side. The cacodemon relaxed
slightly as night, little darker than the storm that just passed, began.
Ardatha glanced nervously toward the horizon where the castle would
soon rise. What was Sestihaculas doing within Darkhaven? He could
enter only if summoned, and that she knew Pandrogas would never
do. Yet the cacodemon would not lie about this. Ardatha looked at
her demon hand and shuddered. She would sooner be hurled into
the Abyss than confront the Demogorgon again—and yet, she had
to know what had taken place in Darkhaven.

She thought of contacting Stonebrow for advice, but the idea of
admitting her failure to him was as frightening as another confrontation with Sestihaculas. Darkhaven's Runestone was a vital part of
the Circle's master plan. There was only one choice left to her.

She looked at Balandrus again. "Bide while I make preparations.
You will carry me to Darkhaven next."

The cacodemon nodded. "This is the second journey," it said.

* * *

Amber stood on one of the many parapeted tower roofs of Darkhaven, clothes and hair ruffling in the clear, rainwashed wind. She could see the features of the stone world about her with uncanny clarity. Everywhere, water poured through gutters and down drainpipes, and spewed from the mouths of gargoyles adorning the buttresses. Darkhaven had been washed clean by the storm—but only on the outside, she thought.

Before her was anchored the dragonship in which she and Tahrynyar had come to Darkhaven. Kabyn and the other servants had restored it to pristine shape, oiling the dragonhide wings and sails, polishing the bone and ivory of its frame, keeping the guys at the proper tension. So beautiful, Amber thought; the builders had managed to overcome the inherent savage appearance caused by the necessity of constructing the entire ship out of dragonbone and hide. She ran her hand lightly over the scrimshaw that ornamented the skull prow common to all dragonships. The small cabin, built of hide stretched over a ribcage, had been stocked with provisions necessary for a journey of a commonweek or more; Pandrogas had no idea how long it would take to find the thief's body.

Amber shifted her gaze from the dragonship to the city of Oljaer, which filled one side of the sky's vault. The air was clear enough for her to see the ant-sized inhabitants going about their business in the miniature streets and houses. Some were removing branches and debris, legacy of the storm, from the streets. The ivory palace dazzled her in the sunshine. Pandrogas had told her that the people of Oljaer considered Darkhaven to be the source of all their woes; doubtless they were blaming the destruction of the storm on the sorcerer. If the Runestone were not found, Amber knew, Oljaer would have reason indeed to damn Darkhaven.

She relived the scene in Tahrynyar's sickroom over and over, feeling fresh pain each time, and yet morbidly fascinated by the depths of his hatred for them both. She knew that the right thing for her to do would be to remain with him while Pandrogas was gone. But his bitterness was more than she could bear. Perhaps, she thought, that was another reason she had turned so strongly on Pandrogas— to focus her own self-anger and guilt upon someone else.

She sensed him standing behind her then, and turned around. The sight of him, the wind whipping his hair and robe, made her wonder how anyone who seemed so self-possessed, so in control and complete, could have any fears at all. But the fears were there, she told herself; and if she loved him, he deserved her help in dealing with them.

"Amber, I'm sorry," Pandrogas said. He looked into her eyes and she had to hold on to the wing's edge at her back to keep from rushing into his arms before his apology was done. "I've laid the healing spell on Tahrynyar. It should speed the mending of his legs, but how well he will walk, if at all, no sorcerer could say."

She put her arms around him then, and kissed him. He embraced her with a reassuring intensity. "Thank you," she said. "Now let's spend no more time on apologies—we have to find the Runestone."

He looked at her in astonishment. "We?"

"I thought we had settled *that* also," she said. "I'm going with you. It may be a mistake but I can't let you go by yourself. I don't care about the right or wrong of it. Tahrynyar will be well cared for, and your healing spell is all that you can do, and certainly more than I can do."

"It will be dangerous," he said, and Amber knew that she had won.

Pandrogas had also fashioned a ring containing a sliver of the Runestone with which to trace it. He hoped that the storm had not blown the thief's body far, and that it had not been found and despoiled by birds or vampires. Perhaps, the sorcerer told himself, it would be a simple search of a day or so, after which they could return to Darkhaven and prepare for the greater problems that faced him. Perhaps he could find the Runestone and return to his sanctuary before Sestihaculas was aware of his leaving. But he did not believe it would be so easy. The gloomy prophecies of the sphere ran through his mind constantly. He had not cast the sphere again before leaving; he did not want to know its forecast. What would happen, would happen—he had no choice but to face it. He was afraid, but determined not to show it; he had shown too much fear already.

And Amber, as she boarded the dragonship to leave Darkhaven for the first time in months, was afraid as well, and just as determined not to show it. But her fear was of a different sort. Terrifying though the thoughts of the Demogorgon's revenge or of Darkhaven's crashing were, she was most afraid of losing Pandrogas.

Pandrogas raised the spinnaker; it bellied full and taut, and the ship lifted free of Darkhaven as the wind rushed beneath its wings. To Amber it seemed as if Darkhaven suddenly dropped away from the stationary vessel, for the ship carried its own Runestone. She kept her gaze on Pandrogas to minimize the dizziness this caused. But watching the sorcerer seemed almost as disorienting, because she felt as distant from him as from the minuscule people she had seen walking the tiny streets of Oljaer.

Chapter 8

Adrift in the Abyss

Beorn awoke in a tranquil hell.

His return to consciousness was an exercise in pain; in addition to the wounds sustained as the bear, he ached in every muscle and joint due to his metamorphosis and the beating he had suffered from the storm. He remembered dimly the mad chaos that had enveloped him when he fell through the hole. He had been hurled about like a leaf in foaming rapids by winds that squeezed him like the talons of Balandrus. They had hurled him straight at the underside of Darkhaven—he had had a brief, terrifying glimpse of the ragged rocks awaiting him—and then another gust as quickly threw him away at the last second. A howling grayness surrounded him as he was helplessly buffeted and tossed about. He was stunned by hail and near misses of lightning. Thunder brought blood from his ears. Once he was trapped in a water pocket and came near to drowning before the winds ripped it apart. Through it all his one overriding fear had not been of death—that was a certainty—but rather that he would pass out and the bear would take over. He did not want

123

to die as the bear. And so he had started the metamorphosis again, which had added to his pain.

He had lost consciousness before it was completed. Beorn looked at his nude human form now with dull wonder. It was the first time he had ever changed back without control from start to finish; he had always assumed that, without his will to force it, he would remain the bear. He was amazed that it had proceeded without his guidance.

The pouch was still about his neck. A few times during the storm the winds had twisted it and nearly strangled him, but he had been unable to release it. He looked in all directions. There was no sign of the storm, nor was there any sight of land. He floated in blue sky patched with a few white clouds, the sun directly "beneath" him, meaning that at the moment he faced away from it. He could hear the humming in his ears that comes with utter silence. The ruffling of his hair and pressure on his skin told him that there was a slight wind, but, being weightless, he was borne along with it and so could not hear it. This was completely different from being in a dragonship, where a Runestone provided weight and stability.

He knew he was a dead man. To be hurled into the Abyss was a common form of execution on most fragments; once set to drift in the void, slow starvation was the inevitable result. Though the world's fragments were many, they were far enough apart that one could drift for years without seeing land. Of course, after a few days it would not matter. The thief faced slow starvation, with no way even to take his own life and end the torture.

The thought was too horrible to contemplate; he panicked, thrashing about, trying to swim in any direction. The only result was a rolling and tumbling that left him nauseated. He screamed in fear and frustration, and the sound was horrible as well—a tiny impotent, echoless noise swallowed by the silence. Angrily he seized the pouch about his neck, tempted to hurl it from him. Much good the Runestone of Darkhaven and Ardatha's magic trinkets would do him now! But he did not. If perchance his free-falling bones were ever discovered, he wanted it at least known that he had succeeded in his last theft.

Perhaps Suchana had been right, Beorn thought grimly. Perhaps there *was* divine retribution—perhaps he was being punished for his life of crime. If so, it was a most cruel and imaginative god that had decreed his fate. To be offered a chance to return the stolen Runestone to the sorcerer with no consequences, to be tantalized for a blessed instant by the prospect of peace, of a way out—and then to be hurled into perdition. For if the Abyss was not hell, then what was?

A period passed in which he thought about nothing; how long it was, he had no way of knowing. He found himself staring into the endless blue void until his eyes ached. He looked at his hands, working the fingers before his face to give himself something on which to focus. He had heard tales of dragoneers sailing the void, where even in the dragonships, many succumbed to rapture. One dragoneer had told him once that the Abyss was addictive, that after a long voyage one felt hopelessly claustrophobic on even the largest fragment. Beorn ran his hands over himself. He was not cold, but still he shivered. He could not seem to focus his thoughts . . .

He was revolving slowly on the long axis of his body. He closed his eyes as he faced the sun, and when he opened them again, he gasped in astonishment. He was looking at the forested surface of a fragment, no more than a hundred feet distant! This was impossible—were he that close to land, the pull would have seized him and he would have fallen. He stared in bewildered fascination. He floated only a few feet above a dark wood. The light was iron gray, filtered through clouds. He drifted slowly, and there came into his field of vision a clearing. He smelled smoke, dry and acrid, and saw below him the smoldering ruins of a small farmhouse . . .

Beorn's throat seemed to close. He clawed at the air frantically with his hands and feet, but could not stop his slow progress forward and downward. He stared at his destination in terrified fascination. He could feel the heat still rising from it, could see tiny licks of orange flame flickering on blackened beams. He was level with the top of the chimney, the only part of the farmhouse that still stood. He settled, gently as a falling feather, toward the rubble.

The cinders stirred directly below him. A charred section of wall was lifted, pushed aside, by a flame-eaten arm. Beorn screamed. The ashen corpses of his parents rose up out of the ruins, burnt flesh clinging in strips to black bones. He could see one eye, obscenely blue, in his mother's grinning charcoal skull—it transfixed him, seemed to draw him down toward their reaching arms. Beorn screamed again and again as he descended toward them. He hid his eyes, digging his fingernails into his forehead...

When he felt no skeletal hand grasp him, he looked down again. He was floating in the Abyss. There was no sign of land at all; certainly none of Aëslovèclan, or of the farmhouse where he had been raised. Beorn wrinkled his nose as the wind informed him that he had soiled himself in his fear. The offal now drifted beside him; he carefully fanned the air and managed to put some distance between him and it. His heart was beating hard enough to shake his whole body. Am I going mad? he wondered. It had been such an incredibly vivid hallucination—he had smelled the smoke, heard the crackling and settling of the ruins. So this is how it ends, the thief thought, with my mind shattered like the world. He shook his head and growled. Something might yet happen, he told himself. After all, he had survived more of this adventure than he would have given odds upon. He had to hold on to his sanity.

He squinted suddenly into the blue distance; there was a spot, a blemish on the perfect depthless sky. It began to take shape—it seemed to have wings, spread to catch the Abyss's winds. Beorn blinked, staring intensely.

It was Ardatha! She floated toward him, her hair a cloud behind her, her green garments spread around her arms like wings. She floated to a stop near him, smiling with evil amusement.

"So, bearling," she said. "You thought I would not come after the Runestone, eh? You thought you could outwit an enchantress?"

Beorn tried not to show the tremendous relief he felt—he wanted to cry with gratitude just for hearing another human voice. "I did not seek this situation," he replied. "Take the damned Runestone. I ask no reward save that you put me on solid ground again."

The enchantress looked at him and smiled again. Beorn realized that his lust for her, more overwhelming than he had ever felt for any woman in years, was very evident. "You shall have more than that as a reward," she said softly. "Your desire is reciprocated, Beorn. Have you not dreamed, as all have, of making love in the deeps?"

Beorn watched, fascinated, as she raised her demon hand to her throat and clasped her bodice. "I grant you your wish," she said to him; "Look upon Ardatha!" She ripped her gown away from her in a single motion. Beorn stared in horror. Only her head and right hand were human; the fabric had hidden the body of a cacodemon, scaled and reptilian, with hissing snakesheads for breasts and a smoking pit between her legs. She laughed and reached for him, pulled him into a cold embrace...

He was wrapped in a blanket, smothering. There was a sharp pain in his neck. He lashed out with one arm in blind panic, felt it strike something leathery and taut, heard a hiss and a flapping sound all about him. The blanket fell away.

Beorn clapped a hand to his neck and felt blood well between his fingers. The thing floating next to him was the size of a child and the color of a corpse. Emaciated, sexless, with a bald head, huge eyes, and pointed ears, it hissed again and bared sharp fangs now stained with Beorn's blood. Its arms and legs were roped with stark muscles and ended in talons and claws. Huge bat wings, folded now, sprouted from its shoulder blades. Beorn, breathing hard, still confused, watched it warily. It might be another hallucination, but he doubted his luck was that good.

The vampire spoke in a dry, sibilant voice. "Not dead blood, eh? Soon. Hungry, I wait." The words were pidgin Dazikahn, a dialect with which Beorn was familiar. He watched the thing hovering out of reach, waiting for him to die.

Yet perhaps there was one slight chance. "I'll make a bargain with you," the thief said. "You look like you need a good meal. Ferry me to a fragment and you can batten on me short of my life. Refuse, and you'll have to wait. I'll take a long time dying."

The vampire smiled. "No time in Abyss," it said. "I wait." It drew its arms and legs up into a fetal curl and hung beside him, using its wings just enough to stabilize itself. The glittering eyes watched Beorn unblinkingly.

To die a lingering death in the Abyss was bad enough, but to have a blood vulture perched almost on his shoulder, waiting—that was too much. Beorn spread his arms open and bared his neck. "Drain me now then, bloodsucker. I'd rather a quick death than a slow one, especially with you as audience." He closed his eyes and waited.

He heard the sanguisuge rustle its wings indecisively. It was suspicious, he knew, but also very hungry. At last it approached him, seized his shoulders with cold talons, wrapped its legs about him, enfolded him in its wings and brought its fangs once again to his neck. Beorn, gritting his teeth, let it have a single long draught— it would need strength for what he had planned. Then he brought his arms up between its chest and his and seized the raptor by the throat. It flailed him with its wings and tried to score him with its talons and claws, but Beorn tightened his grip on the reed-thin neck, and the vampire grew still.

"You've had your drink," he said tightly. "Now take me to land, or by the Necromancer, I'll break your neck."

The vampire was motionless for a long moment. Then, slowly, it spread its wings and let the wind fill them. Beorn could tell by the difference in air pressure on his skin that they were moving. He hung on. Another chance, he thought. Once again, another chance.

Ardatha chose as her egress point upon Darkhaven an open turret above one of the several libraries of the castle. The entrance spell she circumvented with a periapt similiar to the one she had given Beorn; it protected both her and Balandrus. The two passed quickly between the high walls stacked with tiers of books. The light of the starcrystals seemed to shrink before the cacodemon's black shape.

Ardatha took from a pouch the spiralspike burglar's tool that had identified Beorn to her. She had not had it long enough for it to lose the essence of its owner. Now she spoke a spell that caused a hemisphere of shimmering silver to appear about the tool. The shimmer remained clear; no other colors tinged it. Ardatha closed her demon hand over the tool in anger. So Beorn was no longer in Darkhaven! As she pondered her next move she felt a slight tremor pass through the library. Dust rose from tables and shelves about

her, and at the far end of the enormous chamber a single volume
fell from its place and struck the floor with an echoing crash. Balandrus growled uneasily. "Come!" Ardatha said, and they hurried
from the library.

In addition to the protection of the amulet, Ardatha had also
surrounded them with the Charm of Aware Air; the bubble of sensitivity would warn them from a considerable distance of any danger
that the amulet could not turn aside. By this she hoped to avoid
Pandrogas rather than confront him. It had been years since Ardatha
had left Darkhaven, but she remembered the location of Pandrogas's
laboratory, and she knew that Pandrogas would remember her. It
was a mad plan, to enter the sanctum of one of her sworn enemies
and there work magic, but she had no choice; she could not return
to Oljaer and her own laboratory. She proceeded almost at a run,
the cacodemon loping behind her. If her suspicion about what caused
the tremor was indeed correct, there was little time to lose.

She did not pause to wonder over the broken doors of the laboratory. Passing beneath the unknowing bronze guardian, she investigated the disorderly sanctum. There was no sign of the Runestone.
Appurtenances and books were piled about everywhere. Ardatha
recognized *The Red Grimoire,* one of the better-known repositories
of Necromancy. She resisted a temptation to delve into its brittle
pages, and continued her search instead. Pandrogas was something
of an eccentric—it would be like him to keep the single most precious talisman of an entire fragment in open view. But she had no
idea where to start looking. *"Secorum,"* she said, holding out her
demon hand and closing her eyes. *"Damarkor tul ebona."* There
was no answering pull on her hand. She muttered a curse. Her fear
was accurate—Darkhaven had lost its Runestone!

"Sestihaculas was here," the cacodemon said. "I sense remnants
of his aura."

"He is no longer inside the castle?"

"No longer."

Ardatha breathed a sigh of relief. "Who summoned him—the
sorcerer, or an acolyte?"

"Neither. My lord came for one with no knowledge."

The enchantress blinked in astonishment. The cacodemon would not lie about the doings of its master, she knew. She looked at her claw and felt sympathy for the luckless fool who had inadvertently summoned the Demogorgon. *If* it had been inadvertent.

First things first, she told herself. On one of the shelves she found a vasculum containing a whole mandrake root. With a grimace, she swallowed a non-lethal bit of the vile-tasting tuber; then, working quickly while the cacodemon watched the entrance, she performed Pandrel's Formula of Mock-life. The root stirred, sprouted arms, legs, and wings, and gave a mewling cry. Ardatha broke off a piece of the spiralspike and gave it to the mandragoras, which devoured it hungrily. "Find him who now lives within you, as you live within me," she instructed it. With a sound like shaken cloth the mandragoras flitted from the room and down the hall, seeking a window.

She thought further on the mystery of Sestihaculas's appearance. She could not imagine Pandrogas allowing a novice to read a summoning spell, unless he, too, were no longer in Darkhaven. She took a risk—she invoked the maximum ectenic force on the Charm of Aware Air.

She felt no answering awareness within the considerable radius of her spell. It seemed safe to assume that Pandrogas was no longer within the walls of Darkhaven. She wondered what sort of novice would have the audacity to contact the most powerful Chthon of all. Perhaps he or she would have information that she could use. The enchantress turned to Balandrus and said, "Find him who summoned Sestihaculas."

Tahrynyar awoke. He was immediately aware of his surroundings and circumstances, but, somewhat to his surprise, no surge of despair washed over him. He reached for the dream tea, then stopped. The pain still throbbed within his knees, but it seemed more bearable now. He decided he preferred the pain with his wits about him to the mazed state in which the tea left him. In a strange way, the pain was almost welcome—it seemed to reassure him that revenge was possible, worth seeking. No matter that he sought the destruction of a tenth-ring adept; somehow he *would* have satisfaction. His certainty surprised him—he searched within his soul cautiously, looking for any sign of hesitancy or weakness. He found none. It seemed to him that, if he prodded and questioned himself hard enough and long enough, he could shake this strange new serenity; but he preferred not to. He laced his fingers behind his head and leaned back against the pillow, smiling slightly.

He heard Kabyn stir in the next bed. "How are you, marquis?" the servant asked.

"I feel like a new man," Tahrynyar said quietly. The statement had required no thought, but as he said it, he knew it was true.

Before either could say anything further, the door to the chamber was suddenly wrenched from its hinges and hurled against the far wall. For a brief, paralyzing second, Tahrynyar thought the bear had returned. But what stepped through the door was far, far worse. The marquis had never seen a cacodemon before, but its appearance left no doubt as to its identity—the black, hulking shape, the folded wings, simmering eyes, and stench of sulphur made his nightmares of the bear seem tame. Behind the shadowy form, which seemed to leech light from the starcrystals, a woman stood, a woman with hair the color of bone and a face as impassive. Behind him he heard Kabyn struggle to sit up. "Ardatha!" the bald man gasped. He tried to speak a spell but his voice caught on his pain. Tahrynyar ducked as the cacodemon leaped completely over his bed and landed next to Kabyn's with unbelievable quickness. The thing seized Kabyn's head in one huge, splay-fingered hand and pressed its lips against the servant's. Kabyn's body thrashed like a hooked fish. Tahrynyar heard a horrible liquid gurgling come from him, and smelled burning meat. The cacodemon lifted his head and grinned at Tahrynyar, who saw with horror that the lower half of Kabyn's face was now a seared mass of flesh. The cacodemon let the servant's jerking form drop back onto the bed, and, pointing at Tahrynyar, said, "He summoned my master!"

The woman stepped to the side of Tahrynyar's bed and, raising a left hand that might have belonged to the cacodemon save for size, pointed at him. "Why did you call the Demogorgon?"

Tahrynyar, fighting a dizzying wave of nausea, saw the ring of rank on her claw. The woman was an enchantress, with nearly as much power as Pandrogas—far more than was necessary to destroy him. And she obviously had no compunctions about doing so. Kabyn had grown still on the bed beside him. Too still. Tahrynyar knew that how he spoke would determine if he lived or died. He thought quickly; Kabyn had tried to stop her, and anyone who used such methods could be no friend of the sorcerer's. "For revenge," he said, and the voice that spoke seemed hardly his own—it was strong and sure. "I used the sorcerer's books to strike against the sorcerer. Unfortunately, my ambition outweighed my knowledge." He stared levelly into the enchantress's green eyes, and waited. He was afraid, he was very much afraid; but from somewhere within came the strength to conceal it.

Balandrus growled at the concept of someone summoning his master to perform a menial task. Ardatha said, "Be calm, cacodemon." She was impressed by the thin, pale man's courage—not many would be able to do much other than babble in panic after what they had just seen. Even the thief had shown more fear at first. "I seek a red-headed thief," she said. "Perhaps you have seen him. He is burly to the point of being bearlike."

"To the point and beyond," Tahrynyar replied, and told briefly of his encounter with the thief, his injuries and the attempt by the sorcerer to heal them. "The thief stole the Runestone of Darkhaven and then was blown away by the storm. Pandrogas has gone to seek him in the Abyss."

"Thank you," Ardatha said, with a slight smile. "In return for your help, I will let you live." She gestured to Balandrus and turned to go, but the invalid's next words stopped her.

"Let me live—until Darkhaven collides with Oljaer? Enchantress, grant me more than that. I seek Pandrogas and the woman with him, and where the thief is, there they will come. I am unlearned in magic, but my hatred will be my talisman. I will aid you however I can."

Ardatha hesitated. There was a desperation about the man that she did not like—he seemed too much like one drunk on some new-found religion, only his godhead was revenge. "You cannot walk," she said. "You would delay me."

Tahrynyar flung the bedsheets back. "I can walk," he said, and stood up. Pain struck like crossbow bolts up the length of him from his legs to his brain, but he stayed on his feet, swaying, teeth drawing blood from his lips. The enchantress laughed. "Pandrogas cast his catagmatism well," she said; "still, your legs are not yet wholly mended." She extended her claw to him—Tahrynyar seized it with a drowning man's grip, and felt warm strength flow from it down his arm, steadying his legs. She led him forward, and he walked, each stiff-legged step agony. But her power sustained him, and he made it to the broken door.

"Hold my hand and walk to the dragonship port with me," Ardatha told him. "By that time your legs will have healed, unless the pain overcomes you."

"I will walk the length of Darkhaven if that's what it takes," Tahrynyar said through grated teeth, and, great as his pain was, his astonishment at himself was greater. "I would walk from here to Xoth were I sure I would see them there."

"You may," Ardatha said calmly. "You may indeed. Now come, and quickly, whether you can or not."

The cacodemon followed them as they made their way down the hall.

Beorn had thought at the time that he would never experience anything more horrible than the ferry between Oljaer and Darkhaven. But, though that one had been painful in the extreme, for Balandrus had nearly crushed his ribcage and almost suffocated him with his stench, it was at least over very quickly. The journey with the vampire, however, involved almost as much pain, and it took the better part of a day. After several hours of holding on to the creature's neck, fingers and arms tensed to tighten at the first sign of treachery, the thief's muscles cramped in knots of agony that were only surpassed by his hunger and thirst. The vampire did not speak, and only moved to alter his wing position occasionally to take better advantage of the winds. Were it not for the passage of air about them, Beorn would have no way of knowing whether they were traveling at all. He lapsed into a kind of stupor, the pain in his arms going beyond agony to a serene, disconnected nothingness.

He did not know what alerted him—perhaps a change in their speed, or a subtle shifting of the vampire's position. His eyes opened, and he saw ahead of them perhaps a dozen fragments, some mushroom shaped, with miles-long stems of bedrock and mantle beneath the sections of crust; others mere megaliths of stone or cooled lava. They floated in a cluster, made hazy by distance; other than that, he had no way of knowing how far away they were. For the next few hours they seemed to grow in size no more than the sun would were they to fly toward that. But, too gradually to actually see, they came to fill most of half of the blue vault ahead. Beorn realized that what he thought were unconnected land masses were actually linked by a threadlike mazework of vines, tendrils, and roots of rampant tropical growth. Insubstantial though they appeared, he had some conception of the distance they still must travel, and so marveled at what their actual size must be—any one of those linking branchlike growths would dwarf Darkhaven in width.

They approached with tantalizing, maddening slowness. Beorn noticed a small rain system over one of the more distant fragments. They were coming in at an angle slightly below the ground level of the nearest land mass. Beorn could see trees and forest growth now, and glimpsed the sparkling blue of a lagoon in the interior, smothered in green. The jungle seemed almost of a malignant intensity; it covered all of the land and cascaded down the sides, rooting in patches of soil aggregated in the titanic cliffs, or trailing free in the Abyss. It was toward one of these twisted tendrils, its growth made crazy by the weightless environment beyond the fragment's edge, that the vampire made. The wind was blowing too stiffly near the edge itself for the creature to risk landing—the thousand years the vampire kind had spent living in the Abyss had left them with little taste for the shackles of land. The creature struggled to free itself of Beorn's grip as they approached the root, which at its tip was the size of a city street, but Beorn held on until he was sure that his trajectory would carry him to safety. Then he let go, working his arms and fingers to speed the return of blood to them. The vampire floated along beside him for a moment, then used its wings to maneuver up and away, catching a crosswind. With a hissed curse at the thief, it dwindled into the blue sky. Beorn barely had time to draw himself up into a tight ball before he slammed painfully into a tangle of vines and leaves. He tore through several of them before he managed to seize one that held. Still weightless, floating above the massive root, he breathed deeply, waiting for the pain of reviving circulation to stop. The island-sized land mass filled the sky "below" him, several hundred yards distant. He knew he would not feel safe until he had his own weight pressing his feet against solid ground again, and so he began, slowly and wearily, to pull himself hand-over-hand through the complicated skein of vegetation.

The return of weight took him by surprise; his stomach rebelled, though it had nothing to eject. He was sprawled on an ancillary branch perhaps ten feet across, running parallel to the main one, which was easily fifty times as large. The light of the sun had been reduced to a dim, green haze. It was hot and humid, and the sounds and scents of jungle life were all he could cope with for some time. He flickered in and out of consciousness, at last noticing a tangle of conical purple berries within reach. He pulled one and sniffed it cautiously. Though the scent made him ravenous, he bit off only a small piece and held it inside his mouth while he counted to a hundred. There was no irritation, and it tasted delicious. He ate several, stopping before he was satiated. They were juicy, salving his thirst as well as his hunger, and he soon felt able to crawl to a nearby nook where his branch intertwined with another. He put his back against wood, curled up and was immediately asleep.

Chapter 9

The Cloakfighter

Pandrogas watched Darkhaven fall away from him. He tightened his grip on the dragonship's railing until he felt his knuckles crack painfully. Breathe deeply, he told himself. It did not help; even the air was different, wild and fresh and free, unlike the sleeping atmosphere of Darkhaven. For five years he had buried himself behind those walls, studying, collating, categorizing, attempting to codify over five hundred different systems of magic in his search for an exegesis of the occult. *Metamagic,* he had named it to himself: magic *about* magic, the purified essence. He was convinced that, could he but discover this metaphysical distillate, the underlying principles of the ectenic force common to the different systems, he would have the power to strengthen it, to save the fragments from entropy, without resorting to Necromancy. For no good could come from using the power of the dead to preserve the living.

He forced himself to look into the infinity of the Abyss ahead. If only there were gods on whom I could call, he thought. But he knew better. Oh, there were those of power for whom supplicants built temples and waged *jihads.* Many considered Sestihaculas a deity, or worshiped the shade of the Necromancer. There were even those on Oljaer, he knew, who prayed to him whenever Darkhaven crossed the sky. It was possible to gain fleeting, temporary power by currying the favor of petty darklings and godlings, but the price was always too high. Pandrogas had remained a free agent—his soul was still his own, for what it was worth. He intended it remain so now. He would ask no god's help in finding the Runestone; that was his responsibility.

Those who had left the Cabal to form the Circle believed that there was a One God, omniscient, omnipotent, who had turned away from the world when it shattered, and who waited now for mankind to put things right again. It was hard for the sorcerer to conceive of an immortal god—not even the world was eternal. But there were times when he wished that they were right.

Amber's laughter roused him from his musings with a start. He looked forward and saw her standing in the prow, both hands holding the mast. She was glad to be free of Darkhaven, he knew; those surrounding tons of rock and wood had been as oppressive to her as they were comforting to him. He felt a burst of love for her; though he called himself weak for letting her come and share what danger there would certainly be, still he was grateful for her presence. She turned and made her way back to where he stood by the rudder sail. She pinched playfully at his cheeks with both hands, trying to shape a smile on his face. She succeeded, though only for a moment.

"How can you continue to be gloomy?" she demanded. "We're sailing the seas of heaven! Is it not beautiful?"

He did not reply. The dragonship leaped through a small cloud— an instant of cold grayness wrapped about them, and then they were out of it. Amber watched the cloud flee from them. "No matter what happens," she said, more to herself than to Pandrogas, "I'm glad to be away from there."

Then she looked at him. "Any sign of the bear?"

Pandrogas looked at the ring on his right hand. The resin was dark. "None yet. All we can do is wait."

"For either the Runestone, or any of a thousand various dooms," Amber finished. Then, thoughtfully, "Pandrogas, might not the sphere's prophecies prove false?"

"A rhetorical question, I'm afraid. The oracle does not prophesize;

the meaning lies in one's application of the interpretation to—"

"Yes, I know," Amber interrupted. She was looking down at the sky again, and so did not notice the surprise Pandrogas registered at her impatience. "Still, it all seems so arbitrary, so acausal. And here in the sunshine and air, it's hard to believe that Chthons even exist, let alone fear their attack." She looked at him again. "From whence comes this enmity between you and Sestihaculas?"

Pandrogas sighed. "From a situation years ago, very similar to the one with Tahrynyar. I was teaching Lorian magic at the time in Darkhaven; a young woman named Ardatha, upon gaining the rank of conjuress, was impatient to test her power. She decided to summon a cacodemon. What she got was a Chthon—Endrigoth, Lord of Rats, second only to Sestihaculas. She tried to strike a bargain with him. Endrigoth thought her pluck amusing, and let her think she had some chance of surviving the encounter. By then I arrived from another part of Darkhaven. I sent Endrigoth back to Xoth, though it was not easy. But in his place rose the Demogorgon, and there I fought my hardest battle. Well, I won—more by luck than aught else. But as a parting gesture, Sestihaculas turned to Ardatha and said, 'Such a lust for power deserves its reward!' He seized her left hand in his and put his brand upon her, changing her hand to a demon claw."

He paused; save for the creaking of the stays and the leathern sails, the silence of the Abyss was absolute. "Did Ardatha blame you for what had happened?" Amber asked.

"Oh, yes. She left, swearing revenge. I received a letter from her years later, saying she had reached the rank of enchantress in another system, and that she realized now that I had saved her life. She had thought—as had I—that she had been cursed, you see; that the Demogorgon held her hand, so to speak. She had even considered having it cut off. But she had had no further contact with him." Pandrogas shrugged. "The Chthons have a strange sense of humor."

"Do you think the Serpent Lord will find us?" Amber asked after a moment.

"It is a matter of honor to him. He will keep his word. Unless we find the Runestone quickly—" He glanced down at the ring again, then suddenly threw the rudder sail hard over. The Abyss shifted about them as the dragonship turned. Amber looked at the ring also; it was barely glowing. The glow increased ever so slightly as she watched.

"We may have a chance," Pandrogas said.

Despite his exhaustion, Beorn awoke quickly and totally, his hand going reflexively toward where a weapon would be if he still wore a belt. He looked about. The leaves and flowers were still wet from the storm; save for their dripping, the jungle, which had been filled with the sounds of animal life when he dozed off, was now quiet. He listened for a repetition of whatever had awakened him, and after a moment it came: the harsh shout of someone in battle, followed immediately by the whistle of a blade through air.

The thief stood slowly, aching from his ordeal and from sleeping in a cramped position. He flexed, bent, stretched, twisted, easing some measure of suppleness back into his cold muscles while he tried to pinpoint the location of the fight. Another shout gave him that. He moved cautiously and silently along the huge branch to investigate.

He parted foliage, seizing it by the leaves to prevent it from rustling. Ahead of and below him, in an open area on a lower branch, he saw three aborigines, daubed with woad and wearing leather breechclouts. They circled warily about a black-clad, cloaked man. The aborigines held swords and spears formed of hardened acinaciform leaves. One of them shouted again, gesturing threateningly with his weapon. The cloaked man's face remained expressionless, almost serene. He was unarmed; he stood with knees flexed, hands lightly holding the edges of his cloak, which was weighted and sweeping and arced to form a stiff, protective collar with two points rising like bull's horns over his head. Beorn felt sorry for him; he had no chance. He felt sorry for himself as well. There was danger on this fragment and, save for a useless phylactery about his neck, he was naked and defenseless.

Then the aborigines leaped forward to attack, and Beorn's jaw dropped as he watched the results.

Almost too fast to follow, the cloaked man spun on one foot, twirling the cloak about him in graceful, circular sweeps of darkness. One of the weighted ends of the cloak struck one of the natives on the temple—Beorn winced as he heard the *crack!* of the impact. The hem of the opposite side seemed to lightly caress the second one's neck—he dropped his spear with a howl and gripped his throat, and Beorn saw blood spurting from between his fingers as he fell. The third native got through, bringing his sword down in a killing arc; the man twisted, and the weapon glanced off his cloaked shoulder with no apparent damage. The man spun again, wrapping a length of the cloak about the other's neck. Fingers clawed and tore at the fabric, and the hands holding it tight, to no avail—his struggles grew weaker, spasmodic, and then ceased. The cloaked man let him drop.

The thief realized now who he spied upon. The man was a cloak-fighter; he had heard of them, and seen once a demonstration in Bagerah. He was about to call to him when he heard a crashing in the underbrush directly beneath him. The cloakfighter heard it too, and turned quickly to face it. He backed up slowly. Beorn peered over the branch and saw emerging from the foliage another aborigine, this one wearing a hauberk and casquetel of leather and riding a saddled, chamfroned basilisk. The lizardlike creature arced its neck and hissed a yellow cloud toward the cloakfighter. Beorn, upwind, nevertheless held his breath; the basilisk could slay even its gigantic winged cousin, the dragon, with a single exhalation.

The cloakfighter quickly enveloped himself in the folds of his cloak, crouching into a black ball. The mist covered him, withering the surrounding vegetation. Beorn looked about him; at hand was a dead branch of substantial weight. He broke it free and, sighting carefully, dropped it squarely on the aborigine's head. The leather helmet was no protection against the heavy branch; stunned, the man dropped from his saddle. The basilisk, reins loose, looked about in confusion for a moment. The cloakfighter leaped up from his crouch, seized a trailing vine and pulled himself hand over hand up it, narrowly escaping another burst of poisoned air. He swung over and dropped down beside Beorn.

"This way," he said. He spoke Talic with an accent Beorn could not place. He set off at a run down the branch, and the thief followed. Behind them, the basilisk nuzzled the body of its fallen rider.

They hurried quickly along branches wider than the canals of Denaris, passing rain-fed jhils collected in giant knotholes and dodging webs spun by hand-sized shadow spiders. The cloakfighter moved nimbly through the profuse growth; at no time did Beorn see his cloak snag upon a branch or leaf. Its color was not black, he saw now, but the blue-black of well water at midnight, as were his clothes. At last he stopped, and turned to look at the thief with intense, measuring gray eyes. He showed no surprise or wonder at how a naked man had come to rescue him from certain death, nor did he show any gratitude. "Kan Konar," he said at last.

As this was evidently a name offering, the thief responded in kind, and asked, "Where is this place?"

"No idea," Kan Konar replied briefly. "I took port here as refuge from the storm. You?"

"The storm as well—though I came without a windship." The cloakfighter showed no surprise at this, as though people drifted to land out of the Abyss every commonday. "The storm hit my ship suddenly," Beorn continued, improvising. "I was stepping into a bath; like a fool I rushed above deck to see what was going on, and was blown overboard." The story did not make him look very smart, but that, he had learned over the years, might work to his advantage later.

The cloakfighter nodded. "I went to forage for food and the aborigines caught me. They took me back to their village on the opposite end of the fragment—a hollow stump the size of a volcanic crater. I had to kill a few to convince them to let me go. I suppose you'd like a ride?" Without waiting for an answer, he continued: "Come, then. Be wary of the weight loss. Hurry—there might be more of them about." He continued his route. Beorn hurried to follow, and a moment later felt his stomach tell him that they had passed beyond the fragment's edge. At no time in his short wanderings had he even seen the ground.

They pulled themselves along through the tangled vegetation, floating from one gigantic branch to another, higher one. At last, ahead, Beorn saw blue sky. The sun was in the same position; evidently this fragment had no night. He was wondering if that might account for the runaway growth when he saw, floating in the shelter of a massive gnarled cluster of limbs, a small dragonship, the hide and fur the same hue as Kan Konar's cloak.

They made sail none too soon; while poling free of the leaves several more natives came upon them. One hurled a spear that penetrated the stretched hide of the hull, and then they were out of range. The cries of frustration faded quickly behind them as the winds of the Abyss seized the dragonship and hurled it away from the fragment.

Now that his stomach had settled into its proper niche again, Beorn realized that he was ravenously hungry. As though reading his mind, the cloakfighter said, "There isn't much food, but you're welcome to half." He opened the stores and brought out meager rations of hardbread and dried fruit. As they ate, the thief tried to make conversation; his sojourn in the Abyss had made him desperate for the sound of another human voice. Kan Konar, however, was not much of a talker. "Sellsword," was his curt reply to Beorn's query as to his livelihood. Beorn gleaned that the cloakfighter had come from Typor's Fist, a small fragment near Zarheena, and that he was bound for Dulfar, capital of Sothan on the fragment of Rhynne. Fortunately he was a better host in more material ways. In addition to sharing his food, he gave Beorn a cloak of supple dragon leather in which to wrap himself, and an unguent to soothe the infection and aches of his several wounds. The thief leaned back against the curved wall of the tiny cabin and relaxed. Once again he had cheated death. Against all odds, he had come out on top. He did not have the Crystal Crescent, but he did have the Runestone of Darkhaven, and that, no doubt, would bring considerable coin in a metropolis such as Dulfar. He had heard that certain adepts, members of a group called the Circle, were willing to pay handsomely for Runestones. Perhaps he could even parlay what he had for a cure of the werespell. Beorn listened to the creak of the rigging and grinned. Life was good—precarious at times, true, but good.

He recalled his near capitulation to the sorcerer and his wench with a grimace; a moment of weakness, to be sure. Best to put the whole disastrous series of events behind him now—forget all about Oljaer, and Ardatha, and Darkhaven. It would make a fine tale to tell some night, interspersed with long draughts of mulled wine, but for now, he would sooner not think about it.

But he could not stop thinking about it—particularly about the inevitable fall of Darkhaven. It would mean the lives of thousands of innocent people. Still, what could he do? To attempt to return to either Darkhaven or Oljaer now was impossible—at the very least, he would have to wait until he had reached Dulfar and had a course charted for him. How would he pay for such a service? And why should he, when going back to either location most likely meant torture and death?

It was not something to worry over now. For now, he was content to be alive and forward-looking, to have come relatively unscathed from an adventure few would believe. There should be no regrets. He looked at the cloakfighter, sitting crosslegged in the stern, staring into the Abyss, one lean-muscled arm on the rudder sail. He looked to be a man at peace, Beorn thought admiringly. No self-doubts, no worries. Whatever the cloakfighter had left at Typor's Fist, or at the nameless fragment they had just quit, was no longer a part of him. So shall it be for me, the thief told himself. So shall it be for me.

But he could hear the sound of a flute faintly in his mind, and the pouch about his neck felt unusually heavy—as though it carried the weight of an entire fragment.

Rhynne was the largest of the seven major fragments, larger by far than Toul, Calamchor, and Salakh. It carried on its three continents over a hundred empires, realms, nations, toparches, and thalassocracies. Here as well were such natural superlatives as Mount Ghandor, the highest peak on any fragment; Raadan Wood, which covered half the land mass of Uland; the sparkling badlands of the Crystal Desert; and Kormalis Glacier. On Rhynne also was the last ocean: the Ythan, a storm-wracked sea more than three hundred leagues across. It was bounded by the continents of Uland, Althizar, and Quy, and at its farthest extent, beyond the sheer cliffs which once marked a strait, the waters poured over the edge in a foaming cataract wider than a hundred rivers.

The largest of the three continents was Althizar, and of the many boundaries scrawled across its map, the longest and widest belonged to the Republic of Sothan. Its capital was Dulfar, also named City of Light, for here was the greatest concentration of starcrystal deposits, mines, and quarries on any fragment. Entire buildings had been covered with the substance, their placement and architecture carefully designed to distribute the light in orchestrated *chiaroscuro*. During the long Rhynnad night the sapphire luminescence bathed the city, which straddled a thin isthmus between ocean and Abyss. By day the skyline gleamed in the sunlight. Spires of hammered bronze and windows of stained glass gave color to the air. It was a city that had been made proud by its artisans; everywhere was the work of enamelers, ivory carvers, woodwrights; from windows came golden glimpses of tapestries, frescoes, and mezzotint, and the varying roofs of marble, shell, and burnished metal made a dazzling mosaic when viewed from an approaching dragonship. The Consistory, where met the Syndic and his Council of Factors, led the rest in grandeur. Beyond a dense topiary of a crouching dragon, whose length barricaded the grounds, it stood. Built entirely of starcrystal and various quartzes that shone silver, jade, ruby, and other shades, it resembled a giant jewel sculpted with parapets, balconies, and fluted columns.

The inner city, constructed after the discovery of the mines several centuries after the Shattering, was laid out in symmetrical perfection, in contrast to the haphazardness of the poorer outlying sections. These areas, with their houses constructed mainly of rough rock and wood, were hidden from aerial view by strategic stands of trees and vast trellises of vines, so that the many dragonships that came and went would sail over a view of unbroken prosperity. Few visitors passed over the slums of the waterfront either, where merchant ships ferried cargo too bulky for transportation by air on trade routes across the Ythan. Fewer still visited the area, where night was more often lit by sputtering torches than by cool clear starcrystal, where refuse and sewage flowed in the open gutters in contrast to the scented sewers of the inner city, and lives were far cheaper than merchandise.

Near a section of rat-ridden warehouses, in a tavern called Dark Skelos', Kustin the Deft sat shivering in a corner away from the heat of the fireplace and the conversation of the other patrons. He was a thin man, with long spatulate fingers that caressed a small goblet of wine. It was all he had had in the way of sustenance for more than a commonday. He was ravenously hungry, but he had noticed a fold of fat the thickness of his little finger on his waist recently, and he would not eat again until he could find no flesh there to pinch. A fat thief was a slow thief—none were quicker, or thinner, than Kustin the Deft.

He watched the others in the tavern from beneath a lowered hat. A longshoreman glanced curiously at him, and Kustin looked away quickly. He silently cursed his nervousness. It was not the thieving, or the selling of stolen goods, or even hunger, that knotted his lean stomach. No, it was waiting that tortured him—waiting for the sorcerer.

The taproom was small, with only a few tables and booths, of which Kustin had chosen the darkest. The rest of the customers clustered about the bar, where firelight glinted from mugs and bottles, and the friendly smell of drink aging in tuns made the long night outside not quite so dark. The light and dark cycles of Althizar were each eight commondays long, though the darkness was relieved halfway through by "Paran's day"; less than an hour of grace granted by sunlight reflecting from Lake Paran on the nearby fragment of Handula. That respite was almost due; the thin thief yearned for it. Though the night was not as dark as legends once told of, it was dark enough and long enough for thieves to ply their trade well, even in a city filled with starcrystal. Usually Kustin was sorry to see the long night end, but now he longed for sunlight. The thought of meeting a sorcerer in the dark was terrifying, particularly one with a name as ominous as this one's. Kustin glanced at a window in the far wall; the firelight made the night pitch black. Please,

Kustin prayed to any deity who might be listening, Let the light come before he does...

No such luck. The tavern door opened; a gust of sea wind rippled the gray armilausa about the shoulders of a short, thin man who entered. The hood concealed his face. Though Kustin had never seen him before, the sorcerer had been described well to him, as the thief evidently had been to the sorcerer, for the hooded man made his way immediately to the booth, leaving a wake of silence as he passed the tavern's other customers, and sat down. Kustin gulped some wine, sending part of it to his lungs instead of his gut and very nearly spraying the sorcerer with it. He choked, wheezed, turned blue and then red, then managed to recover. The sorcerer waited patiently. Kustin still could not see his face; all he could see was the crystal ring on the tenth finger of his hand, an aged hand, with brown spots and ridged veins. When the thief was through coughing, the sorcerer said quietly, "You wish to sell something?"

Kustin nodded. "A treasure no lesser thief could hope to steal. It was concealed in the deepest vaults beneath the Temple of the Crawling God, guarded by his Mystes, serpent women whose kiss can kill a man in the time it takes him to fall, and a snake the size of—"

"I am aware of the difficulties involved," the sorcerer said. He turned the ringed hand over, palm up, in a quiet demand.

"Of course," Kustin stammered. He fumbled in his belt pouch and at length brought out a small object wrapped in cloth. "The Runestone of Sagar. I think five thousand crystals is not too great a price to ask."

"Ask no price until I verify its authenticity," and, with a quickness that left Kustin the Deft gaping, the sorcerer plucked the Runestone from the thief's grasp. He unwrapped it quickly, while Kustin gripped the table's edge and subtly shifted his body to bolt if necessary. He never got the chance. The sorcerer's other hand struck, seizing Kustin's wrist like a mongoose seizes a snake, in a bone-cracking grasp that belied his age. Kustin turned pale with pain and fright. "This is not the Runestone of Sagar," the sorcerer said, his voice quieter, and somehow more frightening. He spun the small, roughly carved stone about on the table; Kustin watched it in hypnotic fascination. "This is the Runestone of some small, out-of-the-way fragment, which you no doubt unearthed without contest from its cavern, or at most filched from a stone idol's grasp. You tried to cheat me, thief." The grip tightened on Kustin's wrist, bringing the sweat of pain to his forehead. "Shall I tell you why it is unwise to do that? Shall I show you?"

It was at this point that the sunlight reflected from Lake Paran rolled across Dulfar. The windows filled with sudden day, to the cheers and toasts of those at the bar. The noon brightness illuminated for Kustin the face within the cowl—he stared, dry-mouthed with horror. He understood now the reason for the sorcerer's name: his face was a mask of gray stone!

"No, Stonebrow," the thief gasped. "There has been a mistake... the wrong Runestone..."

"A mistake, to be sure," Stonebrow said, "and you have made it. I came all the way from Graystar Isle for what is very nearly a piece of rock. Oh, never fear; I shall pay you what it is worth," and he dropped ten faceted pieces of the crystalline currency used in Sothan on the table. "And I will generously add, since you are obviously undernourished, Duand's Incantation of Abundancy. *Alxacan ul maen, pactaeon nasius!*" He released Kustin's hand and sealed the spell with several precisely executed gestures. The thief slumped dizzily back against the wall of the booth. "A simple cantrip that makes certain changes in metabolism," Stonebrow said. "You will have to work harder, in coming years, to stay nimble and quick. Perhaps that will make you less likely to cheat prospective customers." Stonebrow stood, drawing his cowl close about him, and left: none barred his way.

Kustin grabbed his goblet and tossed off what was left. The entire horrendous affair had left him too weak to even stand. He knew what he needed. "Ale—the biggest flagon you've got!" he shouted hoarsely to the taverner. "And food!" A huge cantharus was set before him, filled to the brim; he grabbed it by both handles and drained it in one long swallow. He still felt hollow as a ghost. A plate of mutton was next, and he attacked it ravenously, though his stomach, shrunken and unused to heavy food, was already beginning to protest.

As the long night began again, Kustin was thrown from Dark

Skelos'. He lay on the cold wet street, vomit-stained, already feeling the hunger beginning again.

The thief and the cloakfighter arrived at the dragonship docks on Rhynne's edge during the latter half of the long night. Beorn was glad to see the voyage end; he had been considerably airsick toward the end of it, perhaps due to the privations he had been through. He had had more than enough of the Abyss. Fortunately there was room and opportunity on Rhynne for a master of direption to make a new life.

They were ferried by wain down the winding road from the hills at the edge, and Beorn could see the glowing, decadent beauty of Dulfar spread out before him. Surely here, with nights so long and riches so abundant, there was good thieving to be had. He could see his breath as he rode; it grew cold in Sothan toward the end of the long night. He hugged the cloak tightly about him. The bear within him did not like cold weather; it made him feel sluggish and sleepy. But he always felt more alive at night, and for this he could endure the cold.

They both took rooms at a caravansary near the gates, and Beorn set about his priorities. A moment's brushing against a fat chandler in the inn's court provided him with a purseful of crystal. He took himself to a local pantechnicon where, after some difficulty, he found clothing to fit his frame. Then he entered a nearby alehouse and, over a wedge of gryphon's milk cheese and a goblet of wine, tried to decide his future.

A few days, or even hours, of judicious listening and questioning—the majority of the populace spoke Talic, so there would be no language difficulties—would provide him with a ready market for the contents of the pouch now hanging from his belt. He would be considerably richer, and perhaps some time in the future he might learn of the cataclysmic result of his sale. Beorn tried to project how he would feel then, to know that he, with whom it was a point of pride never to have killed, was responsible for the deaths of thousands.

His alternative was to attempt to return to Darkhaven—an expensive proposition, requiring a chartmaster's aid in preparing a course through the complicated choreography of the fragments, and the purchase of a dragonship. The only way he could amass the money for such a journey quickly, he realized with an ironic grimace, would be to sell the Runestone.

Such indecision was new to him, and he did not like it. He found himself staring moodily at the hearth, where a bearskin rug was spread before the fire. As usual, he felt he had escaped being totally possessed by the bear only by the narrowest of margins. He had changed back just in time. The chances were good that he could buy himself a cure for his curse, if one existed. Why throw such an opportunity away?

It was then that he overheard part of a woman's conversation from a nearby table. "... ever since he met with that sorcerer two commondays ago, all he's done is eat! Already he's put on five pounds and made himself sick a dozen times. I think it's a curse, levied by Stonebrow for trying to foist that Runestone off as Sagar's ..."

Beorn listened carefully. Another thief's misfortune, it seemed, might prove his fortune. The sorcerer Stonebrow, of Graystar Isle, was in the market for Runestones. Another puzzle piece, to make the solution still more difficult. The thief paid his bill and left.

He was no closer to a decision in his room. He paced restlessly about its confines and brooded over the view of the glowing city from the one window. He thought dawn was finally approaching, though the cold blue radiation of the skyline made it difficult to tell. He removed the Runestone from the pouch and looked at it, traced with one fingernail the runes on it, feeling the barely perceptible tingling of power locked within them. Suchana, he thought; what would you do? Throw away a chance at Tamboriyon to save unknown, faceless people, none of whom were likely to do the same for you? He looked in the tiny glass over the basin and pitcher; in the warped reflection and the blue light it seemed he could see the bear's face, superimposed over his own. With a snarl he struck the mirror a backhanded blow; it shattered, cutting him. He stared at the blood in surprise, then licked the minor wound until it stopped bleeding. No one had ever offered *him* altruism, after all. Society lauded as heroes those who committed spoliation in times of war, or rewarded with power and public esteem those who robbed under the guise of politics or mercantilism, while condemning his relatively minor infractions. He had never done anything before this that had drastically affected the lives of more than a few people...

Beorn sat down on the bed, pressing the heels of his hands against his temples to stop the chaotic thoughts. There was always a way out; Suchana had taught him that, if nothing else. This was no more complicated a problem than deciding which of two vaults to plunder. Faced with that choice, his answer was usually to rob both. He caught his breath then. This Stonebrow was a sorcerer, but he was still human—and so could be tricked. The fate of the other thief did not worry him; obviously the man was a dolt, to try such a thin deception. But, Beorn thought, a master thief like himself could surely find a way to visit Graystar Isle and leave the bear there, escaping with wealth *and* the Runestone! After which he could see it returned to Pandrogas if he still felt squeamish about it. He slammed a fist into a palm in satisfaction and relief. It was at least worth investigating. He had never asked for more than a chance—given enough preparation he was sure that he could rob and cheat even the Demogorgon.

He did not have to make a plan now. He could go out and sample the varied delights of Dulfar, partake of the impromptu celebration he could faintly hear beginning in the streets below to welcome the long day. Soon, perhaps, he would have all he wanted, and a clear conscience to boot. He opened the door—

And stepped back in surprise. Kan Konar stood in the narrow hallway, his cloak highlighted by the starcrystal that also gave a surprising pallor to his face and hands.

"What is it?" Beorn asked warily; his brooding had intensified his normal suspicion of humanity. He realized he was standing in a protective stance. Kan Konar raised one eyebrow slightly at the thief's attitude; his only other gesture was an almost imperceptible tilt of his head that beckoned Beorn out into the hallway. Beorn hesitated, recalling the ease, both physical and mental, with which the cloakfighter had killed the aborigines on the jungle fragment. Then he shrugged and stepped forward, closing the door behind him.

"Trouble," Kan Konar said in a low tone, evidently in answer to Beorn's question. "Come on." He turned and moved silently toward the stairs. The thief followed.

The cloakfighter led him down a narrow flight of stairs and stopped before the door of his room, which was directly below the thief's. "I heard something above my window," he told Beorn, "on the ledge below yours. Thought you might like to know," and with that, he led the thief into the small room. Moving as noiselessly as ghosts, the two of them approached the open window. Beorn leaned cautiously out and looked up. Only his training prevented him from voicing his astonishment. Above him, crouched on a narrow strip of starmolded masonry, was a creature seemingly rough-hewn from a stick or root, with twisted limbs and wings the size of Beorn's hands. Though the thief made no noise, it evidently sensed his presence; it glared at him and emitted a sound halfway between a croak and a hiss. Then it hurled itself from the ledge and was gone into the light of the newly risen sun.

Chapter 10

Neccopolis

Tahrynyar held on to the taffrail, a length of line made of dragon's sinew, to keep his balance. The deck did not yaw or pitch, as the ship's Runestone kept it as stable as the largest fragment. His occasional dizziness came from seeing the clouds and the sun turn about him. He shifted his weight, and pain stabbed deep within his right knee, making him wince. The walk from his bed to the dragonship port had been a march of agony—he had bitten his lips until they bled, and the walls and columns of Darkhaven had wavered in his vision like the rippling sail of the ship. But he had walked, holding Ardatha's claw as he had once held Pandrogas's hand, anchoring himself to his grim reality. And, after a very long time, the pain had begun to subside. The memory of it made him feel ill; but he had made the walk. His legs were not completely healed; he limped badly, favoring his right side. But he could move now without aid. The sorcerer's spell had done that much good, at least.

But more amazing to him than the results of the spell was his new found confidence in himself. It was as though the pain had forged armor for his soul. Even when they had been attacked that night at the tower port by Undya he had not panicked, but had done what he could to aid Ardatha by casting off and raising sail on the only remaining dragonship while she and Balandrus held off the servant woman. He had only a dim memory of their magical battle, mazed as he had been with pain and confusion. He had heard them shouting spells and phrases at each other, had caught glimpses of complicated forms and gestures, and had sensed the tension of power in the air. He had seen, or imagined he had seen, a series of glowing rings, their color a violet that hurt his eyes, surrounding Ardatha at one point—a niveous flash from her claw had evaporated them. Balandrus had torn a barrel-sized stone from a nearby casement and hurled it at the tower entrance where Undya had stood, causing it to collapse. He did not know if she had been injured or not; they had launched the dragonship immediately.

It was only now, thinking about it, that he felt surprise at Undya's magical prowess. He had not known any of the servants to be adepts; yet Kabyn had attempted to say a spell, and Undya had shown sufficient ability to momentarily stand off an enchantress and a cacodemon. He thought of the times he had brusquely ordered them about, and grimaced wryly. He would have been more circumspect had he known he was dealing with such power.

The marquis's nostrils wrinkled as a breeze brought him the sulfurish stench of the cacodemon. Balandrus was crouched within the tiny cabin; Tahrynyar could see his eyes glowing in the dim interior. Tahrynyar avoided the cabin. It was no hardship—the sun felt good after months of living in Darkhaven.

He looked at Ardatha, who stood with her demon hand resting on the carved skull prow. They had been floating aimlessly for the better part of a commonday—waiting for a mandragoras, Ardatha had said. Tahrynyar had no idea what a mandragoras was, and the enchantress had not enlightened him; she had only said that it would lead them to the thief. That was enough for Tahrynyar; where the thief was, the sorcerer and Amber would also be.

They had spoken little, the enchantress and he. He watched her now, admiring the body that the wind outlined in her green robe. There was little privacy aboard a dragonship, but even so, she had remained distant. Not that he particularly desired intimacy with her— he admired her only in the abstract, he told himself. Still, she was so calm and self-assured; so much unlike Amber. Though Amber had also been remote over the last few weeks, before he had learned the truth.

He had no trouble visualizing his revenge on her. He would find a way to see her lover destroyed, and make sure she knew who was responsible. Then he would simply walk away. The thought of it at times gave him great pleasure, and at other times great pain. But he was firm in his resolve. He had always wavered before on decisions, but he would not turn from this one, no matter what the cost. It was the one certainty now in his world.

He made his way forward and stood beside Ardatha. She did not acknowledge his presence—her gaze remained fixed on blue infinity. "How long must we wait?" he asked. "If this is a chase, should we not play our part and pursue?"

"Patience, marquis." He had told her his name and erstwhile title, and it seemed to please her now to use it. Her faintly ironic tone irritated him, but he saw no reason to antagonize her. "The more I know, the more I can help," he said.

"I am not convinced you can help me at all. Perhaps I should have Balandrus pitch you into the Abyss."

"That would be foolish. I am your link to Amber and Pandrogas—and where they are, the thief will be."

She turned to look at him with cool green eyes. "Tenuous. I do not wish to find Pandrogas; rather, I wish to avoid him. But you have showed courage and resourcefulness so far. I will soon have to give up Balandrus's service—he is beholden to me for only one more task. Let us see how well you can replace the cacodemon."

"I smell better, at least." He saw her smile slightly at that.

"We share a common experience," she said; "perhaps that is why I brought you along. We have both made the acquaintance of the Demogorgon. He left me with this," and she held up her claw. "It can give strength, as you well know. Mark what else it can do," and she seized the bronze finial of a nearby stanchion. Tahrynyar saw a silver glow flash for a moment about the scaled fingers, and heard a hiss. Ardatha released a lump of melted slag.

"Impressive," Tahrynyar said. He tried not to think about that claw pressed against his face, about what the cacodemon's lips had done to Kabyn's. He thought instead of the talons locked about Pandrogas's throat.

"It is nothing compared to Sestihaculas's full power," Ardatha told him. "Only one ever dwarfed the Chthon's strength—the Necromancer. For he could call upon the combined power and knowledge of all the dead that ever were. Not all the magic of all the adepts alive could reverse his power and restore the world. The Necromancer shattered it, and only the Necromancer can restore it."

She seemed to be speaking more to herself now than to him. Tahrynyar suspected suddenly that this woman, this enchantress, was a member of the Circle, the sect whose avowed goal was to reassemble the world. In a flash of insight he realized the reason she sought Darkhaven's Runestone. Before he could consider the advisability of the question he asked, "But would not restoring the world to a sphere cause catastrophes as bad as the Shattering?"

Ardatha looked at him; he noticed that her eyes seemed to glitter like the black scales of her demon hand. "It would be worth it," she said softly, "to have the One God smile on us again." She traced a circle in the air before her with her right hand.

Tahrynyar decided it would be wise to change the subject. "Tell me more about this shapechanging thief. Why did he steal the Runestone?"

To his surprise, he thought he saw a slightly discomfited look in her eyes. "I hired him to do so. I promised to rid him of his beast-brother. But there is no cure for a werespell. It is a relatively simple casting—a conjurer could do it—but with time it seeps into the soul. Spells dealing with the mind or the body are often thus. They are unpredictable."

The marquis remembered Pandrogas's warning him of this before casting the healing spell. He felt a fleeting, surprising kinship with the shapechanger. Oddly enough, he bore him no ill will for breaking his legs, though in his previous life he had feared and hated thieves with a passion common to the wealthy.

"It was the only way," Ardatha said softly. She was gazing into the Abyss again. He wondered why she had felt it necessary to make this confession.

Before either could say anything further, Tahrynyar heard the sudden flutter of bat wings over his head. The sound was so out of place in the clear bright Abyss that he did not even duck as a dark, misshapen creature, winged like Balandrus but scarcely the length of one of the cacodemon's horns, dropped down and landed on Ardatha's upraised claw. The enchantress lifted it to her ear, and the marquis could see it clearly against her white hair. It was dull black in color, and despite its form and movement seemed to be made of wood or root rather than flesh. It whispered to Ardatha in a hissing tone. The enchantress nodded, then spoke three words in a language Tahrynyar had never heard, and whose pronunciation he would not even attempt. The creature wavered like oily smoke, and then Ardatha held in her claw a black root, anthropomorphic in shape. She looked at Tahrynyar. "The waiting is over," she said. She dropped the root to the deck. "Come."

They entered the cramped cabin, Tahrynyar holding his breath. "Balandrus!" Ardatha said. "We go now to Dulfar, City of Light!" Before Tahrynyar could turn about, he was seized about the waist in a burning, tight grasp. He heard the cacodemon's guttural voice say, "This is the last journey." Then a whirlwind of sulfur and darkness enveloped him.

"This is beautiful," Amber said. They walked on an esplanade by the Ythan Sea. To one side was a carefully cultivated grove of trees and topiary, and on the other the shining towers and minarets of Dulfar rose in the distance. Further south could be seen the shabbier buildings of the wharf, the warehouses and dockyards. The sun of Rhynne's long morning hung just above the water, slowly dispersing the wisps of night fog that still clung to the ground. Above them, filling more than half the sky, hung the emerald and sapphire fragment of Handula. Amber looked at Pandrogas, squeezed his hand reassuringly. The sorcerer was quiet, and kept his eyes fixed upon the grass, looking at none of the majestic vistas above or to either side. He pointed to a tavern in the distance. "We'll take our dinner there."

The building was a ramshackle graywood affair decorated with sharks' jawbones, ichthyocentaurs' skulls, and gulls' mottled droppings. Amber suppressed a shudder as they drew near it. Months ago, in the height of her glory as Marquise of Chuntai, she would not even have suspected the existence of such an eatery, let alone consider dining there. But now she was very hungry, and the scent of chowder that wafted from Dark Skelos' smelled better than the finest honeyed breast of nightingale.

They took a seat in a secluded booth, away from the laughter and oaths of the sailors and longshoremen at the bar who eyed them curiously. Pandrogas had changed his robes in favor of a simple cross-belted tunic, leggings, and capelet, but his height and appearance were still conspicuous. He relaxed visibly, Amber noted, once he was surrounded by the reassuring high walls of the booth. He said apologetically to her, "The food will be simple but filling. It is all we can currently afford."

She knew he had taken a fair amount of gold and silver with him from the vast coffers of Darkhaven, but she also knew there was no telling how long it would have to last them. "Why do you not fill your purse with magic?"

"It would be only an illusion," Pandrogas said. "To create something lasting out of nothing is impossible, even for a sorcerer. I would sooner not pay for food and fare with coins that fade—such things have a way of coming back to one."

The tavern owner put two bowls of steaming chowder before them, and Amber began to spoon hers up. Between mouthfuls she said, "It was said that the Necromancer was richer than all emperors of all time."

"True. With his magic he could create—and destroy. But no good can come of using the power of the dead."

To her surprise the certainty of his tone bothered her slightly— only a commonweek ago she had considered his apothegms the final authority on any matter. "You are so open-minded on all subjects— you even once defended Sestihaculas himself against me. You have taught me that magic is not good or evil, but only a tool to be used. Why then are you so adamantly against Necromancy?"

Pandrogas indicated with a slight nod of his head a tall, sun-bronzed man at a corner table. The man was dressed entirely in supple leather of a rich brown, from boots to the patch over his right eye—dragon leather, Amber realized.

"Dragoneers hunt dragons," Pandrogas said. "From the bones and skin of the beasts they construct dragonships, and the magic of adepts creates Runestones that enable them to sail the Abyss. Dragonships are necessary to commerce, communication, the civilization of this fragmented world. Yet dragons are now in danger of extinction. Should we cease hunting dragons, cease building dragonships, let our fragile system of trade and travel collapse? Should we cease practicing magic because it is used, at times, for an end some see as evil? There are no easy answers, for much good comes of magic as well. I have taught you to beware absolutes, and so you should. But all rules have their exceptions. I tell you now that no good ever came from Necromancy. To make the dead live is far worse than making the living dead."

Amber looked silently at her mentor and lover. His attitude, which in Darkhaven had seemed at worst avuncular, now struck her as condescending. She was faintly shocked at herself for feeling this way. This is the man you love, she reminded herself; this is a sorcerer who has forgotten more than you will ever know.

Pandrogas continued: "His knowledge and power, stolen from the world's dead, warped him, drove him to destroy the world when it would not acknowledge him as its ruler. And now Thasos and the others of the Cabal wish to use that corrupting power to save us." He shook his head. "It can't be done." He knitted his fingers together nervously, an action very unlike the calming hand forms Amber had seen him use so many times. He pushed the bowl of chowder aside, half-finished. "We must find the Runestone and return to Darkhaven. I must continue my studies, before it is too late!"

"Calm yourself," Amber said, aware as she spoke that these were words she thought she would never have to say to him—words she had spoken far too often to her husband. "We will find the thief." She finished her chowder, hesitated, then took his bowl. She was ravenous; she felt as if she would never be full.

"Easier said than done," Pandrogas said darkly. "He is a cunning one, and he holds a large portion of my power." He spread his hands and looked at them.

"Why do you think he has stolen the Stone?"

"There are ways to tap and drain the ectenic force within it."

Amber nodded. "And he is an adept, as witnessed by his shape-changing."

"Not necessarily. Metamorphosistry is more often a curse than a gift; those who know magic do not seek it. Two beings cannot comfortably inhabit the same hide. The physical stress of the change is very hard on the body, and there is a constant war of identities as well. If our friend stays a bear too long, its bestial nature will subsume his own and he will become a bear in mind as well as in body."

"Then perhaps that is why he has stolen the Runestone—he hopes to use its power to somehow cure himself."

The sorcerer raised an eyebrow. "Astute deduction! Of course, such a cure is impossible if he has worn the bearskin for any length of time. The bear would be too much a part of him to be exorcised. But I'll wager he does not know that. He would seek a sorcerer or enchanter who would be interested in having the Runestone, and that means a member of the Circle." Pandrogas thumped the table lightly in satisfaction. "It is worth trying." He looked at Amber, who was scraping the bottom of the second bowl with her wooden spoon. "Are you through?"

Oddly enough, Amber realized, though the chowder was a tor-minous pain within her, she was still hungry. "The sea air has done wonders for my appetite," she said with a slightly embarrassed laugh. "Either that, or I'm cursed to be forever hungry."

Pandrogas looked slightly startled at her words. He closed his eyes and put out a hand toward her, fingers spread wide, feeling the air. Then he signaled the tavern owner. Skelos, a tall man, approached, wiping his hands on a towel. "Has anything odd or un-toward happened at this table recently?" Pandrogas asked him.

"There has, and not long ago. A thief near ate himself to death after speaking with Stonebrow of Graystar Isle. I've never seen a crueller curse given a man. You're the first customers brave enough to sit here since then."

Pandrogas pressed a coin into the man's hand. "Come, Amber!" They were gone from the tavern by the time Skelos realized that he had been paid enough for a commonmonth's worth of dinners.

* * *

Tahrynyar could not have guessed how long he was in the cacodemon's grasp—the shrieking, wrenching passage seemed endless
while he endured it, yet after it was over he realized that they had
crossed the great gulf in a remarkably short time. The burning talons
released him, and he staggered and fell to the slimy cobblestones
of an alley. As he tried to get his breath he heard the rumble of the
cacodemon's voice.

"Three journeys you have had from me, Ardatha. Release me
now to Xoth."

"Only if you swear by the name of the Demogorgon to take no
revenge against me or my plans."

"I swear. More, I offer you a sooth: that before your quest is
done, you will seek aid from he who gave you your hand."

"You overstep yourself, Balandrus!" Ardatha said angrily. "Are
you a Chthon, to vaticinate thus? Would you like this hand raised
against you?"

"You call me into the light and make me a burden beast, then
threaten me for resenting it? It does not take the knowledge of my
masters or the casting of the sphere to see where your quest is taking
you, Ardatha. To Xoth!"

A burst of stinking wind from the cacodemon's wings washed
over Tahrynyar, causing him to choke. Then the air cleared. He
looked about—there was no sign of Balandrus. He and Ardatha
stood in a winding cloistral passageway, overhung by tall, dilapi-
dated buildings. Tahrynyar wrinkled his nose as the scents of gar-
bage, till now masked by the cacodemon's smell, reached him. He
had heard stories of the beauty of Dulfar, but all cities have their
slums, and they were evidently in the middle of one. The long night's
fog still coiled and eddied in the dampness. Rats skittered in fright
about the refuse that lined the walls. A lump of shapeless rags in
the shadows nearby stirred and coughed; the moist racking sound
made the marquis's gorge rise. No starcrystal helped alleviate the
darkness, but a hint of gray light told them that it was early morning.
"Come," Ardatha said.

"Gladly." They hurried down the alley. They had only taken a
few steps, however, when the slippery paving suddenly shifted be-

neath Tahrynyar's feet. A deep rumbling seemed to vibrate in his bones, and he felt dizzy. Then he fell, landing full length and cutting his cheek on a shard of crockery. One hand, groping for balance, sank into the soft remnants of a long-dead cat. He cried out in disgust, rolled over, and staggered to his feet.

The temblor had subsided, but now it began again; he saw Ardatha, who had managed to retain her footing, taken by surprise and fall to her knees in a puddle of sewage before a gate. A vase atop the gate pier toppled forward.

"Look out!" Tahrynyar cried. He leaped across the alley, his knees cracking painfully in response to the sudden movement. He slammed into the enchantress, pushing her back against the gate's rusting bars. The vase shattered on the cobblestones at their feet.

They held on to each other as the fragment of Rhynne rocked about them. The second temblor was stronger than the first; a window shattered in the building across from them, and they heard distant screams and a crash. Then the ground steadied again. From the alley's exit, around the corner, came confused shouts and cries for help. Tahrynyar realized he was holding Ardatha in a protective hug; the enchantress's silver mane was next to his bleeding cheek, and the skin between his shoulder blades tightened as he felt the pressure of her claw on his feathered cloak. He could also feel her breasts against his chest—the layers of fabric between them did nothing to lessen the sensation. At the same time, apparently, she also became aware of the intimacy, because she stiffened and drew away from him.

"Are you all right?" she asked him, and he realized he had been holding her out of fear as much as out of protection. He nodded, noticing a spot of red blood from his cut standing out on her white locks. She sniffed the air, full of noxious scents stirred by the quake, and grimaced at the same time he did. They both smiled at the simultaneity of the action; later, Tahrynyar would reflect that it was the first time he had seen her smile without a hint of cruelty in her eyes.

"You acted wisely," she told him. He nodded; he had experienced temblors before. There was no fragment of the world's debris that did not still occasionally echo the Shattering. "There will be more quakes," Ardatha continued quietly, "as the ectenic force weakens, as the paths of the fragments decay. We must find Darkhaven's Runestone and bring it to Stonebrow."

"How will that help?"

"It is one of many; if all in the Circle find and bring the Runestones they have been assigned, we will have the power to restore the world before its destruction, begun so long ago, is finally completed." She straightened her green robes, brushing as much of the filth from her as possible. "Your revenge may be nigh, marquis," she said. And, without looking back at Tahrynyar, she started toward the alley's exit. Tahrynyar watched her walk for a moment, tall and proud, her demon hand hidden in a fold of her dress. You have allied yourself with a maenad, he told himself. But that did not matter; he would have signed a pact with Sestihaculas himself to have his revenge. And, fanatic or no, she was beautiful. This he had known abstractly, intellectually; but holding her had made it real. He wanted to hold her again, this time with nothing between his flesh and hers. He wanted to seize fistfuls of that white hair, to learn if it matched in color the curls between her thighs. At this moment, he felt he would willingly help her any way he could in her quest to save the world by destroying it, if only he could have her while fragments collided and cities were ground to dust.

He sighed and limped after her, dabbing at his cut cheek, bemused by this latest of a series of passions. There had been a few advantages to being a pampered milquetoast, he thought wryly. Surely one of them had been a calm, quiet life.

Beorn hurried through the twisting avenues of Dulfar. He had abandoned after a short time the cariole he had hired, realizing he could make better time on foot; the streets were narrow and occasionally blocked by celebrants still welcoming the long-awaited dawn. Beorn seemed to be unique in having a destination; he moved swiftly past buildings of rich and varied purpose: merchant- and craft-halls, ordinaries, theatres, manufactories, a university. He shoved his way roughly through knots of protesting citizenry, venting some of his

anger and fear in this way. He had thought himself safe from retribution; surely not an outrageous assumption, given his precipitate
exit from Darkhaven and his meandering and unorthodox journey
across the Abyss. And yet, somehow, someway, he had been traced
by either the sorcerer or the enchantress, or possibly even both. This
implacable pursuit unnerved him. He was an old hand at dodging
the chase; he had once hidden in an unused hypocaust beneath a
rectory, lying full-length in the ashes of the crawlspace and stifling
sneezes while the margrave's men turned the place upside down in
vain for him. "Give me the grace of a gopher's hole in an open plain
and I can escape an army," he had once boasted. And now, though
provided by pure chance with the most foolproof escape route he
had ever followed, he found himself still on the run.

Beorn slowed his pace until his breath no longer came in gasps.
There was no sense in wearing himself out. He had been through
considerable hardship and injury in the past several commondays,
and they had taken their toll. Despite a good meal and sleep he was
still tired, and the ministrations of the cloakfighter had done only
so much to alleviate the pain of his wounds and speed their healing.
But there was no time to rest; his enemies persecuted him, dogged
him relentlessly, would not grant him the time he so badly needed
to make decisions about his future.

He had passed several street musicians, playing either for money
or for the joy of greeting the new day; the harmonies of ocarinas,
psalteries, flageolets and the like followed him, one blending into
another. Now from a window above him, he heard a melancholy
flute. He listened; the slow, wistful notes seemed to slow his progress
like water. Then the melody stopped abruptly, in mid-refrain. Beorn
turned away with a growl. He lifted the pouch that held the Runestone, tempted once again to hurl it from him. It had to be the
lodestone that drew them to him. Instead he doubled his pace.

He scanned the people he passed warily, seeing an enemy in every
face. As always, he was alone against the world. He had thought
of asking Kan Konar for aid; the man was a mercenary, after all,
and his talents might have been useful. But he had decided against
it—he knew too little about the man. The cloakfighter had repaid

him for saving his life; they were now even. I need no help, the thief told himself. Let them bring every sorcerer who lives against me—let them resurrect the Necromancer himself—I will win through.

He was not far from his destination now—the docks, and beyond them the blue Ythan Sea. Between them and the thief was a portion of the city's cemetery, a wide expanse surrounded by a high wall. Rather than go around, he leaped nimbly to the top of the bricks and swung himself over, dropping to the soft, rich earth within. Once at the docks he would find a way, somehow, to reach Graystar Isle. Let sorcerer battle sorcerer for the Runestone of Darkhaven— he would soon be safely out of it, at least with a fortune, and perhaps with peace for the first time in his life.

"In here," Pandrogas said. They stood before the torii entrance of the cemetery, the sorcerer's ring shining in the dawn light. Its glow had increased after they had entered the city proper, and had led them a twisting route that eventually turned back toward the docks. "He must be making for the shipyards."

Amber peered past the black timbers of the gate. The night fog that still clung to parts of Dulfar seemed thicker within those walls, and there was no sign of the starcrystal radiance that brightened the rest of the city. Headstones and stelae rose dim and indistinct, like beckoning fingers. She shivered, and turned the involuntary reaction into a shrug, attempting to throw off her fear. "Let's hurry," she said. "We don't want to lose him."

Pandrogas looked dubiously at her. "Perhaps I should go alone. He is dangerous, after all—"

"You need me with you." She did not elaborate on this absolute, nor did he question it. She started forward, and the sorcerer followed. She was afraid, though not nearly as much as she would have been months before at the thought of hunting down a dangerous criminal within a boneyard. *That* Amber, the Marquise of Chuntai, was as dead as the citizens of this necropolis, and she had had little time to mourn the passing. Still, however, she was afraid. She was very much aware of her physical weakness and ignorance of magic—she was wholly dependent on Pandrogas for protection. The thought,

which a commonmonth ago would have seemed perfectly right to
her, now was upsetting. It was not that she loved Pandrogas any
less, she told herself, or lacked any confidence in his ability to handle
a situation. But she wanted to be able to defend herself.

Pandrogas's hand on her shoulder stopped her. "Take this," he
said, and she felt pressed within her hand a thin stylet. She gripped
its pommel, which was grooved to match curling fingers, and felt
her breath within her, sharp like the blade. The knife seemed to
meld itself to her grasp, a slender finger of metal, sharp and pointed,
noiseless, an instrument of very intimate death. She had never held
a weapon before in her life.

They hurried on through the cemetery, led by the pulsing glow
of the ring, past crypts, mastabas, and ossuaries, and graves covered
with thick grass and trees. The fog was thicker within, and the
morning sun cast long, sharp shadows. All was silence; even their
footsteps, deadened by the soft loam, seemed unreal to her. She
found herself reflecting on that other life, now so far away in both
time and experience; was she really the same woman who had been
mistress of a province, whose slightest whim had commanded scores
of courtiers, who had awakened every morning to the scents of
delicate pomanders, of gardenias and camellias floating in crystal
bowls? She remembered bathing in an alabaster tub, followed by
serving girls brushing carmine and kohl on her lips and eyes, and
finally attending balls wearing velvet and brocaded silk, and jewels
of amethyst and phoenix feather. It was all especially vivid to her
now, and equally unreal—as though she remembered staring, home-
less and frightened, through a window at someone else's life.

Pandrogas had taken the lead now, striding through the layer of
ground mist like a spirit through a netherworld, and she hurried to
keep up. The fog seemed thicker. She blinked and paused; there had
been a moment of flickering light at the edge of her vision. Pandrogas
had not noticed it; he continued on, disappearing about the edge of
a large mausoleum. Amber hurried to catch him, and then the ground
suddenly spasmed beneath her, groaning like a live thing. She staggered and fell. The earth cracked; a nearby tumulus split open, and
tree roots like grasping hands rose from it. Amber scrambled away

from the fissure. The temblor subsided, and she was able to gain her feet. But she had no sooner stood than the ground shook again, harder, and sent her sprawling again, this time into the shallow trench created by the shifting earth. Momentarily trapped, unable to push against the soft ground, she looked up and gasped in fear—a nearby monument, the statue of a tall, bearded man, toppled toward her! There was no escape, it would crush her. Amber closed her eyes and screamed, fear of death an almost orgasmic burst, an explosion of which she was the core.

But she felt no impact. The quake was over. She opened her eyes, then stared in astonishment—the statue was nowhere to be seen. After a moment she saw it a good ten ells from the pedestal on which it had stood. Amber rose shakily to her feet. The scene reeled about her; for a moment she thought another quake had struck. She put a hand on the empty pedestal and waited until the dizziness passed.

The statue had fallen directly toward her; there was nothing that could have diverted its course. Her immediate thought was that Pandrogas had saved her. She called his name, but there was no reply, and now a new fear took her. She looked about, confused, not sure what direction to take. Nearby was a sepulchre crowned with a tall criosphinx; she climbed to the top of it, sitting on the broad head and holding on to the curling horns lest another quake strike, while she scanned the graveyard in all directions. The ground fog was finally lifting; only pockets of it, like gray silk, remained in the dips and hollows. Ahead of her she saw the far gate, and beyond that she could glimpse the blue of the Ythan Sea. Then she caught her breath as she saw the silhouette of a figure dart quickly through the open gate.

Amber dropped back to the ground. The glimpse had been enough to tell her that she had seen the thief; the outline was as bearlike as manlike. But where was Pandrogas? Was he lying injured somewhere nearby, a victim of the quake as she had almost been? She called his name again, and the sound of her voice in the brooding silence was unnerving. She searched quickly through the surrounding maze of monuments, finding no trace of him. What was she to do? She recalled his admonition to think of the quest over their personal concerns. Should she trust him to be equal to whatever setbacks might have arisen, and pursue the thief before the trail grew cold?

Amber breathed deeply, making a conscious effort to relax. She had found him once, on the Warped Stairs. She closed her eyes, waiting for some deep intuition to set her on her way. But the indecision remained—no one direction tugged at her.

"*Pandrogas!*"

No reply.

She thought of playing her alicorn flute again, but realized that if he could not hear her calls, he would not hear that either. Make a decision, she told herself. The Runestone must be recovered. There was only one way open to her, she knew. She gazed about one final time, then turned and hurried toward the gate.

Someone was shaking the sorcerer roughly, calling him back from the warm darkness. He blinked, coughed, and then felt a sudden blazing pain on the side of his head. Instead of dropping him back into unconsciousness, the shock cleared his senses. He opened his eyes. He lay in a pool of fog, his hand held in a callused, grimy grip; a ragged footpad crouched beside him, trying to tug his ring of rank from his finger. Another one stood over him, cudgel upraised for another blow. "Hit 'im again!" the first one said in a rasping voice. The truncheon fell; Pandrogas seized the descending wrist in his free hand, at the same time mumbling the Spell of the Shifting Senses. He knew before he finished the cant that it would not work— his pronunciation was not clear enough. The ruffians, instead of being caught in synesthetic confusion, were unaffected, but they hesitated at what was obviously a spellcasting. Pandrogas quickly brought his leg up and hooked it about the neck of the one who held his hand, tumbling him over backward. The other, truncheon hand still held, reached for the sorcerer's throat with his other hand. Pandrogas grabbed that wrist as well and used the man's momentum to pull him off balance, then shoved him toward the other, who was getting to his feet. The two went down in a tangle of arms, legs, and shouts. The sorcerer staggered upright. It took all of the discipline learned over thirty years of study to gain control of his spinning head. He drew himself straight, arms describing an arc, hands joining over his head. *"Assegan delundis senarum!"* There was a thundercrack, and he was outlined for a moment in auric fire. He watched the thieves react in horror, then turn and run. In a moment they had disappeared into the cemetery's depths. The sorcerer collapsed against an obelisk and retched.

When he had brought up the last of his meal he felt somewhat better. He managed to stand again, though his head now felt as though all the hordes of Xoth clamored within it. He investigated, gingerly, with his fingertips: there were two bloodied bruises on either side, above each ear. One, he knew, was the result of being thrown off balance by the temblor; he had struck his head on a menhir and passed out. The other wound was from the blow that had helped to awaken him. Luckily it had been a glancing strike; had the aim been better, Pandrogas knew he would be dead now.

He braced himself, hands spread wide against the carved face of the obelisk, and that was when he saw that the resin's glow was gone from his finger. He had kept his crystal ring of rank, but they had gotten away with the other that was his link to the Runestone.

Pandrogas sat down, overwhelmed. Then he gasped and stood up quickly, paying the penalty by almost passing out again. *"Amber!"* He shouted. He looked about; she was nowhere to be seen. He listened intently, but the silence was complete, ominous. Had she been attacked as well? He swallowed to moisten a suddenly dry mouth, and with the appropriate gestures, began to design the Charm of Aware Air. The orb of sensitivity would help him find her. But the passes and phrases would not gel for him; the harder he tried, the more elusive the spell proved to be. He was having difficulty focusing his vision. He cursed, slamming the flat of his hand painfully against a grave marker. He could not remember the last time he had cursed in frustration. You have never been worthy of your ring, he told himself—not from the beginning. To bungle such a simple spell, upon which so much depends! He had barely managed to save himself from the ruffians by the most basic of illusories. And now Amber might be hurt, in peril, and he could do nothing!

Pandrogas forced himself to perform a calming ritual. After all, he told himself, I am injured, mazed by those blows to the head. Self-recriminations and panic will not help. He took a few experimental steps, and found he still felt dizzy and nauseated. The thought occurred to him that such injuries would not have affected him this badly ten commonyears ago. Well, he would have to work with what he had.

He sat down again, and performed a dangerous rite: a cantrip of strength and stability with himself as both donor and recipient. He drew from the only reserve open to him: his own life. He felt new vitality inspire him; the weak sickness was gone. But he would pay for it later, he knew. He hoped he could stave off the inevitable reaction until the time of emergency was past.

He tried a number of spells to find Amber, including the Charm of Aware Air and the Whispered Shout, but none produced results. He searched, to no avail. At last he was forced to give up. He had no idea how long he had been unconscious; it was still morning, and the sun would not move appreciably for the better part of a commonday. The fog-shrouded depression in which he had lain had no doubt concealed him well—she could have passed within a foot of him and not seen him. He would have to operate on the assumption that she was alive, and pursuing their quest as he had told her to do, because any other alternative was too horrible to contemplate. He felt guilty because she had not been his first thought upon awakening, even given the peril in which he had been. She did not know enough to use the power within her, strong though it was. He thought with wonder of how she had been sensitive enough to have been affected by the spell in the tavern, cast a day before—and again, a small, guilt-coated stab of jealousy made him wince.

All he could do was turn his course toward the docks once again, hoping that he would find her there. He felt he had had no right to allow her to come with him. But the thought of facing the vastness of the Abyss and the world beyond had simply been too much for him. A fine sorcerer am I, he thought: afraid of the outdoors, consistently misspeaking spells a warlock would not think twice about, letting my own Runestone be stolen out from under me! A proper hero for saving the remnants of the world, indeed! He thought of the quiet, assured mastery apparent in every gesture, every syllable, of Thasos's thaumaturgy; of his expression, quiet and serene as that of the stone statues in this cemetery, when he performed rites. *There was a sorcerer!* He could not imagine Thasos's ever being plagued with such doubts as he wrestled with now. He had always felt that true mastery had somehow eluded him; had oftimes of late brooded on a masochistic fantasy that involved his Lorian mentor's appearing in a puff of smoke and telling him it had all been a mistake, that he would have to return the ring. These feelings of insecurity and incompetence had plagued him since—and here he stopped as though thunder-struck, the thought reverberating in his mind: *Since first I took Amber to my bed.*

Fast upon that came a sense of someone watching him. Pandrogas turned quickly, hands upraised in a protective gesture. Before him, appearing like an eidolon, was a statue, faded and weathered. The sorcerer looked wonderingly at its face—it could have been Kabyn, his servant, transmuted to marble. The serene countenance beneath the bald pate was similar to an uncanny degree. Pandrogas stared at it, wondering to what extent Darkhaven's course through the sky had disintegrated already. Did the people of Oljaer now point skyward in panic as the fragment dipped lower on each pass? How soon would the turrets of Darkhaven begin to rake the tallest towers of Oljaer? He hoped Kabyn's injuries would not prevent him from escaping with Undya and the others, if it came to that. For five years he had lived with them, and yet he knew so little about them. They were simply there, a part of the castle as though they had always been, instructing him in its mazelike complexity, serving him quietly and efficiently as he studied the ancient tomes. He found himself wishing Kabyn were here now. He needed the man's calmness and assurance.

He recalled something Yaladin had said when Pandrogas had taken custody of the castle from him. Speaking of Kabyn, Undya, and the others, his fellow adept had told him, "You may learn as much from them as from all of Darkhaven's libraries." Certainly he had learned much about Darkhaven over the years from them. But now, suddenly, he wondered if he had asked the right questions. What would the servants have said, he wondered, had I asked them their opinion on my cuckolding Tahrynyar? "She must go with you," Kabyn had said in the caverns, and he had not questioned the statement, though he did not know why. The man had spoken with such authority—and, as he had said, he had never been wrong before.

He continued on his way through the cemetery. He knew now that since he had given in to the loneliness, the longing, that he had felt since he first saw her, he had had doubts about his work, about his purpose and his abilities. He tried to recall if he had consistently miscast simple spells before bedding her. It did not seem so to him... he stopped and leaned wearily against cool stone again. I love her, he told himself, and within him something replied, *You are a sorcerer, with a sorcerer's responsibilities. You have not the right.*

He looked up and realized he was leaning against the wall next to the gate. Beyond the cemetery wall were the dockyards, and beyond that the sea. He was almost reluctant to exit the graveyard; in a subtle way it reminded him of Darkhaven. The silent and grim surroundings felt oddly comforting now that he was about to leave them behind. The dead did not threaten; they offered none of the overwhelming complexities and choices that the living did. Instead, Pandrogas seemed to feel a vast and reassuring power that dwelled, patient and complete, beneath the crumbling edifices and monuments. For a moment he could sense, locked within coffins and caskets, a potential source of energy, knowledge, strength, beyond any that he had ever known. And more: he knew it was possible to tap into that power, to awaken it and channel it, and by so doing, to hold the fate of all who breathed in his hands.

Pandrogas shuddered, turned and almost ran through the gate, back into the world of life.

Chapter 11

"The Serpent Waits..."

"Ah, the burly one," the caravansary owner said with a knowing
nod. "I'm afraid you are just a wink and a whistle too late, gentle
dayfolk. He left in a great hurry, as though pursued by the Demogorgon himself. But his companion is still here, and might know
more than I. You'll find him in the central court."

"Most gracious of you," Ardatha said, and smiled, though it took
an effort. Her quarry had escaped her by mere moments again.

The enchantress and the marquis turned away from the desk, and
the owner's parting words faded behind them: "Take care in your
speech—he has the look of a nightfellow about him, and no mistake!"

The court was empty, save for a packtrain near them of onagers
and dromedaries in the final stages of journey's preparations, and a
lone man, dressed in darkness, performing what Ardatha at first
thought was a dance of adjuration on the far side of the hard-packed
earth. His cloak swirled about him as he spun and leaped with
incredible grace and celerity about a tethering pole. Ardatha heard
the soft, somehow sinister passage of the cloak through the air, and
blinked in surprise at the sound of impact, like stone against bone,
as one end of it connected with the top of the pole.

172

"A cloakfighter," Tahrynyar murmured in admiration. "I once saw two fight in Quy. They are supreme among warriors; it is said that one can defeat five soldiers armed at all points."

Ardatha raised an eyebrow. "This I find hard to believe."

"Watch him. There—note the curl of wood shaved from the pole by the passage of his cloak? There are sharp slivers of bone or ivory set in the hems. He can strike with the weighted corners, or use it like a whip. The material is woven from unicorns' manes, so they say, and treated with certain herbs; it is marvelously supple, and yet strong enough to turn a thrown dagger. In some cases the inner lining contains panels of phoenix feather, which can reflect the sun and blind an opponent. See those circular movements? Thus he shields himself, and confuses an opponent. The cloak can also be thrown like a net, or used to trip—"

Ardatha held up her human hand. "I am convinced, marquis," she said dryly.

"And I haven't yet mentioned the uses of the clasp chain."

As though cued by this, the cloakfighter whipped the silver chain from about the high collar—which, Ardatha noticed, rose in curved spikes that protected his face—and, grasping the morse, snapped the linked silver about the post as though about a neck. Then, his practice form evidently completed, he readjusted the deadly garment about his shoulders. He stood for a moment in silence, breathing deeply, then turned to leave.

"Cloakfighter!" Ardatha shouted. Though they stood in the shadows of the atrium's cloister and the acoustics hurled her voice about in echoes, the man turned unerringly toward them. He made no reply, but stood quietly as they approached.

"A most impressive display of skill," Ardatha said to him with a smile. The cloakfighter did not return the smile, but merely nodded slightly. "It is a quotidian ritual, madam, to which I have adhered for over fifteen commonyears. But then you are no doubt acquainted with assiduous practice, being an enchantress."

Ardatha felt her jaw drop; it took her a moment to regain her self-possession. Her silver ring of rank was on her left hand, which she as a matter of course had kept hidden in the folds of her robe, saving the sight of it until when it might be needed. "It would appear," she said at last, "that I am not the only adept in this court. How do you name me so accurately?"

"You conceal your deformity from me now, but it was evident as you and your companion watched me from across the court. I saw the sun glitter from the ring on your ninth finger." He folded his arms and waited her reply. Though he had just put himself through an intense physical workout, Ardatha noticed, his breath was even, and his skin dry. I must have this man on my side, the enchantress told herself.

"You astonish me, sir." She introduced herself and Tahrynyar, and learned in return the cloakfighter's name. "We seek the whereabouts of one Beorn of Osloviken, late of Oljaer." As well be honest; obviously one could not lie successfully to this man. And not even the greatest warrior could defend himself against a surreptitious mesmerism, if that proved necessary.

Kan Konar shook his head. "You are no doubt she who sent the mandragoras. He saved my life and I saved his; I owe him nothing, but I see no reason to betray him."

"Perhaps, then," Tahrynyar said, "we might discuss a number of reasons—a large number." He and Ardatha had stopped at a money changer's booth on the way to the caravansary; he tugged slightly at the drawstrings of his purse, which loosened to allow the sun to sparkle on the crystalline currency of Sothan. Kan Konar's gaze dropped to the scintillating fortune. "I am," he said slowly, "always open to discussion."

Judicious picking of pockets during the course of his crosstown journey had supplied the thief with more than enough crystals to buy passage to Graystar Isle. After some bargaining he convinced the captain of a small caravel named the *Elgrane* to grant him a hammock in steerage and to alter the ship's route enough to include Stonebrow's redoubt. The arrangements thus completed, Beorn relaxed and watched the complicated and confusing preparations for getting under way, staying within the shadow of the lateen sail and taking care that he could not be seen from the dock. He sat crosslegged atop a coiled hawser, congratulating himself upon yet another aleatory escape. By the sphere, he would turn a profit from this venture yet! He patted his pouch where the Runestone was hidden.

The creaking of wheels and the cursing of laborers drew his attention; he looked up to see the first of three wagons being pulled up the gangboard by a team of sailors. The wagons were open on two of their four sides, and laced with iron bars. In the first cage was a centaur, holding on to the bars with horn-palmed hands, four hooves braced, widespread, against the lurching floor. Long, greasy locks framed the brutish face. It snarled, its mouth foaming slightly. The second wagon housed a huge anaconda, which lay coiled and immobile. Beorn watched, fascinated, as the third cage was drawn up onto the deck. It contained by far the most impressive of the three beasts: a gryphon. As its cage was pulled into place beside the others, it shrieked, a cry of rage that sent clouds of gulls and eiders from the masts and caused the sailors blocking the wheels to cover their ears in pain. The gryphon raked its beak against the bars, drawing sparks visible in the bright sunlight. The huge feathered wings could not extend to their full length in the cage's confines, but they moved nevertheless, and the sound they made was like surf, or the drums of an army's march. Beorn stared into the yellow fearless eyes, fascinated.

A fourth wagon followed, this one with paneled sides; a legend, in faded paint, proclaimed all of this to be Cardolus's Carnival of Wonderment and the Bizarre. The Talic script, all flowing words with extravagant serifs, contained in the voids and counters of the letters pictures of the caged creatures, as well as that of a dwarf, two women, and Cardolus himself. Beorn grinned as he compared the illustrations to the realities, which followed the last wagon. Cardolus was a fat man in faded robes with a wizard's pearl ring on his fourth finger. His mustache was not nearly as dark or as sinister as painted, Beorn noted with amusement, as the carnival owner stopped to argue with the captain. The dwarf, an old man barely waist high, made his way from cage to cage filling the beasts' tins with slop. Beorn did not listen to the argument; his attention was drawn instead to the two women who stood in the center of the deck, looking about them. They were as dissimilar as two members of the same sex could be—and one of them was a shapechanger. This he could tell, even without reference to the wagon's legend, though he had never been able to explain the subtle sense that enabled him to recognize other werefolk. She was tall and voluptuous, with a mane of hair the color of obsidian that flowed back from a widow's peak and ended below her waist. The name beneath her picture on the wagon was Mirren. Her brocaded gown and abundance of costume jewelry, which no doubt was part of the show, added to her meretricious attraction. Her lips were very red, her eyes dark and cold. Beorn watched the muscle-play in her neck and shoulders as she glanced about the ship, and he wiped suddenly damp palms on his knees. As always, desire met with fear within him. But, he thought, this Mirren is a beastling also—she might understand.

The other woman, compared with Mirren, seemed not much more than a child. Ia, as she was named on the wagon, was thin and pale, with brown hair as listless as wet silk. Her large eyes and face had all the life of painted china. She was not a shapechanger, but neither was she human, Beorn realized. The painted advertisement named her a dryad. He felt no desire for her at all; on the contrary, he felt a surge of sympathy. Her attitude was that of a starving child; but, although thin, she did not appear malnourished. Her starvation seemed more spiritual than physical. She took no interest in their surroundings as did Mirren; instead she stood and shivered, though the sun was warm.

Mirren's roving gaze now came upon Beorn—the two locked stares for a moment. Beorn smiled, and she smiled in return. He stood and walked over to where she stood by the centaur's cage. Mirren watched him approach, taking him in with a frank appraisal that added to his desire. "Let me guess," she said in Talic, when he stood in front of her. "A bear." Her voice was exactly as he had expected: as rich as Bageran coffee, a voice made, he thought, for the whispers and cries of lovemaking.

"And you," he replied, "could be naught else than a wolf." She smiled again, her teeth very white against her lips, surprisingly even and straight. They said no more, but simply stood there, enjoying the moment of carnal agreement. With her I can let happen what might, Beorn told himself. Far from a catastrophe, she might even take it as added excitement. And he knew she felt the same way; felt that here at last was a man with whom she could be as abandoned, as savage, as the wolf within her cried to be.

The centaur rattled the bars of its cage and sounded a deep, lusty growl. Beorn glanced at the beast and saw that it had a huge erection. The chestnut flanks trembled. The centaur looked at him and Mirren, and slowly licked its lips.

Amber hurried along the wharfs and piers, past barques, carracks, galliots, and galleons. It was, perhaps, her sense of absolute urgency and haste that prevented her from being detained by the mariners and dockworkers as she asked repeatedly for any news of either a tall grayhair or a stocky redbeard. At last a comprador directed her to a small ship called the *Elgrane*; it was, he said, making ready to sail.

When Amber saw the thief standing amidships, talking to the dark-haired woman, she was not sure what to do. She had still found no sign of Pandrogas, had no idea where he was. She knew she could do nothing against the thief by herself. But the sailors were already reefing lines and making ready to draw up the gangboard; in a few moments the *Elgrane* would weigh anchor. As she pondered, she glanced up again at the ship—and saw the thief looking straight at her. Quickly she ducked behind a stack of cargo. She was not sure if she had been seen or not.

At any rate, she had done all she could, she told herself. It would be easy enough to learn the ship's destination, and Pandrogas could no doubt contrive some method to meet it there. But first she would have to find the sorcerer. She turned to make her way back toward the cemetery—and gasped. The thief stood before her.

When Pandrogas learned that the *Elgrane* had sailed over four hours before his arrival, he was as close to frantic as he had ever allowed himself to become. From what he had been told by the stevedores and sailors, Amber had been taken on board by a burly red-haired man immediately before the ship's departure. The sorcerer stood on the continent's edge, staring at the demarcation of sky and sea. Once again the Runestone was beyond his reach, and now the woman he loved was in danger as well. Previous to this his anger against the thief had been submerged by his concern over the disaster inexorably approaching Darkhaven. But now he felt rage rushing through his veins, filling his ears with a silent, dizzying roar. To recover the Runestone was no longer enough; the thief must be made to pay for the pain and upheaval he had caused. The sorcerer looked at the crystal ring gleaming on his fist, and swore that he would see it happen.

He would need a boat. He turned back toward the warves, but before he could begin his search a carriage, drawn by two lathered horses, pulled up at the dock. Two men and a woman got out. They saw Pandrogas at almost the same time that he saw them. One of the men was a cloakfighter. The woman was tall and strikingly beautiful, with hair like hoarfrost. Both were unknown to him, though there was a tantalizing familiarity about the woman. But he spared both of them only a passing glance. His disbelieving attention fixed immediately upon the other man: Tahrynyar, Marquis of Chuntai.

The sorcerer was literally paralyzed with astonishment for a moment. There could be no mistake—he recognized the tattered cloak of feathers and the silken clothes, as well as the face, though it was lined and haggard. But he had left the marquis a bedridden cripple in a castle several fragments distant; the man was quite probably the last person he would ever have expected to see standing before him now. And so, while the sorcerer stared, Tahrynyar was able to shout to the cloakfighter, "Stop him before he destroys us!"

Almost before the marquis had finished, the cloakfighter had whipped the cloak from his shoulders and sent it whirling, spread upon the air like the wings of a cacodemon, toward Pandrogas. The sorcerer automatically put one hand up to ward off the enveloping darkness, and one of the bone blades that lined the hem laid open the palm of his right hand. Then the cloak wrapped about him like a live thing; he felt a staggering pain on his left thigh as one of the weights struck him. He dropped to one knee, and that saved him, for Kan Konar had hurled himself after the cloak, leaping forward and aiming a spinning kick at the blinded sorcerer's head. Pandrogas felt the murderous blow pass over him and, reacting from his own years of training, swept his arm through the folds of the cloak before him, striking the cloakfighter's supporting leg at the ankle with a hammerfist blow. Kan Konar fell, slapping the sea-worn timbers and shouting to absorb the impact, but before he could roll to his feet, Pandrogas flung the cloak onto him. The sorcerer rolled backward and gained his feet an instant before his opponent.

Tahrynyar and Ardatha were still in the same position; the exchange between the cloakfighter and the sorcerer had happened in the time of two breaths. Kan Konar leaped to his feet, the cloak about his shoulders again. He did not continue the attack, for he saw that the sorcerer stood ready for him, legs firmly planted in a wide, wary stance that matched his own, hands upraised and fingers crabbed in poses of power. Blood dripped from his right hand.

For a moment the tableau held; then the enchantress shouted, "Surrender, Pandrogas! You are no match for the cloakfighter's deadly art and my magic!" She held up a left hand that belonged in Xoth; it glowed, even in the sunlight, with silver fire. The dockside workers who had stopped to watch the battle now took to their heels at this evidence of magic.

"I know you now," Pandrogas replied, keeping his eyes on the cloakfighter. "Ardatha Demonhand, whom I saved long ago from Endrigoth and Sestihaculas. I have heard of pupils attacking masters; now I know how it feels."

"I did not want a confrontation," Ardatha replied; "only the Runestone of Darkhaven. But now this must run its course. The cloakfighter can and will attack before you can finish a syllable or make a sigil. And though my rank is below yours, my spells are no less deadly."

"It appears I am stymied," Pandrogas said. "Now I know what you would have of me, Ardatha. And what about Tahrynyar?"

"I would have your death, sorcerer!" Tahrynyar shouted. Pandrogas risked a glance at him and marveled; the marquis's forehead was beaded with perspiration, his fists clenched, his entire body trembling. He would have never thought Tahrynyar capable of such passion.

"So you might, Tahrynyar," Pandrogas said. "And I salute your tenacity and perseverance in that quest. First you enlist the Demogorgon against me; then, failing that, you seek help from one of his minions!"

"Sestihaculas does not own me, Pandrogas!" Ardatha cried. "Nor does anyone, man or Chthon!"

"No? Do you not serve the Circle?" It was nothing more than a guess, inspired by her desire for the Runestone and his memory of the young conjuress's intense interest in the group. But he knew he was right when he saw rage contrast her skin with her hair.

"You will speak respectfully of them!" the enchantress shouted.

"I will speak as I feel! You may defeat me, or even destroy me, Ardatha, but you will never surpass me!" He kept his eyes on the cloakfighter as he spoke. He felt an odd kinship for the man who stood, motionless and ready, watching him, for he was the only other one who was keeping his head. The sorcerer knew that what he was trying to do must be fairly obvious to his opponent, but Kan Konar made no attempt to stop him; instead, the sorcerer thought he saw the faintest ghost of amusement cross the impassive face.

Pandrogas continued quickly. "And you, marquis," he said, using the title in a baiting tone. "Tell me, are you always going to let others fight your battles for you? Are you not afraid that someone will take this woman from you as well?"

His taunts were the bowstring, and Tahrynyar the arrow; with an inarticulate cry of rage the marquis ran toward him, fists raised. Simultaneously Pandrogas realized the cloakfighter's intent—to allow the sorcerer his desperate ploy, and then defeat him anyway. The weighted end of the cloak snaked toward him, faster than a whip, and he had no chance of dodging or blocking it. It caught him in the ribs, and pain took his breath away. But somehow he caught the end of the cloak in his bleeding hand before the cloakfighter could snatch it away; caught it and yanked it toward him. The cloakfighter's feet slipped the slightest bit on the wet timbers, just enough to throw him off balance. He moved to one side to recover, and Tahrynyar ran full tilt into him from behind. The two fell.

Even as he had tugged on the cloak, Pandrogas had begun shouting the phrases of Zhoar's Sixth Spell, also known as the Spell of Rebellious Attire. Every word burned like fire in his side—where ribs were surely broken—but when he released the cloak it suddenly seemed to wrap itself about both Kan Konar and Tahrynyar, abruptly manifesting the perversity all inanimate objects occasionally show, magnified a hundredfold. As the cloakfighter and the marquis tried in vain to disentangle themselves, Pandrogas leaped over them and ran straight at Ardatha. The pain in his side and his thigh almost caused him to fall, and the effort had started his head injuries throbbing again as well. He saw the enchantress hurl at him a ball of odylic energy the color of polished steel, and deflected it with a gesture of his right hand, though he felt the vitiating force enter him through the cut on his palm. Nevertheless, somehow he pushed past her, sending her sprawling. The carriage that had brought them had long since fled, but there had to be safety somewhere. He could hear Ardatha shouting words behind him, but could not understand them—they seemed to shake the ground beneath his feet, or was that merely his own vertigo? He was confused; he felt as if he stood once again on the Warped Stairs, unable to tell up from down. He seemed to hear once again Amber's voice, telling him the translation of the spherecasting she had made: *From confusion and disorientation come loss and destruction.*

There was nothing at all now but the pain of all his wounds overwhelming him; he could no longer tell if he ran, walked, or crawled. And then there was no ground beneath him anymore, as though he had somehow tumbled over the edge of Rhynne; though that, he knew, was impossible. Nevertheless, he was falling, falling down a great whirling funnel of dark clouds, and he could hear his throbbing pain, which sounded more and more like laughter.

Clouds consume all of worth.

Of course, he thought, quite calmly. *The serpent waits within the darkness.* It did not refer to the hydra at all.

Then from the swirling mists a voice spoke, a voice a snake would have, were it given a snake to speak.

"So, Pandrogas," Sestihaculas said. "Did I not say we would meet again?"

And then the clouds overwhelmed him.

Chapter 12

The Wolf Woman

Amber stood in the fantail of the *Elgrane*, breathing deeply of the salt air in an attempt to recover from the ordeal she had just passed through. The weather was fair, the sun a hand's breadth above the horizon and beginning finally to warm the long day. She watched the continent of Althizar recede over the horizon, hoping perhaps to see some sign of rescue, though that seemed impossible to her now.

She had awakened in a deserted section of the hold, lying in a wide, swaying hammock, her hands and feet tied securely and her mouth gagged. She was dizzy and nauseated by the ship's motion and the sickening smell of bilgewater. Confused at first, she had then recalled her confrontation with the thief, how he had dug a thumb painfully into the junction of her neck and shoulder before she could recover from her surprise, and how her surroundings had dimmed and spun away from her. She struggled, attempting to loosen her bonds; this action served only to overturn the hammock and drop her into a tangle of sea-soaked rigging and spare sails. Several rats of dismaying size had fled at this, but they returned quickly to investigate; Amber could see their red eyes glinting in the dim light. She was helpless; the thief's bonds were too tight for her to escape.

Nausea came again, and she realized that if it overcame her, the gag would cause her to drown in her own vomit.

The rats, quite fearless now, were getting closer.

She was not sure what had happened next. She had been dazzled by a blue glare, had felt a searing pain at her wrists and ankles and in a band about her jaws, and then she was free. She picked up a nearby belaying pin from the welter of storage and hurled it at the rats, who scattered. As she threw it, what felt like a bracelet of ashes broke from about her wrist and drifted to the floor. There were ashes on her bodice, too, and her feet. The ropes and gag had burned away from her, without leaving a mark upon her skin.

She had made her way above deck quickly. Few of the sailors paid any attention to her, being concerned with the ship's myriad duties. Her nausea had left her soon after she had reached the open air; it had not been due to seasickness as much as to the foulness below. She had not seen the thief. Looking at the rough countenances of the crew and officers and hearing their comments concerning her had convinced her that she would get nowhere pleading her case to them; her best course seemed to be to stay out of their way.

Standing alone now, looking over the white and blue of the sea, she allowed herself to think about what had happened below. She had no more explanation for it than she had for her inexplicable survival in the cemetery; or, rather, she had the same explanation. It came from within me, she thought wonderingly. Pandrogas said that I had power, untamed, unknown power. She looked at her hands, half-expecting to see them seething with barely restrained odylic force. She seemed to be able to draw upon it only in the last extremity of need or fear, and sometimes not even then. What good does it do me, then? she wondered. How can I use it when I cannot control it?

It occurred to her then to check her robes for the knife that Pandrogas had given her; it was gone, of course. She had not even had the chance to think of using it. Her flute was still with her. Perhaps I can play my way to freedom, Amber thought bitterly.

She wondered where Pandrogas was; if, indeed, he was still alive. She tried to convince herself that he would somehow find a way to rescue her, but that belief did not come easily. He had lost more than just a major portion of his power after the theft of the Runestone; he had somehow lost confidence in himself. And so she had begun to lose confidence in him. Before all of this began—years ago, it seemed; so hard to believe it had been less than a commonweek— she would have said he was capable of anything. Now she knew she had to depend upon herself for escape. Yes, and I've done so well so far, came the ironic echo of her thoughts.

She turned and made her way forward, keeping her balance upon the shifting deck with difficulty. She had to find the thief, to learn their destination and his plans for her. She was not dead yet; perhaps, then, he did not intend for her to die. She passed the wagons containing the carnival beasts. The gryphon stood defiantly, its eagle eyes seeming to burn through her. She wanted very badly to open its cage; such a majestic creature had no place behind bars. The dwarf lounged before the anaconda's cage, basking in the sun as did the serpent; he watched her pass with one incurious eye. As Amber passed him she heard weeping ahead. Half hidden behind a tar barrel, a young woman, seeming scarcely older than a child, sat upon the deck, hugging her white knees to her chin. She wept quietly. Amber looked at the tears falling from those enormous eyes, and felt that sense of sympathy which is partly relief born of the realization that others also suffer. She crouched beside the weeping woman and attempted to mop the tears with her sleeve. "Are you a prisoner like me, then?" she asked.

The young woman looked straight ahead, past the wale and into the sea. "I am a prisoner, but not like you." The voice was high and delicate; If my flute could speak, Amber thought, it would speak in that voice. She looked at the woman's eyes, at the paleness of a face that had never been burned by the sun. "You are with the carnival," she said; "I saw your picture on the wagon. Ia, you are called."

The other seemed to take no notice of her words. "Cardolus holds my wood, you see," she said sadly. "He had it from an enchanter in Jareem, who stole me from the forests of Prasan." One delicate hand, white-veined with blue like glacier ice, stroked the varnished deck beneath her. "It has been so long since I have touched living wood..."

"You are a dryad," Amber said. Ia made neither acknowledgment nor denial. "Why are you his prisoner?"

"We are all prisoners of the carnival; the beasts, and Mirren, and myself. My task is to prophesy. You and yours are like thin down to me; through you I see, dimly at times, clearly at times, what lies beyond you." She sighed. "It comes from the wood, you see. Trees live a very long time; they gain a dark, rich, solid sort of knowledge; it isn't expressed in words or thoughts, but it is there nonetheless. As I can point to where a leaf will fall, blown by the wind, so I can tell you, at times, where your course will take you." Her voice had become slightly singsong, as though she were reciting by rote.

"This is not a show," Amber told her. She laid a hand gently upon the other's; the dryad flinched. Her flesh was the temperature of fresh-cut timber—Amber hastily withdrew her touch, sure that her human warmth had burned the wood nymph. "You do not have to say my sooth." She was not sure she wanted to hear it.

The dryad looked at Amber for the first time. "But it is all I have left. I still hope that, perhaps some day, I will look at someone and see my own release." Her eyes, the color of mahogany, focused on the marquise. In addition to the sadness in them, there was also a great calmness and patience. Then that gaze, holding her own, slowly filled with wonderment. "And I believe," the dryad said softly, "that you are the one."

"What do you mean?" Amber had to look away; the sense of gentle, patient waiting and suffering in those eyes was too much for her. "How am I the one?"

"I can sense a storm's approach, but I cannot tell where each raindrop will fall. Similarly, I cannot forecast with exactitude how you will save me. But I see a bright and terrible danger approaching, and in the midst of it, you shall reunite me at last with the wood that is part of me." She was quiet then, but she kept her gaze, now full of a hope even more disquieting than her previous despair, fixed on Amber. Amber did not know how to reply to this. At last she said, "I...I will do what I can, of course." She stood, intending to continue her search for the thief, but the dryad's quiet voice stopped her. "You wielded considerable power once," she said. "You will wield much more soon. I see you in the hand of darkness. But you have light within you."

Amber stared at the dryad's wan face in astonishment. She recalled clearly the reading of the sphere's fragments lying on Pandrogas's laboratory table: *The hand of light is raised. To escape its fire, one must bring darkness to its grasp.* But that prediction had been cast for another; it had not been meant for her. Or had it? She thought of the statue in the cemetery, the rats in the hold. "What do you mean?" she asked.

"What I say; no more, no less. A vision comes and fades as you stand before me; I put it into words as best I can."

The deck rocked beneath Amber, almost causing her to lose her balance. She hesitated, feeling that she should say something further, then turned and quickly continued her way forward. She hurried, bumping into sailors and muttering apologies, trying to keep her mind carefully blank, trying to let it be filled only with the crackling and rustlings of the great sails above her, the creaking of the blocks, the hiss and slap of waves against the hull. But she could not escape the echoing of the dryad's cryptic words; nor could she discount them, considering the eerie similarity between the sphere's augury and Ia's.

The possibility of new dangers threatening was far too much to contemplate now. She had to find the thief, to learn her fate. She almost smiled at the thought; it was blackly amusing that she was now seeking what meager solace she could from hearing the sentence he would pass on her.

He was as eager as he was afraid. It had been a very long time since he had bedded a woman; indeed, there had been only five since Suchana. He did not intend anything to stop him in this. When he had seen the sorcerer's woman on the dock, the red anger that had filled him had been faintly shocking in its intensity. He had been sure she had led the sorcerer to him, but this had not been the case. He had not wanted to kidnap her, but the only alternative was to kill her. The urge he had felt to do so had been frightening.

He and Mirren had agreed to meet in the steerage at the end of the third watch; he had found an empty storage locker far from the crew's quarters. The room was relatively large, and had a hatch that could be roped shut. In addition, it was high enough in the bow to avoid the stench and vermin of the hold. A piece of crystal had purchased from the steward a starcrystal rod, a flagon of wine, and a pile of soft oakrum. Now the thief waited, sitting crosslegged. He passed a coin along the backs of his fingers, deftly manipulating it from knuckle to knuckle while he breathed deeply, using the same mental exercises that had always aided him in preparing for thievery. They did not help this time.

His codpiece chafed him; he had been in an almost constant state of arousal since first he met the wolf woman, hours before. For the first time he might be with someone who could understand, truly understand; someone with whom he would not have to hold back. Years before, he had given in to Suchana's seduction after much hesitancy, but he had never allowed himself release with her. He had pretended instead, shouting and groaning in mock ecstasy, then finding relief later by himself. If she had ever wondered at the lack of physical evidence of his orgasm, she had not mentioned it, nor had the few other women he had bedded over the years. There had not been many, for the fear of what could happen—what once *had* happened—had never entirely left him, and he preferred abnegation to the risk. He did not, he had told himself, really care what happened to whatever woman he dallied with. But the fewer who knew of his coeval the better. But now at last, at long last, here was a woman who might understand his reticence, with whom he might at last be completely free...

A low chuckle interrupted his thoughts. "You look as nervous as a lad awaiting his first whore," Mirren said. Beorn looked up in surprise—he had not heard her approach. True, the sounds of the waves against the hull were loud, and no doubt she walked with the silent gait of her lupine alter ego, but he still felt uneasy that he had not sensed her coming. The state of his art, he thought, seemed to have degenerated badly over the last two commonweeks.

Mirren stepped forward into the light of the starcrystal, and Beorn forgot his worries at the sight of her. Her hair shimmered with blue highlights in the light, and her eyes were darker than onyx. She sat down beside him. Beorn inhaled, and her scent made him feel lotus-drunk. He wanted to grab her, to pull her down immediately, but now that the moment was here he felt strangely reluctant, almost shy. He offered her some wine. She tilted her head back for a long swallow, and he admired the muscles in her neck.

"How did you come to be with that sideshow?" he asked. He was postponing it, he knew; it was the old hesitancy, the old fear.

The lycanthrope looked at him with amusement. "So, you make conversation before love? How considerate. Very well; I joined Cardolus's motley troupe for regular meals and a chance to travel. I have few talents other than shapechanging; how else to turn a profit on it?"

"How did you—I mean . . ." Inwardly he cursed; where was the confidence and smoothness that had always served him so well?

Mirren smiled at his stammering. "I bought it," she said, "for revenge. My family and I were serfs; we tilled our seignior's demesne, paid him for the majority of our crops and hunts, and lived at the mercy of his whims. My father attempted to keep me hidden, but one day our lord saw me, and had his myrmidons fetch me to his keep." She chuckled, as though the memory were a pleasant one. "Well, I was young, and gave no thought to consequences; afterward I stole some money and paid a nearby conjuress for the spell. Hothoth, I'd no idea how painful shapeshifting could be! But it was worth it; that night, when he sent for me again, I waited until he slept and tore his throat out with my teeth." She chuckled again. "Afterward I learned that my she-wolf would be with me for good. Well, I do not mind all that much. We roll into a town and Cardolus does his spiel, Ia tells fortunes and makes branches bud, I snap and snarl for the yokels, and we usually come away with full purses. There used to be much more to our caravan. We had a vampire and a unicorn, and a wagonful of other wonders: a piece of mushroom from fabled Xoth, and the mummified tentacle of a kraken; a skull that sang, and the hilt, supposedly, of the legendary Starsword . . ."

The wolf woman looked almost wistful for a moment. Then she turned a sardonic gaze upon Beorn. "And you, bear man? What brought out the animal in you?"

"My parents," Beorn said softly. He took a long swig of the wine. It seemed almost that he could smell the burning farmhouse, the stench of charred flesh...

"I am a thief," he said, changing the subject abruptly—he was not ready to talk about the other yet. "A very good thief. I can tell you how many people are in a dark room by listening to their breathing, or pull a string of bells from a pocket without ringing one. I've robbed crowns from the heads of kings, and Runestones from sorcerers' laboratories. I've stolen jewels from the eyes of idols and the navels of concubines. I'm a thief; it's what I do, it's my life." He shrugged. "And then there's the bear."

"It must be helpful," Mirren said. "Particularly if you've just stolen a jar of honey."

He glanced sharply at her; the amused smile on her face infuriated him for a single instant. Then he took another swallow of wine and laughed. He set the flagon aside and reached for her.

Mirren responded with such enthusiasm that he was momentarily taken aback; in little more than a moment she had discarded her gown and undergarments and was helping him with his buckles and knots. He was content to let her do the work at first; her beauty fascinated him. He had guessed her to be in her mid-twenties when he first saw her; now he knew that she was his age or even older. Her breasts, while large and firm, did not jut as aggressively as he had imagined they would, and her skin was beginning to lose its resiliency. But there was little enough to complain about, Beorn thought; nor, evidently, did Mirren find much wrong with him, judging by the way she caressed his limbs and tangled her fingers in the hair of his chest and beard. He kissed her, then jerked back in surprise as her sharp teeth stung his lip for an instant. She grinned and pulled him back to her again, tugging free the last of his clothes. Even in this extent of his desire, he kept his eye on the pouch containing the Runestone as she tossed it into a corner. To his relief, he was still hard; there had been times before when the anticipation

Michael Reaves

had made all his worry meaningless. She took hold of him, squeezing rhythmically, and guided him gently toward her. The wiry hair between her legs was even blacker, if possible, than that which now framed her face, and her body hair, though like down, was dark as well. It suited her, and added to his lust. She seized his shoulders as he stretched himself on top of her, raking them with her nails. The pain aroused Beorn even more, something he had not thought possible. "Now," he gasped, pushing her knees apart.

But Mirren held him back with hands on his chest. "Not this way," she whispered; then, while he watched in surprise, she rolled over quickly and crouched on her knees, facing away from him. The thief grabbed her hips and pulled her roughly against him. She laughed, the sound wild and exultant, as he entered her, and it increased his own fever. He could feel the fire building within him, and almost reflexively pushed it down, willed it to fade. He wished he had told her first of his fear. Now it was too late. He would have to hold it back, as he had always done. Then she laughed again, a laugh that was half scream this time, and thrust her hips hard against him, and he felt himself responding to her movement in spite of all he could do to prevent it. And why should he prevent it? He thrust harder, abandoning himself, hearing Mirren's cries growing harsher and harsher. They sounded almost like the howls of a beast now. And then he realized that the fine, sparse dark hair on her back was thickening, becoming coarser beneath his hands. He stared at his arms—was the hair on them growing as well?

What he had feared was happening, and it was too late to stop it! With a cry Beorn pushed Mirren forward, breaking their union and sending her sprawling onto the loose hemp. Her shout of shock and anger echoed his cry of pleasure turned to pain as he ejaculated. He fell forward, feeling the pains beginning in his bones and joints. Each breath was that of fire; his legs and arms felt as though they were breaking. His vision was beginning to blur, but he could see Mirren metamorphosizing even as he was. "*No!*" he cried, and the word was half bestial roar. He hurled himself against the wooden wall painfully, feeling the shock momentarily subdue the other, deeper pains. Again he struck the wall, then fell to the floor, gasping.

He caught a glimpse of Mirren glaring at him, eyes glowing in the blue light; heard the crackling and stretching of flesh as her face began to distend and those white teeth grew sharper, longer. It occurred to him that he might need the bear's strength to defend himself. But at that point it did not matter if Mirren tore him apart with claws and teeth; *he would not let the bear win again.*

And it did not. He felt the bear within him, snarling, enraged, but nevertheless retreating. For a long moment, there was nothing but the pain; when he came to himself again, he was lying on the oakrum, which had been torn and scattered. He ached in every muscle, but he was still human. He had won.

He looked up, expecting to face a she-wolf; instead, Mirren crouched as he did, looking at him. Her expression surprised him; he expected anger, and saw instead surprise and concern. "Why did you do it?" she asked, her voice husky.

"The bear," he said dully. "Couldn't you tell?"

She shook her head. "You were not changing."

He blinked. "Impossible—I felt it!"

"I cannot say what you felt, Beorn, only what I saw. You were no less or more than what you are now."

Beorn felt unaccountably angry. "You were somewhat occupied yourself—you could not have seen what was happening to me!"

Mirren shrugged. "Have it as you will."

"Why did *you* begin to change?"

She stared at him in surprise. "What are you talking about?"

He lurched to his feet. "That was why you wanted me, wasn't it? To try a perversion only two shapechangers could attempt!"

She looked shocked. "I would never dream of such a thing!"

"I don't believe you," he snarled, pulling on his clothes. Mirren began to dress also. "Beorn, are you mad? Even if I wanted it, how could a bear mount a wolf?" She came close to him, put a hand on his arm. "My lust for you had nothing to do with the beasts within us! I wanted *you;* I don't care about the bear—"

The thief pushed her away from him roughly; she staggered back and fell. "But *I* care!" he shouted.

He pulled the hatch open and left her final words behind him:

"Go, then! I hope the bear keeps you warm nights, for you'll never have anyone else who'll want to!"

Amber, descending the steps of the companionway, was nearly knocked over by the thief as he came storming up them. He stopped and glared at her like the bear that was his alter ego, his wide chest heaving with rage, and another emotion; after a second Amber realized it was shame. Both of them stood for a moment thus, framed by the narrow stairs. The only other person in the immediate vicinity, a young mariner swabbing that portion of the deck visible from the hatch, prudently took himself and his mop elsewhere.

Amber discovered that, to her surprise, she was not afraid. She faced the man who had stolen her lover's power, who had left her husband a helpless cripple, who had been responsible for her undergoing hardships and privations she had not known had existed before, and she was not afraid. Instead, she was angry. The anger came upon her suddenly, but nonetheless with a feeling of profound and absolute righteousness. It was nothing like the red rage that so obviously burned through his veins; this was a cold and implacable emotion, a buckler and sword if needed. It seemed to focus behind her eyes, burning brightly, fortifying her. "At last," she said. The timbre and words seemed to her to belong to some valiant heroine of a child's tale, rather than to her. But there is power within me, she told herself; as much as any legend's paragon. "You have much to answer for, thief," she said.

She saw him take a step back, and the blind fury in his eyes was dimmed—not by fear, but by astonishment. She realized he had not even recognized her before this point. He looked carefully at her, inspecting her, she knew, for some form of weapon. Then she saw the fury begin to well up within him again.

"Get out of my way," he growled, and raised an arm to push her aside. Amber made no movement or sound, but the thief did not lay a hand upon her. Puzzlement struggled with the anger within him; anger that Amber somehow knew had nothing to do with her.

For Beorn, the sudden appearance of the sorcerer's woman on the stairs had initially only intensified his hurt and rage toward

Mirren. He had not recognized her at first, had made no differentiation between her and Mirren; she was simply another representative of the sex that enticed him, brought out the beast in him in the worst, most literal way. He very nearly struck her, but the expression on her face had stopped him. She was not afraid of him, and the sheer surprise of that served to temper him. He was glad that it had; Jikran, the ship's captain, was willing to overlook much that happened aboard the *Elgrane* for the proper amount of crystals, but murder would be hard to explain, and harder to conceal. The thief gripped the companionway railing and took a deep, calming breath. He could not let his rage rule him; not now, not ever. He had to remain in control. He faced one of his enemies, and all enemies, regardless of appearance, must be considered dangerous. She had been resourceful enough to escape her bonds, after all. He doubted that she was an adept, for she had made no attempt at magic of which he knew. He had the upper hand; only by remaining calm would he keep it.

He said slowly, "You are a long way from Darkhaven, sorcerer's lady, and—"

"I am the Marquise Amber Jaodana Chuntai Lhil, you agrestic oaf!"

"—and Pandrogas is not at your side. You have pursued me; you must expect me to do what I can against you. Nevertheless, I have no quarrel with you."

"And what are your plans concerning me?"

"The *Elgrane* is bound for Cape Uloth; the captain has been paid to ferry you there and release you. I'll be getting off somewhat sooner. Until then, I will respect your privacy if you respect mine."

"Such a gentleman," Amber replied, surprising herself by the venom in her voice. "Your actions condemn the people of two fragments and perhaps more to destruction, and yet you see yourself as persecuted!"

She saw anger boiling up in him again. A voice far in the back of her mind warned her against antagonizing him too far. She could not depend upon her quixotic power; did not even know for certain if it existed.

"You had best hold your peace," Beorn said in a voice that was half growl. "I warn you, marquise—"

He was interrupted by a sudden thunderclap from above; he felt the companionway tremble slightly. The peal was followed immediately by another, louder one. A storm? the thief wondered. But there had not been a cloud in the sky when he had gone below. Then he heard shouts and a babble of excited conversation from above them. Footsteps pounded across the deck. He became aware of a change in the light about him; it seemed brighter, sharper. The marquise noticed it also; she glanced up.

He heard a sailor shout, "A second sun! A second sun!"

They climbed quickly out of the hatchway. Beorn blinked in the actinic glare. There was a strange, surrealistic aspect to the ship, and after an instant he identified it. The masts, the spars, the ropes and rigging, spikes, stanchions, and pins—everything, including the sailors and officers themselves, frozen in a skyward stare—everything had two shadows. And one set was moving, a thousand gnomons charting the mysterious sweep of light above them.

Beorn looked up, squinting. The sun was just above the horizon, as it had been for most of the commonday. But crossing the zenith was another sun, smaller but much brighter. It dropped quickly toward the horizon, leaving a trail of fire behind it that dazzled him. He closed his eyes, waiting for the luminous patterns to fade. Then there was another sound of thunder, this one much deeper and much louder; a long rumble, as if Rhynne itself had groaned. And simultaneously with the sound the *Elgrane* was struck by an angry giant. Beorn felt himself gripped in an invisible fist even larger and hotter than Balandrus's, and was lifted and hurled across the suddenly canted deck. He collided painfully with the bars of the gryphon's cage; an instant later Amber fell against him, knocking the breath from him. Almost unconscious, he nevertheless managed to grab a bar with one hand and her wrist with the other, as the deck tilted more and more. Above him he saw the sails bellied taut, as though in a stiff wind, though there was no wind. A tear split the length of the huge, triangular mainsail, and the relentless roll of the ship abated slightly. Faintly, through a ringing in his ears, he could hear screams and cries of pain. Then a wave broke over him and Amber; the *Elgrane* was taking on water. The deck began to settle, and another wave broke over the wale. Coughing to clear his lungs, the thief managed to scramble to his feet and to help Amber to hers. "What is it?" Though he screamed the words at her, he could barely hear himself. She looked at him blankly, and he realized she could hear no better than he; they had both been temporarily deafened. He saw a trickle of blood starting from one of her nostrils. She pointed toward where the ball of fire had fallen. The ship had settled sufficiently now to provide a view of the horizon. Beorn stared, feeling his insides turn to water. What he saw might have been the end of the world, had that not happened a millenium before.

Rising from the horizon, spreading out over them in the shape of a mushroom, was a gigantic column of steam and smoke. Flashes of fire played within its base, and lightning arced and crackled the length of it. The cloud atop it was rapidly covering the sky; already the sun was dimmed by fog.

The ship was rising and falling on long, high swells that rushed out from the pillar of destruction. A breeze began to blow toward the livid chaos, increasing quickly into a stiff wind. The opposition of wind and water whipped the waves into huge whitecaps. Already half full of water, the sails torn and several masts broken, the *Elgrane* took on more and more as the waves struck it broadside. Beorn saw Cardolus, standing upon the poop, washed overboard by a wall of water that passed completely over half the ship. Those few members of the crew still able to stand clung helplessly to ropes and spars, too stunned and terrified by this attack of the elements to do anything. The centaur hurled itself mindlessly against the bars of its cage, roaring in fear.

The roiling clouds settled down on the ship. Rain struck with a monsoon's fury, and Beorn shouted, more in shock and surprise than in pain as the wind-driven rain pelted him; the water was hot enough to sting his already reddened skin. The deck shifted beneath him again, and he realized that the *Elgrane* was sinking. Several sailors were trying to lift the longboat over the side; a wave crushed it against the hull, hurling it and most of the men into the foaming

sea. He saw the roof of Cardolus's wagon split open by a falling
yardarm. Have I come through so many trials and triumphs, he
wondered, only to drown without even knowing the cause of the
cataclysm? There was no escape; within moments the Ythan would
close over the broken masts.

Then, from the cage behind him, he heard the scream of the
gryphon.

For Amber, the remembrance was like a nightmare, fearfully
experienced and then forgotten, but called to mind with shattering
clarity by a chance word or occurrence the following day. She recalled approaching Rhynne in Pandrogas's dragonship during the
last hours of the long night, looking down at noctilucent Dulfar. In
the abyssal depths she had seen a streak of light, visible momentarily
against the dark surface below, and had asked Pandrogas what it
was. "Part of the decline," he had replied. "A fragment, perhaps no
larger than this ship, perhaps much larger, plunging so fast that the
air itself ignites it."

She had realized when the fire first crossed the sky what had
happened, but there had been no time to tell the thief, nor would
the telling have improved their chances of survival. Now, standing
in the maelstrom with him and hearing the gryphon shriek, she knew
that the winged beast represented their only course of escape. The
thief must have come to the same realization, for she saw him reach
for the latch and open the cage. The tilt of the deck swung the gate
back. The gryphon, fur and feathers soaked, still looked majestic.
It opened its beak, which was large enough to decapitate either of
them with a single snap, and made a sound that was half roar, half
screech. Then it lunged at the thief. The thief dodged with incredible
quickness for a man his size, but still the beak grazed him, hooking
for an instant in the rawhide thong that held his belt pouch and
tearing it free. The thief grabbed the pouch before it struck the deck.
The golden gaze of the gryphon threatened him. Amber felt a moment
of despair. How could they ride this savage creature to freedom?

She could think of only one thing to try. As she had done on the
rain-drenched roofscape of Darkhaven, months before, she put her

flute to her lips and began to play. She was not even sure what melody she produced; at any rate, her ears, still slightly deafened from the shock wave and the storm, could not make out much sound. But the gryphon turned toward her, and she could see the fire in its eyes dim slightly. She kept playing, one arm hooked through the bars to keep from being washed overboard. The thief, still holding his pouch in one hand, cautiously reached into the cage with the other and patted on the gryphon's neck, urging the beast gently toward him. The gryphon ruffled its feathers and lashed its tail slightly, but it stepped forward, out of the cage. The thief swung himself onto its broad back, ahead of the wings. He knotted the thong holding the pouch about his neck. "Come on!" he then shouted to Amber, extending one hand. She started forward, then was suddenly shoved aside. She fell to one knee, looked up and saw her assailant: a tall, dark-haired woman, lithe and muscular, pulling Ia with her as though the dryad were a recalcitrant child. The woman leaped toward the thief's outstretched hand. For an instant, it seemed to Amber as though the thief hesitated, was about to withdraw his hand; but before the woman could grasp it, another wave cascaded over the ship, washing both her and Ia overboard.

"No!" Amber screamed. She scrambled to her feet. The wave had also flooded through the broken roof of Cardolus's wagon, bursting open the door from within and washing out a potpourri of his belongings. Amber saw, wedged in the doorway, a glossy black log about four feet long. "Come on, marquise!" she heard the thief shout behind her. There was an ominous creaking sound all about her, and the deck seemed to drop beneath her feet. She saw that the prow had dipped beneath the waves. She took two steps, put both her hands against the log and pushed with all her might. It shifted, came free, and Amber barely avoided being struck by it as it rolled across the deck and into the sea.

The ship shifted again, and she stumbled backward. She fully expected to feel the sea receive her, but instead the thief's arm went about her, and he pulled her up behind him onto the gryphon's back. The huge wings spread, and the wind almost hurled them off of the deck and upward. Amber, looking down, got a single, lightning-bright glimpse of the *Elgrane* disappearing beneath the waves. Some distance away from it the dryad's wood floated. She thought she saw, clinging to it, two figures, one fair-haired, the other dark. Then the fog closed in beneath her.

For Beorn, it was a repetition of the madness he had endured when he had fallen from Darkhaven. He held to the gryphon's neck, and felt Amber's arms locked about him. The wind blew them toward the inferno; he could see it, ahead and below, a red glow in the fog. Then there was a wrenching blast of warm air from beneath them that hurled them upward. The gryphon shrieked, wings beating furiously in an attempt to stabilize itself. Beorn locked his legs about the feathered thorax. He felt the marquise's grip loosening and realized she was going to fall.

Amber, falling, reached out frantically. Her fingers found and seized the rawhide thong about the thief's neck. Then she slipped off the gryphon's back.

Beorn felt the thong snap. He saw the pouch containing the Runestone hover for an instant, just as Amber's hand, outstretched in desperation, also hung before him. He could save only one. There was no time to weigh the consequences. He reached, grabbed—and pulled Amber back to safety, while the Runestone disappeared into the ocean's fire.

BOOK III

Xoth

That we are capable only of being what
we are remains our unforgivable sin.

—Gene Wolfe,
The Book of the New Sun

Chapter 13

Graystar Isle

On a moucharaby woven by ivy to one of the many walls of Darkhaven, two figures stood. One was a man and one a woman, though their thin forms, clad in green livery, and their calm faces made one seem almost the doppelgänger of the other. They watched with little change of expression as the glittering city of Oljaer filled one side of the sky, close enough seemingly for them to reach out and pluck the weathervanes from the tallest spires, or to hurl bits of crumbling mortar from Darkhaven's towers into the river that divided the city. They could plainly see the animalcular inhabitants fleeing in panic. From the perspective of the two observers it was Oljaer that seemed to move, hurtling toward them; but the two servants knew that it was Darkhaven's route through the Abyss that had shifted, and which now spiraled closer and closer toward destruction.

The wind of the castle's swift passage plucked at Undya's robe; she huddled closer against the machicolations for protection. The fragment was not moving swiftly enough for friction to ignite its wood and stone, as she had heard had been the fate of some; not yet. Lambas, her companion, turned toward her, moving slowly; the particular aspect of the Runestone's magic that kept one's weight constant was also beginning to decay, and sudden movements could betray one's balance. "We have to do something," he said.

"There is only one thing that can be done," Undya replied, "and we have neither the power nor the right to do it. We are caretakers only. The power lies with Pandrogas, though he does not yet realize it."

"And if he does not realize it in time?" Lambas asked. "Is this how the centuries end?"

"You and I, of all people, should not fear death," Undya told him calmly. "One of us has gone already; I think that more will join him soon."

Lambas looked up. The two fragments were at their closest, and the landscape of Oljaer was spread before them like an infinitely detailed tapestry. Then it began to recede, slowly, almost reluctantly, as Darkhaven's speed once again overcame the pull of its neighbor. Lambas pointed toward a mote that hovered over the palace of Oljaer, growing steadily larger. "Another dragonship comes."

"And, as before, they will find nothing," Undya said. "Darkhaven could hide an army; it will hide us easily enough."

"Could we not meet them, tell them—"

"Tell them what? That their fate—and ours—lies in the hands of a sorcerer crippled by his humanity, blinded by his love, and the decision of a thief with the soul of a beast? That will be little comfort to them. We can only wait; and how can they do more than we?"

Lambas watched the approach of the Lord King's dragonship. Sunlight glinted on polished blades and helms. "I think," he said softly, "that Kabyn might have been the lucky one among us." He turned then and re-entered the cold maze of Darkhaven's corridors.

Undya stood for a moment longer, watching the fragment below recede for another, brief passage. Her eyes were bright with tears—from the wind, perhaps. She raised her hands, touching her index fingers and thumbs together for a moment. Then she turned and left sunlight for shadow.

On the fragment of Rhynne, in the Ythan Sea, a twisted and fluted spire of gray rock grew from the ocean's floor to rise above the waves. In one of the topmost of the many caverns and chambers that honeycombed the spire, Stonebrow had built his laboratory. He considered Graystar Isle an excellent retreat for a sorcerer, particularly a sorcerer embarked on so momentous a project. Here he was safe from the prying of curiosity seekers and would-be magicians seeking quick and easy knowledge. Here he had assembled a library that, though by no means as exhaustive as the miles of tome-laden shelves of Darkhaven, was nevertheless most impressive. He had managed to acquire over the years most of the texts penned by the Necromancer himself, which had been banned since the breaking of the world. And within their dry, dusty pages he had devoted himself for three commonyears to a search for the location of the Necromancer's tomb.

Stonebrow untangled his spectacles from the gray hair about his ears and wearily rubbed the pinched bridge of his nose. His skin felt as stiff and brittle as the stone mask he wore to disguise his identity, and from whence he had taken his pseudonym. He glanced at where it lay upon a nearby table. It had been no less than a gift from the One God; a vision had told him where to find it, in an ivy-choked temple on Aum. More than just a mask, it was also a talisman which greatly augmented his power. Without it, the speed and strength he had evidenced in the Dulfar tavern would have been utterly impossible; though as it was, Stonebrow thought wryly, he had paid sorely for even that small bit of theatrics. He rubbed his eyes. The Necromancer had unquestionably been a genius, standing to a sorcerer as a sorcerer stood to the most bumbling warlock or apprentice. Still, Stonebrow wished that the man's handwriting and indexing had been clearer; it was nearly impossible to make sense of the texts. But he believed he had determined beyond reasonable doubt that the latest Runestone brought to him by his agents, from the fragment Godspur, was not the one he sought. He stood, stretched, scratched a spot of flaking skin on his neck that had stubbornly resisted all cataplasms, cicatrizants, and catholicons known to him, and carefully placed the Runestone in the bottom of a nearby crucible. Into this he poured a measure of treated hydrargyrum. *"Ladmandium diris,"* he said, and made a sign; the liquid metal immediately began to boil. "Seek your rightful place," Stonebrow said in Payan, carefully shielding his eyes. There was a brilliant yellow flash, a sound like a hive struck with a stick, and a stench of ozone; when he looked again, the crucible was empty. Stonebrow nodded thoughtfully and crossed to a window, an irregular crack in the stone spire through which he could see the ocean. The tranquil beauty of a sunlit sea never failed to soothe him. At times he could see whales spouting, or porpoises and selchies at play. The salt breeze was rejuvenating.

He sighed. If only travel from fragment to fragment were like apporting Runestones; a spell as easy as triggering a crossbow. Instead his agents had to move at the sluggish pace of a dragonship's sails. At this rate it would take years to test each Runestone. And, though he returned them immediately to the fragments they supported, there was still the possibility that the long and often circuitous route the Stones took to reach Graystar Isle might result in the collision of one fragment with another. It had already happened more than once, though how many cataclysms had been due directly to the Circle's theft of Runestones, and how many to the general decay of the ectenic force itself, he was not sure. He regretted the possibility of innocent people dying, though he knew that mass destruction would be inevitable once the process of re-formation was started. All the more reason to avoid as many deaths now as possible; the One God deserved more than a world empty of worshipers. It was a funambulatory effort, for at times he had to deal harshly with those who served him. He thought of the ectomorphic thief who had attempted to trick him. The irony was that the nameless Runestone Kustin had tried to foist upon Stonebrow might well have been the right one. But he could not allow duplicity to go unpunished. He had to maintain fear and respect. A pity there were so few acolytes he trusted. The thought brought to mind Ardatha, the enchantress of Oljaer, she whom others called Ardatha Demonhand. There was a woman the One God smiled upon, and no mistake. She was driven with fine fervor and zeal. He wondered if she felt the weariness that he occasionally experienced, wondered if she at times questioned— only momentarily, of course, and with great trepidation—the righteousness of their cause.

Stonebrow pushed the thought aside. This was weakness; worse, it was blasphemy. The One God had turned His face from the world when man's knowledge broke it apart—it was only right and fitting that the same knowledge bring it together again.

His research and studies had lately indicated a likely location for the tomb: a small fragment in a far orbit called simply Nigromancien, an archaic term for Necromancer. Assiduous study of the complicated charts and orreries involved in navigating the world's remains had given him a route to it that would be viable for at least a commonmonth. He was seriously tempted to investigate the fragment himself instead of assigning it to one of his aides, though the journey would require well over a commonweek. But he still did not have the Runestone that was the key to the tomb. According to the *Scroll of Dust,* only one of the thousands of Runestones contained the power to revivify the Necromancer's corpse, to make his knowledge once again available.

Stonebrow took a deep breath and looked at the sky. The sun was finally above the horizon, and the air was warming, but still he felt cold. He took from a driftwood cabinet a sphere carved of interlocking pieces of coral. He fixed his mind upon the uneasiness that had plagued him since rising, and dropped the sphere onto the table.

The configuration's translation was not one he recalled offhand; he was forced to consult *The Book of Stones.* "One journey ends where another begins," he read. "Seek knowledge at its heart." Stonebrow pursed his lips in annoyance. The oracle was all too often vague to the point of incomprehensibility; the reading could mean anything. It did not seem a dire portent, and yet he could not rid himself of the suspicion that something was about to happen.

It was then that he heard thunder. A second, louder rumbling followed the first, and his insides seemed to reverberate in time with it. He crossed quickly to the window. Before he reached it, he had to squint against the sudden glare. He stood quite still, watching the descent of the fireball. Oddly, the only thought that occurred to him as he watched it fall was whether children had once played on its green hills. He had the presence of mind to close his eyes before it struck; even against his closed lids, the light was dazzling. He stared in awe for a moment as the roiling cloud climbed toward the sun, then he turned and quickly gathered his navigational charts, his mask, and the *Scroll of Dust,* which contained the quickening spell that might revive the Necromancer, should Nigromancien indeed be his tomb. He wondered why he bothered; without the particular Rune-stone needed as catalyst, it was all futile. Still, he could do no more than try. The One God expected no less from him. It was his duty to aid however he could in returning the world to a state of grace, no matter what the cost.

He marked the place in the ancient volume he had been studying at the mention of Nigromancien; there was always the possibility that another of the Circle might somehow find it. Then he sealed it within a protective spell and hurried from the room.

As he climbed the winding, rough-hewn steps he felt Graystar shake slightly about him. At the same time, he could hear a rising wind outside. For the first time in years he thought of games he had played as a child; particularly of dropping stones in water to watch the splash and the ripples that spread out in concentric circles. What sort of waves might not result from such a stone as this one? They could quite possibly drag Graystar down.

It took him almost fifteen minutes to reach the apex of the spire, and by then he was breathing raggedly. There was a pain in his chest that alarmed him slightly. He was no longer a young man, and even the magic of the mask could only do so much for him. He looked about as he caught his breath. Damp, ill-smelling straw was scattered about the floor of the chamber he entered. The walls and floor were pitted and scarred. Already fog and warm rain obscured the room, which was open on the side facing the disaster. A warning hiss sounded over the sound of the storm; two lambent eyes regarded him through the fog. Stonebrow stepped forward, one slipper crunch-ing a fish skeleton. His cockatrice, at best a sullen beast, was ob-viously put out of sorts by the sudden storm and the temblors. Stonebrow quickly chanted the incantation known as Armor of Light; no sooner had he done so than the cockatrice reared its wattled head and spat a stream of acid at him. The corrosive liquid struck the nimbus surrounding the sorcerer and boiled away into steam, save for a few drops which left smoking pits in the rock floor. "Dung-bred creature!" Stonebrow muttered, and spoke a calming mesmerism. He dismissed the protective spell and strapped a saddle about the now quiescent winged serpent, which was twice the size of a python, then dumped the few belongings he was taking in a saddlebag. At this point Graystar shook again, harder this time. With a groan, Stonebrow mounted his steed, then looked toward the area of the aerolith's strike.

What he saw took his breath away; a wall of water easily half the height of Graystar was even now rising up before the spire. It had arrived sooner than he expected. A word of command to the enspelled cockatrice caused the beast to coil and then hurl itself from the chamber, spreading its wings and catching the wind, which hurled it forward with a burst of speed that made Stonebrow's neck crack painfully. Behind him he heard the crashing inundation as the wave struck. He could glimpse below him, through a break in the mist, another, even larger wave following it. He tried to see what damage had been done, but the fog and steam had already hidden the isle from view. His home, if not already broken and gone, would surely be so soon. He felt no regrets for its loss; though he had the soul of an eremite, he had never been particularly territorial in nature. The setback in his quest to find the Necromancer's tomb and perform the One God's work disturbed him far more. It is in His hands, Stonebrow told himself, attempting to be as serene as possible under the circumstances. I will find another sanctuary, and continue my work.

The cockatrice was moving along the edge of the cloud, which still rose from the boiling ocean. Stonebrow was about to urge the beast upward, as to drop any lower would be to risk injury from the steam and heat. But at that point he sensed something—a concentration of ectenic power, below him. His long work with Runestones had sensitized him to their subtle ethereal vibrations, and he knew without a doubt that a stone of great power lay at the bottom of the Ythan. Without a moment's hesitation the leader of the Circle urged the cockatrice downward into the maelstrom. Hot wind and rain lashed at him; he held grimly on to the barrel-sized neck of the serpent. There was no time to formulate a protective cant for him and his steed; all of his power was needed to find the Runestone. The steam was almost unbearable now. Through gritted teeth, Stonebrow recited an attrahent. He held the cockatrice in a tight circle above the power locus, despite the creature's hissing objections; its trance was beginning to wear thin, and he could not spare the concentration to renew it. Then, from the clouds below him, a small black object shot upward; he reached out his hand and felt it smack his palm. Another moment and it was in his saddlebag.

"Upward!" Stonebrow shouted to the cockatrice, and the reptile hurled itself toward the cooling atmosphere beyond the clouds. Stonebrow held on, eyes closed, feeling the rush of air in his hair and beard. The One God be praised, he thought. There could be no doubt of it; this was the Runestone for which he had been searching these three long years. There was no need to apply the determining thaumaturgies he had learned. The power within this Runestone dwarfed all others he had seen, even those of fragments like Rhynne or Typeror. He had found the key to the Necromancer's tomb—and a new age was now begun.

Chapter 14

Aboard the Dark Horizon

Amber stared into the gray cloud through which the gryphon flew. They were beyond the wind and rain, but the fog apparently went on forever. It was as though they were the only motes of life in the vast, azoic nothingness that had existed before the world was formed. The setting matched the bleakness she felt. The Runestone was gone. The struggles that Pandrogas and she had gone through had been in vain; Darkhaven would fall, and it would only be the first of many. She had wanted to wrest the sorcerer from those endless corridors and chambers, but not at this cost. Whereas before she had looked upon the quest primarily as a means to escape the castle, she now realized what the loss of the Runestone meant, both to the inhabitants of Darkhaven and Oljaer, and, in a larger sense, to the world. She hoped that Kabyn, Undya, and the others would be able to escape, and that they would take Tahrynyar with them. She felt guilty when she realized how little she had thought of her husband over the past few days.

A tear fell from her cheek into the void, to mingle with the

211

uncounted raindrops so far below. When she had been a young girl, she had thought of the rain as the tears of sky-dwelling spirits, shed in noble grief over the imperfections and sufferings of humanity. Now she knew better; tears, no matter where or how they fell, came only from flawed and miserable people like herself, in response to the vicissitudes of a life of which they had no understanding or control.

Her arms were clasped about the waist of the thief, who sat before her on the gryphon's back. She had no idea how to feel about him at this point. He had chosen to save her over the Runestone. She might tell herself that logic dictated it be saved over her; the lives of so many depended on it, and that far outweighed her right to live. But she was still glad to be alive, and glad the thief had grabbed her instead of the Runestone.

She had no idea what the future held now, nor could she force herself to be overly interested in it. She tried to tell herself that there was hope while life persisted, but she could find no hope within her. Where was her sporadic power when she needed it? Why could she not have arrested the Runestone in its fall? As well ask why she could not have stopped the hurtling fragment that had plunged, white-hot, into the ocean.

She bowed her head against the thief's broad back, and felt the tears start again. The world was quite literally falling apart, and there was nothing that she, or anyone, could do to stop it.

There was no similar conflict of emotions raging within the thief; all he felt was anger, both at himself and at the woman clinging to him. After all the hardships and narrow escapes, he had *thrown the Runestone away* in favor of saving one of his enemies! Beorn remembered it very clearly; the Runestone hovering before him, and Amber as well, her terrified gaze locking with his, the moment frozen in time. He had not thought; he had simply acted.

Suchana, Suchana, he thought; do you twist and turn in your coffin at my choice? Do I hear ghostly vilification from every thief who ever lived? There is no more question; I have lost whatever skill I once had. I am a thief no longer; I am not even a man. I am only a fool, flying through a fog no less dense than my own stupidity.

He had to make a decision about their destination; at this point the gryphon was merely flying aimlessly. They were no longer within Rhynne's field of attraction; still, the enormous wings would tire eventually. His best choice would be to make for nearby Handula, but to do that he had to escape the mist. He pressed his knees into the feathered neck before him, urging the beast upward, expecting it to turn and pluck him from his precarious seating and hurl him into the clouds; He was not sure if he would regret the action. But the gryphon responded to the command, surging upward. For several long moments there was no change in the uniform grayness about them; then it began to lighten ever so slightly.

But one patch of darkness beneath them seemed to be growing instead of fading. At first only an irregular blotch, it was now taking on a definite shape. Beorn heard the marquise gasp as she recognized it at the same time that he did. He slapped the gryphon's furred hindquarters in a vain attempt to elicit more speed. But it was no use; behind them, breaking through the fog, the grim skulled prow of a huge dragonship appeared. Beorn could hear snatches of commands and excited shouts from aboard the craft, and caught glimpses of silhouettes dashing about the decks as the ship rose parallel to them. "Look out!" Amber cried. Beorn saw a whirling network of black lines gyring toward them. Before either he or Amber could move, the net was about both them and the gryphon, entangling them. The gryphon shrieked as its wings thrashed against the heavy ropes. Beorn hung on to the ropes. He felt their drifting arrested with a jolt as the net's line came taut, and he could clearly hear the creak of the capstan as they were hauled in like a catch of fish. The gryphon's wings battered him; he felt a line of pain drawn down one leg as a hind claw's talon scratched it during the angry creature's struggle. Then the huge beak slashed through the ropes like a sword through a spiderweb, and the gryphon was free. In an instant it had vanished into the mist, leaving behind only a fading roar of triumph.

Hands grabbed the net, tugging it roughly; Beorn felt his weight return as he was tumbled onto a cold, damp surface. He was seized and pulled to his feet. He looked about the wide deck, which gleamed, ghost-white, in the fog. The crew surrounded them, wearing belts, boots, gambesons, and breeks of tanned dragon leather. Beorn saw the giant crossbow cannons, with stacks of ivory harpoons beside them. He and the marquise had fled one ship, only to be picked up by another—but this ship sailed the infinite ocean of the Abyss, its purpose a far more bloody one than mercature. They had been captured by dragoneers.

Amber had heard legends all her life of the dragoneers, those magnificent sailors of the sky who stalked the mightiest of all beasts. She looked about her in astonishment. All dragonships were constructed primarily from the bodies of dragons; for some reason she did not understand, the magic behind the ships' Runestones demanded it. But dragoneers carried this necessity to an extreme; it was a source of pride to them that everything, from the smallest needle to the largest mast, from the cutlery to the harpoons, from the hammocks to the sails, were constructed of the relics of their quarry. Looking about her now, she saw that this certainly appeared to be so. The deck she stood upon was shellacked bone, planed and jointed, as were the bulwarks and the wales; everywhere she looked, the creamy color of bone and ivory seemed to glow with a numinous light, which, together with the gray mist, gave the impression of a ghost ship. The masts were formed of vertebrae; Amber watched them give slightly as the sails filled and slackened. The sails themselves were a rich brown, patched and stitched; she assumed that they were leather.

She had time to observe all this only for a moment, before she was abruptly aware that this spectre vessel was hardly crewed by revenants. They gathered about the thief and her, and most of their comments seemed to concern her beauty and the lack of same during a long voyage in the Abyss. Suddenly, from behind her, she felt two rough hands grab her buttocks and squeeze. She jerked free and spun about with a cry of outrage, to see several men laughing. She looked at the thief—he gazed back at her levelly. He showed no amusement at her violation, but neither did he make any offer of aid. One of the dragoneers, somewhat bolder than the rest, stepped

forward, speaking in heavily accented Perese. "Here be as fine a
catch as ever I've seen in the net!" He thrust his pelvis forward in
exaggerated rutting, driving Amber back before him. Another seized
her arms from behind and held her, laughing, while she twisted and
struggled futilely to free herself. The first dragoneer strutted up to
her, posturing for the amusement of his comrades. He was close
enough for Amber to smell his rum-scented breath, when suddenly
a long poleaxe shot into her vision, the hook slipping neatly about
her tormentor's arm. He was jerked off balance and sent staggering
into a pile of rigging, to the laughter of the rest of the crew. He
came to his feet livid and cursing, holding a kris he had pulled from
his belt. "Come ahead, then!" he shouted, looking about for the one
responsible. "I'll split ye from baldric to buskin, whoever ye be; I'll
flense ye like—"

"Ye'll crawl back below, Grycikul, and be happy doing it," a
cool female voice to Amber's left said. The speaker stepped into
her view—a wide, solidly built woman, still holding the poleaxe.
She was dressed like the others, in dragon leather. She shot a glare
at the one holding Amber, and the marquise was immediately released. Amber rubbed her arms, looking at the female dragoneer in
grateful amazement.

Grycikul hastily thrust the kris back into his belt. "A bit of fun,
was all, Cap'n," he mumbled.

"Have your fun with yourself; they tell me ye're best at that,"
and a shout of glee rose from the crew at the barb. Grycikul slunk
away aft, into the mist.

The woman he had named captain turned toward Amber and the
thief. Though she had saved the marquise from harassment and
probably worse, there was no sign of friendliness in her face. "I'll
be naught but honest," she said. "We flung the net more for the
lionhawk than for its riders; though we be dragoneers, we're not
adverse to making a profit from other types of beasts. But here ye
be now, so welcome aboard the *Dark Horizon*. My name is Asran;
I be captain."

"I be the Marquise Amber Jaodana Chuntai Lhil," she replied,
speaking quickly before the thief could, fearing he might revile or

reject her, "and this be Beorn, a gentleman of Aëslovèclan. We barely escaped when our ship was capsized by the waves from a fragment's strike on the Ythan Sea, the smoke and steam of which still surrounds us."

An excited babble broke out at this, which Asran stilled with a wave of her hand. "The watch did speak of this," she said slowly; "of a gout of fire bigger than the flame of the largest skyworm ever that lived. But only he saw it; all seemed well to us ere we drew nigh the edge of Rhynne to take on supplies. Then came this damned fog." She turned to the crew. "Well, then, looks like it's hardtack and salt meat a while longer, lads! I'll not risk the flame oil and ivory already in our hold for a few days of fresh chowder! Back to the sun and the Abyss, and the work we do best!"

There was lukewarm agreement to this as the crew returned to their duties. Asran turned back to Amber, looking at her while she spoke to both of them. "What's to be done with the two of ye, then?"

"I can pay for my passage to Handula," Beorn said. "I cannot speak for the marquise."

"Payment or nay," Asran said, "such a sidejaunt would take too much time from my schedule. I have a quota to fill for my employers on Xhrann, and I must be prompt, or lose the commission. 'Twould appear the both of ye have signed for a dragon-hunt."

"Consider, Captain," Amber said, choosing her words carefully. "What possible aid could I be to a dragon-hunt? I will gladly work for my passage to the nearest fragment, but—"

"Ye will work, as ye say," Asran replied. "There is neither room nor food for shirkers, and while we be not barbarians who would hurl ye overboard, still, accidents can happen. Ean will see ye squared away." She gestured toward a small, copper-skinned lad who watched them from behind a water butt. He hurried forward; his eyes, large and of an almost luminous violet, regarded Amber with awe. Asran turned away, but the thief's voice stopped her. "Captain," he said, his voice friendly, almost suave, "might I ask how long we can expect this voyage to last?"

"Until we find one last skyworm. Near nine commonmonths it's taken to scare up the two now cut and dried in the holds. Find and kill us a dragon, my fine gentleman and lady, and we'll turn our prow toward port again. Until then, we roam the Abyss," and, so saying, Asran turned and left them.

The boy, a tatterdemalion who barely came to Amber's waist, touched her fingers hesitantly. "Come along, mesire and madam," he said. His voice was a hoarse whisper, as though a rusted hinge had spoken. Amber looked down at him and caught her breath at the sight of a large scar, pink against his tanned skin, that crossed his throat. She glanced at Beorn, and saw that the thief had noticed it too. She followed the cabin boy, feeling suddenly completely exhausted. All she hoped for was a quiet corner with some straw for bedding, where she could curl up and, at least for a time, find escape in sleep from the relentless world.

Beorn had given up, for the time, trying to analyze his own actions. Though he told himself repeatedly that he did not care what misfortunes befell the marquise—would, in fact, like nothing better than to see her suffer to a degree commensurate with the trouble she had caused him—still, after they had both been fed meager rations of dragon jerky and dried citrons, and he had received a poultice for the scratch on his leg, he had watched her collapse, exhausted, in a hammock slung beneath the lashed bones that supported the quarterdeck, and had stretched himself out on a woven mat beneath her. He told himself that his choice of repose was not so that she could sleep protected; he was tired as well, that was all. But he did not sleep; instead, he lay there, hands clasped behind his head, staring up into the darkness that was almost complete, so carefully had the skeletal planks been fitted. Amber had said that the maelstrom had been caused by a falling fragment, fired by its passage through the air as one's hands could be scorched by sliding down a rope. Had he been given a graphic re-creation of how Darkhaven would come to its end—assuming it had not already done so? Was this the disaster of which he was the cause? He tried not to think about it. Nothing could be done about it now, after all. He wondered if Mirren had survived the deluge of waves and rain. He tried to enjoy the memory of her clinging desperately to the log, tossed by the whitecaps, but satisfaction would not come. Instead he remembered the panic on her face as she had reached for his hand, begging with her eyes to be saved.

Had the werewolf been right? he wondered. Had he really only imagined the bear's onslaught—was he that terrified of intimacy with anyone? Such a fantasy had never occurred during his beddings with Suchana, or with the few other women he had been with. Because you had never granted yourself release, he told himself— never, since the first time.

He looked upward at the outline of the hammock. One of Amber's hands hung over the edge; he thought of feeling that smooth, cool hand caressing his cheek. He thought of seeing the marquise on her back beneath him, her breasts against his chest, feeling her hips moving against his, her legs locked about his waist. He undid buttons surreptitiously, glancing about to make sure no sailors were within view, feeling faintly amused at his adolescent paranoia. He masturbated, keeping his gaze fixed on that dangling hand, imagined Amber rising against him, eyes closed in pleasure. Then, with an inevitability provided by years of fear, he imagined her eyes opening wide, saw her stare at him in disbelieving horror, saw her face blur and begin to lose its sharpness, its color, as she screamed, and screamed, and—

He groaned, rolling over on the rough matting. At least this was safe—but not satisfying. The tension that was always a part of him was still there; it would always be there. At times he felt that he was only a pseudomorph; that the bear was the reality. Was he a man who became a bear or a bear that, at times, assumed the guise of a man?

Amber awoke to the sound of a groan; she sat up quickly, forgetting that she was in a hammock. She fell squarely on top of someone, knocking the wind from both of them. A moment of thrashing limbs and confused sounds, and then she felt herself seized in an iron grasp by her wrists and pulled roughly upright.

She recognized the silhouette of the thief before her. "It's all right!" she gasped. The thief hesitated for a moment, then released her with a growl. "Can't you do anything right?" he asked her; "even sleep?"

"You woke me. Were you having a nightmare?"

He rubbed his face with the back of one hand; she was struck by the bearishness of the gesture. "I think so."

She smiled despite herself; at least it was not another emergency. "We have enough nightmares to contend with, without inventing more of them." He did not reply to that. After a moment Amber said, "What will happen to us?"

The thief shrugged. "I will be a dragoneer until the *Dark Horizon* makes port. After which I shall return to being a thief. I do not know what will happen to you, marquise; nor do I care."

The remark stung her. "Fair enough. And I suppose you would tell me there is no hope of escape?"

"I would think you smart enough not to have to ask the question."

She asked, "Why did you steal the Runestone?"

At first she thought he was not going to answer her. The only sounds were the hollow thump of dragoneers' feet on the deck above them, the creaking of the sails and rigging as they responded to the wind, and the shouts of the mate giving orders. Then the thief said, "For money, of course. Why else?"

"Why else, indeed? Perhaps to cure your animal self?"

He swung quickly toward her; she gasped involuntarily and drew back. She could not see the expression on his face, and was glad of it. But he made no threatening motion; he merely stared at her. It occurred to her that they were both in the dark; she was as much an enigma to him as he was to her. "I could have killed you," he said at last. "If you push me, perhaps I still will."

"Then I'm right. You thought the power within the Runestone would rid you of the bear."

"Are you telling me it would not have?"

"I don't know. There are no rings on my fingers."

Beorn looked away again, staring into the darkness of the hold. He remembered how he had felt standing at the edge of the storm that had raged about Darkhaven, exhausted and wounded, ready to give up his prize to the sorcerer and this woman. It seemed an eternity ago. He had wanted then to tell her how it felt to have the bear always looming over him, the prospect of the pain increasing as he grew older, the ever-present fear of being overwhelmed by the beast. He wanted now to explain the dull, continuous ache of always being alone, of moving through the world silent and apart, self-contained, supremely skilled at staying alive but with no knowledge at all of how to live. "I'm a thief," was all he said.

Amber nodded. I blamed him for destroying my life, she thought; but in truth, I am more responsible than he. It has been my decision from the start to be affected by his actions; I put myself in the path of the bear. "Tell me," she said, "about being a thief."

And Beorn, having ceased now to even wonder anymore at his actions, spoke of his career. He told her of his apprenticeship on Thieves' Island in Bagerah; of the arduous physical and mental training he had begun as a youth and continued all his life. How he had developed his senses, achieving excellent night vision (How well can he see me now? Amber wondered), hearing acute enough to count the people in a room by their breathing and the rustling of their garments, and a sense of smell that, while not the equal of the bear's, could still let him remember and identify someone by their pomade. He could walk a branch blindfolded, and his toes were dexterous enough to tie knots in ropes. He spoke of the various tricks and tools of his trade; how powdered mela leaves, cast into bushes, will keep crickets chirping while one moves through shrubbery; that the best time for robbery is between midnight and dawn; that dark-seed oil will let a knife slide silently from a sheathe, and keep mail and leather from creaking while one walks. He told her how Suchana would at times deliberately complicate jobs for him to test his quick-wittedness, and how the two of them had planned to retire with stolen wealth to Tamboriyon. He described some of his greatest depredations, such as the stealing of the Frozen Flame from the lava-encysted ruins of Kommorian in the Crimson Desert, which was guarded by packs of fierce cynolycus, and how he and his team of accomplices breached the strongroom of Jitu Tyk, which lay at the center of a pyramid constructed beneath the waters of a loch. He spoke until his voice began to pain his throat, and not once did he mention those things he most wanted to speak of: loneliness and fear, and his increasing desire to warm her body with his.

And Amber, in spite of her anger toward him, was intrigued by the tales. They were endlessly fascinating in their wealth of lore and their adventure and intrigue, though his attempts to justify them only increased her contempt for him. "You think me, perhaps, merely a conscienceless blackguard," he told her at one point. "But I have my code, marquise, even as you have yours. I would not rob from anyone who had less than I, or from one disabled in any way. Though some have argued that it is only robbery of a different sort, still I would not stoop to kidnapping—"

"Yes," Amber interrupted sarcastically, "you obviously sensed my desire for a long sea voyage."

The thief paused, then continued: "Unless my enemies leave me no choice."

"What a convenient set of morals you possess, thief! They adapt themselves to every circumstance! Still, I suppose one could expect no less from a chameleon such as you."

She saw his shadowy hands tighten for a moment into fists, and cautioned herself against pushing him too far. But she was determined to try to force some realization of his crimes into his awareness, though she knew it was futile.

Beorn continued: "I have never killed, as man or as bear."

"You do not know this. My husband was disabled by your bestial counterpart. He may have died by now. Or shall you amend that code to say, 'I have never killed that I know of'?"

She had thought he would protest, threaten, perhaps even strike her; she was prepared for that. She was not prepared to hear him say, in a quiet, almost plaintive tone, "Please don't." Surprised, she was silent, and he continued: "Try to understand me. What I have done to you and yours, I have done not so much out of greed as out of desperation. The bear . . ." He hesitated, and Amber realized that she was at last seeing the thief as close to honesty as she likely ever would. "I fear the bear," he said at last; the words came in a rush. "I must grant it freedom every so often, or it will take it from me; and the longer it holds sway, the stronger it becomes. I dread the possibility of its dominance. Someday I may forget that a man lives within the bear, and then that man will be lost—don't you see?"

She nodded, slowly. "How long has this werecurse afflicted you?"

"Since I was thirteen. I was—" Amber heard a gasp that sounded like a harsh sob. "They thought I could make some money, you see. They paid a conjurer for the spell, and planned to take me to Denslèven to show me at the fair. But I couldn't change—not at first..."

"Who?" Amber asked quietly. "Who bought the spell, Beorn?"

She could see the outline of his shoulders shudder. His reply was almost too low for her to catch. "My parents."

After a long moment of silence he sighed and said, "When I could not change to a young bear upon their command, they beat me. I ran away. I lived for a time by stealing from the neighboring farms, and off of the generosity of my friends. One of them, a girl—Jatta was her name—took pity on me and one day gave me more than food. It was my first time with a woman. It was also the first time I became the bear."

"Did you kill her?" Amber held her breath.

"I told you I have never killed. She was hurt—I did not know what was happening, and I clung to her—my claws scratched her. She ran away, screaming. Still the bear, I fled back to my parents. My father was chopping wood by the cabin door, feeding a fire which my mother would use, I imagine, in making soap or dye." He gave a sharp, bitter bark of laughter. "I suppose he did not recognize his son, and thought instead that I was a real bear bent on attack. Here," and he pulled his tunic open, seized Amber's hand and guided it to his flesh before she could object. She felt a scar on the long muscle covering his ribs. "The mark of his axe. My father ran inside and barred the door as I stumbled against the cauldron, spilling it and scattering the brands. The grass against the cabin wall was dry—it caught." He took a deep breath. "They did not realize the cabin was on fire until it was too late. They were afraid, you see—afraid of me. I tried to warn them, but my voice was that of the bear..."

He bowed his head, and Amber impulsively put her hands on his shoulders. The touch galvanized him; he put his arms about her, pulled her into an embrace. She pushed against his chest, with no more luck than if she had resisted the bear. He kissed her; it was gentler than she had expected, but there was no gentleness in his grip. She swung her two open palms against his ears, causing him to release her and rock back on his heels with a howl of pain. For a moment, Amber thought he would attack her again.

He did not. The *Dark Horizon* had evidently finally crested the cloud, for more light now gleamed through the interstices of the hide and bone boundaries of the hold. By it, Amber could see Beorn looking at her reproachfully, almost like a child who has been punished without knowing why. "Nothing will happen," he said softly. "I promise you, Amber..."

There was such a yearning in his voice and eyes that she looked away. "I do not fear the bear, Beorn," she said. "Nor do I fear you. I sympathize. I have not lived a life without love, but I have returned little, I think, of what I have received. I sympathize, but I cannot bed with you."

"Say rather 'will not,'" he replied bitterly. "I have opened my soul to you!"

"And so I must open my legs for you?" She thought briefly of how at one time such a statement would have made her blush. "I fail to see how this follows. I offer you this: that we are no longer enemies, unless you must have it as such. But neither are we friends, and we are certainly not lovers. At most we are allies, until the *Dark Horizon* returns to land. I will help you, if you will help me. But do not lay hands on me again." She stood, as did he, and he gave her a look of such hatred that she wondered that her face did not chap as in a hot wind.

"And if I do?" he asked, his voice almost a snarl. "If I take you now? What will happen?"

"I don't know," Amber replied. "I honestly don't know. And I fear the learning."

A chorus of shouts and the cadence of running feet above them caused them both to glance upward. Whatever the thief's reply to her would have been she was not to know, for the next voice that spoke was not Beorn's but that of Ean, the cabin boy. The lad came clattering down the scuttle and raced across the hold to them, breath-less with excitement. "Fire in the sky! Fire in the sky!" he shouted. "All hands topside, quick!" He left as quickly as he came.

Confused, Amber looked at Beorn. "What does he mean?"

His tone was surly as he brushed past her. "He means we're about to earn our keep, marquise. They've raised a dragon."

Chapter 15

The Land of Night

In a land of eternal darkness, four people crouched shivering beneath the umbrella of a giant toadstool. All about them rose a profusion of twisted, mottled fungi, far exceeding in size the familiar mushrooms and toadstools on those shards where humanity dwelt. In the distance could be heard the flap of wings, and dark shapes could be seen dimly through the clouds and mist overhead. The refugees could not make a fire; there was nothing in the mycetoid forest that would burn naturally, and they dared not use magic. They could only hide, and await the inevitability of capture.

Pandrogas huddled into himself for warmth, knees pulled close to his chest, breathing shallowly to minimize the pain in his side. How long they had hidden thus, he could not say. There was no cycle of day and night here; the fragment moved perennially in the shadow of another. The air was damp, with a chill breeze constantly blowing. He felt he might have been here for a commonday; it seemed a commonmonth or more.

When he had felt Sestihaculas's spell enveloping him and the others, he had used the last of his strength in an attempt to disrupt it. He had been only partially successful; instead of appearing before the Demogorgon, they had materialized deep within the mushroom forest. At Ardatha's suggestion she and Pandrogas had combined their waning strength to perform Eiton's Cloak. It had worked, at least so far; the shielding spell kept the Chthons' magic from finding them, as long as they used no magic themselves. But nothing could protect them from the more conventional means of detection, and so they cowered beneath the bloated stalks and caps as cacodemons prowled the sky.

Though the forest was silent, it was not still; rather, it was a nidus of abhorrent life. The sorcerer watched a slug longer than his leg making its way slowly across a lichen-covered rock, leaving a trail of phosphorescent slime. Huge insects flitted or crawled everywhere; Pandrogas recoiled in disgust as a fly as large as his fist hovered suddenly before him, inspecting him with faceted eyes the color of verdigris. The air reeked of decay and corruption. Worst of all was the certainty of no escape. They were on Xoth, a name synonymous with hell.

The sound of the cacodemons' wings faded. Tahrynyar rose, keeping close to the stalk to avoid the fetid water dripping from the cap. He said to Pandrogas in a low voice, "Would I had the power of the Necromancer, that I might kill you slowly for each of your crimes, and revive you to suffer still another death. You brought us here, and I will see that you pay for it."

"He did not bring us here," Ardatha said wearily, much to Pandrogas's surprise. "If any one of us is to be blamed, it must be I." She looked at her claw. "In my fear that Pandrogas would escape, I dared to use for the first time all the power latent within Sestihaculas's gift. He sensed it, and came for us."

"For just such a contingency as this he gave you that gift, years before," Pandrogas said. "It is the sort of deviousness the Lord of Snakes delights in."

"I still blame you!" Tahrynyar said. "For everything!"

"So you have managed to make abundantly clear," the sorcerer said wearily. The marquis lurched toward him, boots splashing slime, but Kan Konar, standing to one side, seized him by the collar. "Keep quiet!" he growled. "A cacodemon can hear a baby's wail the length of a fragment."

"The cloakfighter is right," Ardatha said. "Survival is the game now."

"He has no right to survive, and I have every right to kill him!"

"Even wounded and exhausted as he is, he is still more than a match for you," said the enchantress. "Of the two, you are by far the most expendable, marquis. Do I make myself clear? Leave off your thoughts of revenge."

Tahrynyar jerked away. He stood with his back to them, staring moodily out at the fungaceous landscape.

"We are enemies, Pandrogas," Ardatha said after a moment's silence. "Yet you must believe I had no desire to deliver you to Sestihaculas, and still less desire to accompany you. I fear the Demogorgon more than most folk. Though we were at odds in our quest for Darkhaven's Runestone, we must now aid each other, I think. I have never heard of it being done, but still, a sorcerer and an enchantress might be able to escape Xoth."

"We cannot bind a cacodemon to our service here," Pandrogas said. "There is only one possibility. Dragoneers, venturing near in their hunts, have noted that Xoth's orbit is shifting, as are those of the other fragments. No longer is it shielded completely from the sun—one edge now lies in light. The dragoneers call it the Cliffs of the Sun. If we could reach this sanctuary—"

"The sun would shield us from the attacks of the Chthons and their minions! But we would still be trapped on Xoth."

"It is also said that dragons have been laying their eggs to hatch in the sunlight. I know a sorcerer who rides a cockatrice. It should be possible to enspell and ride a newborn dragon."

"It could work," Ardatha said slowly. "The One God willing, we might escape Xoth! But how are we to find the right direction?"

"We must try," Pandrogas said. He stood with difficulty, wincing at the pain of his various wounds.

The cloakfighter said quietly, "But perhaps not all of us want to leave Xoth."

The others stared at him. He continued imperturbably, "I have not yet thanked you, enchantress, for rewarding me with far more than money. You have made immeasurably easier the achievement of my life's goal. For over a commonyear I have been journeying toward Xoth. Now I am here. Now I will have my revenge at last."

"Against whom do you seek revenge, cloakfighter?" Pandrogas asked.

"Against Zhormallion, Lord of Spiders, the Chthon who, for idle sport, destroyed my master, the Daimyo Ras Parolyn."

"An impossible vendetta," the sorcerer said. "For a sorcerer such as myself to face a Chthon in my own sanctuary is still to risk almost certain defeat. To beard one in his place of power, where he may call upon the aid of his vassals and peers, with no knowledge of sorcery is insanity incarnate! You face death and worse than death."

"Due to Zhormallion my life has already been destroyed," Kan Konar replied. "Because of him I am ronin; I may honorably offer my services to no one; I have been reduced to selling my skills to survive and to further my quest. I must destroy the Lord of Spiders, or die trying."

"It will be the latter," Pandrogas assured him, "if you are lucky. Lend your talents toward the possibility of escape, toward a new life. Your death will not bring back your daimyo."

The cloakfighter did not reply. He gathered his garment and weapon about him, seeming almost to disappear within its depths.

After a moment, Ardatha chuckled. "A fine crew," she said. "We all hate each other, and we all need each other. I do not give us much of a chance for reaching the sunlight that is the hoarstone of Sestihaculas's domain, but as you say, sorcerer, we must try."

"Then let us try now," Pandrogas said. "I grow steadily weaker, and I can no longer bolster my strength by spells. If only I knew which of these fungi were edible, if any."

"I can tell you that," Kan Konar said. He looked about them. Though most of the growths were uniformly fulvous and ashen, there were splashes of colors that, even in the murky light, seemed almost incandescent: royal purple cilia covered a nearby boulder, and several stalks that grew higher than their heads were tipped with bright orange. In the distance they could see a huge morel, easily twenty feet high, as scarlet as fresh blood. The colors accentuated the predominately corpselike hue. Kan Konar stepped to a nearby mushroom and, stretching to reach, broke off a handful of the green pileus. "I have lived off smaller versions of this," he said, breaking it and handing half to Pandrogas. The sorcerer bit into the fibrous mass with difficulty. The taste nearly made him ill, but he managed to swallow it. The effort it took to chew seemed to leave him more exhausted than before. He thanked the cloakfighter. "We must travel while we still have the strength," he said. "Will you not aid us in our search for the sun?"

"I am bound for the city of the Chthons, and Zhormallion," the cloakfighter said. "I will follow the flight of the cacodemons. I wish you luck in your quest, and promise you I will do nothing to bring you to the Chthons' attention."

"Very well," Pandrogas said slowly. "You will need all the help you can get; allow me to place upon you Alohan's Charm of Anonymity, which may aid you in reaching Zhormallion's side. It is a minor spell; I doubt that Sestihaculas or the others will sense its casting."

The cloakfighter hesitated, then nodded. Pandrogas placed his hands on his temples and began to speak in Payan. At the first word Ardatha glanced sharply at him, but said nothing. Then the cloakfighter's body jerked spasmodically. "No!" he cried. He seized his cloak in both hands, preparing to spin about in a deadly arc, but then Pandrogas finished speaking. The cloakfighter stood still, his muscles lax. His voice was calm and composed when he spoke, but there was a great anger beneath it.

"I trusted you, sorcerer," he said. "Why have you betrayed me?"

"I am sorry," Pandrogas replied. "But the emergency warrants it. Sestihaculas may not even be certain that we are on Xoth at this point—we cannot take the chance of his tracing the rest of us through you. Also, we may need your abilities to win through this hostile place. When we reach the Cliffs of the Sun and subdue a dragon, should this come to pass, I promise you release from the geas."

"Until then I must obey you," Kan Konar said. "But I warn you, Pandrogas: take care not to be within reach of my cloak when you free me."

Pandrogas made no reply. Ardatha looked at him and said, "Which way, do you think?"

"Does it matter? If we walk far enough, we will come to the edge of this shard. If we follow the edge long enough, we will find the Cliffs of the Sun."

"Xoth is not a large fragment," Ardatha mused, "but neither is it small. This could take weeks, even months."

The sorcerer shrugged. "Again—what choice do we have?"

It was not an easy journey. The paludal swamps and marshes made for slow progress. Footing was treacherous; apparently solid ground would turn out to be but a thin crust of scum over quagmires, and the mushroom growth was often thick enough to block their way. A pity none of them carried a sword, Pandrogas thought. He tried to remind himself that there was nothing inherently evil about his surroundings. He tried to see Xoth simply as an ecology, as beautiful in its own way as halcyon Tamboriyon, for example. Were not some of the growths as complex as the sculptured limestone of caverns, as colorful as an artist's palette? But then he would smell a particularly noxious putrescence, or step in a puddle that filled his boot with black oily water, and the temptation to start a cleansing conflagration that would scour all of Xoth to bare rock was all but overwhelming.

Kan Konar had, upon Pandrogas's command, found more edible growths to nourish them all. None could even charitably be described as tasty, but they were revivifying to a surprising degree. But the pain of the sorcerer's wounds still sapped his endurance. He kept his slashed palm wrapped in a swath of cloth as best he could, lest it become infected. His head throbbed unmercifully from the grave-robber's attack, and pain stabbed his side with every breath. The others, with the exception of Kan Konar, were not in the best of shape either, he noted. Ardatha seemed as weak or weaker than he; he suspected that giving her demon hand full rein had drained her reserves considerably. As for Tahrynyar—the marquis, Pandrogas thought, was truly amazing. He still limped, obviously painfully, and of the four of them was by far the least physically fit for such marathon efforts. Yet he did his part in forcing his way through the mildew and mold of the forest, grim-faced and uncomplaining, seemingly sustained entirely by his hatred for the sorcerer.

He has a right to that hatred, Pandrogas thought. When they had first arrived upon Xoth, the marquis had demanded to know where Amber was. Pandrogas had lied; had told him that he had left her safe at a Dulfar inn while he had sought the thief. He was not sure why he had lied; whether it was to spare Tahrynyar any more pain, or to escape himself, however briefly, into the fantasy that she was safe. Not knowing was the greatest of the many pains that plagued him. He missed her terribly, though he was glad that she was not here to undergo the tribulations of Xoth.

But another part of him, a part he was ashamed to acknowledge, was glad of her absence for a different reason. He had felt less of a sorcerer while in her presence. To know that she possessed such potential power, and to be unable to shape it, to mold it, to use it, was frustrating, particularly in a situation in which such power could aid him. He looked at the enchantress as they wended their way through a copse of swollen sporangia which burst into pulverulent clouds at the slightest touch. Her knowledge was less than his, her abilities not so finely honed. But she possessed the demon hand, and not even she was sure how much power dwelled within it. He frowned. Two of his erstwhile students had the potential to surpass him, and he was not sure how he felt about that. He had been acknowledged for so many years as a master—Sestihaculas himself had not been able to breach his citadel. Now he was overshadowed by two women, one by virtue of a gift that was half curse, and the other due to an inherency she did not even understand, much less appreciate.

He should never have invested so much of his power within the Runestone. True, by doing so he had intensified it, used it to increase his knowledge and abilities even more; but he had paid the price when it was stolen. For the first time in years he had been vulnerable—and the vulnerability kept getting worse.

Ardatha's demon hand had taken him by surprise, he told himself. Prepared, he would still be her master. There was more to magic than knowledge.

He had to believe that, if he was to go on.

*   *   *

It would make their progress so much easier to use just a little of its power, Ardatha thought. Just enough to burn through this tangled jungle, instead of having to claw and slash for each precious inch. She looked at the hand, its talons dripping with excrescence from their hard-won passage. Its power seemed to be inexhaustible— she had once tested its light over the course of several of Oljaer's days, going about her business wrapped in a fulgent nimbus that dazzled all who saw her. For three days and nights the hand had blazed. It showed no sign of dimming, and neither did she feel any weakness that indicated it was drawing upon her strength. She had wondered if its power came directly from Xoth; if it drew upon the strength of the Demogorgon himself. If so, to use it now would be tantamount to lighting a beacon for Sestihaculas. And so she clawed her way through the mucid growths before her with it.

She feared the hand now, for the first time in many years. Upon receiving it, she had, of course, been terrified; had even contemplated having it removed. But when it made no threat or attack upon her she had grown less fearful, and eventually had ventured to draw upon the power she could feel within it. With the use of the hand her confidence had grown, and she had incorporated it into the systems of theurgy she knew, finding that its power enhanced many spells, and even provided new and unknown results to some. She had taken what Pandrogas and others had taught her and enlarged upon it, illuminated it with the silver fire of her demon hand.

Oddly enough, it was the hand that had been in part responsible for her introduction to the Circle, and the Way of the One God. She had felt polluted by the power it had given her, felt her soul to be stained with the evil of the Chthons. But the hand was a part of her; she could not stop using its power any more than she could stop using her human hand in daily life. If she was to use the hand, she had reasoned, then let it be used to further a righteous cause, and so expiate its evil origins. No sooner had she made that decision, it seemed, than a vivid dream had shown her where to meet other acolytes of the Circle. Their doctrines were what she had been searching for, and she had quickly come to be one of Stonebrow's most trusted allies. Until now, Ardatha thought grimly. Until now.

She had come so close, and failed. Even if she escaped somehow from Xoth, where among all the myriad fragments of this shattered world would she search for the thief and his precious cargo? Stonebrow had trusted her with the assignment to steal one of the most powerful Runestones of all, and she had bungled it completely. She swiped at a turgid growth before her, then exclaimed in disgust as a jet of sebaceous liquid splattered her gown. "This is hopeless!" she cried. "It has taken us hours to come this petty distance! Look— we are still within view of where we started!"

The others looked in the direction she pointed. It was true; they stood upon a slight knoll at the moment, and through the dusk they could see, across a depressingly short span of the agaric jungle, the scarlet morel near where they had been.

"The enchantress is right," Tahrynyar said. He swatted wearily at a cloud of midges, each the size of his thumbnail, which buzzed about him. "There has to be a better way."

"If you have a suggestion, make it," Pandrogas said.

Tahrynyar smiled slightly. "Very well." He turned to the enchantress and said, "Use your demon hand, Ardatha! Use it to call Sestihaculas to us! Call him, and let us give him the sorcerer!" The marquis spoke rapidly, as though afraid the sorcerer would attempt to stop him; Pandrogas, however, merely leaned against a massive stipe, his eyes closed. "The Demogorgon does not want us," Tahrynyar continued. "He only wants Pandrogas! You have, in effect, been his servant, by bringing him the one he despises most—"

Tahrynyar stopped in surprise as the enchantress glared at him. "I have said before that I am the servant of neither man nor Chthon! Do you propose to ask the Serpent Lord for a palanquin and cacodemons to bear you where you would? Fool! Have you forgotten how casually he would have taken you from Pandrogas's laboratory? Or how he once tried to take me?"

"In both cases, his goal was to take Pandrogas. Besides, we can bargain with him. We can offer him something I'll wager he wants as badly as Pandrogas."

"What?" Ardatha asked. Pandrogas, she noticed, had opened his eyes and was watching the marquis.

"Access to Darkhaven," Tahrynyar said. "There is knowledge there even a Chthon must covet." He took a deep breath. "Offer him the Runestone."

"We don't have it," Ardatha said slowly.

"But we know who does. And not even our shapechanging thief can hide forever from Sestihaculas's demonic legions."

Ardatha said nothing. Pandrogas smiled. "Most clever, marquis," he said. "You are right—while Sestihaculas could enter Darkhaven after disposing of me, not even he could prevent its course of destruction without the Runestone. He would most certainly be interested; and I will tell you frankly that, as well as I can predict the mind of a Chthon, the chances are decent that he might even trade your lives for the information, instead of forcing you to divulge it by excruciations the sight of which would make a torturer ill. It might well be worth the risk." He looked at Ardatha. "But it puts you in a quandary, does it not, my colleague? To escape this living hell by betraying your trust, by offering to the Demogorgon what might be the key to the world's salvation?"

"Be quiet, sorcerer," Ardatha said in a low voice.

"The chances are thousands to one against this Runestone's being the one the Circle seeks!" Tahrynyar argued. "It is a gamble to be sure, enchantress, but what alternative is there other than death in this miasmal pit?"

For a long moment, Ardatha was silent. The other three watched her, Tahrynyar anxiously, Pandrogas with a cryptic smile, Kan Konar, as usual, unreadable. Then, slowly, the enchantress nodded. She raised her left hand toward the dark sky.

But before the claw could shine its lambent beacon, Pandrogas said, "Let me save you the trouble." He thrust his right hand upward and it flashed as golden as the sun, the light cleaving the nebulous air. Both Tahrynyar and Ardatha remembered that light once raised in their defense against Sestihaculas. Then the glare was gone, leaving all save the sorcerer blinking in dazzled shock.

"That was your death warrant!" Ardatha said in disbelief.

"Who better than myself to put the seal to it?" Pandrogas replied. He seemed somehow to have accrued new strength from the action; he no longer slouched under the pain of his many wounds, but stood

straight and tall. He stepped away from the sheltering cap and into
the open, looking up in all directions. Already the flapping of wings
could be heard. "They are coming," the sorcerer said. He looked at
Tahrynyar; the marquis stared back at him, triumph in his gaze.
"You have grown strong, Tahrynyar," Pandrogas told him, "but it
is the gnarled strength of a stunted tree, rather than a straight, clean
growth. You are more crippled now than ever your broken legs
would have left you."

"And you, Pandrogas, are a dead man," Tahrynyar replied, "and
I am your carnifex. Remember me as such. It is only just, for you
helped to murder the man I once was. He is avenged now."

"He is avenged, and your life's work is done. What will you do
now? Where will you go? What will keep the breath in your lungs,
the blood in your heart? When my life ends, Tahrynyar, yours will
have no more meaning. I hope," Pandrogas said, "that you are
prepared to deal with that." He turned to Ardatha. "And you, my
lady—can you deal with the knowledge of what you would have
done? How shall your god judge you now? I would speculate upon
it, were I you, for you may be meeting Him very soon." He looked
at the cloakfighter then, and spoke the Payan words that released
him from the geas. "Kan Konar, your will is your own again. I trust
you will leave my destruction to Sestihaculas, as it is in your interests
to do so. Seek Zhormallion if you will. But consider; if, by some
cosmic fluke of luck, you accomplish your goal and survive, then
you will be in the same position as your companions—your life will
be over, and you will still be alive." The sorcerer shook his head.
"Not an enviable situation. I think perhaps that I am the luckiest
one here."

No one replied to him. Then the sound of nightmares descending
made further talk impossible, as two cacodemons, graceful for all
their rough-hewn bulk, settled down beside them. Ardatha looked
at one of them and stifled a gasp—it was Balandrus.

"So," the cacodemon growled. "My prophecy is fulfilled. Join
me, Ardatha, on one last journey!" He seized the enchantress by the
waist in one monstrous grip and Tahrynyar in the other, while his
companion lifted Kan Konar and Pandrogas. They sprang aloft as
one and disappeared into the darkness.

Chapter 16

Dragon-hunt

When Amber first saw the dragon, it was rising from the sea of clouds which had by then spread far beyond Rhynne. She caught her breath at its beauty. Sunlight gleamed in parhelic splendor from the ribbed wings and the graceful curve of body and tail. The dragon moved slowly, majestically, and she caught a glimpse of its shadow rippling beneath it over the milky waves. The huge wings stroked the wind, scattering crescents of foam from the clouds below. The narrow head lifted, and a gush of flame, so bright it hurt Amber's eyes, issued from its mouth, rising in a sweeping arc before dissipating. She understood now the dragoneers' cry, "Fire in the sky!": it referred to the breath of dragons, the fire that, it was said, could burn through almost anything. At last she realized why the dragonship and everything aboard it was fashioned from the beasts the dragoneers hunted; only dragonhide and dragonbone could withstand the withering blasts of dragonfire.

She heard Asran shouting orders to her men. "Skysails up! We've the wind with us, and she's not yet got our scent! Ready cannons! Prepare to stoop!"

There was a chaos of activity about her; Amber huddled to one side as dragoneers rushed past, bent on various duties. She noticed how their faces gleamed in the sun. Of course, she thought; they have covered their skin with the oil of the great creatures for some small protection against the flame. The dragonship was in the bright eternal light of the Abyss now, and she looked about, really seeing it for the first time. She wondered how many dragons the *Dark Horizon* had accounted for in what had obviously been a long and arduous existence. The marlined halyards of dragon sinew had grooved the sun-bleached bone of the masts, and the leather and peritoneum of the sails and wings were patched and stained from years of storms. The masts, hatches, and cabin walls, the skull prow, and many other surfaces had been inscribed with scrimshaw and intaglio. It was a colorful ship, matched by a colorful crew, she thought. She watched dragoneers moving agilely about the rigging and crossarms, setting sails. Others cranked the huge crossbow cannons tight, and made ready the smaller chase boats so like the one that had carried her and Pandrogas from Darkhaven. She saw Grycikul and another applying grease to the capstan. The small sun-wizened man winked at her, and she turned away to stare once again after the dragon.

The beast was higher than them now, and for a dizzying moment seemed to be flying backward; then she realized this was the effect of the ship's Runestone, which, in providing weight and stability for those on board, made the dragonship seem motionless relative to the clouds and the dragon. She found that this could be overcome somewhat by a focus of will, not unlike the effort she made on the Warped Stairs. The *Dark Horizon* was, in fact, overtaking the dragon slowly. As they grew nearer, Amber began to comprehend the enormous size of the creature. The scaled body was at least twenty feet in length, with another ten or fifteen feet of tail, and this was dwarfed by the wingspan, which she overheard a crewman estimate at over ninety feet. The dragon's color was a rich brown, shading to a light cream on the plated belly. The tail ended in a barb like a ship's anchor. The two massive, bowed legs were drawn close, and ended in gleaming black talons. The neck was shorter, less serpentine than she would have imagined. Twin serrated ridges ran from the horned head to the tail.

She was so fascinated by the dragon that she was taken by surprise

THE SHATTERED WORLD   238

when cottony mist suddenly enveloped her. The *Dark Horizon* had dipped down into the cloud cover once again. She realized Asran's intention was to hide their approach until the last moment. She thought to look about for the thief, but he was not within the limited view now afforded her.

She heard Asran's disembodied voice from the forecastle: "Steady keel, Sythor. Let naught but the eyes of the masthead stand above these clouds! By the fangs of Kul-Zi-Thash, this skyworm's half flensed and carved already!"

For a long moment there was silence, with nothing but the cold caress of the mist about her. Then Amber faintly heard a voice far above her call something, though she could not make out the words.

"Now!" Asran cried. "Hard port the rudder sail! Tilt wings! Bring her up, lads!"

Nothing indicated that they were rising, but after a moment the clouds broke away from about the ship. Amber gasped—above her, as large seemingly as a fragment which could support empires, the dragon loomed. She could see the muscles that drove the mighty wings working beneath the armored skin. Several birds, roosting or searching for mites beneath the scales, took panicked flight from the broad back. *"Fire!"* Asran shouted, and the tendons that were the crossbows' cables hurled three spears, their heads coated with poison from manticores' tails. Their lines followed through the cannons' grooves, fast enough to ignite were water not poured on them. But, lightning though the harpoons were, they were not fast enough for their target; the dragon suddenly dropped her wings and slowed. One harpoon tore through the thin membrane of a wing; the other two missed entirely. The wings scooped air again, and the dragon dropped below the deck's level, the thunder of her pain reverberating on the quiet air.

Asran ordered the dragonship brought about. This was a difficult proceeding in a weightless environment, as they could not successfully tack against the wind. But the air currents in the Abyss were as myriad as the coursings of a restless ocean; the masts were tilted, the wings lowered, and Amber saw the clouds apparently shift about her as a wind from the other direction began, ponderously, to turn the *Dark Horizon*. She looked around and finally saw the thief, helping to reel in the drifting lances. Those of the crew who could peered over the sides, shading their eyes and looking in all directions for their enemy. The cloud cover came into view again, now at right angles to the dragonship, a wall of billowing white that faded into the blue distance in every direction. Asran gave the order to climb, and the wall began to tilt away from them; no sooner had it done so than the dragon burst from it as though hurtling through a curtain, mouth open, teeth gleaming. Another flameburst blinded Amber; she felt a moment of intense heat, and opened her eyes in time to see wisps of smoke curling from the prow. The dragon thundered past the ship, and this time the slipstream hurled Amber to her knees. She heard the crossbow cannons fire again. A chorus of cheers from the crew told her that they had scored a hit. She felt an arm about her shoulders, pulling her to her feet. "Let's get below!" Beorn shouted in her ear. "We wear no dragon leather or oil to protect us from the flame!" They hurried toward one of the hatches, but stopped when they heard a crewman shout, "It's over! Yonder she goes!"

Amber saw Asran, her fists white on the railing, staring into the Abyss after the disappearing dragon. "How many bones have we in her?"

The voice of the first mate was quiet. "One, Captain. She caught the line on her horns and snapped it."

Asran swore. "Hard about then, and after her. She'll not fly far with a lame wing and a wound full of poison!"

Amber, standing beside the thief, watched as the Abyss revolved about them, bringing the rapidly shrinking outline of the dragon into view. She felt sorry for the beleagered creature, which had no idea why it was being hunted. How did it feel, she wondered, looking at Beorn, to know that any stranger could be your enemy, to lead a life of constant suspicion? When she had thought about this before, she had felt no sympathy for the thief—it had been his choice to be an outlaw, after all. But after listening to him talk at length about his origins, of the cruelty of his parents and the hard street life of Bagerah, she had realized that he could not be judged so simply. She tried to imagine how the woman she had once been, the Marquise of Chuntai, would have reacted toward this man. With horror and revulsion, undoubtedly; she would have seen him as no more than a feral brute whose only law was that of the jungle. It had come as quite a shock to listen to him talk, to realize that he possessed a considerable, if eclectic, education, that he spoke five languages and several dialects better than she spoke three. She was seeing him now as more than just the cause of her woes; she knew that he was as frightened, as lonely, as human as she.

He looked down at her then, as though affected by her thoughts. She asked then the second of the two questions that were uppermost in her mind. "Why did you save me, instead of the Runestone?"

Beorn glared at the marquise, hoping that she would turn away in fear or abashment, and that he would not have to deal with the question. But she did neither. He would have to be the one to turn away, to give up, and he did not want to do that. "Because I am a fool," he growled at last, and started to leave.

She seized him by the arm; he was surprised at her strength. "I have not thanked you for being a fool, then," she told him. "I owe you my life."

Any further conversation was cut short by the appearance of Sythor at their side. The first mate said shortly, "I have a duty for both of you; follow me."

Amber and Beorn went with him to the forecastle, where, much to their surprise, he led them into his quarters and bade them sit. With the practice of long habit, Beorn scanned his surroundings surreptitiously yet thoroughly as he settled into a hide-bound chair. He noted the charts, the log books and fragments of sphere scattered on the ivory table beneath the hanging oil lamp, the cabinets above the bunk, the accessibility of the portholes. He had no desire or anticipation of robbing Sythor; it was simply reflex, as natural to him as breathing.

Sythor sat with his chin resting on his fist, in the attitude of someone who wrestles with a dilemma. The first mate was a huge block of a man, burly enough to make the thief look slender, with a great patch of pink and puckered scar tissue on his left arm which

told of a bad burn once. Beorn wondered how many living there
were who could speak of being burned by dragonfire.

"Your pardon, Sythor," he said, "but what assignment requires
our presence here?"

"A most easy and yet most difficult one," Sythor said heavily.
"Ye present yourselves as educated and learned folk, and 'tis seldom
enough I have the pleasure of conversation with such. I would discuss
a matter that's been on my mind of late. This ship has sailed the
Abyss now for near a commonyear, and we've raised three dragons
and conquered two. In my father's time, their numbers would darken
the clouds; aye, fire a harpoon blindfolded, and ye'd land one. But
now we've hunted them near out of the sky. And I wonder about
the rightfulness of this."

Beorn suppressed an urge to laugh. The dragoneer was asking
them for absolution! He glanced at Amber, saw by the expression
on her face that she was giving the matter serious thought. How
absurd! He could not see how the possible extinction of dragons
could matter in any way; there were enough dragonships to provide
trade and commerce for years to come, and even were there not,
one could easily lead a comfortable life without traveling the Abyss.
It surely would not affect him if the creatures were no more. True,
they were spectacular beasts; he recalled the altivolant flight of the
dragon, its graceful sweep across the sky. He had heard somewhere
that on land they were as awkward and ungainly as gigantic bats,
dragging themselves about on shinbones, tethered by their size and
weight. But in the air they were beautiful, and it suddenly occurred
to him that, if he knew that they had ceased to exist as a species,
some of the beauty would be gone from this shattered world.

"Much good comes from dragon-hunting," he heard the marquise
say slowly. "In addition to allowing us to travel the Abyss, their
carcasses serve us in myriad ways, of which ye are far more familiar
than I. I would not see the hunting stopped. But perhaps some form
of quota could be imposed?"

"Easier to say than to do," Sythor replied. "And what of dragoneers such as myself and the crew, whose livelihood depends on
bringing in as many skyworms as we can? I see nothing to be done

about it, and yet, I do not wish to be in part responsible for wiping them out."

"There is always something that can be done," Amber said. "There is always another occupation to which one can turn one's hand, if the desire be strong enough. Everything we do affects others—it is for ye to reflect on the relative good or ill of it. For my part, I doubt I could pursue a trade that brought suffering to another living creature—in any way."

She did not look at the thief as she spoke, but Beorn had no doubt that her words were intended as much for him as for the first mate of the *Dark Horizon*. He pushed himself out of his chair. "Excuse me," he said to Sythor. "I fear I am not qualified to judge such philosophical niceties. But, do not dragons, on occasion, slay dragoneers? They have no compunction about doing so. When a thief robs a house, it is not his responsibility that the owner had not the foresight to hire guards. If pressed for an opinion, I would say do what the gods gave you the strength and talent to do, and by so doing honor them." He looked at Amber, bowed slightly, mockingly, and left the cabin.

Outside, he stood breathing deeply of the cool, crisp air, watching crewmen lubricating the sails and ropes with dragon grease. How dare she judge him! he thought with rage. She was like all other members of royalty he had ever seen or encountered—priggish, judgmental, condescending...

He shook his head and growled.

Amber apologized for Beorn's precipitate exit, explaining that he had lost someone close to him in the destruction of the *Elgrane*. The first mate shrugged. "I am in a reflective mood," he said, "and so excuse it. But he would be wise to heave to and seek out some duties from the crew; they do not take well to a man lazing about when there's work to do—and there's always work to do."

They discussed further Sythor's uncertainty about dragon-hunting, but reached no decision. For all his ecological concern, Sythor was afraid to turn his hand to some new and unknown livelihood,

and afraid also of the opinion of his captain, who most emphatically
did not share the mate's worry about the trucidation of a species.
"What can I do, after all? My loyalty's to my captain. A dragon's
only a beast, and a man deserves to live more than a beast, does he
not? I have to look out for myself—Laadan, the second mate, covets
my position."

It was fairly obvious to Amber that all Sythor really wanted was
reassurance that he was doing the right thing. When Amber refused
to offer such reassurance, stating again instead that she could not
make the choice for the mate, he became moody, and refused to
speak further. Amber gave up and left the cabin.

She did not see the thief on deck. She sighed, leaning on the
railing and looking out into the blue haze. She had not really expected
her little sermon in the cabin to have much effect on either of them.
Perhaps she expected too much of Beorn. At least he seemed willing
to come to her aid when she needed it. She disliked looking upon
him as a protector, but she was still grateful for the fact. She would
have to be content with the uneasy truce which now existed between
them.

If she knew how, she would attempt to steal one of the longboats
and sail to Darkhaven, in hopes that Pandrogas would return before
it was destroyed. But she was only slightly familiar with the me-
chanics of guiding a dragonship, and even if she could steal one,
she had no idea at all of how to find one small piece in the ever-
changing cloud of fragments that composed the world. She felt
frustrated by her lack of knowledge.

But perhaps the thief could help her—perhaps he could be per-
suaded to attempt an escape. Certainly there were riches enough in
Darkhaven to tempt him. It was worth a try. Galvanized by the
thought, she determined to search for him. But as she stepped away
from the rail, she felt a hesitant tug on her arm. She looked about
to see little Ean, hesitantly proffering a large piece of sandstone.
"Excuse me, milady," he said, "but the captain says you are to help
holystone the foredeck."

Amber sighed and smiled. "I'm afraid you'll have to show me
how," she said. "I've never done anything like that before." She

watched Ean's violet eyes grow wider still in amazement. She had a moment's vivid recollection of charwomen scrubbing the floors of Tahrynyar's manse, and wished wryly that she had paid more attention to them.

Beorn was working as best he could at the varied and tedious shipboard duties assigned to him. His agility and excellent balance volunteered him for setting up the rigging of the topsail and spinnaker and making taut the guys that held the wings. He piled oil and grease rendered from dragons' fat until it seemed he could taste it through his pores, and floated, weightless, at the end of a tether polishing the teeth of the skulled prow, that their ominous gleam might bring fear to the ship's quarry. It was hard work, all of it, but not too hard for one in his condition, and it was work well suited for him: arduous enough to work the accumulated tensions of the long pursuit and the stiffness of his newly healed wounds from him, and uncomplicated enough to let his mind relax while he toiled. The clean air and food helped as well.

Oftimes during his labors he had seen the marquise working also. He passed her once, and, though he still burned with resentment at her sanctimony, he could not help but smile at her appearance: the sad tatters of her once beautiful traveler's gown were covered with daubs of varnish and oil, as was her face. It was not a smile meant kindly, but she evidently took it as such, for she smiled back at him ruefully and made a mock gesture of attempting to fix her hair as she went on about her duties. This bit of friendliness surprised him greatly; he stopped and stared after her for a moment, trying to decide if he should read condescension or snobbery into it. He had to admit that none had been apparent. She is brave, he thought. There is no question of that. He wondered if even Suchana could have borne up so courageously under the hardships and trials that Amber had undergone. We shall see, the thief told himself. There are more hardships yet to endure.

At the end of his duty Beorn was more than ready for sleep, and he found it the calmest and most refreshing since he had been arrested for stealing the Crystal Crescent.

* * *

The *Dark Horizon,* wings and sails bellying full in the wind, sailed the endless sea of the sky, following the distant batlike silhouette of the dragon, which flew toward the sun. A watch passed, and then another. Captain Asran stayed in the bow, watching as intently as did the eyeless sockets of the dragonskull on which she stood. And Beorn began to notice a nervousness among some of the crew concerning their destination. He had no idea where the ship was, of course—even his superb sense of direction was confounded by the infinite blue depths surrounding them. But the dragoneers began whispering among themselves, and Beorn overheard references to the Cliffs of the Sun. He held his peace, rightly assuming that he would learn more by listening than by asking. At last Grycikul made bold to question Laadan, a thickly muscled Jaskandar with a bald, tattooed head. "Yon skyworm's heading straight sun'ard, sir," Grycikul said. "And we all know what lies that way that she might make for, don't we? Ye can't be telling us that we're chasing her to the Cliffs of the Sun?"

"Captain Asran means to make the quota," the second mate replied briefly. "We're overtaking the beast; there'll be no danger to the ship."

"So ye say. So said the captain of the *Savage Star* too, no doubt, and they found her gutted hull floating in the Abyss, with not a soul left on board, and the decks swabbed with blood."

"Ye signed to hunt dragons, Grycikul, wherever we may find them, be it Tamboriyon or—"

"Or the Cliffs of the Sun," Grycikul finished. "Ye give us small choice, Laadan. But not a man on board will pursue her into shadow—depend on that!" There was muttered agreement from the other men nearby. The second mate turned on his heel and left the group.

"I am not familiar with the Cliffs of the Sun," Beorn said to Grycikul. "What is it?"

Grycikul regarded him and spat over the side. "It's the land of death, mate, is what. Know ye not that we're headed for the sunny side of Xoth?"

Beorn continued braiding lengths of ligament into serviceable lines while he considered this. So, Asran's determination to fill her hold had put the dragonship on a course to hell. He had never known anyone who had seen the legendary fragment of the Chthons, was not even sure he believed it existed. But there had been a time when he would have doubted the existence of cacodemons too. He felt no great desire to learn for certain if Xoth were real or not, but it seemed the decision was not his to make. It was impossible to steal a long-boat, and even if he could bring that off, he had no charts or guide to aid him—as well leap into the Abyss. He shuddered at the thought. He did not want to go through that again.

There had to be some way out of it, however. He did not intend to be led tamely to the darksome mushroom forests if he could help it. He would think, and he would plan. There had to be a way.

No doubt of it, he told himself; if he managed to live through this adventure, he would be assured of free drinks for the telling as long as he lived. Already he had robbed a magician, fought a brace of monsters, survived the Abyss, dodged a falling fragment, leaped from land to land like a man crossing a stream by stepstones, and now, unless his wits served him, it seemed he might pay a call on the Demogorgon himself. Truly, his life was anything but dull.

Amber, despite doing her share of exhausting work, did not sleep well. Several times she awoke in her hammock of dragongut, some-times jerked from sleep by an unfamiliar noise or shout, but more often by her own restless dreams. A recurring image throughout them was that of Ia, the dryad. In her dreams, the wan face and wistful eyes looked up once more at Amber, and she heard again her prophecy: *You wielded considerable power once. You will wield much more soon.* The light illuminating the dryad—from what source Amber could not say; all was roiling gray clouds about her—began to dim, and she huddled within a dark, cowled robe that hid her face. The figure raised one arm, and Amber saw at the end of the sleeve not a hand, but a black and hideous claw, talons flexing slowly. It began to glow with a cold silver fire. From within the cowl now she could hear the hissing of snakes. The claw reached up, seized the hood, threw it back—

Amber gasped, sitting upright in the hammock and barely avoiding another fall. Her heart was pounding; she took a deep, slow breath, then another, feeling the race of blood within her slowing reluctantly.

The face within the hood had been a writhing mass of snakes.

She shuddered at the memory of it. Who had the mysterious figure represented in her mind? At first she thought of Sestihaculas, but one of the spectre's most frightening aspects had been its elusive yet unmistakable femininity. Its identity was an enigma to her; but she felt quite strongly that the claw represented both the "grip of darkness" and the "hand of light" she had been warned against by both Ia and the sphere. She also had the feeling that, despite her enforced voyage and separation from Pandrogas, she was not yet done with the matter of Darkhaven's Runestone. The thought was frightening rather than comforting. She felt more exhausted now than before she had slept. She wished she could play her flute—the music, hard-won over so many years of practice as a child, never failed to soothe her nerves. But there were others sleeping in the hold; though the darkness was too complete for her to see them, she could hear their snoring nearby. They would not take kindly to being disturbed, she was sure, and she was not in a position to antagonize or annoy anyone.

She heard a distant, muffled groaning, two voices intermingling. The sounds of passion were unmistakable, and she realized that some of the men did not need women to satisfy their needs. She felt a small measure of relief—perhaps they, at least, were not threats to her.

She swung out of the hammock and felt her way cautiously toward the scuttle, forcing herself to move slowly, teeth clenched against the thought of feeling cold, reptilian talons from her dream close upon her shoulder from behind. It was an eternity before she finally opened the hatch and let the cleansing sunlight wash over her. She sat crosslegged on the deck, feeling the cool air on her face and skin, wondering vaguely how she could ever force herself to go below again.

Then a hand fell upon her shoulder.

*   *   *

Beorn had been oiling the bowstring on one of the crossbow cannons when he saw Amber stagger from the hatch. There was no officer around to object, so he crossed the deck and stood behind her. She looked drawn and upset, and his first thought was that she had been attacked while below. That did not bring him the pleasure he had thought it would. Impulsively, he put his hand on her shoulder; she jerked as though wasp-stung and spun about. He seemed to see her outlined in livid blue fire for the barest instant, and then, though she made no further move, Beorn felt himself hurled backward across the deck as though kicked by a horse. He struck a scuttlecask hard enough to splash water from it, and lay there, gasping for breath, hearing dimly the laughter of the crew about him, who evidently thought he had simply tripped. The thief stared at Amber, who stared back at him in amazement for a moment before coming to kneel beside him.

"Let me help you," she said, tugging at his arm in an attempt to lift him to his feet, and succeeding no more than if she had tried to pull a tree stump from the ground. Where could she have gotten the strength to hurl him like a toy? Beorn wondered dazedly. He held up a hand to stop her efforts, and got to his feet, still dizzy, keenly aware that he would soon be wearing a bruise over most of his upper back.

"How do you feel?" she asked, her tone one of concern for an accident of which she knew she was the cause.

"Empty. Strike me and I'd echo like a drum." He looked at her, too stupefied even to feel fear of her. "Blue fire," he murmured.

He heard her catch her breath. "What did you say?"

"You glowed, blue as the sky, for an instant—as though you wore a cloak of fire, just before you—"

"Before I struck you," Amber finished softly. There was wonderment in her voice. "I'm sorry, Beorn. You took me by surprise."

"You lied to me," he said, feeling absurdly hurt. "You *are* a sorceress."

"I said there were no rings on my fingers." She held up her unadorned hands. "I did not lie. I have had no training—well, none of which to speak. Pandrogas had barely explained some of the basic tenets of magic to me before . . . before all of this."

"Then where did you get such power?"

"From me—within me." She looked confused. "I have always had it, evidently. Pandrogas said once that I was born with more power than most mages could ever hope to achieve. But I cannot control it; only when I am in danger, or think I am, can I call on it, and not always then."

Beorn tried to look at her, and found he could not meet her eyes. He could still feel the terrifying strength of the power that had hurled him across the deck—Balandrus had not gripped him more strongly. He wondered if she could somehow sense the desires of revenge and lust that he had felt for her. He realized that he was now afraid of her, afraid of triggering her power again. It was a galling sensation.

"Forgive me," he said in a low voice. "I did not mean to startle you."

She did not reply, and, despite his expertise in such matters, he found he could not read her expression. "I will try to be more careful as well," she said at last. "We need each other's help—for now."

He did not know what to reply to that. A shout from the masthead saved him from it. "Fire in the sky!" The words triggered a thunder of pounding feet and shouts, as dragoneers rushed to their stations. Beorn swiftly climbed up a nearby rigging and sighted into the sun, shading his eyes with his hand. It was true; the manticore poison had at last weakened the dragon. She no longer had the strength to pull her weightless body through the air with strokes of her wings, and the more efficient windgear of the dragonship was slowly winning the race. Captain Asran stood upon the bridge, bellowing orders. Dragoneers loosed the hawsers binding the three smaller chase boats, setting their sails and cocking the cannons. More members of the crew began reefing sails, decreasing the wind resistance and slowing the ship. Sythor ordered the wings angled and the rudder sails thrown hard over. The *Dark Horizon* began to dive slowly, banking in a wide turn, gaining almost imperceptibly on the dragon's side.

The chase boats, each manned by ten men, were launched; their sails, proportionately larger than the ones on the dragonship, caught the wind, which hurled them toward the huge creature in wide arcs.

Beorn saw the dragon fold her wings suddenly, instantly slowing her forward momentum and presenting as small a target as possible. The lead boat overshot her, and Beorn lost sight of it in the sun's glare. The dragon turned her head and flamed at the second boat, a candent blast of such intensity that, though it did not reach the boat, heated the air about it to such a degree that the disturbance caused the craft to veer away. The recoil hurled the dragon backward, on a collision course with the third boat. A harpoon hurtled from its cannon, the sound of the shot coming faintly to Beorn's ears a breath later. It missed the dragon, and there was no time for a second attempt; the dragon's body crashed into the chase boat, splintering it and hurling the men into the Abyss.

"Come around!" the captain shouted. "Reef sails!" The crew hastened to obey, but too late; the dragon caught the wind on her wings again, and was quickly swallowed in the sun's glare. The *Dark Horizon* took up the chase once again, overtaking and securing the two chase boats, who had managed to rescue four of the men from the shattered boat. "Stay on her!" Asran ordered. "Blood for blood it is now; we'll have her if she flies to the sun itself!"

"It's not the sun she's making for, Captain!" Sythor shouted from the deck. "Can't ye see?" and he pointed sunward. Beorn squinted upward, as did Amber and everyone else. An apprehensive murmur arose from the crew. Barely visible in the solar brightness were the outlines of two fragments, a larger one and a smaller one in its shadow. "She's bound for the Cliffs of the Sun!" Sythor continued. "And she'll make it, with the lead she's got! We've lost, Captain! We're dragoneers—we'll stand against one with naught but a needle and thread to cast at it—but we can't follow her to Xoth!"

"We can, and we will! Fill me every yard of leather with the wind—say ye that all the dead dragons that make up the *Dark Horizon* cannot overtake one wounded?"

"Think on the consequences should we stray into shadow!" Sythor argued. "'Tis the sun only that protects us from the cacodemons! It's too risky!"

The crew agreed in a heartfelt chorus, but Asran's single voice drowned them out. "We cannot afford to spend more months of searching! I'll hear no more on it! Up sails! This skyworm's ours,

251   *Michael Reaves*

or we are hers!" She spun about and entered her cabin.

Beorn watched the crew move about their tasks sullenly. He felt
fingers touch his arm, and looked about to see Amber beside him.
"We have to escape," he said. "If you could use your magic, somehow, to steal one of the boats—"

"I told you I cannot control it like that!"

Forgetting for a moment his new-found fear of her, Beorn seized
her by the shoulders and shook her. "I've never asked help of anyone
in my life before! I must ask it of you, now. I cannot lie or cheat
or steal my way out of this, and the bear cannot help me! Only you,
with your magic, can stop Asran's plan!"

Amber pulled free of him. "I have no magic—only power! You're
the thief. *You* steal the boat!"

They had been speaking in Talic instead of Perese; a low voice
from behind them spoke in the same tongue. "You cannot steal the
boat; but I can."

They turned to see Sythor beside them. "I've made my decision,"
the first mate continued. "I'll not be a party to Asran's mad plan.
At the middlewatch, then, when most of the crew's asleep. The
boats are stocked with provisions, water, and charts, should they
become lost in the Abyss. Are you with me?"

"Most assuredly," Beorn said. He looked at Amber.

Amber felt one moment of reluctance—there was the slightest
possibility that, where Sestihaculas was, there Pandrogas might also
be. But to seek him in Xoth was madness, she realized. She had to
face the fact that she would undoubtedly never see him again; she
had to find and make a new life now. "Yes," she told Sythor and
the thief. "I am with you."

Sythor found garments of dragon leather for both Beorn and
Amber, including a leathern casquetel and cloak to hide the marquise's hair and figure. Taking the chase boat, he assured them,
would be easy; the few sailors about would assume that Sythor was
testing its airworthiness, a common enough procedure. Unfortunately, the theft did not come off so smoothly. Amber and Beorn
had stepped into the small craft, and Sythor was untying the lines
from the bone cleats, when a shadow fell over them; looking up,

they saw Laadan, a belaying pin carved from a dragon's tooth in one hand. "Have ye spied a dragon, then, Sythor?" the Jaskander inquired sarcastically. "Or might this be a small pleasure cruise?"

"Asran has ordered me to test the maneuverability of both ships," Sythor replied. "Go and ask her, Laadan, if ye do not believe me."

"Perhaps ye should all accompany me," Laadan said. "I confess to being sorely confused, Sythor, since the captain did tell me, not a quarter watch before, to make certain the chase boats were not disturbed for any purposes by anyone. I think she may fear mutiny and desertion—what say ye to that?"

Sythor hesitated, looking up at Laadan. Laadan smiled, slapping the pin suggestively into his callused palm. Sythor stood up slowly. Laadan looked down at Beorn and Amber in the chase boat. "Out of there, both of ye," the second mate said. "I don't doubt ye'll wind up in the Abyss for this, though not the way ye intended."

Amber saw Beorn glance at her; hoping, she knew, that she would somehow use the power within her to save them. She looked back at him helplessly. He sighed, and turned as if to grab the lines and pull himself back on board, then instead seized a harpoon, spun about and swung the sharp edge of it against the lines, once, twice, severing them, then rammed the weapon's butt against the dragonship's hull, pushing the boat away from it. The craft tumbled away from the *Dark Horizon* and into the void. Its sails were reefed, and so the larger ship quickly left it and the shouts of alarm that were raised behind. Beorn saw Laadan leap to one of the crossbow cannons and swivel it toward them. "Get down!" he cried to Amber. He pulled desperately on the sheets and the peritoneum sail bellied out full and taut against the wind. The Abyss tilted about them, and the harpoon whistled across the bow. Then they were out of range.

The two fragments' silhouettes were now clearly visible below the sun. "Change course!" Amber cried. "We are being blown toward Xoth!"

Beorn jibed quickly, then threw over the rudder sail and raised the wings to a dihedral position. He could not closehaul the weightless craft against the wind; his only hope was to rise and find another current of air. The chase boat came about slowly, rising; the sails began to luff, then filled again with a crosswind. The *Dark Horizon* was now nowhere to be seen. They looked at each other in relief, but it was short-lived, for suddenly a swift-moving shadow passed over them, and the wash of air caused the Abyss to spin crazily about them. The chase boat's Runestone prevented any danger of their being hurled overboard, but the sudden vertigo caused them both to cling to the mizzen. Beorn looked up and saw the dragon banking, wings spread to catch another gust that would bring her back toward them. He could see a dreadful intelligence and purpose in the yellow eyes. The dragon flamed again; the blaze would have engulfed the craft and incinerated both of them had not a stiff crosswind changed its arc. The dragon shifted her wings as she hurtled toward them, turning her body and bringing her tail around in a destructive sweep toward the boat. Beorn angled the mainmast quickly, and the craft dipped slightly in response, but not enough; they ducked as the tail skimmed over them, crashing into the mizzen and main masts and shattering them, flinging the tangled sails into the Abyss. The sharp fragments of the masts tore through one of the wings.

Amber leaped to the crossbow cannon as blue sky and clouds spun about her. She had never killed anything in her life before. But she knew that if she did not do something, in another moment she would be impaled on those talons even as she had seen rabbits snatched by the kestrels and peregrines of Chuntai's gentlefolk in their gaming sports. She aimed the stock at the dragon and fired, realizing as the harpoon hurtled outward that she did not know how to compensate for the deceptive stability of the chase boat. The lance, instead of striking a fatal blow to the great beast's body, buried itself near the tip of her tail.

The dragon roared, and her wings hurled her forward again. The chase boat, tethered to her by the harpoon line, followed. Beorn sawed quickly through the tough sinew with a harpoon, and the dragon, freed, fell away from them toward the sun.

But, quick as the thief had been, his action had come too late. The damage had been done. With no sails and only one wing, the chase boat was now a derelict, drifting irrevocably in the direction the dragon had pulled her—toward Xoth.

Chapter 17

Sestihaculas

During her tenure in Oljaer Ardatha had caused many prisoners to be sent to the dungeons. Those occasions when she had been forced to descend there herself, such as when she had rescued Beorn, had required a considerable effort of will on her part. The bright finery of the palace had been quite easy to grow accustomed to, and the dank, noxious atmosphere and vermin that pervaded the lowest levels had always sickened and frightened her, though she had tried to convince herself that an enchantress should be above such feelings. But those dungeons had been the very courts of heaven compared to where she, Tahrynyar, and Kan Konar were now incarcerated. The oubliette was composed of cells that were no more than rough, irregular cavities in the base of the cliffs in which the Chthons and their demonic servants dwelled. The walls and jagged ceiling dripped with an incrassate slime which pooled on the floors and shone like isinglass in the metallic light of her hand, the cell's only source of illumination. Occasionally, no matter where they tried to shelter, drops struck them, burning like weak acid and leaving itching sores. The charnel stench made it a battle for Ardatha to keep down the food the cloakfighter had found earlier for them in the mushroom forest.

254

Ardatha sat on a slippery boulder, watching her companions. Kan Konar had attempted to compose himself through meditation; the cloakfighter sat crosslegged on a relatively dry area of the black floor, huddled within his all-purpose garment, his breathing slow and regular. Tahrynyar had initially prowled restlessly about the cavern, seeking vainly some escape from the slime and the smell, but now had given that up and simply stood, arms folded and head bowed, in the center of the chamber. His entire body shivered when a drop hit it. Ardatha wondered if the marquis's sanity would hold— of the three of them, he was least used to such privation. Occasionally he would mutter the name of the sorcerer in a hateful tone. This is good, Ardatha thought; as long as he fixates on a desire for revenge, he will survive.

Pandrogas had been separated from them when they had been brought to the basaltic cliffs that formed the warrens of the Chthons. Ardatha assumed that her time to face Sestihaculas would come soon enough. The thought no longer filled her with the terror it had for so many years; she had passed beyond all feeling save despair. She had betrayed the One God by agreeing to trade her knowledge of Darkhaven's Runestone for a chance of personal safety. True, she had not actually done it—Pandrogas's strange, suicidal action had saved her from that. But she could not deny that the intention had been there. She felt she was no longer worthy to be a member of the Circle, to take part in the restoration of the world to a state of grace. Let the Chthons do with her as they would—she deserved it.

She looked once again at Tahrynyar, feeling vaguely sorry she had helped to bring him to this pass. True, it had been his choice— his desire for revenge had become an elemental force within him, as basic as the power behind all magic. It had resculpted him like water on limestone, hollowed him and filled him with hatred. A pity, actually, Ardatha thought. Though she had been no less devoted to her cause, she had not put aside completely her human feelings. It had been a very long time since she had been with a man she cared for; her couplings with Troas had been politically expedient, but she had enjoyed them no more than she enjoyed a chirurgeon's

palpations and probings. She thought now about that moment during
the earthquake in Dulfar, when the marquis had saved her from
injury in the alley and they had sought protection for a moment in
each other's arms. She had wanted him then, but there had been no
time; there was never any time. And so that moment had passed,
and now would never come again.

Now, in this last extremity of her failure, it was easy to wish that
things had been otherwise—to imagine wistfully how different her
life might have been had she turned on another path. If she had not
foolishly experimented, so long ago, with the summoning spell that
had brought Endrigoth to Darkhaven...if she had allowed more
time in her life for love, and been less afraid of the vulnerability it
brought...

She looked at the cloakfighter, sitting calm and self-contained on
the cold rock beneath her. So much more and so much less than a
man he seemed; possessed of amazing physical prowess and skill,
and yet robbed, by these very superhuman attributes and the fanaticism necessary to achieve them, of his humanity. He would willingly
sacrifice all that hard-won ability and knowledge to avenge his dead
master—an empty gesture. At least she would be expending her life
for a noble cause; though she had failed, it was with the knowledge
that her death meant something. Surely the One God would forgive
her her moment of weakness at the end. Perhaps, after all, she might
not have gone through with it...

Useless to speculate, Ardatha told herself. A faint smile tugged
at her lips as she recalled an anecdote she had heard long ago: A
sorcerer, a soldier, and a scholar had once journeyed together to a
fork in the road, and argued as to which route to take. The sorcerer
cast the sphere, and its reading advised the right fork. The scholar
consulted his scrolls of learning, and decided upon the left fork. The
soldier could not make up his mind, and so sat down in the dust of
the road while the other two continued their separate ways. After a
time a traveler approached from the right-hand road, and the soldier
asked him for news of the sorcerer. "He has met with a terrible
fate," the traveler replied; "for a phoenix attacked him from the sky,
and, though he fought with every spell he knew, the jeweled wings
enveloped him and their searing embrace burned him to a cinder."

The soldier thanked him and continued his vigil. After a long time, a peddler approached from the left-hand road, and the soldier asked him for news of the scholar. "Ah, yes, most unfortunate," the peddler told him. "He encountered a band of brigands who, when they found he carried only papers and books, became enraged and killed him." The soldier thanked him and, rising, returned the way the three of them had originally come. He settled down in a village and lived a long and happy life. Ardatha looked at her two comrades and thought, Here is certainly the making of another story. Three fanatics in a dungeon, each with their own particular *jihad* . . .

And what would be the ending of this fable? She suspected it would not be nearly as tidy as the one she had just recalled. The Chthons were known for their gruesome imagination, so the legends said. She wondered if it might not be easier to use the power within her hand to kill herself. Even more than the dampness of the cell, the thought brought a chill to her skin. But she forced herself to look at it. With the Runestone lost, was not her only reason for living now gone as well? Did it not make more sense to save herself the torture and degradation that was sure to follow?

The temptation was appallingly strong. She regarded her glowing claw with fascination. She had no doubt that she could use it to turn her strength against herself. It seemed she had been struggling, running, fighting for so long . . . perhaps it was time she granted herself peace . . .

A heavy grating caused her to whirl about with a gasp. Tahrynyar and Kan Konar looked up also, and the three of them watched the massive stone wheel that imprisoned them slowly moving aside. Two cacodemons rolled it back far enough to shove a human silhouette into the cell, then replaced it. The new prisoner staggered forward. His features were indistinct in the darkness, but there was something familiar about his burly shape. Ardatha increased her hand's glow. The figure stopped, squinting in the sudden blaze of light, and Ardatha gasped as she saw the heavy features of the thief.

After a moment of silence, Kan Konar rose. "So you have found us, Beorn, instead of the other way around," the cloakfighter said. "All roads lead to Xoth, it seems."

The thief looked from one to another of them; the initial flicker of astonishment in his eyes was quickly replaced with resignation. "Ardatha recruited you, then," he said to the cloakfighter. "It seems there is no one in what's left of the world whom I can trust."

"I tend to agree," Ardatha said wryly. Beorn turned his gaze to her; she could not tell how much of his pallor was due to the light. She held out her claw, automatically tempering the radiance to achieve the proper dramatic highlighting of her face. How easily she slipped back into the old patterns of power, she thought. "The Runestone, shapechanger," she said. "With it I might be able to free us all."

Beorn took a deep breath. "It is safely hidden, enchantress. And only I know where it is."

"For the moment, perhaps. But a simple spell can lift the knowledge from your mind as easily as you lift the coins from a dowager's purse."

"Not so simply," Beorn said; his voice was steady, though he was obviously frightened; in spite of herself, Ardatha admired him for that. "I learned at an early age how to hide a fact in my head well enough to withstand mesmerism. I can forget where it is, and then it will be truly lost. It would be easier for you to cooperate with me."

"This is all academic," Tahrynyar said. "The Runestone is not here, and we cannot escape. What is the point of fighting over it?"

Ardatha saw the thief look closely at the marquis. "I recognize you," he said. "The fop whose legs the bear splintered. You have made a remarkable recovery."

"In more ways than one," Tahrynyar replied. "How came you here?"

"We were adrift in the Abyss; Xoth seized us, drew us into its shadow. A swarm of cacodemons took us before our wrecked boat could crash. They brought me here; my companion, they said, was to be taken before Sestihaculas." The thief's voice was even—too even, the enchantress thought.

"Who was your companion?" she asked.

"The Marquise of Chuntai."

Tahrynyar staggered as though struck. Then he leaped forward, seizing Beorn by the shoulders. "You are lying, thief! Amber is safe in Dulfar!"

The thief shrugged free of his grasp and stepped back. "I wish that were so," he said quietly. "But she is here on Xoth. Why she faces the Demogorgon and I face the three of you I do not know."

"It is the Serpent Lord's humor," Ardatha said. "He will stage some form of drama for his amusement with Pandrogas and your wife, marquis."

"We must escape!" Tahrynyar shouted. "Do something, enchantress! Use your power! Free us!"

Ardatha looked at him with raised eyebrow. "You told me once that you would gladly see the two of them face the Demogorgon. What brings this change of heart, Tahrynyar?"

She regretted the taunt immediately; long years of using words as weapons, both in spells and sarcasm, had made her say it. For a moment she thought the marquis was going to attack her. But he controlled himself, though she could see the pulsing of a vein in his forehead. She looked again at the thief, then at her hand. A few moments ago, she had been on the verge of using it to take her own life; now, miraculously, there was hope again. She wondered how she could ever have been in such an extreme of despair. "Yon door cannot be moved by might," she said; "perhaps it can by magic. It is worth a try." She turned and extended the claw before her; its silver blaze increased, becoming refulgent, blinding, forcing the others to shield their eyes. *"Enoz machan terica,"* she said, speaking the Payan words of the spell known as the Wallbreaker as she gesticulated, her hand trailing cometary fire. *"Chand tauran!"* There was a thunderclap; the ground shook, and a sharp scent of ozone momentarily overpowered the cell's foetor. The light from the hand dimmed. Ardatha staggered, suddenly weak; Tahrynyar caught her before she could fall. "It's done!" she gasped. They looked at the door and saw that it was so—the huge stone had been split down the middle.

Tahrynyar started to rush forward, but the cloakfighter caught his arm. "Wait," he said softly. "There is someone out there."

Ardatha looked up to see a shadowy figure standing in the corridor beyond the rock. "A cacodemon, no doubt," she said. "We shall learn now if Sestihaculas's gift can still sway his minions." But before she could raise the hand again, the figure laughed. Ardatha felt her spine become ice. Such laughter could never have come from the rough throat of a cacodemon. Soft, velvety, rich with power, it nevertheless had a faint undertone of chittering, like mirth somehow filtered through the throats of thousands of rats.

"My compliments, Ardatha," the voice said. "Your power and knowledge have increased considerably since I last met you." The figure stepped forward, and the light illuminated him a bit more. Ardatha caught a glimpse of short silken fur that gleamed, blue-black, and of red eyes. She gripped the clammy rocks beside her to hold herself up.

"Who is it, Ardatha?" Kan Konar whispered.

Her mouth was almost too dry for speech, but she somehow managed to name him. "Endrigoth," she whispered. "Endrigoth— Lord of Rats."

Endrigoth laughed again, revealing a flash of sharp, white teeth. "You do not seem anxious for a rematch, Ardatha! Come, surely you did not expect such an easy escape! To pass the door was easy— now you must pass me!"

Kan Konar leaped forward without warning, his body spinning, the lethal edges of the cloak slicing the air. No human warrior could have responded quickly enough to avoid his attack. But a flash of purple light struck him like a stone from a ballista, hurling him against the boulder where he lay stunned. "All in good time, cloak-fighter," the Chthon said. "You had best preserve your strength for my colleague, Zhormallion." To Ardatha he said, "You have feared me for many commonyears, enchantress. Why I am not sure, for I bear you no malice or ill will. I am not a grudgeful sort, like Lord Sestihaculas. Even he cares little for your fate; you were but an expedient by which to find Pandrogas. You may keep the Demo-gorgon's gift to you, and your life—if you can survive my little entertainment." He laughed again, and the laughter seemed to echo about Ardatha; then she realized that the susurrant ripples of sound were coming from the innumerable cracks and openings in the rock walls about her. Within them she could see the glow from her hand reflected, like torchlight dancing on waves, coming closer...

Ardatha bit down on a scream as rats began to pour into the

cavern. The wriggling bodies dropped from the holes in the ceiling and walls, and welled up through the fissured floor, their fur streaked with slime. Tahrynar and Beorn quickly joined the enchantress on the boulder as the crepitating horde poured toward them. The tick of thousands of claws on the rocks merged with the Chthon's laughter, mesmerizing, somehow almost inviting. The glittering eyes lusted for them. Ardatha saw the wave of brown and black bodies roll over the cloakfighter's recumbent form. Beorn reached down, managed to grab Kan Konar's cloak, and with Tahrynyar's help dragged him to their temporary sanctuary. The rats scrabbled at the smooth sides of the boulder, climbing upon each other, clawing toward their prey.

"Do something, Ardatha!" Beorn whispered between clenched teeth.

Ardatha shook herself free of her paralyzing horror, raised her glowing hand and enspelled the boulder with Armor of Light. To her amazement, the rats surged through the light without even slowing. She heard Endrigoth chuckle again. The enchantress raised her hand once more, but a shout of disgust from Beorn distracted her— a rodent the size of a small cat had dropped from the ceiling onto his back, clawing for a grip on his tunic. Tahrynyar, teeth set, struck at the rat, knocking it into the undulating mass. Another one leaped at Ardatha's foot, fangs bared; she kicked it away. The creatures continued to pour from the walls, inexhaustibly, their weight crushing those beneath them, their foul odor overwhelming. The squeaking was deafening by now. Ardatha could no longer hear Endrigoth's laughter, could no longer see him standing beyond the rats.

Another moment, she knew, and they would be dragged down, and their bones picked clean a moment after that. She raised her claw again—and something heavy and pulsating struck her head, claws digging into her scalp, knocking her off balance. Ardatha felt herself falling. She prayed that she would lose consciousness before she felt their teeth.

When he at last stood in the court of the Chthons, deep within the stark, warren-riddled cliffs, Pandrogas was vaguely amazed at his own calmness. He had heard that such serenity as he now felt comes at times to condemned men—that only when at last the hideous uncertainty over death has been resolved can one really begin to live. There was something of this in him now, though he had not yet resigned hope. His summoning of the cacodemons had not been an admission of defeat—at least, so he hoped.

He stood in the center of a vast cavern, obscurely lit by an all-pervasive phosphorescence. Its crepuscular glow showed him hints of columns and boulders strewn everywhere, cruciate formations and obelisks which might be natural or the result of rough-hewn sculpture. He could dimly make out, in the galleries and recesses of the hall, an assemblage of Chthons and cacodemons silently regarding him. Some of them he recognized: Trisandela, Lady of Bats, her folded wings rising above her like the pinnacles of a dark cathedral; Breelorand, Lord of Wolves, his bushy gray tail twitching with restrained bloodlust; Shaikor, Lord of Flies, the myriad facets of his eyes glittering in the shadows. Each was surrounded by an entourage of cacodemons of nightmarish variety: cynocephalic, tenaculate, vermicular. Even in this vaulted cavern the air was thick with their stench. They waited, silent, expectant. He had no idea how long he had been there; hours, perhaps. He remained on his feet by will power alone—his weakness and wounds had sapped his strength almost completely. He stood with knees slightly bent, head down, breathing deeply of the fetid air. He would greet his fate, whatever it was, standing.

Then something—not a sound, for the funebrial silence had not been broken, not a movement, for nothing had disturbed the autochthons of darkness arrayed about him—told Pandrogas that the waiting was, at last, over. He realized now that he had been waiting far longer than the time spent in the hall of the Chthons for this moment—he had been waiting since that time, so long ago now, when he had first crossed Sestihaculas, when he had saved Ardatha from the Serpent Lord.

And now the waiting was over.

Pandrogas turned, and faced the Demogorgon.

The saurian body stood well over nine feet. The mottled patterns of his scales gleamed like enamel even in the dim light, in colors of yellow, red, and black, shading to a deep green on his ridged belly. Slowly writhing tentacles rose from the vertebrae of his back and tail, and from his shoulders; two tiny ones also sprouted from his temples and two from his chin. He was naked, and between his legs hung not a male member, but a viper with gleaming fangs. At the sight of Pandrogas it began to hiss, porrecting in a vain attempt to reach him. Sestihaculas smiled, stroking it casually as he looked down on him. "Welcome, sorcerer," the Serpent Lord said. "I have long looked forward to this meeting."

"I cannot say I have," Pandrogas replied. "I presume you seek reparation for your past defeats by me?"

For the first time there was noise from the multitude within the shadows; a cacophony of growls, hisses, shrieks, and moans as the Chthons and their servants reacted to this insult. Sestihaculas raised his head, and silence instantly resumed. Then the Demogorgon returned his ophidian gaze to Pandrogas. "Could you blame me if I did?" the courtly voice inquired. "In all my life, which has been longer than yours and a score of your ancestors', I have never before been outmatched in sorcery. Now I have been brought low not once, but twice, and by one whose kind were responsible for our subterranean world being destroyed. Surely you can understand why I would desire revenge—not only on you, but on all your kind?"

"I am not answerable for the Necromancer's folly," Pandrogas said wearily, "only for my own."

"Nevertheless, you will answer. Are you prepared?"

"As I recall our agreement, I was to meet you in a place of equal power. The hall of the Chthons seems hardly that."

"It was your colleague that brought you here, not I. Still, I would have some satisfaction from this match. I see also that you are wounded, and that your power is at a low ebb. None, not even humans, should say that my victory was due to luck or circumstance. Step forward, Pandrogas."

The sorcerer took a deep breath and did as he was bid. The penile viper struck, burying its fangs in his arm below the shoulder. Pandrogas gasped, feeling a burning, bitter acid spreading through him. For a moment he was consumed with agony; then it faded, leaving him on his hands and knees, gasping. He stood, realizing that the exhaustion and the pain of his wounds had disappeared. He did not feel wholly rejuvenated, but neither was he any longer on the verge of collapse. He looked at his hand, and saw that the slash across the palm was now a thin scar. He met the eyes of the Demogorgon once again. "Thank you," he said.

The barest hint of a smile tugged at the thin, cruel mouth. "I grant you the choice of arenas," Sestihaculas said. "My only stipulation is that we remain on Xoth."

"I ask for one other consideration. This contest is between you and me, Serpent Lord. Let it be viewed by none else."

Sestihaculas's laughter was dry and papery, and it filled the immense hall, cuing his minions. Pandrogas put his hands over his ears until the ear-splitting mirth subsided. "What good is a contest without an audience?" the Demogorgon asked. "No, Pandrogas— this is really too much to ask. But you are a human, and so expect creation to cater to your outrageous demands. So be it. I will limit the size of our audience drastically; in fact, it will consist of no more than one." He gestured with a hand the size of Pandrogas's chest. There was a thunder of wings from one of the balconies, and the dark form of a cacodemon landed beside the sorcerer, a grin splitting its rugose face.

Pandrogas cried out. The vast chamber seemed to grow darker yet about him, until all he could see was the woman in the creature's grasp. "Amber!" he shouted, and his anguish was drowned by the renewed laughter. The cacodemon released her; she ran to Pandrogas and they embraced.

"Now, Pandrogas," Sestihaculas said, "make your choice. Should you survive, you and she may go free. If not..." he smiled again, and the serpent hissed.

The sorcerer said, "Then I choose the desert on the edge of your domain, Sestihaculas. We will do battle on the Cliffs of the Sun."

He did not know what Sestihaculas's reaction would be; the Serpent Lord simply said, "An excellent choice. Not even I can survive more than a few moments' exposure to sunlight. This will be a most satisfying contest." He raised both arms, and scarlet fire burst from his talons, sweeping over both of them in a cloud. The sorcerer closed his eyes during the moment of vertigo as the apportation spell did its work, and then he felt hot, dry sunlight on his face. He heard Amber gasp, felt her press against him. A dry, sibilant hissing broke out all about them. In the instant before he opened his eyes, Pandrogas realized the mistake he had made. The desert was the land of the sun, it was true.

But it was also the land of snakes.

Beorn saw Ardatha fall forward. He lunged for her, missed, lost his footing on the slippery rock also and tumbled after her. The enchantress had managed to turn about so that she landed feet first in the sea of rats; her heavy gown afforded her a few moments of protection against their teeth and claws. The thief landed on his back and was inundated in an instant; he felt the filthy creatures scrabbling over him, biting and scratching. He had covered his face with his hands and drawn his knees up into his chest, but still he felt himself being lacerated. Then a silver glow flashed about him, and the rats were flung away like leaves in a gale. He knew they would overrun him again in a breath's time. Beorn staggered to his feet. Ardatha had her back to the rock, and was standing in a momentary space cleared by the power of her claw. Before the verminous army could attack again, she looked over the thousands of beady eyes, at the silhouette of Endrigoth.

"We will all die together, Endrigoth!" she cried. "But by my hand, not yours!"

Beorn saw her close her eyes, and then her demon hand seemed to explode, filling the room with its glare. He cried out, dazzled. He heard her shouting once again the words of the spell she had used to shatter the door, but this time each syllable crashed like surf in a storm. The glow faded slightly, and he could see the Chthon clearly for the first time, etched in stark black and white, humanoid and yet ratlike, the muzzled mouth gaping wide in surprise. Then the cavern rocked about him like the ground had in Dulfar; he stumbled, and found himself holding on to Ardatha's human hand for balance. Her face was rapt, transfigured, in the supernal glow.

He heard the grinding and crashing of rocks about him, saw a barrel-sized stone strike the floor beside him, crushing a score of rats. And then Endrigoth moved his hands in the patterns of a spell, and purple light warred with silver. The purple struggled, overcame, surrounded them both; Beorn felt an instant of wrenching dislocation and dizziness . . .

Then the only sound was a rushing and scrabbling, rapidly fading. He opened his eyes.

He stood, with Ardatha, Tahrynyar, and the groggy Kan Konar, in a corridor of glistening obsidian. The rats were vanishing into the various crannies and cracks of the walls. A few paces from them, in the shadow of a huge column, stood Endrigoth. Rats ran up his legs, clustered on his shoulders. He stroked one in his hands protectively.

The enchantress leaned against Beorn, exhausted; her demon hand still glowed slightly, dripping motes of silver. She looked about her, first in confusion, then in triumph.

Endrigoth spoke. "My compliments, enchantress. Both your power and your will far surpass my gauging. I could not let my pets be crushed, and there was no time to be selective in my spell, as you knew would be the case. You tricked me most cleverly, and I grant you now your right, as I said, to leave Xoth."

He spoke no words of summoning, but a cacodemon appeared between them, curtained by fumes of brimstone. "The gift of the Demogorgon has served you well, Ardatha," Endrigoth continued. "But any weapon is only as strong as the arm that wields it. Remember that," and with those words, the Chthon vanished in a burst of purple light, as abruptly as the cacodemon had appeared.

The cacodemon turned a surly, hate-filled face toward them. "Three journeys you may have of me," it said with obvious reluctance. Ardatha, weak as she was, nevertheless burst into laughter, for the servant provided by Endrigoth was none other than Balandrus.

Tahrynyar was supporting Kan Konar, who was slowly shaking off the effects of Endrigoth's defense. "What happened?" the cloak-fighter asked.

"Be glad you don't know," Beorn replied. His clothes had pro-

tected him somewhat from the rats' attack, but he was still scored
with many tiny cuts and bites on his arms and face. He was worried
about the possibility of infection; already he felt dry and feverish.

Ardatha looked exhausted, but also exultant. "I defeated him,"
she said wonderingly. "I stood against Endrigoth, and won!" She
looked at Beorn. "Now, shapechanger, you will lead me to the
Runestone."

"Only if you swear by your ring to take no reprisal against me
for my flight."

Ardatha smiled. "Done. I feel magnanimous this day." She looked
at Tahrynyar and Kan Konar. "Prepare yourselves, gentlemen—a
cacodemon's route through the Abyss is quick, but scarcely comfortable."

The cloakfighter shook his head. "I am here on Xoth, and here
I shall stay. I still have a debt to settle with the Lord of Spiders."

Ardatha shrugged. "You know best how to end your life, cloakfighter. You have been of aid to me, and I would repay it. Perhaps
a spell of—"

Kan Konar held up his hand. "My thanks, enchantress, but I have
grown understandably wary of such offers."

"As you wish. I grant you luck."

The cloakfighter nodded, and with no further words gathered his
garment about him, turned and seemed to melt into the shadows, so
quickly and silently did he vanish. Ardatha looked at Tahrynyar.
"And you, marquis? What is your decision?"

The thief looked at Tahrynyar, noticing once again, even despite
the pain of his lacerations, the vast difference between the fop who
had opened the doors of Pandrogas's laboratory and the man who
stood before him now. The marquis had grown harder, leaner, and
infinitely more acquainted with suffering. He looked at the enchantress now from eyes newly lined, and said, "No more can I leave,
Ardatha. My enemy and my wife are here. I must do what I can to
find them. It is the reason I accompanied you on your quest, you
will recall."

"I remember," Ardatha said softly. "Still, I had hoped..." She
was silent for a moment, and then stepped forward to him. Tahrynyar

took her in his arms, and they kissed. It was an embrace of uninhibited passion, no doubt of it, the thief thought. He watched the marquis's fingers stroke the enchantress's back, saw the strength with which they clung to each other, and felt a surprising welling of sympathy for them both. He knew, as did they, that they would never see each other again.

Ardatha stepped back, her eyes moist. "Let me, at least, grant you the protection of my art," she said. He nodded, and she quickly spoke the words of a spell.

"There is little I can offer you of offense or defense in a land of adepts. But this will ensure that you do not become lost in this maze of corridors, and also that you will find those whom you seek." Silver fire leapt within the upraised palm of the claw and formed itself into a miniature phoenix, with wings like tongues of flame. It hovered in the air above them, filling the corridor with light.

Tahrynyar took Ardatha's demon hand tenderly in his. "May your world some day be one," he said to her. Then he turned and left quickly, following the phoenix. Ardatha silently watched him go. Then she turned to the thief. She said nothing, simply waited, her eyes and face once again hard, shielded. The enchantress he had known and feared was back.

"It is at the bottom of the Ythan Sea," he said, and explained what had happened. She showed no change of expression; merely turned to Balandrus and said, "We go now to Graystar Isle, on the fragment of Rhynne."

"This is the first journey," Balandrus snarled, and seized them once again in his burning grasp.

Chapter 18

The Cliffs
of the Sun

Tahrynyar hurried through the dungeons, not daring to look back lest his resolve weaken. All of his senses and emotions pleaded with him to turn back, to escape from Xoth with the enchantress and the thief, to abandon his self-imposed geas. And yet he continued on, following the darting bird of fire that led him through the catachthonian maze, leaving behind the only one who could save him, a woman he had wanted and who had wanted him, though they had both realized it too late.

One question repeated itself like the echoes of his footsteps in the corridors: Why was he doing this? Why, beyond all sanity or purpose, did he persist? His quest for revenge had led him to the very bowels of hell, through tribulations of which he could not even have conceived in his other life. He could still smell the nauseating odor of the rats, could still see their thousands of unblinking eyes, feral and full of bloodlust, shining up at him, could still hear the murmurous sound of their siege on the rock... he stopped walking, racked by a shudder of reaction. How could it possibly be worth it?

269

The phoenix perched upon a shelf of stone, waiting with the patience of a magical being, while Tahrynyar pondered. He still wanted to see Pandrogas dead, but the desire felt curiously cold now. Instead, the thought that came unbidden to him was: This quest will end in my death.

It was truly the first time he had acknowledged the possibility. Much as he hated to accord his enemy any credit at all, he knew that Pandrogas had been right in saying that he, Tahrynyar, would have no further reason to live once the sorcerer had died. And yet, he could not abandon the quest—his hatred of the sorcerer was by now as instinctive as breathing.

And then there was Amber, whom he had thought safe on Dulfar. Honor, if naught else, demanded that he attempt to find her. And after that, what? He told himself that the wrenching pain he had felt when Beorn had told him of her fate had been due solely to disappointment, that he was simply sorry he could not have had a more personal hand in her death. But as he walked down his silent path, he found himself remembering the music of her flute, and seeing her in a hundred different idyllic scenes from their life together. And a shock cold as the walls of the dungeons gripped him when he realized he was having difficulty remembering what she looked like.

He continued walking, following the enchantress's guide, lost in his musings. Suddenly he was brought up short by a dark-clad arm that reached from the shadows and seized him by the collar, stifling the shout of surprise that arose in his throat. He turned, and found himself facing Kan Konar.

"They could hear your blundering steps all the way back on Typor's Fist," the cloakfighter said in a low voice. "Do you wish to bring the Chthons down on us, you leadfoot?"

Tahrynyar apologized. He was so glad to see the cloakfighter that he did not even notice the insults. Walking the empty corridors alone had been oppressive in the extreme; he hoped he could convince the man to be his ally, at least until they reached the surface again.

Kan Konar pointed at the luminal. "Can you get rid of that?"

"Why—what for? Ardatha generated it to lead me—us—out of—"

"I don't need a guide, and certainly not one that will draw ca-codemons like spoiled meat draws flies." Kan Konar flung a fold of darkness over it, gathered the end of his cloak about it until no radiance escaped. "Now let's go."

Tahrynyar blinked uselessly in the ebon gloom. "But we'll be lost within five paces!"

"I won't be, and neither will you if you hold on to my cloak. I remember the route the cacodemons followed when they brought us here. Come on! We're wasting time."

Tahrynyar found such a talent unbelievable, but he kept his opinion to himself and took hold of the cloakfighter's garment. He stumbled along behind him, trying to be as noiseless as his comrade and failing miserably; were it not for the material, lighter than the finest cloth-of-gold, that he held in one hand, he would not even have known that the cloakfighter walked a pace before him. The man proceeded with a sure, steady step, not groping or hesitating at all as far as the marquis could tell. They turned this way and that, now climbing, now descending, for a considerable length of time. Tahrynyar's knees began to crack painfully, the sound as loud to his ears as a whiplash. At last Kan Konar paused for a moment. When he continued, it was more slowly and, Tahrynyar thought, more uncertainly. The marquis strained his eyes, and at last seemed to discern the faintest lessening of the darkness ahead. Kan Konar stopped. "What is it?" Tahrynyar whispered.

"I seem to have lost my way," the cloakfighter replied softly. "Still, it is an exit. Let's see what it is also an entrance to."

They continued. The faint grayness grew stronger and became a soft glow that radiated from an irregular crevice in the rock ahead. They stepped forward, onto a tiny ledge overlooking a gigantic shaft. The pearly luminosity that lit it came from far overhead; an equal distance below them, the shaft narrowed into a dark throat, from which a slight wind, laced with scents of corruption, rose. Fog and mist shrouded the walls of the huge infundibulum, and filmy strands and sheets, like decaying curtains, hung from the sloping walls. It reminded Tahrynyar uncomfortably of the cloud-lined vortex over which he had dangled in Darkhaven. The ledge on which they stood was scarcely wide enough to accommodate them both. Tahrynyar took another step forward, to peer into the darkness—and felt his boots stick to the floor of the ledge.

Kan Konar unwrapped the phoenix from his cloak. By its flickering light Tahrynyar could clearly see the soft ankle-deep grayness in which he stood. It was not fog. It was silk—spider silk. Web cocoons, in which they could dimly glimpse the encysted, desiccated remains of animals and humans, lined the spiraling shaft—a cornucopia of death.

They stood within the funnel of an enormous web.

"So," Kan Konar said, almost to himself; "it appears my way has been decided for me."

Tahrynyar turned to dart back through the crack—then froze as it disappeared under a layer of silk even as they watched. Tahrynyar could see thousands of tiny bulbous forms busily at work; in a matter of moments the last hint of an opening faded beneath their warp, and the spiders vanished into the depths of the silk.

Mouth dry with fear, he looked back at the cloakfighter. Kan Konar turned slowly, his face expressionless. He stepped to the edge of the shaft and looked down into its depths. "Zhormallion!" he cried. "You who slew the Daimyo Ras Parolyn! Step forward and make reparation!"

A voice answered him from the depths of the web. Like the voices of Sestihaculas and Endrigoth, there was the merest creatural undertone to it: a brittle, crackling note that also somehow hinted of a terrifying, sanguinolent hunger. "Ah, it is a belligerent gnat in my web! Fool, do you not realize that your blood is already drained?"

The first syllables of that voice had struck Tahrynyar with a fear far outmatching even that which he had felt when surrounded by Endrigoth's horde. There, at least, the threat that had surrounded them had been warm-blooded, mammalian, not the verminous horror that lurked all about them, just out of sight, now. And Endrigoth, though a monster, was not nearly so terrifyingly *alien* as the thing that lurked in the breathing darkness below. All that kept him from fainting in his fear was the knowledge that he would fall directly into the maw from whence that voice issued. He looked at Kan Konar. The cloakfighter's face seemed paler than usual, or perhaps that was simply the glow of the phoenix. He stood in a ready pose, knees slightly bent, hands grasping the seams of his cloak. "I challenge you, Zhormallion!" he shouted again.

"And I accept." Upon those words, Tahrynyar felt movement over the tattered doeskin of his boots—he looked down and choked back a scream. Thousands of spiders had surfaced from the depths of the silk; as though guided by a single mind, they poured toward the chasm, silk streaming behind them. The ledge on which the marquis and the cloakfighter stood began to grow, extending like a blindly questing pseudopod across the gulf. More spiders cast themselves onto the lifting air, their webs extending like ectoplasm toward the opposite wall from which a similar lip was extruding. In a matter of moments a silken bridge spanned the chasm, and the spiders once again faded from view.

The hanging folds that laced the far wall then opened like curtains, revealing a dark lacuna. And in that darkness, something large moved. In form it was humanoid, with two extra sets of limbs, but its movement was utterly inhuman—so quickly did it step from the recess to the foot of the bridge that it seemed almost to materialize. The light of the phoenix was not strong enough to illuminate it clearly, but Tahrynyar could see eight shining, unblinking eyes, mandibular jaws and pedipalpi. The head seemed to merge into the body, which was sheathed in chitinous armor and black, silken hair.

"Come and face me then, gnat. Attack and defend—set your heart to pounding. Your blood will taste the better for it."

Kan Konar stepped out onto the bridge and approached Zhormallion. Tahrynyar noticed that his boots did not stick to the scaffolding web. The cloakfighter walked with his head high, shrouded in his flowing cloak. Zhormallion advanced also, with a flickering movement that started and ended in complete immobility. They faced each other in the center of the bridge.

"When I take a form approaching human, I find myself touched by human curiosity," the Spider Lord said. "Why have you come thus to die, gnat?"

"You sent a plague of your vermin upon my master, the Daimyo of Typan. I mean to avenge his death."

"Ah, yes, I seem to recall. One of those whom I choose to cherish bit him, and he ordered a purge of them within his house."

"For his death, you shall now die."

A dry, rattling sound that might have been a chuckle came from the Chthon. "I think not."

Kan Konar spoke no further; instead, he leaped forward, his cloak cutting like a scythe toward Zhormallion's cephalothorax. The motion was almost too fast for Tahrynyar to follow, but Zhormallion avoided it easily, scuttling to one side. From its abdominal spinnerets poured viscid strands, which its many-jointed arms, tipped with claws and scopulae, hurled toward the cloakfighter in a blur of speed. Kan Konar whirled his cloak about his head, the razored hems severing the fibers as they looped through the air. He lashed toward his enemy with the silver chain from about his neck, but a limb flickered out to block the blow, entangling the chain and jerking it from the cloakfighter's hand, to hurl into the darkness below them. The Chthon rushed at the cloakfighter then with the phenomenal quickness of his subjects; Tahrynyar caught his breath as Kan Konar sprang into the air, executing a complete flip over Zhormallion. His adversary turned as he landed, but the cloakfighter managed to sweep the weighted end of his cloak against Zhormallion's legs, entangling them. The Spider Lord fell from the bridge into the chasm; Tahrynyar felt an instant of jubilation before he saw the Chthon swinging from a thick cable of silk. Before Kan Konar could attempt to cut it, Zhormallion had swarmed back onto the bridge and renewed his attack.

Tahrynyar had seen a great many demonstrations of martial prowess in Turrith, but none that could touch Kan Konar's skill against the Spider Lord. But it was obvious from the start that the battle could have only one conclusion. Though it seemed to take a lifetime, it was in reality over very quickly. Kan Konar struck again, his cloak flickering like dark lightning; Zhormallion's pedipalpi caught it and pulled it free of the cloakfighter's body, dropping it on the bridge. Kan Konar leaped forward to attack barehanded, but before he could cover half the distance between them gray tendrils shot forward and wrapped about him, encasing him quickly in silk. Zhormallion drew the struggling cloakfighter in while Tahrynyar watched in horrified fascination, and embraced him with black, jointed limbs. A single scream of hopelessness and terror burst from the cloak-fighter as the Spider Lord's fangs pierced him. Then Zhormallion, carrying the lifeless form, scurried quickly back into the darkness of his lair.

Tahrynyar felt himself very close to madness at that point. He looked about frantically for escape. How long would it be before Zhormallion returned for him and left his shriveled corpse dangling alongside Kan Konar's?

It was then that he felt something crawling, feather light, beneath the sleeve of his torn dolman. Gingerly he lifted the material away from his arm, exposing a spider with a body as large as the end of his thumb and the color of a corpse. Revulsion shook him, and he thought he saw the loathsome thing tense ever so slightly, felt the tiny claws grip his crawling flesh as it prepared to bite. He bit his lip, tasting blood, and did not move, though every nerve within him sang with the urge to crush it. But to do so, he knew, would be to invite the wrath of Zhormallion, and so he gritted his teeth and waited.

The spider turned and crawled slowly back down his forearm to his fingertips. There it dropped off, descending on a thread back into the grayness. Tahrynyar was drenched in chilling sweat. He forced himself to walk forward on the web bridge, Ardatha's luminal following him, and pick up the cloak from where it lay. He dropped his torn feather cloak in its place and wrapped the heavy garment about him. It was irrational, he knew, but he felt safer within its folds.

No sooner had he donned it, however, than he suddenly felt a swarming movement at his feet, moving up his legs. He looked down and saw uncounted spiders swarming up from the interstices of the web like an army attacking out of a fog, covering his feet with grayness, enveloping him in a pall. He screamed and tried to run, but already his legs were bound, and his panic-stricken efforts only caused him to sprawl full-length upon the narrow isthmus of silk. More spiders crawled over his face, scrabbling through his hair; he glimpsed the eight eyes of one staring into his an instant before his vision was veiled by the thickening shroud. His screams were gagged in another moment, his nose stopped, his ears covered with the filmy substance and his arms bound to his sides. His lungs labored for air; he grew dizzy, felt himself floating...

Something vile spattered in his face, causing him to cough and choke. He rolled over, shook his head and looked up.

He lay, still swathed in silk, in the mushroom forest. Above him a lacteal discharge dripped slowly from the underside of a toadstool. It had dissolved the cocoon where it had struck it.

Tahrynyar maneuvered until his bound arms were beneath the pituitous growth and waited for the next drop. It came, and his arms were freed. He managed to extricate himself from the rest of the webbing, and stood shakily, drenched in foul-smelling grume.

During the process of freeing himself he had not attempted to think about how he had gotten there. He did not think at all for some time, save for vague feelings of gratitude. Abhorrent though these surroundings were, they were the forests of Tamboriyon compared to where he had been. But eventually the question had to be faced— how had it happened?

He finally concluded that it had been Zhormallion's doing, but why, he did not know. Perhaps the Spider Lord had rewarded him for staying his hand instead of killing one of the Chthon's minions. Or perhaps Zhormallion, sated for the moment on the cloakfighter's blood, had cast him out of the nest for some unknown reason, as he had sometimes seen spiders and other creatures do. No doubt he would never know. But he was alive, and no longer in the city of the Chthons, though he was still on Xoth.

And so, perhaps, were Pandrogas and Amber.

He realized that he was ravenously hungry; the fact surprised him, considering what he had just been through. He managed to swallow a few bites of one of the mushrooms which the cloakfighter had identified as nutritious. He thought about Kan Konar. The cloakfighter had journeyed all the way from Typor's Fist on a mission of revenge for his dead lord—a mission he had no chance of accomplishing. His blood now nourished Zhormallion, his shrunken body would forever be a trophy on the Chthon's wall, and for what? Not even for the empty satisfaction of honor.

Shall I now do the same? Tahrynyar asked himself. Shall I return to that den of nightmares, seeking two human beings who are in all likelihood dead, and most likely die myself as well? He had already looked into the eyeless sockets of several most horrible and lingering deaths. He had thrown away one chance at escape—perhaps he had now been offered another. He looked up; above him the huge mass of Xoth's shielding companion blocked the sun. But at one edge was a line of fire, and he could see the shaft of sunlight hanging like a curtain in the fuliginous air.

He was near the Cliffs of the Sun.

The drive to seek out and kill the sorcerer seemed at last leeched from him, burned away by the horror he had passed through and the sight of his companion's death. And what of Amber, Amber his wife? Should he seek her now, and if so, for what motive—revenge or rescue?

When Beorn had told him that she was on Xoth, for a moment he had felt once again the incandescent, desperate love for her that he had once known; had been fired to seek her and rescue her, to prove to her once and for all that he, not the sorcerer, was the man for her. But the horrors interposed between then and now had torn his courage, so new-found, from him. He was neither the old marquis now, nor the new; he was a shell, incapable of any feelings, any desires.

He shivered and tugged the dark cloak tighter about him. He would go to the Cliffs of the Sun. There he might find succor; there he would be safe from the Chthons and their cacodemons. There, at least, he could let the cleansing light warm and protect him while he decided on his course. And from there—he did not know. It was enough to have a destination, at least for a time.

Once again I have erred, Pandrogas thought wearily. Once again I have proven myself unworthy of my rank. And this time, the error has been fatal.

When he had opened his eyes the dry chorus of hissings and

rattlings had increased. He stood now with Amber on the adust red sands of Xoth's edge, amidst outcroppings of cairngorm and other crystalline formations. The land fell away from him in a series of terraces and drops to the precipice; they were near enough to feel the updraft from the Abyss. Not far from them was the ancient wreck of a dragonship; Pandrogas could see the mummified corpse of a dragoneer sprawled on the sands next to the hull, parchment skin stretched tight over bones, a sword still held in the skeletal grasp. Above them, on the top of a bluff, the demarcation of shadow and sunlight lay, and beyond its boundary squatted the Demogorgon, framed against the dark sky and the fungoid growths of his domain. And all about Pandrogas and Amber clustered his pets. A bushmaster coiled within easy striking distance of Amber's leg, the gray and brown diamond pattern of its dorsal scales shining in the sunlight. On a rock beside Pandrogas's head lay a hooded hamadryad easily fourteen feet long. As far as they could see lurked other venomous serpents: mambas, fer-de-lances, asps, kraits, adders.

"If you move," Sestihaculas said, "they will strike." The Demogorgon grinned, showing fangs. The viper at his groin coiled about one of his legs. "You seem to have outsmarted yourself, Pandrogas."

The sorcerer did not reply. He kept his gaze fixed on the Serpent Lord; from the corner of his eye he saw Amber watching him. She knows I have given up, he thought. There was nothing he could say or do to assuage her; the Demogorgon had won. He could cast no magic of consequence here—his first attempt at the movements necessary to formulate a spell with even a hope of defeating Sestihaculas would result in the snakes striking both him and her. He could only wait helplessly until the Chthon decided to end his cruel game, and their lives.

I have been a failure from the start, he told himself. He thought with bitter regret of all the years he had wasted hiding in Darkhaven, searching futilely for a codex to magic. He had been afraid to admit the truth—there was no such codex, no way to stop the inevitable decay of the fragments' paths. The world was doomed, and he could not help prevent it—he could not even save his home from destruction. He could not even save the woman he loved. He could not even save himself.

Amber touched his arm, the movement brought a warning hiss from the bushmaster coiled at her feet. "My power is yours," she whispered. "I cannot control it, but you can. Take it, shape it, use it to defeat him!"

He shook his head. "I cannot. At my first motion we will both die."

"There must be *something* you can do!"

"There is nothing! Don't you understand? *I do not have the skill!* I am on his territory, my power is weakened. He has won!"

Amber stared at him, and he saw in her gaze not the anger or the contempt or the fear that he had dreaded, but only a vast sadness and regret. He wanted to explain to her what he had never been able to tell anyone—that he had sought the codex not so much to save the world as to save himself. He had never been able to master fully the single most important precept of magic, the one rule he had reiterated to his students endlessly throughout the years—he had never believed fully in his ability, in himself. And now she knew that, and, knowing that she knew, he was ready to die.

The Demogorgon stood. "Enough of this," he said. "I must say that you disappoint me, Pandrogas. I thought you would make some attempt, however futile, against me. Is that not, after all, the supposed definition of humanity—to strive against hopeless odds, to seek a light when all about you is darkness?" He laughed then, and raised his left hand. A ball of roiling odylic energy, glowing like lava, began to form within the palm.

Pandrogas watched the sphere of destruction grow. It seemed to take quite a long time. He stood there, overwhelmed by his helplessness, waiting to die.

Amber cried: *"No!"*

He felt the heat of the power that rose from her, like the flames behind the opened door of an athanor. Blue fire seemed to burst from her, expanding in a wave, crisping the snakes about them to ash in an instant. He heard Sestihaculas bellow in shock and rage as Amber collapsed weakly against the rock in reaction. Atop the cliff, the Demogorgon raised the crimson fireball to hurl.

Behind him the sorcerer saw Tahrynyar, wearing Kan Konar's cloak, emerge from the jungle. He recalled something Kan Konar had said at one point during their journey through the mushroom forest: "Every time I fight, I think of myself as a dead man. One can only lose that which is precious."

He was now free to move, to cast with words and gestures the mightiest spells he knew. But there was no time. Sestihaculas's words echoed in his thoughts: *To seek a light when all about you is darkness.*

"*Limnus diam,*" he said quietly.

The fireball in Sestihaculas's hand flared in a burst of incarnadine brilliance that blinded all of them. Pandrogas staggered back, rubbing his eyes frantically to clear his vision. He looked up, and through luminous scotomata he saw Sestihaculas, his hands still clawing at eyes unaccustomed to light. The Demogorgon staggered forward, and Tahrynyar hurled Kan Konar's cloak toward him from behind. The heavy garment struck him, wrapping about his horned head; already off-balance, the ruler of the Chthons stumbled and fell, with a hissing scream, into the sunlight.

The cloak dropped away from him as he tumbled down the cliff; the Demogorgon sprawled on his back in the burning sand, arms out, crucified by the merciless sun. He did not cry out, though Pandrogas could see the scaled skin immediately beginning to sear and crack. The sorcerer stepped forward. Sestihaculas looked up at him with lidless eyes.

"You have won," he croaked. "But you could not have done it alone."

"I know," Pandrogas replied. "But the result is the same."

"I ruled the Chthons when the world was shattered, sorcerer. I fled the burning sun with my people, saw them consumed by the chaos and fire. I led them here, where we awaited the time that the world would once more be one, and its caverns ours again. It is soon at hand. I regret I will not see it."

"What do you mean?"

"Even in winning you have lost," the Demogorgon whispered.

Smoke was beginning to rise from his blackening skin; Pandrogas could hear the bubbling sound of roasting meat. He held his breath at the nidorous scent. "Even now," Sestihaculas continued, "the repository of your power, and of the greatest power this world has ever known, is in the hands of one who will serve my dream, though he knows it not. Ever so subtly have I manipulated him and his followers, feeding them visions, coming to them in disguise while they dreamed, expounding my orthodoxy, tending the fires of their fanaticism. Look upon the deity of your enemies, Pandrogas. Look upon the face of the One God."

Pandrogas nodded in astonished comprehension. "Of course," he said slowly. "The gift of the demon hand to Ardatha, who had the makings of a fanatic."

"My kind were too limited by the loss of night; we could not search for the Necromancer's tomb. But the Circle could. And Stonebrow has found it!"

"Do you think the remnants of your race would survive the cataclysm of a re-formation?" Pandrogas asked. "Think of it, Sestihaculas! The Shattering nearly wiped out both Chthon and humankind! To fuse the fragments together again would wipe them clean of life! There can be no going back—the world is as it is."

"Whether you are right or wrong matters no longer," the Serpent Lord said faintly. Pandrogas had to concentrate to understand the words; the Demogorgon's cheeks and tongue had withered like paper in a flame. "I die; the sun has claimed me." The huge frame was beginning to shrink, showing bones. The penile viper was now only a shriveled, twisted stump. Sestihaculas's eyes were sightless cusps, sunken in their sockets.

"Aid me and you shall not die," Pandrogas replied. "Swear that you will cause no harm to me or those with me; agree to aid me in my quest, and I will let you live. Refuse, and I promise you that your kind will not long survive you."

The Demogorgon hesitated only a moment. "Agreed," he hissed through fleshless jaws.

"*Sushha mand palowen sandai,*" Pandrogas said then, calling upon the Hands of the Wind. With a stirring of sand and dust the cloakfighter's garment lifted into the air, following the sorcerer's pantomime, to hover and cast a protective shadow over Sestihaculas. For a moment the charred husk was utterly still, and Pandrogas feared he had been too late. Then a shudder convulsed the frame. The flesh began to swiftly reconstitute, swelling and rehydrating as the sorcerer watched. The hide regained its colors, firmed as muscles bunched once more beneath it. The forked tongue flickered once, twice. Then Sestihaculas slowly rose to his knees, his breathing harsh with effort.

"Remember your pledge," the sorcerer cautioned, as the Demogorgon towered over him once more.

Sestihaculas looked at him, his ophidian gaze unfathomable. "It is remembered," the Chthon said. "Ask of me what you will."

"What is Stonebrow's destination?"

"He journeys to the fragment called Nigromancien, there to use Darkhaven's Runestone to awaken and control the Necromancer."

"You will provide us with transportation there, and thence to Darkhaven. You will make no interference of our actions."

"Call upon Taloroth the cacodemon," Sestihaculas said heavily. Without further words, he turned and began climbing the escarpment. The cloak followed him, shielding him from the sun. He moved slowly, effort apparent in his every motion. Amber, recovered, joined Pandrogas, and together they watched him struggle toward the darkness. When he reached the safety of the shadows he turned and looked down at them.

"Farewell, sorcerer," he said. "If you value your life, do not leave Darkhaven again!" He reached above his head and snatched the cloak from the sky, rending it with his talons. Then he vanished in a burst of erythrean flame.

Pandrogas felt Amber relax against him. He lifted a hand and stroked her cheek, feeling the reaction to the tension leave him exhausted. For a long moment they simply stood there, silent and together, feeling the heat of the sun on their skin. Time enough to speak of their adventures since they had been separated in the cemetery; time enough to plan the journeys and the battles that still lay ahead. I am still alive, Pandrogas thought in wonder. More won-

derful still, he was glad that he lived. Whether or not he could have
defeated Sestihaculas alone did not matter. They had acted together,
and so survived.

They, and Tahrynyar . . . even as he remembered the action of the
marquis, he heard a voice behind them.

"It's not over yet. Now you must deal with me."

Amber whirled about with a gasp of shock. Pandrogas turned
also, to see Tahrynyar standing on a large slab of sandstone at the
cliff's edge, holding a pitted sword in one hand and a marteldefer
in the other. "The weapons of dead men," he said to Pandrogas,
who realized he had obtained them from the wreck of the dragonship.
"They will suit one of us very well very soon." He held them up.
"Choose, sorcerer. Fight like a man, for once in your life."

Pandrogas saw Amber staring at her husband, and remembered
that she had last seen him an unconscious cripple in Darkhaven. The
change in his appearance must be quite a shock to her, he thought.
He had metamorphosized, and the tattered rags that had once been
finery were the least part of it. He was gaunt now, his face lined
with pain and sorrow. As he stepped forward, Pandrogas saw that
he still limped slightly. But more than all this, what set him apart
from the old marquis was the look in his eyes—the desperate,
yearning look of one who has driven himself past hatred and into a
kind of madness.

"Tahrynyar," Amber murmured, her tone that of horrified disbelief. "Am I mad, at last? How came you here?"

"Is not the edge of hell an appropriate place to see me again,
Amber? I have followed the two of you across what's left of the
world for one reason—revenge! And I intend to claim it at last."
He looked at Pandrogas again. "If you will not choose, than take
what is given you!" and he hurled the marteldefer at the sorcerer,
who caught it by the haft. Tahrynyar advanced, sword held ready.

"I am the one your quarrel is with, Tahrynyar," Amber said, "not
Pandrogas. Do you intend to kill me as well?" The marquis hesitated
slightly at her words, then stepped forward again. Amber stepped
in front of the sorcerer, but Pandrogas pushed her aside gently. She
looked at him in quick anger. "This is no time for gallantry!"

"True," Pandrogas said quietly, "but it is a time for sorcery.

"Tahrynyar," he continued, "I will not battle you. With a word and a motion I can melt your blade from its hilt, or bend your will to mine. Put down the sword. This insanity must end."

"It will end with your death!" and Tahrynyar raised the sword to strike. Then he shouted in pain and dropped it, for a quiet phrase from the sorcerer had made good his threat; the blade ran like silver oil upon the sand.

Tahrynyar looked at him, tears in his eyes. "Damn you," he said softly. "Damn you both! I had almost given it up! I had almost walked away from it! And then, I saw you together..."

He launched himself at Pandrogas, fingers hooked into claws. The sorcerer sidestepped instinctively, and the marquis stumbled as one knee twisted beneath him. Amber cried out as Tahrynyar fell, sliding down the escarpment even as Sestihaculas had done earlier. He seized an outcropping of quartz and dangled, half-floating, in the updraft from the Abyss.

"Don't move!" Pandrogas shouted to him. Steeling himself against his fear of the limitless gulf, he approached the edge and started to speak the words to summon the Hands of the Wind once more. But Tahrynyar shouted, "No! Not again! *You won't save me again!*"

He released his grip. The wind seized him, hurled him up and outward. Like a leaf, like a tear, like a final breath, he fell into infinity.

Pandrogas stepped back and turned to Amber, who stared, face drawn and white, into the uncaring sky. "Can you do nothing?" she whispered.

He shook his head. "He is gone."

"It should have been me," she murmured.

Pandrogas felt the meaning of her words chill him. "Amber," he said. "Amber, no."

She turned away from the Abyss. He tried to touch her, to take her in his arms, but she stepped back, the wind whipping the cloak of dragon leather about her shoulders. "How can I love," she asked softly, "when someone has hated me that much?"

"He didn't hate you," Pandrogas said. "He saved your life; he

threw the cloak at Sestihaculas. The three of us defeated the Demogorgon together."

"He did it that he might kill us himself." Her tone was lifeless.

"You don't know that."

"I only know that he was my husband; that I loved him once,
and that he is now dead. There seems little point in going on."

"You have to," he said, his voice harsh in his ears. "Our quest
is not yet over, and your power will be necessary to finish it. We
must stop Stonebrow before he awakens the Necromancer. I told
you once that magic offers no escape from pain, Amber. Nor does
it offer escape from responsibility."

She raised her eyes to his at last. "We made a mistake, didn't
we?"

His throat was too dry to speak. After a long time, he nodded.

"How? How did it happen? When did it start? Somewhere there
was a point where it all went wrong. How did we miss it?"

Pandrogas did not reply. He remembered standing on the Warped
Stairs, so long ago it seemed now, and wondering the same thing.
He wondered now if he would ever know the answer.

"I told you I could teach you about magic," he said at last, "not
about life."

Amber said nothing. Pandrogas turned away, and began the spell
that would summon Taloroth the cacodemon.

Chapter 19

Stonebrow Unmasked

Beorn, Ardatha, and Balandrus stood within the highest room of the spire on Graystar Isle. The thief looked about him at the sea-soaked devastation. Brine encrusted the walls, and seaweed was looped and festooned everywhere. Dead, bloated fish had been piled in corners by the evaporating water. Through the open wall they could see rain pouring from the leaden sky. The cacodemon sought the darkest corner, where he crouched, glowering, his stench almost lost in the reek of decaying marine creatures.

"What could have sent a wave so high?" the enchantress murmured in amazement.

"A fragment," Beorn told her. "It fell from the sky and swamped the ship we were on. That's when I lost the Runestone. It must have splashed half the ocean onto this Isle."

"There is no time to lose," Ardatha said, more to herself than to him. "The world is falling apart." The thief watched as she evoked the Charm of Aware Air. *"Secorum damarkor tul ebona,"* she said, closing her eyes and waiting for a long moment.

"Stonebrow is not here," she said at last; "nor do I sense the Runestone within a considerable radius of the Isle."

"As for that, I told you—it is on the bottom of the Ythan Sea."

"Perhaps; perhaps. But Stonebrow's search for it was conducted from here; he would be here now, restoring his sanctum to a workable state, unless he had what he had been searching for." She turned toward the stairs. "Come," she said briefly over her shoulder as she descended. The two of them followed, the cacodemon growling softly. Beorn hardly noticed the monster's truculence so close behind him. He was exhausted, both physically and mentally. He was worried about infection from the rat bites and scratches he had sustained; his mouth felt dry, and he was dizzy. But more than that, he felt he had reached the end of his endurance. How long could he keep up this insane leaping from fragment to fragment, constantly facing death in its most terrifying forms?

Perhaps the worst is now over, he told himself. After all, he had been to Xoth—what fate could be more horrible?

Ardatha noticed his state when they reached the laboratory, which was still knee-deep in water. With the aid of a cantrip she walked across its muddy surface, and from a coffer in the wall's recess took several ampoules. From them she mixed an electuary, which she handed to the thief with an admonishment to drink. Beorn, expecting a nauseating draught, was pleasantly surprised by its sweet taste. He drained the cruet and began to feel better almost immediately. Meanwhile, Ardatha strolled about the top of the flood, picking up floating scrolls and parchments from the debris. She looked through them quickly, then cast them aside. At last, sitting crosslegged as though on an undulating couch near where Beorn and Balandrus waited on the stairs, she spoke a phrase; the thief watched a silver shimmer rise from her hand, like heat waves from a flat rock. After a moment the water between them bubbled, and a sphere of green force broke the surface. Within it was a leather-bound volume. The sphere floated to Ardatha's demon hand, and upon contact with it vanished like a bubble. She opened the book to the place marked and read it, then stood quickly. Beorn saw excitement in her face.

"He has found it!" she exclaimed.

"The Runestone?"

"I would not doubt it. But this tells me he has found Nigromancien, the tomb of the Necromancer!"

Beorn could see on the page of bound vellum an emblem that appeared familiar to him: a portrait with two profiles, one a bearded face, its opposite a grinning skull. "What does that device represent?" he asked.

"It is the escutcheon of the Necromancer," Ardatha replied somewhat impatiently. "Why do you ask?"

"I have seen it before—in a haunted bedchamber in Darkhaven..."

The enchantress made a gesture of dismissal. "We have no time for your reminiscing!" She looked at the cacodemon triumphantly. "Our second journey, Balandrus, is to Nigromancien!"

"Let it soon be over," Balandrus snarled. Ardatha lifted her hand at his words. "Beware, cacodemon! I have loosed the full power of Sestihaculas's gift before—I fear it no longer. Would you like a taste of it now?"

Balandrus lifted Beorn once again and lumbered forward through the water, which hissed and steamed about his loins, to Ardatha. "Enchantress," he said, "know this: by your hand you command my actions, but never my loyalty. Your goals are the goals of my master, and I would see them accomplished. But beware the day your power over me ever wanes."

Ardatha slapped him then, and a platinum flash seared his cheek where she struck. Balandrus howled in pain.

"To Nigromancien," the enchantress said softly. The cacodemon lifted her, his eyes like flaming arrowheads.

Stonebrow's journey to Nigromancien had taken a long time— how long, it was difficult to tell, since there was no way to measure time in the Abyss. But he had stopped for food and rest many times before he saw the fragment. The sight filled him with awe. It was an odd, almost forgotten feeling; as a sorcerer, he had witnessed and performed miracles and magicks to such an extent that he had thought himself too jaded to ever be impressed again. Even the

cataclysm on Rhynne he had viewed primarily in terms of the in-
convenience it had caused him. But as the details of the Necromancer's tomb slowly resolved from a distant silhouette and the sheer
size of it became evident, he stared in disbelief and wonderment.
Nigromancien was no less than a floating statue shaped from an
entire fragment by the hammers and chisels of countless forgotten
workers. As he drew closer, the gargantuan proportions became more
overwhelming; it was hard to determine the scale, but the masked
sorcerer estimated it at no less than ten miles from the sandalled
feet to the cowled, bearded head.

He closed upon it with maddening slowness, but at last the cockatrice, wings spread against the wind, glided alongside its peninsular
length toward the head. The likeness was that of a man lying in
state. The declivitous folds of his robe, some the width of a ghaut,
were green with lichens, sedge, and scrub. His hands, folded across
the tableland of his chest, were ridged tors of stone, dusted with
snow. The weightless cockatrice had no need of rest, but it was still
several hours before they drew level with the head. There Stonebrow
hoped to gain entrance to the interior of the fragment via one of the
orifices; after all, was not the sphere's reading *Seek knowledge at
its heart*? As they approached it he saw several giereagles hurtle,
shrieking, from nests in the ear. The cockatrice moved over the
cheekbone, using its wings now to support its returning weight, and
settled down at last beside the nose.

With the flap of the cockatrice's wings now quiet, the desolation
of the locale was intense. Stonebrow traced a circle in the air, but
drew little comfort from the gesture. He looked about him. From
here the sculptured nature of the fragment was not so apparent; the
nose was, at this range, a monticule that reached on the one hand
toward a distant crest that was the lower eyelid, and on the other
terminated in the cavernous opening of the nostril. The rock beneath
his feet rose gently upward toward the striated ridge that represented
the mustache. Stonebrow touched the base of his own nose lightly
with the tip of one finger; then, moved by an obscure impulse, he
retrieved his mask from the cockatrice's saddlebag and donned it.
How strangely appropriate that he, Stonebrow, should be the first

one in ages to stand upon this granite icon. The One God's plans are not without irony at times, he thought.

He reinforced the cockatrice's trance and then climbed up the slope and entered the nostril, the winged serpent slithering obediently behind him. He unpacked a starcrystal rod, and wondered if the forgotten artisans had devoted the same conscientious detail to the interior of the tomb as they had to its exterior. Could he in fact follow the echoing nasal passage to the shaft of the pharynx, and from there down the trachea and into the vast caverns of the lungs? Would his goal actually end in a huge aortal or ventricular chamber? There was only one way to find out. He started walking, keeping close to the towering wall of the septum. Within his pouch he could feel the power of the Runestone, waiting to be unleashed. It would not be long now. Soon the Necromancer's sleep of ages would end— soon he would rise again, brought back by the magic he had used to revivify so many others. Stonebrow would have to perform the ceremony alone, and that would increase the danger of losing control. But that could not be helped. It would be several commonmonths before all the members of the Circle could be gathered at Nigromancien, and by then more fragments would have fallen, and the delicate balance of the orbits damaged beyond the ability of any magic to restore. It had to be done now.

He kept walking, feeling sharp aches now in his hips. He had not gone to this much physical effort in years, Stonebrow thought ruefully. There was a time when he could have run the entire length of the fragment and still have energy enough for strenuous hours of spellcasting. But his isolation and studies—and most of all, of course, the inexorable, relentless years—had taken all that from him. Still, should he be attacked by some feral creature that lurked in the depths of these caverns now, he had his sorcery and the acidic venom of his cockatrice to defend him. It was a comforting realization. True, he had smelled no fumets, seen no devoured remains to indicate that this was the lair of a beast. But one could never be sure...

Something moved in the shadows ahead.

Stonebrow stopped. Whatever it was, it loomed huge and ominous in the edge of the crystal's radiance. There was a hint of wings as large as the cockatrice's rising from a hulking, anthropoid form. Suddenly it rushed at him with appalling speed; the masked sorcerer caught a glimpse of sulfurous eyes and yellow fangs before he threw himself to the cold stone. From behind him the cockatrice hurtled forward, hissing. A jet of acid spattered against the cacodemon's impervious hide, and ricocheting droplets left tiny craters in Stonebrow's mask. The cockatrice's body wrapped about the cacodemon's, its tail seeking the other's thick neck. The cacodemon clawed at the winged serpent, talons shrieking over the armor of the scales. Stonebrow was about to shout a spell that would put an end to the struggle, when silver fire flashed in the darkness. *"Let be, Balandrus!"* a voice shouted—a voice that sounded familiar to him.

He shouted a similar command to the cockatrice; the two creatures reluctantly broke their deadly clinch. Stonebrow rose stiffly to his feet and saw, standing before him in the starcrystal's light, a burly man with red hair and beard and a tall woman, whose left arm ended in a demon claw. Stonebrow felt a dizzying sense of relief rush over him. "Ardatha!" he cried thankfully. The two of them embraced.

"I did not make good my pledge to deliver Darkhaven's Runestone," Ardatha told him, smiling. "But I have done the next best thing—I am here to help you awaken the Necromancer!"

"With my most valued assistant beside me we cannot fail," Stonebrow said. "Thank the One God, who brought you here! Now we must find the tomb! The sphere has told me where it is: *'Seek knowledge at its heart.'*"

"We shall find it," Ardatha assured him. "The One God smiles on us." The sorcerer and the enchantress moved forward then, carrying light into the darkness. Balandrus, grinning as if at a private joke, followed his master, as the cockatrice followed his.

Beorn followed the blue light of the starcrystal. He followed reluctantly. The instincts of the thief, honed over the years to an almost extrasensory sharpness, warned him that all was not as it should be. And Balandrus made him increasingly nervous; it was obvious from the way he had attacked Stonebrow's cockatrice that the cacodemon was boiling with repressed hatred. But still he followed; he had no other choice. He could not leave Nigromancien save by their aid.

The stench of brimstone, the brutal force of the wind, the crushing grip of the talons—these were the only impressions Amber had of her journey. It lasted only a very short time, but when it was over she dropped to her knees, nauseated and dizzy. Pandrogas helped her to her feet. They stood in a corridor of naked stone, lit by occasional starcrystal rods. Ahead of them the passage curved toward the right, and behind them, toward the left.

"Are you all right?" Pandrogas asked solicitously.

She managed to catch her breath and gasped an affirmative. The vertigo passed slowly. "Where are we?" she asked.

"Within the fragment called Nigromancien, I expect," the sorcerer replied. "According to the Demogorgon and the mysterious Stonebrow, this is the tomb of the Necromancer."

Quite suddenly, the silence and oppressiveness seemed to settle on Amber with suffocating intensity. She felt as if she were back in Darkhaven again, with the sense of great weight above her, pressing down on her. The shadowy form of Taloroth the cacodemon, lurking nearby, did not improve her mood. Exhaustion flooded her, and she leaned against the wall. She had not even had time to really register the fact that Tahrynyar had suddenly appeared before them on the Cliffs of the Sun, much less comprehend his death. And now they were abruptly thousands of miles away from him, where he was floating in the Abyss, doomed to slow starvation...

Pandrogas held her gently by the shoulders. "We have no time for this, darling."

She twisted out of his grasp. "He's *dead*, and I don't even have time to mourn!" she shouted.

"You didn't love him," Pandrogas said, and she saw him wince as he realized the thoughtlessness of his remark.

"I was not only mourning for him," she said quietly.

Pandrogas hesitated, then was about to say something in reply when suddenly Amber gasped, shivering as though struck by a cold blast of air. She had felt *something*, the way a change of air pressure in the inner ear causes sounds to suddenly shift, or the way the suggestion of a scent long forgotten will bring vivid memories back to life; so in such a way she had been told, by no sense she could name, that the first words of a spell that could literally change the world had been spoken somewhere within these anfractuous passages. An instant after she reacted, Pandrogas felt it. He wheeled about and faced the cacodemon. "You will help us stop this ceremony!" he ordered.

"I am bound by Sestihaculas to ferry you on three journeys," Taloroth replied. "I will do nothing to otherwise aid you."

Pandrogas shouted, "Then take us to it!"

"This is the second journey," Taloroth told him. This one lasted only an instant, and when her vision cleared Amber saw that they stood within a shadowed narthex which opened into a huge crypt, bounded by columns the size of redwoods. At the far end, on a dais, was a sarcophagus of onyx, carved in the Antaean likeness of a bearded man in final repose. On the wall above it was a strange emblem—a portrait, within a triangle, of two faces, one of them a death's-head. The scene was lit by starcrystal, which illuminated the two who stood on either side of the tomb. Amber saw a woman with silver hair, her clawlike left hand upraised in a nimbus the same color. She felt her blood run cold at the sight. Her dream aboard the *Dark Horizon* was suddenly vivid once again in her memory, and now, at last, she made the connection. Ardatha Demonhand!

The man, she knew, had to be Stonebrow; a mask of stone covered his features. This also glowed, with emerald luminescence. Between them, on the onyx forehead of the Necromancer's image, the Runestone of Darkhaven lay, along with a crumbling scroll, and over them the enchantress and the sorcerer wove, with thaumaturgic dactylology and phrases of ancient Rannish, a spell of Necromancy. Amber knew this to be the case, though she had never heard or seen such a spell cast before. She felt the words resonating in her bones and her blood, pounding her senses like drum mallets. Each motion that they made struck her like a blow. She saw that Pandrogas was affected the same way; the very power of the spell battered them like the surf of a storm. And, rising from the Runestone and surrounding Ardatha and Stonebrow, an aurora of light was beginning to form. It seemed no one color, but was rather a shifting rainbow of hues. Amber stared at it, mesmerized for a moment by its beauty.

"Stop!" she heard Pandrogas shout, saw him thrust out with both hands as though attempting to topple the supporting pillars themselves. Dazzling golden flame outlined him momentarily. Then she glimpsed a shadow hurtling at him from the darkness above them, and leaped forward, colliding with him and sending them both sprawling. A stream of acid ploughed a smoking furrow in the floor where the sorcerer had stood. Pandrogas rolled to his feet and surrounded them both with Armor of Light, just in time to turn aside another searing attack by the cockatrice, which swooped over them like a gigantic, grotesque bat.

"The spell!" Amber cried to him. *"They are finishing the spell!"* She could sense that it was so—her very heartbeat, it seemed, pounded now in cadence with Stonebrow's and Ardatha's thunderous syllables. The aurora rising from the Runestone was blinding now, washing away the starcrystal light and the glow of claw and mask, even paling the luminence that protected them from the harrying cockatrice. Then, to her astonishment, Pandrogas spoke a word that caused the shielding light about them to vanish. The cockatrice dropped toward them again, eyes glowing, mouth open. *"Pyrus anemaetar vas,"* Pandrogas shouted; *"unam projam!"* An aura of gold enveloped the cockatrice. Amber felt a burst of intense heat, saw the creature outlined for an instant in an agonized pose—then its lifeless body crashed to the floor beside her.

She looked again toward the sarcophagus and saw that the spell was complete.

Ardatha and Stonebrow stood motionless, their arms at their sides. The coruscating ectenic force exploded away from the Runestone with a rushing sound as of all the world's winds. Amber saw Pandrogas stagger suddenly, as though struck a crippling blow. The gale reached a climactic scream as the huge lid of the sarcophagus *melted* into black smoke. Then the rainbow vanished, and all was silence, with only the dim light of the starcrystal sconces providing illumination.

Ardatha and Stonebrow looked at one another, dumbfounded. Amber glanced at Pandrogas, and saw that he, also, was confused. He ran forward, Amber following. Their battle momentarily forgotten, the four of them peered inside.

There was no coffin within.

"His body has been stolen!" Stonebrow shouted in despair. Ardatha looked closer into the depths of the sarcophagus. Something metallic gleamed in the shadows, next to the *Scroll of Dust.* She reached for both of them as Pandrogas spoke.

"All your effort has been for naught," Pandrogas said. "Without the Necromancer's aid, you cannot reconstitute the world."

"But the prophecy," Stonebrow whispered. *"Seek knowledge at its heart."* He buried his masked face in his hands. "We have failed the One God."

"He is an impostrous god," Pandrogas said. "Your visions and portents have come from none other than the Demogorgon himself."

"Blasphemer!" Stonebrow cried.

"It is the truth," the sorcerer said heavily.

"Truth?" Stonebrow said. "Yes, you were always the one who sought the truth, Pandrogas—in all matters save one. You have fought me on every step of my quest to save humanity; you have never believed in the good that can come from the dead. But I believed, Pandrogas. I still believe."

"Your voice," Pandrogas said slowly. "It is familiar..."

"It should be." Stonebrow lifted the stone disguise from his head. Pandrogas stared in shock at the face revealed. *"Thasos!"*

At that moment he was off guard, as was Amber; both realized it too late as a quickly shouted spell produced a lattice of silver fire from Ardatha's claw that wrapped itself about them, hurling them away from the dais and into the center of the burial chamber. Ardatha turned to her companion then, her expression full of a great realization. "It has not been stolen! It was never here!"

"What do you mean?"

Ardatha lifted from the depths of the sarcophagus a golden medallion. On its obverse was embossed the image of a mountain, and crowning the mountain was a castle the size of a city. A line of cabalisms arced over it. The enchantress pointed to the emblem on the lid of the sarcophagus. "The thief told me he saw this blazon in Darkhaven! Recall your prophecy: *One journey ends where another begins. Seek knowledge at its heart!*" She turned the medallion over, revealing a finely etched, complex map. "A map of the Labyrinth, which no mage has ever penetrated! Nigromancien is but a cenotaph, a false lead! The Necromancer lies where he once ruled—in Darkhaven!"

She whirled about, her demon hand glowing. "Balandrus! This is the final journey—we go now to Darkhaven!" The cacodemon stepped forward from the shadows. "And this time," Ardatha continued, "none will follow us!" Nitid power arced from her claw to one, then another, then yet a third of the columns supporting the roof of the burial chamber. They shattered like trees struck by thunderbolts, and, as Balandrus lifted the acolytes of the One God and vanished in smoke and flame, the ceiling above Pandrogas and Amber caved in.

Amber, still slightly vertiginous from the cacodemon's mode of travel, was thoroughly disoriented by the net of power that spun them about like a whirlwind as it deposited them in the center of the vault. She heard only a few words of Ardatha's declamation, and when the avalanchine roar of the collapsing ceiling and pillars reached her, she did not know at first what was happening. They were still enwrapped in Ardatha's spell; Pandrogas dispersed it with a countering phrase, but by then the destruction had already been done. She looked up and caught an instant's glimpse of death hurtling toward them. Her reaction was totally instinctive; the power burst from within her, and then darkness took her.

Beorn, watching from the shadowy depths of a nearby alcove, barely had time to dodge backward as the spell shattered the ceiling. He thought himself beyond the range of the rocky shrapnel, but then there came a flash of blue radiance, and a boulder the size of a serf's hut slammed against the alcove's entrance, blocking it. The reverberation of air within the tiny space hurled him to the floor, where he lay motionless.

* * *

Pandrogas had started to hurl himself to one side in a futile attempt at escaping the disaster, when he felt a wave of force pass around and through him. An azure glare dazzled him, and each hair on his body strained to uproot itself. He felt fine powder enter his nose as he inhaled. Coughing, he held his collar over his mouth, vaguely wondering why he had not been crushed. He opened his eyes, and saw that they lay in a circle filled with gray powder. He realized it was granite that had been pulverized into dust. And beyond that, scattered like the fragments of the world about them, lay pieces of the ceiling and the columns, ranging in size from pebbles to rocks the size of a dragon's head.

He looked up. Above him most of the ceiling had fallen, leaving an opening into cavernous darkness.

Pandrogas crawled to Amber's side. She was motionless, and not breathing. His own breath stopped then, and he fought down an urge to seize her, to cradle her in his arms. Instead he pressed his fingers lightly to the side of her neck, and when he felt the slow pulse of blood there he rocked back on his heels, put his face in his hands and sobbed. In that moment, when he had thought her dead, he had realized that he would have done anything to save her, including raising the Necromancer himself. He looked at Amber again, and saw that her eyes were open. They were dazed at first, but when she saw the tears on his face her expression filled with concern, and she raised herself quickly, reaching toward him before he could stop her. "Are you all right?" she asked at the same time that he said, "Don't move! You might be injured."

"I'm not," she said, and rose quickly to her feet, then helped Pandrogas to his. "What happened?"

"You saved us," Pandrogas replied, looking closely at her, "as you did on the Cliffs of the Sun. Do you remember?"

She seemed oddly embarrassed by his query; she looked down for a moment, then nodded. "It first happened in the cemetery in Dulfar, just after we became separated," and she told him what had happened during the temblor, and aboard the *Elgrane* and the *Dark Horizon*. "I cannot control it, and it seems to come only in dire emergencies."

"I've never seen such power before," he said. He had known her innate talent was great, but seeing her destroy the snakes and disintegrate the collapsing ceiling had showed him the full scope of it. She shrugged. "But I cannot control it," she repeated.

"You will," Pandrogas told her. "No one could stop you." He was silent then, analyzing his feelings. He could not deny the fact that he was jealous; that he had known before. But now he also felt fear, and this he did not know how to deal with. He was afraid of her power, afraid of it being turned against him—and did not that mean he was afraid of her?

He remembered then that he had tried to escape when the ceiling fell, instead of attempting to shield her. It would have been a futile gesture, of course, but no more futile than had been his frantic lunge on his hands and knees to get away. And while he had panicked, she had acted. She had saved his life and hers, and Pandrogas realized with shame that he resented her for it.

She turned then, moving slowly, almost somnambulantly, toward the dais, picking her way through the rubble. A boulder had broken the sarcophagus in half; she climbed over it and reached into the broken shell. Then she rose, holding a small black stone in her hand.

"I saw it fall," she said as Pandrogas joined her. "It is the Runestone, isn't it?" She handed the stone to him. The sorcerer held it in his hand, feeling its cold, dead weight on his palm. Even the luster of it seemed dimmed. He remembered the weakening, draining sensation he had felt when the necromantic spell had been completed.

"It *was* the Runestone," he said. "Now it is nothing but a bit of black rock. The spell drained its ectenic force. Now its magic— and most of mine—is gone.

"Now Darkhaven is truly doomed."

BOOK IV

The Tomb of
the Necromancer

We shall not cease from exploration
And the end of all our exploring
Will be to arrive where we started
And know the place for the first time.

—T.S. Eliot
Little Gidding

Chapter 20

Demonhand

"The fools," Lambas said in a low voice as he stared into the depths of the mirror. "Don't they know that Darkhaven is in the last hours of its existence? Why do they not flee?"

Undya and several other servants of the castle stood before the glowing surface, watching. Within it, images moved; images of soldiers tramping the dead halls of Darkhaven, yanking open doors, peering into chambers, weapons ready, telesms fingered nervously. They moved slowly, with an almost dreamlike languor, for the weight of each grown man within the castle was now that of a small child.

"They are brave men," Undya said, "and their king is a brave king." She murmured several words in Palic and the scene within the speculum changed to show an image of Troas, Lord King of Oljaer, at the head of a detachment of his men, about to pass through the broken doors of Pandrogas's sanctum. Though no sound accompanied the image, they could see the bronze lips of the guardian over the door move as it asked its eternal question, and the frightened faces of the soldiers as they heard the metal head speak. They could see Troas shouting defiantly back at it, and ordering his men forward. Undya murmured a dismissing spell, passing her hand over the polished metal surface. The guardian's features stilled before it could speak the words that would immobilize the soldiers.

Lambas looked at her, as did several of the other servants. "Why do you let them pass?" one asked.

"What good to let them wait helplessly for the end?" Undya straightened, stepped away from the mirror and into the darkness of the small coverture.

"Is that not exactly what we are doing?" Lambas said. "We watch them from within the walls, peering from eye slits cut in paintings and tapestries, hiding in tunnels and unused sewers, moving among them like ghosts. You will let us do nothing to save either them or ourselves. Time is running out, Undya," and with a phrase he changed the picture within the mirror, showing a view of the outside. Smoke obscured the towers and battlements of the castle, smoke that arose from the many fires ignited by atmospheric friction as the castle plunged toward doom. "Perhaps as little as five more orbits," Lambas said. "We have no more than that." As though to underscore his words, the dark chamber about them shivered slightly in a minor quake caused by the fading residual magic. "The Lord King of Oljaer cannot save us; Pandrogas cannot save us," Lambas continued. "Only one can prevent Darkhaven from colliding with Oljaer!"

Undya sighed, closing her eyes. She touched her index fingers and thumbs together, forming the outline of a triangle. "If it is to be, then it will be," she said. "I admit that I had hoped Pandrogas would have returned by now from the cenotaph with the key to the Labyrinth. But there is still time—"

Lambas started to interrupt her, but then all were suddenly silent, attitudes tense as though alerted by a sudden sound, though no sound had been heard. "A cacodemon arrives!" one of them whispered. Undya quickly caused the mirror to shift scenes in a flood of colors. The scene cleared, to show a man, a woman, and a cacodemon standing in a corridor not far away, the sulfurous smoke of their apparition still clearing. The man wore a stone mask, and the woman's left hand was a demonic claw. In it she held a bronze medallion that glinted in the starcrystal light.

A murmur of dismay arose from the servants. "Ardatha Demonhand and Stonebrow," Undya said, feeling the fading flame of hope

within her flicker to a new low. As bad as things had been, they
had just become much worse.

Ardatha looked jubilantly about them. They stood in an ancient
passageway, no different from a thousand others of Darkhaven; stark
and bleak, the floor an inch thick in dust. But to Ardatha it was
beautiful. She glanced at the medallion held in her claw. All would
be right now; they had already won. All that remained was to perform
the ceremony again, this time with the confidence that they had
found the Necromancer's tomb at last. She felt like laughing out
loud. Such cleverness she had been witness to this past hour! She
looked at Stonebrow, who had replaced his stone mask; Stonebrow,
the mysterious leader of the Circle, now revealed by his own hand
to be none other than Thasos, formerly the leader of the Cabal of
Mages! It lent added substantiation and credence to her cause; if
there had ever been any doubt that she was following the right course,
it was gone now. But even this had not amazed her as much as the
complexity of the Necromancer's plan. Especially devious had been
the concept of using the Runestone of Darkhaven to unlock the
cenotaph. It had started sand flowing in a glass, so to speak; if the
medallion was not found and used before the time ran out, the secrets
of Necromancy would be lost forever.

But there is still time! she told herself. She spun about and looked
at Balandrus. "Carry us now to the heart of the catacombs," she told
the cacodemon. "Past the Warped Stairs and the Labyrinth; to the
vault of the Necromancer's tomb."

But Balandrus, instead of obeying, threw back his head and
laughed. "This has been the third journey, Ardatha," he snarled,
"and now I am free of you at last. Find your way yourself!"

His laughter transmuted the joy she had felt to rage with a swift-
ness and virulence that astonished her. How *dare* he thwart her plans,
stand in the way of her triumph! "Begone, then, hellspawn!" she
shouted, and scored him with a whiplash of power. Balandrus roared
and leaped at her, talons curved for her throat, but the semiweightless
condition prevailing in the castle caused him to overshoot her and
collide against the wall with stunning force. Thasos quickly shouted

the words of Balkar's Gyves of Dust, and the grayness coating the floor rose in a choking whirlwind of green light, then quickly coalesced about the cacodemon, forming shackles that pinioned him to the walls. He frothed, howling obscene threats of revenge until the sorcerer added another band across his mouth.

"It will take him some time to free himself," he told Ardatha. "By then, if all goes well, we will have found the tomb."

Ardatha nodded, and, without another look at the cacodemon, started down the corridor, Thasos following, the scroll in his hand. The burst of anger she had felt had shaken her; she had not lost control like that in longer than she could remember. Make no faulty judgments now, she cautioned herself. You are too close to victory to lose it all now.

They hurried on, moving in swift, elongated steps and leaps, seeking the lower levels which led to the Warped Stairs. It had been long commonyears since Ardatha had walked the halls of Darkhaven, but she had learned them well when she was there; she made only a few wrong turns. One of them, however, resulted in their coming face to face with a detachment of soldiers from Oljaer. The sergeant leading the men stopped and stared in fear and amazement. "Ardatha Demonhand!" he shouted.

"None other," Ardatha replied, blinding them with a burst of argent light before they could move. By the time their vision had cleared, the sorcerer and the enchantress had gone.

The two reached the stairs, but before they could descend them there was a shout from behind them. Ardatha and Thasos turned and saw more soldiers running toward them carrying crossbows, and leading them was Troas, Lord King of Oljaer. Ardatha turned to face him. Thasos put his hand on her shoulder. "We have no time for this," he whispered. "Dazzle them again and let us begone!"

"I will do more than dazzle them, this time," Ardatha replied in a low tone. "Troas has much to answer for to me."

"Spill no blood in the cause of the One God if it can possibly be helped!" he urged, but she turned away from him to face Troas.

The Lord King stopped twenty paces from her. In one hand he held a falchion. "Ardatha," he said, the slightest tremor in his voice. "Is it you, then, who is responsible for the castle's fall?" The en-

chantress did not reply. Troas ran the thumbnail of his other hand
nervously up and down the blood gutter of his weapon. "Our memory
of our last encounter is a bit unclear, enchantress," he continued.
"But we believe you did some violence to the person of the king."

Ardatha smiled at him then. Those who survived later said that
it was a smile terrible to behold. Awed and frightened whispers
broke out among the men behind Troas as they saw the demon hand
begin to smolder with a light like starcrystal on snow. "I did no
violence undeserved," the enchantress said softly. "How well is your
memory, Troas? Do you recall your attempted ravishment of me
while I labored against time in an attempt to provide redemption for
all the people of the world? Do you remember the many other times
you lay with me against my will, which I endured *for the ultimate
sake of your soul?*" She raised her claw then, and its icy brilliance
caused Troas to drop his sword and cover his eyes in pain. "Crossbows!" he shouted, dropping to the floor. The quarrels hurtled toward
the sorcerer and the enchantress, but the glare of the demon hand
melted them to streaks of flame in midflight. Troas started to leap
to his feet, but at that moment the walls shuddered and groaned
about them. The shifting floor dropped from beneath the Lord King's
feet and he hovered helplessly for a moment, arms and legs wind-
milling, suspended by the temblor's movement and his inability to
cope with lessened weight. Before he could reach the floor, a bolt
burst from Ardatha's palm and caught him, the nimbus outlining
him for an instant in a rigid spasm of agony before he exploded, his
bodily fluids evaporating in a cloud of greasy steam. Then there was
nothing, not even so much as a drift of ash to mark the passing of
Troas, the Lord King.

The rest of the men, after staring for a moment in stupefied horror,
took to their heels, and, despite the collisions and falls resulting
from their attempts to run in a partly ethereal state, were not long
in vanishing into the depths of Darkhaven's corridors. Ardatha turned
to Thasos triumphantly. "Did you see it?" she cried. She shook her
glowing fist. "The full power of the Demogorgon's gift is unbelievable! And *I* control it, Thasos! I fear it no longer! It is mine to
command!"

Thasos simply looked at her, his expression one of great sadness, until her exuberance waned slightly. Then he said quietly, "Your power is for the One God to command; not you."

Ardatha found she could not meet her mentor's eyes. "I meant to say," she said at last, "that the power is mine to command in His name."

"He would not have struck in revenge," Thasos said, "but in dispassion." He turned toward the curving staircase that led to the lower levels. "We have work to do, Ardatha—His work. And we are running out of time."

Ardatha followed him. She looked at her claw, flexing it, feeling the power within it and the reverberations of it through the rest of her body. No, old man, she thought; there will be time. I have been through too much fire for it to be over now. She could remember once feeling sorry for Beorn because she had deceived him, had sent him on a mission that was to have resulted in his death. Now she had abandoned him to slow starvation, alone in Nigromancien, and the thought of it had not even occurred to her until this moment. She thought of Tahrynyar; the marquis was almost certainly dead by now, but though she tried to feel a sense of loss she felt none. She could not even recall how it felt to take leave of him in the dungeons of the Chthons.

So be it, she told herself. There would be time enough to mourn the loss of those feelings. And not all of her emotions had been anesthetized; she still relished the fierce satisfaction she had experienced upon seeing Troas fall before her power. She wondered how much more power Sestihaculas's gift would be able to wring from the spells of Necromancy. The thought made her shiver with anticipation.

They reached the iron gate that opened onto the Warped Stairs. Ardatha led the way, the light of her claw illuminating the steps, which remained solid and firm in that relucent glow. "They will lead us to the Labyrinth," she told Thasos, "and the medallion's map will show us the safe route to the catacombs, and the real tomb of the Necromancer. Pandrogas and his wench will not be able to stop us now."

"So we thought before," Thasos replied. "And yet we were wrong."

"We will not be interrupted again," Ardatha assured him. "I will see to that," and she stroked her claw with her human hand, delighting in the sensuous smoothness of the scales.

Amber sat on a section of broken pillar, watching Pandrogas. The sorcerer had sat for some time staring at the empty husk of the Runestone in his hand. He had told her what he had heard Ardatha say before they left: that the Necromancer's tomb lay in Darkhaven. "Any fool could have deduced it," he had said, more to himself than to her. "The spells of protection that lay about the Labyrinth and the catacombs beyond them; the sheer amount of knowledge in Darkhaven's libraries. Now we know at last, too late, who built the castle." He laughed. "I fled from him into his moldering arms. It has always been thus; I lose what I want most, and gain what I fear most. My life, my knowledge, my friends betray me. Stonebrow, my enemy, reveals himself to be Thasos, my friend and mentor. Truly, the dead have more power than I." He had said nothing further then. He has withdrawn from me once more, she thought; this time further than ever before. And this time she could not bring herself to care. She was too exhausted, mentally and physically, to feel anything at this point; she wondered if she would ever feel anything again. She could not care, at this point, if Darkhaven did fall; all she wanted was for it all to be over. She had been hurled from fragment to fragment, from peril to peril, for so long that it seemed she knew no other existence. She had lost a husband, and now, it seemed, she had lost a lover. In fact, nearly everyone she came in contact with seemed to meet disaster in one way or another. Amber thought of the thief, of how he had tried to prevent the chase boat from drifting into the shadow of Xoth. The cacodemons had poured up from the black, glistening crags of their citadel and seized them, separating them. He had shouted a wish of luck to her as they had been carried down to the surface. Then she had been incarcerated in a cell that had been little more than a tomb of stone and slime, where she had waited, fighting with all her will not to go mad. She had tried to use her power to shatter the huge boulder that had imprisoned her, but the cleansing fire would not come. She had crouched, shivering, in the darkness, wondering if she would ever see Pandrogas, or sunlight, or anything of life again. When she had been brought to the great chamber and realized she was to be reunited with the sorcerer again, she had felt such joy and relief that even now it shook her with the echo of its intensity. But it was a cold, sterile memory. Between it and her stood Tahrynyar, and her plunge into the depths of his hatred had, it seemed, frozen all feelings within her.

She wondered about the thief. Did he still languish in some forgotten pocket of hell? Or had his part in this endless nightmare finally come to an end? If so, Amber hoped it had been quick and painless—though she doubted such a death was possible on Xoth.

She looked again at the sorcerer. Something should probably be done, she told herself, or they would die here. She tried to feel some concern at the thought. Part of the reason for her lassitude was hunger; it had been almost a commonday since her last meal aboard the *Dark Horizon*. The thought of death no longer frightened her as it once did, but death by slow starvation seemed particularly unpleasant. "Pandrogas," she whispered to the sorcerer, but he did not respond. She was overwhelmingly tired; it would be so easy simply to lie down and sleep. Instead, something within her made her take out her flute and begin to play. As before, when she had played to soothe him, it was not a light or frivolous air, but rather calm and stately, its cadences replenishing, strengthening. It seemed to hearten her; the music occupied her reflexes and brain, and she felt herself becoming involved in it. It was working for Pandrogas as well, she noticed, penetrating the armor he had laid about himself. He blinked and looked blankly, as though she was some stranger come to serenade him for obscure reasons. Cheered more than she had thought possible a few dark moments before, Amber played on. Perhaps we will come out of this alive, she told herself. Perhaps, at this moment, she even wanted to.

Then, letting the music lift and turn her, she stood to finish the piece—and dropped the flute with a gasp. A shadow stood in the darkness beside the tomb. Before she could do anything further, however, it stepped forward quickly, and the thief stood revealed before her.

Amber stared at him in astonishment; she had been so sure that he was either dead or one of the damned on Xoth that he seemed a phantasm standing before her now. "How did you come here?" she asked, then continued before he could reply: "It does not matter. I'm glad you're still alive." That surprised her; not that she felt so about the thief, but that she felt anything at all.

"The sentiment is returned," he said, with that trace of courtliness that always surprised her. She saw then that Pandrogas was watching them both. He stood, facing Beorn.

"So, thief," the sorcerer said quietly. "We have finally run you down—too late, it seems."

"I make no excuses and no apologies, sorcerer," Beorn replied. "I am a thief; I did what I was hired to do."

"We will not waste time in recriminations. It is all academic now, at any rate. The essence of the Runestone is gone, and we have lost."

Amber saw Beorn pale for an instant before his face resumed its noncommittal mask. "What do you mean?" She glanced at Pandrogas; when it seemed he was not going to speak, she explained briefly the circumstances. Beorn sat down, and despite his efforts to conceal it, she could tell that the news had shaken him. She remembered the theory she had espoused in the Dulfar tavern, that he had stolen it as a cure for his curse. She felt a burst of sympathy for him.

"And so Darkhaven will fall," she finished. Beorn looked at his hands, then at the two of them. "Is there no way?" he asked.

"To reinforce the Runestone requires more magic than I am currently capable of," Pandrogas said. "I do not have access to such power."

It was then that Amber realized she had the solution. The realization struck her with such quiet force that for a moment she was unable to say anything. At last she murmured quietly, "Yes, you do."

He looked at her. "What do you mean?"

"The power within me," Amber said, feeling both fear and joy at the thought. "Is it not enough? Can you not take from me what you need?"

He was quiet for a long moment, and she saw conflicting emotions in his expression. At last he said, almost reluctantly, "Yes, it would be enough, and more than enough. But it cannot be done."

"Why not?" She tried to ignore the feeling of almost personal rejection that his words had caused.

When he spoke again, his tone was surprisingly harsh. "Because you do not know how to release it willingly, and I have not the strength to take it."

"There has to be a way—"

"*There is no way!* You are too strong for me!"

Amber stepped back, amazed at the vehemence in his voice. "I'm sorry," she said, not sure why she was apologizing.

"There must be something we can do," Beorn said.

Pandrogas looked at him. "Oh? And what would you do, thief?" he asked bitterly. "How would you plunder your way through this?"

"I'll tell you how!" Beorn returned hotly. "You say you have access to a cacodemon for one more journey, even as Ardatha had Balandrus. They have gone to Darkhaven to awaken the Necromancer, have they not? Well then, take me there, and I promise you I'll loot his secrets as I did yours!"

"Impossible," Pandrogas said. "We could never make our way through the gauntlet of the Labyrinth!"

"I can pass any defense, and steal any treasure! It's at least worth a try!"

Amber looked at Pandrogas, and found the sorcerer's gaze soliciting her opinion. And what shall I advise? she wondered. Life seemed to be a part of her again—or, if not life, at least the fear of death, for the thought of pursuing Ardatha and Thasos to the catacombs of Darkhaven terrified her. But she also knew that she had no other choice. If she urged Pandrogas to use the last journey granted them by Sestihaculas simply to escape the cenotaph, she knew the decision would haunt them for the rest of their lives. She said softly, "You told me once that the hardest part of magic is believing in yourself."

Pandrogas looked down at the dead Runestone, then at the thief again. "I must tell you, thief, that even if we should succeed in this mad venture, I cannot use the Runestone to divest you of your curse.

Not even Necromancy can accomplish that. If I chase the bear from your soul, you will die; it is too much a part of you, and you of it. There is no cure; do you understand?"

Beorn had grown pale again at the sorcerer's words, but he merely nodded in response.

"Very well." Pandrogas made a gesture and spoke in the Whispered Shout; his summons echoed about them. "Taloroth!" The cacodemon appeared before them. "To Darkhaven," the sorcerer said. "To the entrance to the Warped Stairs."

Amber took a deep breath and prepared herself mentally for the hellish transit. She looked at the thief, and smiled at him. He smiled back, and she thought, At least we have one fewer enemy now.

"This is the final journey," Taloroth told them then, and Amber felt Nigromancien vanish from about them.

Undya, Lambas, and the rest watched the drama unfolding before them in the speculum's polished surface. "He is returned, at last," one of them murmured.

"But is he in time?" Lambas said. "The Runestone, and his power, are impotent. How will they survive the perils of the Labyrinth?"

"They may not," Undya replied serenely.

"Undya," Lambas said in a low tone, almost as though he were ashamed. "I was afraid of death. I still fear it."

She smiled at him, a sympathetic smile, one that said without words, This is no secret shame of yours alone. So do all, even those who face it but once.

"Is there no way in which we can aid them?"

"We *have* aided them, as much as we can. They must win through by their courage and talent now. The world deserves no less." She made the sign of the triangle again. "One way or another, our waiting will soon be over."

Chapter 21

The Labyrinth

Taloroth deposited them within Darkhaven and vanished. Though all three were acutely aware that time was running out, Pandrogas suggested that they detour through the kitchens for food to strengthen them for their coming ordeal. He and Amber took pieces of bread and cheese and jerked venison, which they devoured hungrily as they half-ran, half-floated through the corridors. The thief refused to eat any solid food, but supped instead on milk. At his insistence, they also sought out the sorcerer's sanctum, so that Beorn could equip himself once more with the tools of his trade, which had been taken from the remnants of his clothes after the bear had fled.

At last, carrying rods of starcrystal, they came to the entrance to the Warped Stairs. It seemed to Pandrogas that he could feel the runaway careening of the castle through the sky, spiraling closer and closer toward Oljaer. His skin prickled in reaction to the cold air that rushed past him on the stairs, his imagination attributing it to an echo of the screaming gale outside, perhaps strong enough by now to tumble towers and ignite fires. The eerie feeling of lightness did not help matters any. It would grow less, he knew, as they made their way deeper into the fragment, where the residuum of the ectenic force was strongest. But that would be the only danger that would subside.

"Lead us, Amber," he told the marquise. "Use your power as you once did to find the caverns, and bring us now to the entrance of the Labyrinth." He saw her nod and close her eyes in concentration. She linked fingers with the thief, who in turn took Pandrogas's hand. And so I have become the merest acolyte at last, the sorcerer thought, as they ventured onto the Stairs. My powers are gone, and I am led by a student and a thief.

He felt like a disembodied spirit. His intrinsicality, the power that he had nurtured and shaped within himself for so many years, was now but the dimmest echo of what it had been. He followed the manuductory guidance of those ahead of him almost without thought or caring. Within the pouch that hung from his belt he could feel the weight of the dead Runestone. It was a light burden, easily borne. The weight of his own soul was far heavier.

Neither he nor Beorn spoke, for fear of distracting Amber from her effort to bend the Stairs to her will. The sorcerer remembered the last time he had stood on these dark steps, with Kabyn and the other servants. He wondered how they fared now, if Kabyn had recovered from his injuries; if, indeed, they were still in Darkhaven, or had wisely fled its impending destruction. He hoped they had chosen the latter; he would hate to feel responsible for their deaths in addition to those of countless others. For he had no real hope that they could stay Darkhaven's meteoric descent. He merely followed, willing to make the attempt, willing to die in the inferno that was sure to come. The alternative was starting over, inculcating once again the power and abilities that had taken him so long to learn. He could not face that again.

He thought about Amber. Her power still lived within her, unshapen though it was, and it was a power far greater than any he could hope to attain. But she also did not understand the enormity of what they faced, as he did. Should Ardatha and Thasos succeed in their vivificative spell and awaken the Necromancer, pitting even her power against him would be like attempting to light a candle in the gale that now howled over the battlements. What mercy could be expected from an omnipotent madman who had destroyed a world that would not acknowledge him as ruler?

Assuming they even made it that far. The Necromancer or his

followers had designed the safeguards to his tomb well. With the map from the cenotaph, Ardatha and Thasos could breach them. But the three of them could wander aimlessly until they died; a fate that would not be long in coming.

He had loved Amber; that had been his downfall and hers. The time he had spent with her in his bed should have been spent immersed in study, in searching for the answer. Had he been working, had he paid more attention to the security of his sanctum, the thief might not have stolen the Runestone, might not have escaped with it, and all of this might not have happened. He had abrogated his responsibilities; he had loved. And now all would pay.

It was easier this time than it had been before, Amber realized. The fact surprised and heartened her; she had feared that, due to the privations she had suffered over the last few commonweeks, she would be unable to wend her way through the surreal complexities of the Stairs and would become lost. She wondered if their power to confuse and disorient was less now because of the fading force that sustained the castle. Be that as it may, she found the steps firmer and easier to navigate now, the turnings and twistings not so dizzying. She saw light up ahead, past a final turn. She sighed, daring to relax the slightest bit. Perhaps there was a chance of success after all. Then she led them about the corner—and stopped, stunned, as she saw the barred gate of the entrance once again before them.

Amber felt strength empty from her like water from an unstoppered vessel, and she sank to her knees. Pandrogas and Beorn were there immediately, one on either side, murmuring encouragement. "We were almost there," she said. "I felt it! If I hadn't let go too soon—"

"All we have lost is time," Pandrogas told her. "We can start again." She put her head against his chest and sobbed for a moment while the thief watched. Then she pushed herself away from the sorcerer. "These damned Stairs are a crueler torture than anything the Chthons have invented," she said, and saw both of them smile slightly at that. She turned then, and faced the long, forbidding arc of the passage once more. It had been so long since there had been any time to rest. No slightest slackening of vigilance was forgiven. She sighed and started again.

This time she did not allow her self-confidence to mar her concentration. She led them through the winding tunnels that rose and fell like the loops of a giant ouroboros, pausing only slightly at intersections before choosing her path. The stairs seemed to move beneath her feet like swells of black water, now resisting her, now pulling her suddenly forward. The silence was so intense that she thought, at those times when they stood motionless, that she could hear not only the breath of her comrades, but the very pulse of blood beneath their skins. She kept her eyes closed most of the time, sliding her hands over the slick walls, not daring to question the subtle sense within her that urged her onward, now this way, now that. Trust yourself, Pandrogas had told her. Amber kept going, somehow, though the passageway seemed at times no less resistant than the stone that surrounded them, though each step was harder to take than the last. She kept going, until finally her blindly questing reach found not stone but wood. She opened her eyes. Before her was a door of oak, with thick hasps and a handle of iron. Once more reaction overcame her, and she felt an arm go about her shoulders for support. She turned and leaned against the broad chest with a sigh of relief, then realized she was leaning not against Pandrogas, but Beorn. The sorcerer stood to one side, looking at them. Amber pushed herself gently away from the thief. "Thank you," she said to them both, hardly hearing the words; "thank you both. We're here."

"Yes," Pandrogas said. "And now the hard part begins." He pushed at the door to the Labyrinth, and the rattle of the bolt in its sheath was very loud in the silence. He looked at the thief. "This is your domain," he said.

The opening of the spring lock was a simple affair for the thief. Pandrogas sensed no jeopardizing magic that would be triggered by the forced entry, and so Beorn slipped the bolt with a piece of tough, flexible cartilage from a dragon's xyphoid. The door swung open, and musty air tinged with the dry scent of death enfolded them as they entered the Labyrinth.

They were in a small chamber of bare gray stone, from which

five openings branched. The floor was paved with flagstones. "The center stone pivots," Pandrogas warned the thief. "I narrowly evaded it when I entered here, years ago."

Beorn nodded slightly to acknowledge the words, and felt forward with one foot. "It feels solid enough," he said. "But I'll take no chances." He stepped to one side, putting his weight on a pavé near the wall. It fell away from him, rotating on a central axis to expose a dark pit; only the thief's reflexes enabled him to turn and seize the edge of the floor in time. Pandrogas pulled him from the pit. "You said the *center* stone!" Beorn said angrily.

"It *was* the center stone when I came here last," the sorcerer replied. "It evidently changes at random. Most ingenious."

"I'll appreciate the cleverness of it all much more if we get through it alive," the thief said.

They made their way with extreme care across the chamber to the entrances of the five tunnels. The center passage was almost totally blocked by a cube of stone which had fallen from the ceiling. A scrap of dark cloth protruded from beneath it. The sorcerer pointed to it. "I chose to investigate the center passage when I was here last," he said. "That was as far as I got. The block caught my sleeve as I rolled free."

"Which way?" Beorn asked Amber. Though he could not see her behind him, he could imagine her with eyes closed, reaching out to sense the correct route even as he stretched forward with his senses, tasting the air, alert with eyes, ears, nose, and skin for any sensory warnings.

"The second to the left," she said at last.

"Wait here," the thief told them. He extended his starcrystal rod into the tunnel, illuminating a narrow passage, the walls of which were cut with estoilés, gammadions, and a confusion of other designs. He entered, took another step forward and felt the lightest of pressure against his instep. Instantly he dropped prone, and from apertures in the wall concealed by the designs worked about them lances of carved ivory thrust forth, interlacing above him. The lowest of them quivered a mere foot over his head. Beorn rolled over and looked at the sorcerer and Amber, who stood at the tunnel's mouth. "Crawl," he said.

They worked their way with maddening slowness into the Labyrinth. Beorn tried to keep his thoughts free of nothing but the constant array of perils before them. He had to call upon every bit of the skill and ability he had learned from old Maenen and the others on Thieves' Island and afterward. The danger was heightened by the fact that his weight was lighter than he was used to, and that threw his reflexes and timing off. This was the ultimate challenge of his career; he had never faced such a series of dangers and tests before. And for what? he could not help but ask himself. The sorcerer had told him that there was no cure possible for him; the bear would be with him for the rest of his life. As he thought of it, he could feel the beast prowling restlessly in corridors of his mind and soul. It had been caged for some time, and would demand its freedom soon—very soon. The longer he kept the bear pent, the more difficult it was to remain in control when it finally roamed free. But he could not worry about that now. Every room, every corridor, every flight of stairs presented some new danger for him to circumvent. The passage they followed now had begun to narrow, its walls angling inward almost imperceptibly, until eventually they were forced to walk sideways. Force of habit made him edge through without touching the walls, as he had been trained to do in a narrow corridor lined with sharkskin—and fortunately so, for a moment later he scented a tarry trace of something on them. He recognized it immediately. "Keep clear of the walls!" he told Pandrogas and Amber. "Do not touch them by so much as a hair!" They were coated with the blood of the madworm, a poison which set fire to the nerves and brought death as a blessed relief after hours of agony. It could have been painted there centuries before, he realized; the unchanging atmosphere would preserve it indefinitely. Both Pandrogas and Amber managed to follow him unscathed. His admiration for them both increased as they continued.

They passed one or two skeletons, picked clean by vermin. The dangers were constant and hellishly varied, and the thief knew the chances were excellent that he would gain nothing by conquering them except the privilege of death at the hands of the Necromancer himself. But—and this, he thought, was the strangest part of this adventure since its beginning in the Land's Edge Tavern—he did not regret urging Pandrogas in this attempt. He wanted to strike this blow, however futile. It did not even have anything to do anymore with Ardatha, with the fact that she had manipulated him, had used him from the beginning. This was an act of affirmation—his greatest act of thievery.

They stopped to rest in a small chamber with two exits: an opening in the ceiling, with hand- and footholds cut in the stone, and a wider shaft in the center of the floor, with an iron pole rising from it. The thief wound a strip of cloth about a shaved patch of skin on his arm; a huge crescent blade at the end of a shaft had swung without warning across the length of the room they had been traversing, and he had barely avoided its lethal arc. They had entered this chamber through a winding tube that had snaked through the rock for an interminable distance. It had been barely wide enough for the thief's broad shoulders, and the thought of running into some menace while wriggling his way through it had been unnerving even to him. Amber, Beorn noticed, was pale and shivering; he remembered her speaking once on board the *Dark Horizon* of how claustrophobic she had found Darkhaven to be. To creep and crawl thus through these peristaltic tunnels must be as bad for her as the oubliette of Xoth, he thought.

He watched her hair shimmer in the starcrystal's light as the sorcerer stroked it. It was almost the same shade that Suchana's had been, he realized abruptly. It occurred to him again, as it had so often in the past, what choice words Suchana would have for him could she but see the situation in which he had put himself, and he smiled faintly at the thought. The smile faded as he looked again at Amber's drawn features. He recalled the burst of joy he had felt when he had seen her in the stone viscera of the cenotaph and had realized that she had not died on Xoth. At the time he had thought it was simple relief at finding allies once again; he would have aided them then, he told himself, but events had moved too fast for him to take a hand in them before the enchantress's spell had collapsed the ceiling. He had felt then as though the falling stone had crushed his own body, in the instant before the burst of blue fire had flung them outward like the shattering of the world. He heard again the

music of her flute, as she had played it among the rubble before the
empty sarcophagus, and that time so long ago when its faint echoes
had mesmerized him in the sorcerer's sanctum. He thought of her
as he had first seen her, standing tall and proud beside Pandrogas
in the nethermost depths of the caverns. Even the memory of her
contempt and anger toward him aboard the *Elgrane* impressed him
with her spirit. He had hated her, and later feared her, not only
because of the power within her but for the same reason that he had
hated and feared all women—for the danger that their love might
awaken within him. He feared her still, but he knew now that he
no longer hated her.

At that moment the silence of the Labyrinth was broken for the
first time by a noise other than the various sounds of the traps they
had evaded. A faint, echoing roar was heard; it was impossible to
tell from which direction it had originated. The thief looked at
Pandrogas. "What was *that?*"

"Remember the hydra in the caverns," the sorcerer replied. "It
appears that beasts roam these areas, too. Once a trap has been
sprung or avoided, I would imagine some of these tunnels and rooms
would make quite comfortable lairs."

Amber shivered, and Pandrogas put his arm about her. Beorn
watched them both sadly. "It is cold here," Amber said, "and it is
more than just the air."

"Ancient spells have permeated this stone," the sorcerer said.
"They sap the power in you, as they would sap mine had I any now
of which to speak. They were placed to prevent the breaching of
this maze with magic."

"It is becoming more and more difficult even to sense the correct
route," Amber said. "But I believe it lies downward."

Beorn moved to the shaft and peered into it, holding the starcrystal
over it. He could see nothing; the pole descended beyond the range
of the glow. The surface of the pole was rough, which would make
it easier to cling to. After a few more moments of rest, they began
the descent.

When they were over halfway down Beorn began to think that
they might pass through this part of the maze without trouble. Then

he inched downward again, and felt his legs suddenly lose purchase. The surface of the pole had changed from rough to a glassy smoothness. He lowered himself the full length of his arms, feeling with his toes. There was only smoothness, too slick to cling to; if he lowered himself again he would slide helplessly down to—what? Beorn wrapped his legs about the rough part of the pole again and leaned over the well, looking down. The blue light of the rod illuminated a floor of spikes perhaps twenty feet below him. The pole ended ten feet below him.

"What is it?" Pandrogas, who was immediately above him, asked. The thief explained the situation.

"I cannot cling here much longer," Amber gasped. "And it is beyond my strength to climb back up."

The thief looked about desperately. In the wall of the shaft parallel to him he saw a dark opening. It was too far to reach. In desperation he changed his hold, using one elbow to brace his hip, and extended his legs and body perpendicular to the pole. He was barely able to hook his toes over the sill. "Climb across!" he whispered harshly, "quickly!" Pandrogas lowered himself and hung from the thief's rigid torso over the field of spikes, moving hand over hand across his legs and pulling himself into the opening. Amber followed, clinging desperately to Beorn's tunic and belt until Pandrogas could reach her hand and pull her to safety. Beorn wrapped his legs about the pole again and waited for his muscles to stop trembling, breathing deeply to spread oxygen through them. Though his weight was slightly less than normal within the Labyrinth, the effect was not as pronounced here as in the rest of Darkhaven. He took a deep breath, then pushed himself away from the pole, leaping toward the hole. He landed half in, half out, and began to slip—Pandrogas and Amber each grabbed a hand and pulled him in.

"I've never seen such a feat of strength," Pandrogas said in admiration. Beorn managed a grin in response.

The tunnel was a short one, and opened into yet another of the small chambers. The walls were featureless gray blocks, save for a series of holes circling them directly beneath the ceiling, and a section of wall directly opposite the entrance, where seven irregularly shaped pieces of semiprecious ores were embedded in the rock. They entered the room warily, watching for yet another trap.

Nor were they disappointed. With the grinding of stone against stone, a thick block of darkness lowered into place behind them, sealing the entrance with so precise a fit that it appeared to be a solid wall. Beorn heard a hollow, rushing sound, and an instant later water spurted from the holes above them. One of the streams struck the sorcerer between the shoulder blades with enough force to stagger him. In a moment's time the floor was covered, the water lapping at their ankles and creeping steadily upward.

Amber pressed her palms to her temples as the water rose to her knees. "The fire!" she cried. "Why can't I make it come? *Why won't it happen?*"

"No one can strike against these walls," Pandrogas shouted over the rush of the flood. "I've tried!"

Beorn felt his feet leave the floor as the water, now up to his chest, lifted him. There has to be a way out, he thought. Every threat they had encountered so far had had some possibility of escape, however remote. He dove, holding his breath and investigating the section of wall containing the embossed stones. They had looked strangely familiar to him when he had entered, and as he looked closely he knew why. Their shapes and arrangement represented the seven principal fragments of the world. He had encountered locks like this before; to open them it was necessary to press upon the pieces in a certain pattern. But how could he determine the proper sequence before it was too late?

Beorn surfaced and took another gulp of air. The water was within two feet of the ceiling now; he had a glimpse of the others' faces before he submerged again. There was fear in their expressions, but also frustration, a rage against the helplessness of their situation. Beorn swam back down, determined more than ever to save them if he could.

He clung to the raised pieces of stone, staring at them, forcing himself to think calmly, rationally. He was in a Labyrinth designed, as far as he knew, by the Necromancer, a man responsible for the destruction of the world. Might not the code have something to do with that? Inspired, he began pressing the fragments from the center outward, starting with Calamchor, then Salakh, Toul, Twilan, Rhynne, Kulareem, and finally Pandor. Each one sank until it was flush with the wall's surface, and when he had depressed the last one, the section of wall rose as the other one had fallen. There was nothing to seize for an anchor, and so Beorn was swept through the opening and into another corridor. A moment later Pandrogas and Amber were also washed through. The water drained quickly through gutters in the stone floor.

The three of them staggered to their feet. At the far end of the corridor, barely visible by the light of the starcrystal, was an oaken door similar to the one through which they had entered the Labyrinth hours before. Behind them were five portals; the flood had washed them through the middle one.

"Is it over?" Amber asked faintly. "Is it finally over?"

"We'll know soon," Beorn said. He started forward cautiously, testing each step before he put his weight down. When he was halfway to the door he suddenly felt dizzy. He waited until his balance returned, then continued until he stood before the massive, iron-bound barrier. He could see nothing ominous about it; there were no tripping mechanisms that his experienced eye could spot. As far as he knew, it was the way out of the Labyrinth. All he had to do was open the door.

But he did not want to open it.

As he reached for the latch he realized that his palm was damp with the sweat of fear, and his mouth was dry for the same reason. The portal seemed suddenly the flimsiest of barriers between him and a horror that had awaited his coming for years, biding with terrible patience until this moment, and which now hovered, grinning, in the dark, with barely restrained bloodlust.

He turned and looked back at his comrades. They seemed to be standing much further away than he had left them, as though the entire tortuous length of the Labyrinth had been stretched out into one long strand, with Beorn at one end and Pandrogas and Amber at the other. They could not help him.

He could hear it breathing. Pandrogas had said that there were beasts even here, in the Labyrinth. There are beasts everywhere, Beorn thought, shivering. Implacable, impossible to escape, they waited for all humanity, lurking in cavernous depths, in sunless lands, and in the darkest region of all: the soul.

Beorn opened the door.

It swung silently into darkness, a night which the light of the starcrystal could not pierce. And in that darkness, two eyes blazed green. A snarl, so deep it shook the stone about him, rose and fell. Yellow teeth glinted.

The bear came toward him.

It moved quite slowly, with the dreamlike languor of motion he had experienced in the upper corridors of Darkhaven. He had no weapon, nothing but the starcrystal rod. And he knew that no weapon could stand against this. He faced the greatest menace of the Labyrinth now; the greatest menace of his life. The bear was separated from him at last and, at last, out of his control.

It rose upon its hind legs, towering over him, saliva dripping from its muzzle. It growled again. He had never seen it so clearly before; when he had looked at his reflection while wearing its hide, his vision had been too poor to make out details. The coat was beautiful, its cinnamon highlights showing even in the blue light. In a fascination of terror, he watched the interplay of muscles as they moved beneath the fur. Every instinct, every nerve within him screamed the urge to run. He did not run. He had been fleeing from the bear his whole life. *He would not run.*

It raised a claw above him. He could see light glinting from its nose and eyes, could hear the heavy respiration, the creaking of the muscles and joints. He could smell— Beorn blinked. He could smell nothing. No breath washed over him, and there was no trace of the thick, musky odor he knew so well; only the arid atmosphere of the Labyrinth.

The bear struck. The claw passed through him without the slightest sensation. The bear vanished before his eyes.

Beorn sagged against the wall, heart pounding. Before him was a dark passage with a low ceiling, the walls of which were set with stone crypts. He was out of the Labyrinth now, and in the catacombs of Darkhaven. He recalled the sudden dizziness he had felt when approaching the exit—the fumes of dream tea, then, concentrated to hallucinogenic intensity. He had somehow triggered a release, and the vapor had permeated the air about him. Beorn's legs gave way and he slid down the wall to a sitting position, unsure whether to laugh or cry. He felt he had just won a great victory, though he was unsure how or why it had been fought. He looked back at his friends. "Come ahead," he called. "But hold your breath!"

Though Amber had seen nothing threaten the thief when he had opened the door, she had felt the tension in the air, and she had known that the thief had seen something she and Pandrogas could not. She had started forward, hoping to help in some way, but Pandrogas had put his hand on her arm. "This battle is his," the sorcerer had said softly. "That much power is left to me; I sense he faces a private demon."

"Can we do nothing to help him?"

"Yes; when he calls us. Until then we must wait."

"How much longer do we have to wait? The spell is being cast; do you not feel it?"

The sorcerer nodded, slowly. Amber could sense the waves of power emanating from somewhere beyond the door, as she had felt them in Nigromancien, resonating in her soul. And she knew that they might not be in time.

She saw the thief slump against the wall, and for a brief moment was afraid that he had succumbed to whatever terror he had faced. The thought enveloped her in ice. Then she saw him turn, and heard him call to them. Relief filled her, and it was an effort to cross the last room of the Labyrinth with caution; she wanted to run to him and hug him, and tell him how glad she was that he had triumphed over whatever devil he had faced.

"What did you see?" she asked him as they left the Labyrinth.

He did not answer immediately. "An old friend," he said at last. "One who was, I have thought on occasion, my only friend." And he said no more about it.

* * *

They hurried through the tunnels of the dead, following Amber's lead. The narrow, twisting passages branched and forked in a complexity almost as bewildering as the Labyrinth, and Amber was astonished at the number of loculi; the walls of every passage were tiered with recesses from floor to ceiling. The inscriptions on the slabs of marble or terra-cotta that sealed them were, for the most part, in Rannish, the language now associated with Necromancy. They passed many vaults and galleries containing sarcophagi also. To be able to call upon the knowledge and strength of these many liches, Amber reflected, would provide a source of almost limitless power. She could feel the solemn, infinite patience of the dead surrounding her, charging the silence with an intensity, not expectant, but simply present.

The thief stopped as they passed through a vault. On a crypt, in a sheath carved for it, rested a curved scimitar. Beorn drew the blade, which was of gleaming black steel. The dry air and constant temperature had preserved it well; save for a few rust spots it had kept its sheen and edge. "This may prove useful," Beorn remarked.

"Do you think it is wise to steal from the dead?" Pandrogas asked wryly.

"I have not found the dead to prove resentful," Beorn said, "and certainly not nearly as dangerous as the living." He swung the curved blade experimentally once or twice, then gestured for Amber to lead on.

They pursued their winding way again. There was no sound save for their footfalls and breathing. And then something broke the silence as they approached a final turn in the cloister. It was the sound of a beast, half hiss, half growl, that reverberated around them. They stopped and looked at each other. The thief lifted his sword, took a deep breath, and peered cautiously about the turn. A deafening roar greeted him, accompanied by the sound of rattling chains—the same roar they had heard earlier, echoing in the Labyrinth.

Amber followed him around the corner, as did Pandrogas. Before them were two gigantic portals of obsidian. And in front of them, straining against a heavy collar and chain anchored to the floor, was

a beast unlike anything Amber had ever seen. It was as tall as
Sestihaculas had been, standing erect on two legs, with a long,
snakelike tail for counterbalance. Its skin was scaled with dark patterns, and its hind legs were goatlike, with cloven hooves. The
forepaws ended in a lion's claws, and the snarling head was that of
a lion as well, but crowned with a goat's horns. Amber saw a forked
tongue flicker between the serpent fangs. It made a slow, rumbling
noise, a strange admixture of reptilian and mammalian sounds. "What
is it?" she whispered.

"A chimera," Pandrogas replied. "Ardatha or Thasos has set it
to guard the crypt while they proceed. I no longer have the power
to defeat it." He glanced at the thief, who stood with the black
scimitar gripped tightly. "Do you think your blade will avail you
against *that?*"

Beorn hesitated. He looks trapped, Amber thought. Desperation
shone for a moment in his eyes. Then he straightened his shoulders,
as though he had made a decision. "No," he said to the sorcerer.
"It will not. But I know of something that will."

She realized then what he planned to do. "No, Beorn!" she said.
"There has to be another way!"

"There is no other way," Pandrogas said, before the thief could
answer. "Only the bear can hope to defeat it, or at least delay it
long enough for us to reach the crypt."

"The sorcerer is right," Beorn said. "The bear is our only chance
now." He handed the scimitar and the starcrystal to Amber, and
took a few steps away from them. He began to disrobe.

Amber looked at Pandrogas, who was watching the thief. "Come
then," she said to him; "let us at least give him privacy." She turned
and stepped around the corner.

Pandrogas hesitated, then said to Beorn, "Beware the chimera's
fangs. They are virulent." Then he followed Amber.

They stood in silence, not looking at each other. Then, from
around the bend, she heard a muffled cry of agony, followed by a
roar from the chimera, and the sound of it lunging against its chains.
She could not stop herself; holding the scimitar, she ran forward.
"No, Amber!" Pandrogas shouted, too late. Amber stepped around

the corner and realized that Beorn was not being attacked, as she had thought. The chimera was still chained, though it hurled itself to the length of its iron tether in a futile attempt to break it, driven to frenzy by what was happening. Amber felt Pandrogas's hands on her shoulders as she looked down at the naked body of the thief, writhing on the floor before her.

The transformation had begun.

Chapter 22

Necromancy

There was nothing in the world for Beorn save the pain; it enveloped him in a blazing cocoon, an inferno that burned along every nerve and charred each bone to ash. Its onset struck like a morning-star to his gut, dropping him to all fours. His hands began to elongate, the carpal and phalangeal bones aching as they twisted and changed, the thumbs shrinking into dewclaws. His nails thickened and curved, and he scraped them over the cold stone as the agony proceeded. He felt the muscles in his legs contracting, and sharp bursts of pain as the large bones and hip sockets re-formed. A memory flashed quickly of once being threatened with the rack as reparation for his thievery, and how he had laughed in response. His feet stretched and re-formed also, the heels becoming hocks. Hair sprouted in runnels over him, a hundred thousand fiery needles. His back humped with muscle, growing as the skeletal support for it swelled, became heavier.

He cried out, a strangled sound, neither human nor animal. He could dimly hear, through the pounding of the blood in his ears, the responding roar of the chimera. Each time it seemed the agony was worse than before; as always, he feared—almost hoped—he would not survive it. And yet, as always, there was a part of him that exulted, gloried in the pain. The bear was emerging, and he welcomed its strength and power even as he feared it. More than thieving, more than anything else, the bear defined his life. He knew then, in this heart of his excruciation, that the creature was a part of him, would be forevermore, and that no magic could sever their bonds.

Amber watched in fascinated horror as the metamorphosis proceeded. Beorn writhed and strained as though he were bursting from his skin. One part of her noticed quite calmly that the transformation was asymmetrical; the right side of his body was changing faster than the left in most respects, although the fur seemed to be growing faster on the left side. Sounds of tearing muscle tissue and tendons assailed her, and more than once she heard the bright *crack!* of bones breaking. She could smell the sharpness of perspiration and urine. The thief, a terratoid hybrid of man and beast now, staggered on all fours. He lifted his head, and she heard him snarl, saw his eyes changing from blue to brown. The forehead sloped back, supraorbitals thickening as reddish brown fur sprouted over them. She watched his face running like hot wax, jutting forward in a series of small jerks to form a muzzle. Blood ran from his lips and nose as they turned black. The teeth lengthened into fangs.

The bear crouched before her, panting, eyes closed. Amber twisted free of Pandrogas's grip and ran forward, kneeling beside him. Laying down the scimitar and the starcrystal, she took the massive head in her hands and lifted it tenderly. The bear looked up at her, eyes still clouded with pain. The human look of suffering in them struck her to her heart. The bear rose slowly, stood with head swaying. Behind them the chimera roared again, hurtling against the restraining links of iron.

Amber felt Pandrogas's hands on her shoulders once again, pulling her back. She looked down at the bear and said, "Beorn—I'm sorry." The bear rose to its hind legs then, towering over them both, gazing at them for a moment. Then it turned to face the chimera.

It approached the creature warily. The chimera still strained against the chains, talons and fangs gleaming in the starcrystal's light. The bear dropped suddenly to all fours, ducking beneath the other's claws, and struck a swiping blow with its own talons, leaving five parallel streaks of blood across the scaled torso. The chimera gave a hissing shriek that caused Amber to cover her ears in pain. Its tail lashed out, striking the bear across the muzzle. The bear roared in pain and backed up, then leaped with astounding quickness at the chimera's neck. The chimera tried to meet its attack with its own teeth, but was too slow; the bear seized its neck in powerful jaws. The impact of its weight caused the chain to pull free of its stone anchor, and the two beasts rolled free, each seeking to disembowel the other with their powerful hind claws. The bear still held the chimera's neck in its jaws, but the thick mane surrounding the neck protected it. The bear broke free and rolled to its feet, glancing for an instant toward Pandrogas and Amber. Then it turned and fled into the depths of the catacombs with the chimera in pursuit. The echoes of their flight faded quickly, leaving silence.

Pandrogas shook himself, as though awakening from a nightmare. "Come!" he told Amber. "He has given us our chance!" He picked up the starcrystal and started toward the doors of the tomb. Amber hesitated; then, realizing she could do nothing now to help the bear, took up the scimitar and followed the sorcerer. It took all of their strength to open one of the doors enough for them to slip through.

They stood within a huge, navelike fault, the walls and ceiling only faintly illuminated by the azure light. At the far end rose a shadow, massive and still, with a patch of gray before it. Pandrogas lifted the rod higher and approached it. Amber followed, feeling cold fear enfolding her. They stood within the tomb of the Necromancer, the world-shatterer, an icon of even greater dread than Sestihaculas.

As they approached, the patch of gray became a figure, sprawled facedown upon steps of rough-hewn black rock. Pandrogas put fingers against the vein in his neck; then, assured that life was gone, turned him over. It was Thasos. His stone mask, webbed with cracks, fell from his face in pieces.

Amber gripped the sorcerer's arm. "The tomb," she whispered to him. His gaze followed hers. Above them, on the dais, was a

tomb of black marble. On its lid was the medallion Ardatha had
brought from Nigromancien. The tomb was identical to the one in
the cenotaph; but this one, Amber knew, was not empty.

The lid was moving.

Silently, with no sound of stone scraping over stone, it slid to
one side, exposing a narrow rectangle of darkness which no light
could ever breach, and then stopped. Pandrogas put his foot on the
first step. Amber tried to restrain him, but he pulled free of her grip.
"I must," he said softly. "He lives again, and only he can save
Darkhaven now."

He ascended the black steps to the sarcophagus, his face pale
even in the light of the starcrystal. Amber watched him raise the
glowing rod over the open tomb and peer within.

Then she screamed, as blackness rose from the tomb and engulfed
him.

"It is the final orbit," Undya said.

She stood with the others about the mirror, now in Pandrogas's
laboratory. The vision it showed of the roofscape of Darkhaven was
one of chaos and inferno. Hurricane winds tore gargoyles and crock-
ets from towers and powdered them against stone walls. The rooftop
orchards and the wooden bridges and buttresses were afire with a
clear bright flame. Through smoke and vapor that tore across the
scene they could see Oljaer rushing toward them. The laboratory
rocked suddenly and violently about them; retorts and containers
were cast from their shelves to float lazily in the air before settling
to the floor. Undya and the others were also suspended momentarily,
grasping at each other for support and anchor. Undya gasped the
words that changed the scene in the speculum. Colors shifted and
whirled, and then the reflective surface filled with blackness.

"He is awakened!" Lambas cried.

"Yes," Undya said, as the laboratory shook once more. "But, I
fear, only in time to die again."

Beorn galloped through the dusty halls of the dead, pursued by
the chimera. He had fled for one reason; to lure the beast away from

the sorcerer and Amber. Now he looked for a suitable place to make his stand against it. He had little doubt of the outcome; already he was bleeding from several wounds inflicted by the chimera's talons, and his muzzle was numb and sore from the lash of its tail. He had managed to avoid its poisonous bite, but more by luck than by skill. He was outmatched, and he knew it. The last time he had roamed these subterranean reaches as the bear, he had faced a hydra, and only escaped by the sorcerer's aid. The chimera was an even more formidable opponent, quicker by far and capable of killing with one bite. He could only hope to delay the creature long enough for Pandrogas to complete his task.

He still ached in every joint and muscle from the metamorphosis. The savagery of the bear was very strong within him; it was an effort to keep from turning and rushing back to close in battle with his pursuer, to hurl himself at the other's jugular again. But he knew his only chance lay in devising some strategy. He heard the cry of the chimera echoing through the catacombs. It was gaining on him, he knew; he would have to face it again very soon.

It would be sooner than he expected, he realized, as the twisting passageway he followed ended abruptly, overlooking a sunken vault. He stood between two pilasters that rose a few inches from the ends of the passageway. A perron of stone descended from a narrow walkway that encircled the vault, but there was no time to reach it. There was no room to maneuver; he would have to jump, a dangerous move for the bear. As nearly as his poor vision could estimate, the drop was over ten feet. He hesitated—and heard the scream of the chimera right behind him.

He turned and saw the monster bounding toward him, its goatlike hind legs hurling it forward in great springs, the ophidian tail trailing behind. Serpent fangs gleamed in the leonine jaws. The chain trailed behind it like a scarf in the wind. He would have to face it here, delay its victory as long as possible, give the others as much time as he could.

The chimera leaped for him. He crouched, then rose, driving his heavy head, backed by the power of his massive legs and shoulders, straight into the thing's midriff. Its breath exploded from it in a whistling scream, and he felt the jaws snap shut, tearing fur from his neck. He had absorbed the chimera's forward momentum, and they crouched on the edge of the vault, struggling. The sinuous tail wrapped about his midsection, squeezing him; the pain was like reliving the metamorphosis. The talons of the forepaws raked over the healed wounds left by the hydra on his shoulder, and he felt blood matting his fur. A droplet of liquid fire seared the wound, spreading agony through his veins; he realized dimly that poison was dripping from the chimera's fangs into his scored flesh. With a convulsive heave he arose on his hind legs, freeing himself from the constrictive tail and lifting the monster's hind legs from the floor. The chimera's writhings overbalanced them, and he toppled backward. He felt himself falling; then he struck the floor of the vault with a jolt that drove the wind from him. Dimly above him he could see the chimera dropping toward him, eyes burning, fangs bared, and knew that in another instant he would feel those fangs driven into his flesh. Then the snarling head snapped backward, and the body suddenly, impossibly stopped in mid-fall, limbs thrashing. Beorn heard a sound he had heard once before, in human form, when awaiting his turn on a gallows scaffold. It was the *crack!* of vertebrae snapping. The chimera hung lifeless above him, swaying slightly.

Bewildered, Beorn peered upward, trying to focus the nearsighted eyes of the bear on his adversary. A final shudder shook the lifeless frame, the head lolled to one side, and Beorn saw what had saved him—its chain had caught between the pilaster and the wall as they had fallen, and the chimera now hung as from a gibbet. Its bowels had voided during the death throes, and the foulness had partially spattered him. Snarling in distaste, Beorn tried to scrape himself clean against the sarcophagus, staggered and almost collapsed. The loss of blood and the minuscule amount of venom that had entered his wounds had left him dizzy and weak. He managed to balance on trembling legs and stagger up the narrow staircase that hugged the wall of the vault.

He had to return to Amber and Pandrogas. The corridor seemed to sway; he could not tell if this was the effect of the poison or the castle itself being shaken to its foundations by the force of its fall. The result was the same, however; he fell, rose and stumbled on, only to fall again and again.

He did not recall falling for the last time; he only knew that he did not seem able to rise. He lay there, panting, feeling his heart pumping alternating gouts of fire and ice through his veins. What an appropriate place to die, he thought with grim humor. The death fear of the bear was very strong, pushing against his reason, clouding it. Beorn fought back as best he could. He wanted at least to die thinking human thoughts.

He heard a scraping sound above him, and saw one of the marble slabs that sealed the tiered loculi moving. Oddly enough, the sight filled him with no fear, but only a dazed wonderment. The corpse of a woman, wrapped in cerement, left her resting place and came to kneel beside him. She tugged the rotting cloth strips from her face, and Beorn saw who it was: Suchana, his Suchana, as he remembered her from years gone, beautiful beyond death. She looked down at him with the amused and faintly exasperated look he had received from her so many times; the look that told him he had made yet another amateur's mistake.

"Beorn," she whispered, kneeling and placing a cold palm on the bear's head. "Ah, Beorn. How many times have I told you not to rob from magicians?"

He felt no amazement at all at being able to answer her with the bear's throat and tongue; it all seemed entirely natural. "It's somewhat late for reprimands now, is it not?"

"It usually is, with you. As usual, you need help, you need Suchana to hold the rope."

He felt the coolness of her hand flowing over him as she stroked him, quieting the temperature extremes that wracked his body. Strength seemed to flow from her to him. Confused, he asked, "How is it you are here, interred in Darkhaven?"

She smiled, and he felt his laboring heart nearly break at the vision of that memory. "Does it matter to you? It does not to me; the dead care not where they lie." She stood. "Rise, love, rise. The job's not over yet, the reward still waits to be claimed. We've stolen

many things together, you and I; let's see now if we can't rob life
from death. Rise."

He wanted to protest that he could not, but he had never been
able to refuse her. He struggled to his feet, and to his surprise found
that, though weak, his legs would support him. Suchana put her
arms around his neck and hugged him. "That's my thief! Hurry now;
they need you."

Beorn hesitated. There was so much more to say, so many things
he had wanted to tell her for so many years. "Suchana, I'm sorry,"
he said. "We never made it to Tamboriyon."

"We will, Beorn, we will. And I will be with you, as I am now—
as I have always been." She kissed the top of his head, and pushed
him gently on his way. He lumbered down the corridor a few steps,
then stopped and looked back. Suchana was gone, and he could not
tell to which of the receptacles she had returned. He tried to call to
her, but the only sounds he could produce were the sharp, coughing
barks of the bear. He felt an overwhelming wave of sadness pass
over him as he turned and continued. But at the same time, there
was joy. She had understood; she had forgiven him, after all these
years. He kept going, pausing several times to lick moisture from
the walls of the tombs in an effort to quell a fiery thirst. He still felt
weak and sick, but no longer as though he were going to die. His
main concern now was the bear—the virulence of the chimera seemed
somehow to have weakened his human will while strengthening that
of the beast; it was an effort to remain in control. He knew he should
return to human form soon, for the struggle to retain his identity
would only grow harder. But instead he kept going, trotting through
the halls of the dead, letting his instinctive sense of direction lead
him back to the Necromancer's tomb—and Amber.

When Amber saw the black cloud rise from the sarcophagus and
flow over Pandrogas, hiding him in absolute darkness, she had rushed
forward, the scimitar held high, in a futile attempt to save him. But
as her outstretched hand touched the boundaries of the cloud, a wave
of polar cold flowed over her, causing her to stagger back. She could
not enter the cloud; in addition to the freezing pain it caused her,

the darkness was somehow *solid,* impenetrable. *"Pandrogas!"* she cried, but there was no answer save the echoes shuddering through the vault. She stepped back. Pandrogas had dropped the starcrystal when the cloud had engulfed him, and its light now illuminated it, rolling sluggishly before her like ink in water. She was unable to decide what to do, unable even to think.

Then she heard a noise on the far side of the tomb: a scratching, dragging sound. Around the corner of the sarcophagus a hand reached, slowly; a scaled horror of a hand that burned with white light as its talons scraped the black marble of the sarcophagus. Amber watched as Ardatha staggered into view, her gown torn and disheveled, her eyes glowing brighter than her hand with a mad fire. The enchantress saw her, and smiled.

"You pursue me to one hell after another," she said, her voice ragged. "But neither you nor I can go any further. Thasos is dead, and I do not know why I still live. The spell is a success, you see; the Necromancer lives," and she looked up at the black cloud hovering over them. "But it was madness to think we could control him. Even as Thasos read the spell, the scroll was consumed in fire, and he fell dead. The Necromancer was waiting for fools like us to liberate him, to restore life to him. And now he will rule again."

She seemed to be speaking more to herself now than to Amber, and her voice was full of sadness. She stared at her glowing claw as she spoke.

The hand of light is raised.

"We will never know the grace of the One God now," Ardatha continued. "The Necromancer will bring back the Age of Night, and we will be abandoned to our heathendom." She looked up at Amber; the light from her flexing talons cast moving shadows over her face, reminding Amber of the nest of snakes beneath the cowl in her dream. "It is our fault; all of us," Ardatha said. "You have helped to bring this about; you and your sorcerous lover. The power of the Necromancer has destroyed Thasos and him; it is fitting that our powers destroy each other!"

An intolerable brightness flashed from her claw, and Amber felt it surrounding her, crushing her. She experienced a moment of bright agony—and then, somehow, she struck back. Blue fire warred with silver fire, ending in a coruscating explosion of light. Amber felt the scimitar's hilt tear from her hand, and then she was falling. She sprawled full-length on the floor next to the dais. Beside her lay the scimitar, with only a foot of its dark blade remaining on it; the rest had been broken into shards. Before her, Ardatha crouched on her knees.

"You are strong, Marquise," the enchantress said. "But strength without skill is nothing. You cannot resist the power of the Demogorgon." She raised the glowing claw again, but before she could strike Amber kicked out against Ardatha's knee. The enchantress shouted in pain and fell backward, both hands outspread to check her fall. Amber rolled over and seized the broken remnant of the dark scimitar.

To escape its fire, one must bring darkness to its grasp.

Without giving herself time to realize what she was doing, Amber seized the hilt and brought the blade's edge down against Ardatha's left wrist.

She struck true; the scimitar, aided by the weight of her body, severed the demon hand at the wrist. Blood painted a crimson swath across Amber's bosom. The enchantress screamed, rolling over and rising to her knees, staring at the stump from which her life was jetting. Her expression was one of shock and disbelief; then the enchantress looked at Amber, who, to her amazement, saw gratitude in the glazing eyes. In that look seemed to be a realization, too late, of a freedom she had not known she had lost.

Then thunder filled the great chamber, and sulfurous fumes choked Amber. A shadowy, batwinged form with lambent eyes crouched over Ardatha. A hand with fingers like black, twisted roots seized the stump, cauterizing it in its grip. Ardatha screamed again, a sound of utter fear and despair. "Balandrus!" she cried. *"No!"* Then the dark form embraced her; the drumbeat of wings sounded again, and all that remained was the fading stench of brimstone.

Amber crawled away from the spattered, congealing blood. She saw the severed claw lying there, slowly flexing and relaxing. Then red fire consumed it, and it flared silently and was gone. She collapsed with her head resting on the first step of the dais, and the last sight she remembered was that of the black cloud still cloaking the sarcophagus.

Pandrogas stood in absolute darkness. He had dropped the star-crystal when the cloud swallowed him, not so much in reaction as from a dim sense that it would be useless to him. He was right; no slightest ray of light alleviated the surrounding blackness. He could not see his own hand before him, and yet, somehow, he *could* see. The darkness seemed at one moment the shifting mass of clouds that had boiled up from the tomb, and the next to be the adamantine columns and walls of a vast chamber cut from solid ebony rock. It was neither cold nor warm within it. He waited in that noiseless, timeless place, for he was aware that he was not alone, and that he was being judged.

At last a voice spoke. It surrounded him as did the darkness, and yet it was quiet, almost intimate. "Do you know me, sorcerer?"

"I do," Pandrogas replied, fighting to keep his voice steady. "You are the Necromancer."

The voice was silent, almost as though considering the truth of this. "That is who I was," it said after a time, "when the world was whole. How long ago was that?"

"A thousand commonyears have passed," Pandrogas said.

"And now I, who have raised so many from their tombs, have at last been raised." There seemed almost a note of irony, of amusement, in that last observation. Pandrogas did not know what to respond to this, and so was quiet.

He had considered himself a dead man when the cloud took him; he did not know what to make of this now. He was not as afraid as he had been initially, and that in itself surprised him. He had expected the Necromancer to be the ultimate horror, a ravening force of evil who, once roused, would complete his scourge of the world. Instead, the voice about him and within him was quiet, almost contemplative.

He asked the question that had been asked by all humanity since the fateful, cataclysmic moment. "Why did you shatter the world?"

The Necromancer did not speak immediately. When he did, it did not seem at first to be a reply.

"I lived for some time after the Shattering," he said. "This part of Darkhaven—less than a tenth of the total—was my sanctuary, and eventually my tomb. I was well aware of the hatred the world held for me. It was not an easy load to carry, particularly since it was undeserved."

After a long moment, Pandrogas asked carefully, "Are you saying you are not responsible for the apocalypse?"

"I was the most powerful mage of all time, and I drew my power from a source vilified by all other magicians. As such, would I not make a convenient scapegoat?"

The sorcerer's mouth was dry. "Why should I believe you?"

"You will believe what you will believe. But I tell you that I did not break the world. The sphere that these fragments once comprised was not the only sphere in the cosmos. There are countless such, all falling forever in an abyss far more desolate than the one you know. On rare occasions their paths intersect, and they collide. That is what happened. It was attributed to me. In truth, I tried to prevent it, as did every other magician alive. But even the power of the dead was not enough to turn it aside; the most I could do was lessen the impact, and save the few pieces to which humanity clings today."

Pandrogas realized his heart was hammering. "It was the Cabal who created the Runestones, established the orbits . . ."

"True. But they worked with what I had salvaged. Without my efforts, all would be frozen dust in the void."

"You killed Thasos and Ardatha!" Even as he spoke, he realized he was attempting to save his crumbling convictions.

"No. The enchantress still lives; the sorcerer was struck down by the weakness of his own heart."

Pandrogas felt himself reeling from this. The Necromancer had been the one figure of unquestioned evil in his world. He remembered Amber's expressing amazement that he could defend the acts of the Chthons and still condemn him, and for the first time he realized how unilateral his prejudice had been. Why? he asked himself. Why had he, who had tried never to deal in absolutes, whose studies and delvings into the complexities of magic had taught him, if nothing else, that one answer was never the only answer, accepted with complacence the ultimate villainy of the Necromancer?

As he asked himself the question, he knew the answer. Because the Necromancer dealt in death, and, in common with the rest of humanity, the sorcerer feared death.

I am not at peace with myself, Pandrogas realized. I never have been. I have always sought mastery of my art, instead of oneness with it. The little spells, the basic foundations that have always eluded me; this is why.

"Sorcerer," the Necromancer said quietly, "your introspection must wait. My awareness grows brighter in me; I know now the reason I have been quickened. It is the reason my servants have nurtured the castle for the last thousand years, and why I left clues to my awakening for those resourceful as yourself to find. The Runestones flicker and fail; the destruction begun so long ago is rushing to completion."

"It must be stopped," Pandrogas said. He fumbled within his pouch and brought out the Runestone. "Thasos wished to re-form the world into a sphere; I seek merely to maintain equilibrium. How can this be done?"

"Equilibrium cannot be maintained; all decays eventually. This world is doomed, as are all worlds. But, given time, mankind may find a way to flee this world for a better one. Let the dead make time for the living, sorcerer."

Pandrogas did not understand what he meant at first; then the cold realization made him shiver. "Necromancy?" he gasped. "I cannot! I know none of your spells, I could not control—"

"It is not a question of control," the voice within him said. "One does not control death, any more than one controls life. Open yourself to the power that is there. It will control you, as it always has and always will."

"I fear this surrender," Pandrogas said quietly. "I fear giving up what control I have, illusion though it may be."

"There is no time for you to fear; even now, Darkhaven plunges toward Oljaer. The dead of Darkhaven surround you, sorcerer. Seek their power. It is all that will save you."

Pandrogas felt the Runestone, cold in his hands. He hesitated, not sure how to begin. *With trust,* he thought. That is always the way to begin.

He opened himself to the power of the dead.

There was no need for recitals and gesticulations, no requirement of rituals and sacraments. Pandrogas felt his awareness extend from him through the catacombs, touching and linking with the strength and knowledge that had fired the thousands of men, women, and children who had once lived and learned and loved within the massive walls. The flashes from a myriad of lives confused and nearly overwhelmed him; he resisted, tried vainly to hold off the onrushing tide. That moment of potential energy he had sensed in the cemetery of Dulfar, he now realized, had been but the merest touch of what he now felt, and what he now felt was the barest fraction of the full power the Necromancer had once known. And he realized then that the strength of the dead could not be used for evil, simply because it could not be used at all.

He abandoned himself to it, let it fill him and absorb him. He ceased then to exist as Pandrogas, sorcerer of the Lorian System, became instead merely a receptacle, a focusing point for the omnipotence. He was all who had ever lived and died in Darkhaven, and, under that compelling charge, the Runestone blazed unseen in his hands like a fragment of the sun. He saw through the eyes of Undya and the others as they gazed into the mirror's depths; saw the mass of Oljaer plunging toward them, winds toppling buildings and laying waste to both castle and city; felt the impact when the tallest towers of Oljaer's palace shattered like glass as the stone parapets of Darkhaven grazed them; saw the city blur by and fall away beneath them as the castle began to rise, charged once more with the full power of the Runestone.

And then he was Pandrogas again.

He stood once more within the atramentous cloud. The Runestone was in his hands, and he could feel the power of it tingling through him. Despite that, however, he felt spent, exhausted, like an empty glove.

"You will sleep," the Necromancer told him. "Not the sleep of death, but not far from it. To serve as the vehicle of the dead is not an easy task, especially when one is unaccustomed to it as are you. You are drained. The Runestone will replenish you."

"And you?" Pandrogas asked. "You are alive again, at last." There was so much more he wished to ask the Necromancer, so much more he wanted now to learn. Was Necromancy in fact the unifying system he had been searching for these past five years? Did the ectenic force rise from it, as it now appeared, rather than the reverse? But already he could feel himself dropping into a vast, dreamless slumber even darker than the sable mists about him. He barely heard the Necromancer's reply.

"I arranged the possibility of my resurrection for just such an emergency as has arisen, and to aid as I can. The power of Necromancy is yours to explore, sorcerer. It will restore the orbits of the fragments—for a time. But nothing lasts forever, and if humanity is to survive, it would do well to find another nest. As for me—do you think I fear death, or seek life over it? How could I? All who live die. The dust of the dead contains, inherent, the power and grace and joy of the living, but revivification is not life. I died, and so can never truly live again. One does not fear the past, only the future—only the unknown.

"I was the Necromancer. Perhaps, one day, you will gain sufficient knowledge and confidence in the power of the dead for your hands to be bare of rings, as those of acolytes are, and as mine were. Perhaps. But until such time, the Necromancer is dead."

The cloud began to flow about Pandrogas again. He saw it pouring back into the sarcophagus, saw the lid sliding shut. Then his eyes closed, and he thought and saw no more.

It was thus that Beorn found Pandrogas and Amber, one lying at the foot of the dais and the other atop it, next to the sarcophagus. The bear staggered into the great vault, and at first thought both of them as dead as the corpse of Thasos which lay between them. He looked down upon Amber's still face, the color of ice in the star-crystal's glow, then raised his muzzle high and howled his grief. He nuzzled her, licking her face with his rough tongue. Her eyelids fluttered, and he would have cried in joy had he been a man. She opened her eyes and looked up at him. Though she could not at first remember where she was or what had happened, she felt no fear at the sight of the bear. She rose unsteadily, and climbed the steps to where Pandrogas lay. He was breathing, though just barely. As she caressed his pale, cold features, a tremor shook the burial chamber. A corbel from some unseen design high above them fell and powdered on the floor with a crash. A jagged crack appeared in the black marble of the dais. Amber saw something clenched in the sorcerer's hand; she touched it, felt the force within it. It was the Runestone, with its power restored. She tried to take it from his hand, but his fingers were locked about it; it seemed almost a part of him.

The chamber shuddered again. She had no idea what was happening, but as she stood again she realized that either her strength had faded or her weight had returned to normal. She looked down at the bear. "Beorn," she called. "Can you understand me?" The bear growled in response. "I think Darkhaven has been saved," she continued, "but the stress caused by that may be responsible for these temblors. Pandrogas needs help; we must get him out of here!"

The bear lumbered up the steps slowly and knelt beside the sorcerer. It took all of Amber's strength to lift him partially and drape him over the bear's back. As she did so her hand brushed fur matted with blood, and the bear whined in pain. She saw the deep furrows that had been dug into his flesh.

She took the medallion from the sarcophagus. "This will lead us through the Labyrinth," she said. The chamber shook again, more strongly this time, causing one of the massive stone doors to swing like a shutter in the wind. They quickly made their way into the antechamber of the Labyrinth, where Amber, following the bronze map, led them through the last door on the right. "We will have to trust to the map's accuracy," she said, as their surroundings shook and groaned again. "There is no time to be wary of traps." The bear growled again; whether it was an attempt at communication or simply an animal sound she did not know. She had gained no rest from her faint of exhaustion; it was an effort almost beyond endurance simply to keep moving, steadying Pandrogas's unconscious form on the bear's back as they hurried through the twisting corridors and turns of the maze. She tried not to think about the infinite varieties of deaths that awaited them if she took a wrong turn. She tried not to think about anything except following the way traced in minute detail upon the medallion.

Thoughts persisted, however, as did the hope that perhaps, at last, it would soon be over, that the terrors and flights that had gone on for so long had now, at last, come to an end. She glanced at Pandrogas and hoped it had not come too late. The emotion was a faint ghost of what she thought she should feel, however. Her sensibilities were numbed. She felt like the fire-eaten shell of a house, still standing only by the merest chance.

Another tremor rocked the Labyrinth, this one strong enough to throw Amber to the floor and to cause Pandrogas to slide from the bear's back. She managed to block his fall and save him from injury, though the impact knocked the breath from her. Ahead, the spandrel of an arch collapsed, the sound reverberating in the narrow passage with half-stunning force. Dimly she was aware of the bear surging forward, straining with his shoulder against the giant block of stone, which balanced in such a way as to prevent passage. With a grunt of effort he managed to topple it, clearing the way. An archstone fell upon his foot, and with a roar of rage he swatted it, hurling the heavy piece against the wall. He turned toward Amber, growling, his nose wrinkling in rage. In that moment he seemed wholly bestial, without the slightest vestige of humanity left within him. She was afraid that the power within her would strike him down, if he did not kill her first. Not knowing what else to do, and recalling that he had told her once of the calming effect her music had had on him, she quickly pulled her flute from its case at her belt and began to play.

The music sounded odd to her ears in the grim depths of the maze. She played the piece she knew best, *The Light upon the Water*. For a long, tense moment it looked as though the bear might charge despite her efforts. Then she could see the visible effort the thief within made to regain control. The lowered head swung violently away from her, and muscles stood out in sharp relief under the pelt. He padded slowly back to her and knelt to receive the sorcerer's weight again.

She continued playing after Pandrogas was once more astride the broad back, and that was how they continued, the starcrystal gripped in the bear's mouth and Amber playing whatever melodies she could remember upon her alicorn flute, leading them past the hazards of the Labyrinth. Several times more the strength of the bear was required to clear the way, until, at last, they stood once more upon the Warped Stairs.

Amber looked down at the Stairs, which glinted blue-black in the light. I cannot continue, she thought. Then she turned and looked at the bear, standing behind her, his gaze fixed upon her, in it human trust and encouragement. She knew that she had no choice but to go on, not only for herself and Pandrogas, but for Beorn, for the thief whom she had once hated, and who now, she knew, loved her.

"Come then, Beorn," she said softly. "We'll yet rob death, you and I." And, lifting the flute to her lips once more, she stepped out onto the Stairs.

The bear was winning, he knew. He could feel it growing stronger within him, clawing and snapping at his human identity, overcoming his thoughts with the mindlessness of the brute. But he could not return to human form now; only the bear could clear a way through the debris the temblors left, and only the bear could carry Pandrogas such a distance. Amber's music slowed the onslaught of the darkness, held the beast at bay for a time. But he feared, in those interludes when he could still think coherently, that it would not be long enough. The combination of his weakness and his wounds and the length of time he had spent as the bear were wearing him down rapidly.

By the time they reached the Warped Stairs he could no longer remember his way back to the man he had been. His path was unlighted now, save for an occasional faint flicker that momentarily illuminated the night. During one of those last lucid intervals, he realized that he had waited too long. Like death, even as the concept was grasped, it was over. His final vision was that of the iron gate that marked the exit to the Stairs. He stared at it, and at Amber framed within it, and felt her music filling him, lifting him—but not high enough.

Chapter 23

Tamboriyon

A stream meandered through the meadow, descending by terraced steps to the overhanging cliffs. The rocks and the water sparkled in crimson sunlight; the tint, Pandrogas said, was due to the dust cast into the air by the fragment's collision with Rhynne. On a knoll overlooking the shallow valley Amber and Pandrogas stood. A spire lifted from the mainland cliff nearby, its junction hidden in mist, its broad cap, crowned with grass and trees, separated from the knoll by a few feet of Abyss. Tethered to a tree on the cliff's edge in that small cove of calm air, the sorcerer's dragonship floated.

They stood together, looking down at the meadowland. Below them the bear moved slowly along the side of the stream, combing through the grass with its paws in search of insects. It drank from the stream, then began eating cloudberries from a bush.

"I'm glad we brought him here," Pandrogas said at last.

"It was his dream," Amber replied. "I thought at least a small part of it should come true."

The sorcerer nodded. He looked out at the distant forest, where a paved road wound through the trees. He thought he saw, for just a moment, the white coat and pearly horn of a unicorn flash among the trees. "The land is as beautiful as the stories have it," he said.

346

She smiled at that. "How strange to hear you commenting on the beauty of nature! The vista, and the Abyss at your back, do not make you nervous?"

"There have been more important things to be nervous about," he said, and smiled with her. They were both silent then, watching the bear.

"What will you do?" he asked her at last.

She did not look at him. "I will learn. I will seek out schools of magic and study; I will practice, and eventually I will control the power within me." She paused. "And you?"

Pandrogas did not answer immediately. "The same."

"In Darkhaven?"

"Yes. I am a novice, even as you. The power of the dead can save the world of the living. Someone must learn the way."

"Would you return there to live alone, without even the cold company of the Necromancer's servants?" She had sought Undya and the others to aid in reviving the sorcerer from his coma, but all she had found of them had been dust scattered among robes on the floor of the laboratory.

He shrugged. "Someone must learn the way," he repeated. They were not the words he wanted to say. He wanted instead to beg her to return with him, to share the loneliness and the burden. He wanted to tell her that when he had awoken at last in his bedchamber to find her bending over him, he had realized what a fool he had been to blame his love for her for his lack of self-confidence and ability. But it was too late then, as it was too late now. *Houses fall,* the sphere had said. He knew now what it meant; not Darkhaven, but those tall and lonely walls he had erected about himself over the years.

He gestured at the bear below them. "He gave up his humanity for us. Can I do any less for the world?

"Besides," he continued, "I will not be alone in my studies. There are those of the Cabal who have already expressed interest in Necromancy. Once it is realized that there is no evil, no corruption in it, Darkhaven will be hard put to contain all the students."

"Martyrdom ill becomes you, Pandrogas," Amber said. "The

Necromancer did not choose you to succeed him. If you wish to take up his mantle, that is your decision."

"And what of you?" he demanded, angry now. "Why can you not be one of those many students who will clamor at the doors of the new knowledge? With your power merged with the power of the dead, there is no limit to what we could do for the world!"

She looked down at the star-flowered grass rippling in the breeze. "I cannot return to Darkhaven, Pandrogas. Not now, at any rate. I cannot face the dead of Darkhaven; Tahrynyar, Beorn, Ardatha, and all the others." She wanted to add, *including our selves that once were,* but she could not bring herself to do so. Why? she wondered. Did she fear that saying it would make it real, irrevocable?

She could no longer look at him with the awe and adoration she had once felt for him. He was no more the mysterious and omniscient sorcerer of Darkhaven to her, but simply Pandrogas, as full of doubts and uncertainties as she was. At first she had been disappointed by this. But now, she thought, if love were to grow again, perhaps it would be stronger than before. They were on equal levels now; perhaps they could rise together.

She looked up at Pandrogas, and saw him looking at her. He stepped to her and took her in his arms, looking down at her, noting for the first time, it seemed, how much she had changed since it all began. She was thinner now, with faint shadings of musculature in her arms and neck where none had been before. There were new lines in her face. All of which made her look more beautiful, more desirable, than ever to him.

"Our paths lie in opposite directions," he said, "and yet we wish to join them, somehow. What are we to do?"

"We might ask the sphere," she said, her tone so dry that he could not help but laugh. "You laugh much easier these days," Amber continued, tracing his jawline with her fingers. "And your skin has browned in the sun. It suits you."

"I must return," he said. "If only for a short time."

"And I must go, if only for a short time."

As one they asked, "How long?" and laughed together.

Amber turned away and picked a flower, regarded it. "In a commonyear," she said, "I will stand again upon this knoll." She looked at Pandrogas.

"Agreed," the sorcerer said. Then, uncertainly, "Much can happen in a year."

"Much can happen in a few commonweeks!" she exclaimed, tossing the flower away. He caught her hand as it swung by him, pulled her to him again, and they kissed.

After a moment, Amber looked down into the valley again. The bear was still there, wading in the stream, looking for fish. "Do you think he will be here too?" she asked.

"I'm certain of it."

She turned toward him then, the sun and the wind in her hair, smiling. Then, without another word, she started down the knoll and across the meadow, toward the distant road. She crossed the stream by a series of steppingstones quite close to the bear, who paid her no attention. Pandrogas watched her until she disappeared into the forest. Then he returned to his dragonship, unfurled the sails, and let the wind lift him up and away from Tamboriyon. In a few moments he had vanished into the blue of the Abyss.

In the valley, the bear neatly flipped a fish from the water. It scratched an ear with a hind paw, then settled down to enjoy its meal in the sunlight.

Acknowledgments

Thanks go to the following people for their advice, encouragement, and otherwise instrumental aid:
J. Brynne Stephens, Lia Amidon, Mikey Roessner-Herman, Steve Perry, Pat Murphy, Diane Duane, David Gerrold, Marc and Elaine Zicree, Evelyn Sharenov, Martha Millard, John Douglas, Mimi Panitch, and David Hartwell.

MICHAEL REAVES has been a freelance writer for ten years. He is the author of six novels, a computer game, and over seventy-five teleplays. His fiction and nonfiction have appeared in various magazines and anthologies, including *Universe, The Magazine of Fantasy and Science Fiction*, and *Heavy Metal*. He lives in Los Angeles, California.